The Last Goodbye

The Last Goodbye

A Novel

FIONA LUCAS

wm
WILLIAM MORROW
An Imprint of HarperCollins*Publishers*

P.S.™ is a trademark of HarperCollins Publishers

THE LAST GOODBYE. Copyright © 2020 by Fiona Lucas. All rights reserved. Printed in the United States of America. No part of this book may be used or reproduced in any manner whatsoever without written permission except in the case of brief quotations embodied in critical articles and reviews. For information, address HarperCollins Publishers, 195 Broadway, New York, NY 10007.

HarperCollins books may be purchased for educational, business, or sales promotional use. For information, please email the Special Markets Department at SPsales@harpercollins.com.

Originally published in the United Kingdom in 2020 by HarperCollins UK.

FIRST U.S. EDITION

Designed by Diahann Sturge

Part title art © Elena Eskevich / Shutterstock, Inc.

Library of Congress Cataloging-in-Publication Data has been applied for.

ISBN 978-0-06-303638-3

21 22 23 24 25 LSC 10 9 8 7 6 5 4 3 2 1

For Amanda, the best partner in crime an author could wish for.

The Last Goodbye

Part 1

Chapter One

Anna was lying in bed with the duvet pulled up over her head. A thing not so unusual in itself, perhaps, except for the fact it was half past seven on a Thursday evening, and she was fully dressed, bar her shoes. Somewhere in the distance, her doorbell was ringing. She was doing her best to ignore it.

She'd climbed into bed about half an hour ago, and she had no intention of getting out again that evening. Maybe not ever. It was nice in her cocoon. White. Calm. The world had been too bright today, too noisy. Just too flipping cheerful. But this was a lovely solution. She should have come up with it sooner.

The letterbox clattered. "Anna?"

Anna stared hard at the cotton duvet cover and began to count the individual threads above her nose. Maybe she should consider some sort of soundproofing?

The voice came again, louder. "Hey there! I'm here. Open the door!"

Deep breathing . . . That was supposed to be good for keeping calm, wasn't it? Anna decided to try it; she wanted so badly to hang on to this velvety, white numbness. The only problem was that it had been a very long time since Anna had been able to take a deep breath. Two years, nine months and eight days, to be exact.

Had it truly been that long? It still felt like yesterday.

She rolled over onto her side and curled into a ball, squeezing her eyes shut.

The voice called through the letterbox again, but it no longer sounded bright and cheery. More irritated. Maybe even a little desperate. Anna blew out a shaky breath. Her bubble of calm was in a precarious state now. Cracks were appearing. She tried to pretend these intrusive noises were happening on a different plane, in a different reality. At least, she did until the voice became softer, more pleading.

"Anna? Minha querida? Are you okay?"

Anna covered her face with her hands and let out a sound that was half-growl, half-sigh, then forced her legs out of her duck-down nest and found the floor with her feet. The rest of her followed a second later and then she walked mechanically out of her bedroom and down the stairs into the hall.

"Thank goodness for that!" her best friend said when Anna opened the front door. "I was worried you'd fallen down the stairs or slipped in the bath!" Gabriela's tone was cheery as she stepped into the hallway, but there was a tightness to the accompanying laughter and there were questions in her eyes. Anna knew Gabi wasn't going to ask them, but she heard them anyway. *You are okay, aren't you? Or do I need to be properly worried?*

Everyone Anna knew had questions in their eyes these days when they spoke to her. Often, the same questions. But they were afraid of saying the wrong thing. Or not saying the right thing. Anna lived in a minefield of eggshells.

Gabi thrust a cake tin into Anna's hands. "I was missing my mother's carrot cake, but I made far too much."

"Thank you," Anna said, receiving the tin and hugging it

into herself. "I'll look forward to it." Her friend's bright-orange Brazilian version of the cake, slathered in chocolate sauce, was amazing.

Gabi's eyes held a mixture of worry and hope. "Will you?" This was more than cake. Gabi had always moaned that her curves were a result of her mother equating loving people with feeding them, but it seemed she was more like her mother than she realized.

Anna nodded awkwardly. "Of course." And then she went and placed the cake tin in the kitchen, out of sight, hoping it would curb any further discussion.

She appreciated that her friends and family cared about her, but she was sick of being watched, of every word that left her mouth, of every gesture, being judged and weighed and measured so they could compare notes, so they could encourage each other with the tiny pieces of evidence they collected that she was finally "getting over it."

When Anna returned to the hall, Gabi squinted at her. "What have you done to your hair?"

Anna reached up and discovered that her shoulder-length brown hair was all fluffed up at the back. She smoothed it down with her hand, trying not to make it obvious. She didn't dare glance in the mirror by the front door. She hadn't left the house since Christmas Day, and she feared she'd see someone when she was scruffy and pasty-looking. In comparison, Gabi looked immaculate. Her hair fell in dark, silky spirals around her shoulders and the cobalt-blue dress she wore complemented her warmer skin tone perfectly.

"You are ready for the party, aren't you?" Gabi's gaze traveled downward to the crumpled little black dress Anna was wearing and to her stockinged feet. "It's only a few hours until we will all shout 'Happy New Year' and I don't want to be late!"

Happy New Year . . .

Oh, how Anna would like to do a little bit of surgery on that phrase. The first word should be chopped off and discarded, for a start. However, "New Year" was a fact. Nothing she could do about that. Time was going to march on whether she wanted it to or not, but "happy" just seemed ridiculous, maybe even a little insulting.

A rush of emotion hit her, engulfing her so completely that she briefly considered sprinting up the stairs and diving back under her duvet. She turned to Gabi, ready to make her excuses, but the look in her friend's eyes silenced her. Although she was clearly perplexed at Anna's disheveled state and more than a little concerned, there was something else shimmering under the surface, a look Anna recognized. "There's someone you like at this party, isn't there?" she asked, because that sparkle behind Gabi's eyes only ever appeared when romance was in the cards.

Gabi blinked at her innocently. "No."

Hmm. Anna wasn't so sure she believed that.

"Don't look at me that way," Gabi added, frowning. "After Joel, I'm done with men, remember?"

Anna nodded slightly. "I do remember you *telling* me that." Whether it lasted remained to be seen. Right at that second, Anna would have bet twenty quid on her friend's lips being locked onto someone else's come midnight.

But Anna couldn't begrudge her that. The breakup with Joel had been almost five years ago. To be honest, Anna hadn't been sad to see the back of him—he hadn't appreciated Gabi nearly enough—but Gabi hadn't seen it that way and she'd been brokenhearted. Since then, there had been a handful of short-lived relationships. Gabi liked guys who were confident, but more often than not, "confident" turned out to be "cocky and self-absorbed." Not qualities that lent themselves to a mature, long-lasting partnership.

"It's true," Gabi added, looking so convincing Anna almost believed her. "Are you ready?"

Anna glanced up at the staircase, beyond which her duvet cocoon lay waiting, and sighed. At least one of them should have something to hope for this evening as they crossed the threshold from this old, tired year into the fresh blankness of the next.

She forced the corners of her mouth to turn up. "Of course. Give me two seconds. I'll just grab my coat and put on my shoes."

Chapter Two

In an ideal world, Anna thought, *I would arrive at every party an hour and a half late.* That way she could skip the beginning, when everyone was buzzing with optimism about the night ahead, full of loud hellos and instantly forgotten introductions.

Gabi worked as a food stylist, in charge of making the pictures of dishes in cookbooks and magazines appear mouthwatering. Over the years, she'd encountered an eclectic mixture of people, from photographers and art directors, to magazine editors, stylists and TV presenters. The party that evening was being hosted by an expat Californian who owned a chain of south London beauty salons. Vanessa lived in Chislehurst, and as Anna drove to their destination, the houses became progressively grander, the streets leafier. It was only a couple of miles away from Anna's semi-detached in Sundridge Park, but it seemed like a different world.

She trailed round the ground floor of the stylish house behind Gabi, a glass of untouched fizz in her hand. Every time Gabi managed to extricate herself from one group of excitable extroverts, she was instantly dragged into another, most of whom Anna didn't know. Anna just hovered around the edges, keeping her expression friendly but neutral, and avoiding eye contact as much as possible.

The advantage of having a more outgoing friend who seemed to know ninety percent of the other guests was that the conversation eddied around Anna, much the same way a stream flowed around a rock in its path, and that was fine by her. Because with small talk came questions, and she wasn't particularly keen on questions, not the personal kind, anyway, and the one question she really didn't want to hear was—

"Hey, Anna! How *are* you?"

She fixed a smile in place and turned to find another of Gabi's creative, interesting friends smiling at her. "Oh, er, hi . . ." Anna trailed off, partly because she couldn't remember the woman's name, but mostly because this one simple question always left her in a quandary. She was basically an honest sort of person, so when somebody asked her how she was, her automatic response was to tell the truth.

Big mistake.

Back in the early days, she'd done just that, launching into a description of how each second of the day was a painful knife-stab in her heart, how she dreaded opening her eyelids each morning. It had been so wonderful to let it all out.

But she'd soon discovered it was a great way to make her friends' faces fall, to cause them to stammer awkwardly. More often than not, they'd invented someone on the other side of the room they urgently needed to talk to and had scurried away.

No one *really* wanted to hear how she was. Not after two years, nine months and eight days. Not even Gabi. Instead, they wanted to hear she was putting herself back together, that it was possible to heal from something that tragic and move on. It was selfish, really, because they were asking her to give them hope. They were asking her to reassure them that if something that awful happened to them, they'd eventually be okay too. But Anna wasn't okay. She wasn't even close.

Gabi's friend was looking at her, eyebrows raised, waiting for an answer.

"Doing good," Anna replied, nodding, and noticed, once again, how grief had turned her into a big fat liar. "How about you?"

The woman—Keisha! Her name was *Keisha*—nodded philosophically. "Oh, you know. Same old, same old . . ." And then her brows drew together. "I heard about . . . you know . . . I'm so sorry." And then she did the worst possible thing: she placed a sympathetic hand on Anna's arm. It burned.

Anna wanted to shrug it off, to glare at Keisha for stepping over an unmarked boundary, but she didn't. "Oh, look!" she said, staring at the air past the other woman's head to the opposite side of the large and glossy open-plan kitchen. "I think Vanessa is looking for you."

Their hostess was actually nowhere to be seen, but two could play at the "invisible friend" game. Keisha looked torn for a brief second, then gave Anna a swift one-armed hug and hurried off. Anna breathed out and escaped in the other direction.

She was glad when the hour hand on her watch slid past nine and people got beyond the "meet and greet" phase and settled into small groups, leaning against kitchen counters, staking out their places in the various seating areas. It made it easier to skirt around the edges of the party, glass of warm fizz in hand, giving the impression she'd just finished a fabulous conversation with one person and was on her way to another, when really—aside from that brief exchange with Keisha—the only person she'd properly engaged with all evening had been Gabi, and that had been in the car on the way there.

They'd barely pulled out of Anna's road when Gabi had said in a very offhand way, "Did I mention Jeremy is coming tonight?"

Anna had glanced sharply across at her friend in the passenger seat. Gabi had been sitting calmly, hands folded in her lap, the hint of an angelic smile on her lips. That had troubled Anna, because Gabi didn't do cool and matter-of-fact. Gabi did squeals and smiles and showers of confetti. Over *everything*. The churning in the pit of Anna's stomach had intensified.

"Oh?" she'd said, deliberately keeping her tone light. "Remind me who he is again?" Even though she'd known full well that Jeremy was a pal of Vanessa's. Even though she'd known he was a graphic designer and had an "amazing" flat in Beckenham.

Anna had known it was only going to be a matter of time before that particular grenade landed because Gabi had been casually dropping his name into conversation for weeks now, almost as frequently as she hinted—not always so obliquely—that it was time for Anna to "move on."

But Anna didn't want to move on. She wasn't ready.

However, the fact she'd said this a thousand times had obviously had no impact on Gabi at all, because there her friend was, smile barely contained, weaving her way through the crowded kitchen with a man in tow.

And the penny finally dropped. It hadn't been her own romantic prospects Gabi had been getting all sparkly and hopeful about earlier on that evening—it had been Anna's.

Anna turned to slip away in the opposite direction but found herself blocked by a gaggle of Vanessa's beauty salon employees, blinged up and colorful like exotic birds. They'd set up camp next to the glass-fronted fridge containing nothing but champagne and didn't seem inclined to budge.

"I thought I'd lost you!" Gabi said, breaking into one of her Julia Roberts–style grins. She glanced over to the man whose arm she had hold of, who, it had to be said, wasn't looking as enthusiastic about this encounter as Gabi was. "This is Jeremy!" Gabi said, with the same degree of fanfare more suited to announcing an Oscar winner. Tall with sandy-blond hair, Jeremy had the kind of sharp cheekbones that reminded Anna of the detective in the Swedish crime series she was currently bingeing on Netflix.

"Remember I told you about him?"

Anna shot Gabi a look. *Seriously? You're really doing this?*

Undeterred, Gabi countered with a look of her own—*Don't mess this up!*—and carried on talking. "You know you were saying you wanted to try salsa classes? Well, Jeremy here has been going to some at the civic center. He can tell you all about them." Gabi then came to the startling realization that everyone's glasses needed topping up and, despite being *right next to* a fridge packed with champagne, skipped off in the opposite direction to find some. That left Anna and Jeremy staring awkwardly at one another.

Anna took a breath, smiled and said, "Hello." Yes, she was feeling a bit antisocial at the moment, but she wasn't rude. That was also why, as they began tiptoeing through the small talk, she didn't tell him salsa classes had been Gabi's idea. Something to get Anna out of the house. Something to take her mind off things. Before that, it had been conversational Italian, and before that, silver jewelry making. Even flipping car maintenance.

And so that was how Anna ended up talking to Jeremy in the kitchen for half an hour. He was a nice man, she decided. Not too full of himself. Not boring. And he'd obviously been blindsided by Gabi's not-so-subtle attempt at matchmaking too. He was trying his best to hide it but not quite succeeding. Anna liked him more for that.

When he suggested moving outside to get away from the crush and noise of the kitchen, she followed him. "So, how did you become such a salsa expert?" she asked, as they made their way out onto the deck overlooking the immaculate back garden.

Jeremy made a face. "I definitely wouldn't call myself an expert."

"No? How long have you been taking lessons?"

He rubbed a hand over his face and laughed. *He had a nice smile*, Anna decided. There was a twinkle in his eyes, a warmth there, something genuine. "Well, that's just it . . . I've only been a handful of times, and that was because my sister was desperate to go and my brother-in-law flat-out refused."

Anna laughed along with him. Not a full-on belly laugh, more a soft chuckle, but it shocked her so much she fell silent again almost instantly. The sound was foreign to her ears, the gentle juddering of her shoulders, alien. How long had it been since she'd last laughed? She wanted to answer "days," but that would be bare-faced lying. "Weeks" was also probably a tad optimistic.

Maybe that was why she threw herself into the conversation with this nice man more fully, why she found herself not just standing there, smiling and nodding in the right places, but talking back, sharing little bits of information about herself. Maybe that was why, when he told her about the salsa classes and said he'd brave them again should she wish to go and not want to walk through the door alone, she said she'd think about it.

It struck her, as she steered the conversation toward another subject, that Gabi had picked well. Very well. Because in another life, another reality, she might be feeling butterflies at the thought of dancing with Jeremy, at the thought of placing her hand in his, feeling the brush of his palm against hers when they moved. As they leaned on the deck railing, Jeremy kept looking at her, and every time he did, delicate wings tickled her inside.

But Anna knew not to pay much heed to the fluttering. Butterflies were short-lived creatures and, given the frost hardening the depths of her soul, they'd probably be dead soon. Frozen stiff, poor things.

Even so, when Jeremy took the glass of warm, flat champagne from her hand to get her a fresh one, their fingers brushed, and the butterflies started to panic.

That brief touch tripped a secret alarm inside her, like a cashier pressing an under-the-desk button during a bank raid. Red lights flashed in the vault of her heart every few seconds. Sirens blared inside the confines of her skull as Jeremy pushed his way through the crowd back toward the kitchen.

Don't care if he's nice-looking, the alarm yelled. *Even* really *nice-looking. He's not Spencer.*

Don't care if he's intelligent, sensitive and gently serious in a way that's appealing, in a way Spencer never was. Don't care that this Jeremy person would never crack a joke every time you tried to talk about something deep or important. He's not him. Never will be.

Anna tried to ignore the nagging alarm when Jeremy returned. She tried to listen to an anecdote about a particularly demanding design client he'd had, but the pulsing warning was there in the back of her head as his gaze began to linger longer on hers, as a little bubble of intimacy began to close around them.

Oh, heck. She knew where this was going.

In less than half an hour, he might gently touch her arm whilst making a point. Maybe, when Big Ben's chimes rang out across the nation, he'd lean in and kiss her softly on the lips. Her stomach plummeted at the thought. She felt hot and prickly all over.

Not Spencer, the warning flashed again. *Not Spencer. Not Spencer. Not Spencer.*

Anna tried to smile and nod as Jeremy kept talking, but she felt sick and giddy at the same time. This really wouldn't do. She had to find a way to make it all stop.

But then Jeremy segued into a story about a stag do he'd been on, where he and his pals had spent an afternoon driving racing cars at Goodwood. Anna grabbed the lifeline he offered without hesitation.

"I bought my husband one of those experience days for his birthday," she said. "Supercars . . . He was mad about Aston Martins."

Jeremy opened his mouth to say, "Oh, really?" but then her words caught up with him, and he faltered. He nodded a couple of times, a filler action, she guessed, designed to give him time to regroup. "Aston Martin?" he finally said, his head still bobbing. "Good choice."

He was momentarily stalled, she realized, but not shocked at the mention of a husband, as most men might have been if a woman at a party had been talking to them exclusively for more than an hour with no sign of a significant other.

"Gabi told you about Spencer," she said. A statement, not a question.

"A little," he replied, and she had to give him credit—he maintained eye contact, didn't look away or do the invent-a-friend routine. Up until then, their conversation had been plain sailing, but he didn't run when the waters got choppy. He stayed

and navigated the lurching awkwardness that followed her revelation. The man had class.

But Anna couldn't let that make a difference, so she launched
into the story of what happened two years, nine months and
eight days ago: How her husband had gone out one evening to
the corner shop to buy a bottle of wine. How he'd never returned because someone else had drunk too much wine the very
same evening, and then that person had got behind the wheel of
a car. It had only been a three-minute walk to the shop.

She'd told Jeremy how she'd heard the sirens as the ambulance
arrived and how she'd just known that something was very, very
wrong. How she'd left the front door open and had run out of
the house in her bare feet, even though it had been March. How
she'd seen Spencer lying in the road, surrounded by paramedics.
How their faces had been white. Grim. How he'd been pro-
nounced "dead on arrival" when the ambulance had made it to
the hospital.

She told Jeremy every last detail while he watched her, not
horrified or embarrassed, but with compassion in his eyes. True
compassion, not pity.

And that was why Anna made sure every word was a brick,
and that she built each brick into a wall. A boundary line. And
when she had finished her tale, she was on one side, and Jeremy
was on the other.

Still he didn't turn tail. Damn him.

"About the salsa lessons . . ." he began. "I get the feeling
they're more Gabi's idea."

"They are," she said simply. Truthfully.

He nodded, understanding there would be no salsa-ing for the
two of them any time soon. Probably not ever.

"It was nice meeting you, Anna," he said gently, looking her straight in the eye. Not in a romantic way (she'd definitely squashed that vibe) but in an honest way, letting her know he really meant it.

Anna nodded in reply and swallowed down the stray words forming in her throat, afraid they might form a request for him to stay, to keep talking to her as if she was a human being and not a walking tragedy that needed gentle handling.

He glanced toward the house. "There's someone I need to . . ." He didn't finish the sentence but gave her a rueful smile before turning and walking back indoors. Anna watched the back of his head appearing and disappearing as he made his way through the crowded kitchen.

He'd fallen back on the old invisible-friend routine after all, but far from hating him for it, she was grateful. He'd done it to save her any further discomfort, not himself. Jeremy had seen her bricks, he'd seen her wall, and he'd respected them. Tears sprang to her eyes.

She was still standing there, staring blurrily through the vast folding glass doors into the house, when Gabi bounded up. "Where's Jeremy?"

Anna was pretty sure her friend was here asking her this question because she'd spotted him back inside the house on his own. "He had someone he needed to talk to," she said, and ignored the flicker of warmth at the idea of being connected to him through this little white lie, a secret just between the two of them. She turned to face the lawn and stared out into the darkness.

Gabi looked crestfallen. "But . . . But it looked as if you were getting on really well."

"We were."

"You were talking for ages."

Anna nodded again. She felt a stab of guilt in her stomach. She really hadn't been fair to Jeremy, chatting to him for so long. And then the knife of guilt, only a flesh wound at that point, plunged itself deeper, twisted and turned. She hadn't been fair to Spencer either. "What were you *thinking*, Gabi?"

Gabi feigned ignorance for only a split second before she crumbled. She looked beseechingly at Anna and shook her head. "I don't know . . . I was just thinking that he's a nice guy and that . . . And that . . ."

Anna's jaw tightened. "If you say I need to move on, I'm going to dump this glass of champagne right over your head."

Gabi's expression grew earnest. "But you *do* need—"

That was it. Anna had had enough. She didn't make good on her threat, but she did fling the glass over the railing of the deck and onto the lawn, where it rolled down the slope and landed under a bush. Vanessa would kill her if she ever found out.

"I don't need to move on!" she yelled. "It's only been two years!"

Gabi opened her mouth, and Anna knew she was going to—quite correctly—point out that it had been closer to three, but she took in Anna's warning expression and shut it again.

"What am I supposed to do? Just snap my fingers and say, *Oh, well! The love of my life, the man I adored with every fiber of my being, is gone, so I'd better just pick a replacement?* As if he was last year's fashion trend?"

"Okay, no . . . I . . ."

Anna could see the hurt in her friend's eyes, but it didn't slow her down one bit. *Too bad, Gabi. You're the one who pushed and pushed, the one who prodded this tiger out of its numb sleep, and now you're going to hear it roar!*

"When you've had a relationship that's lasted more than eighteen months, maybe *then* you can start telling me how to live my life!"

Gabi flinched. Anna knew she'd hit below the belt, that she was going to feel horrible about this when she calmed down, but she had to make Gabi stop. She had to make her *see*.

There had to be an end to the Italian lessons, to the jewelry making and the salsa dancing. To the *Jeremys*. Because Anna knew there would be more of them paraded out for her to meet if she didn't stand up for herself now. She had to make Gabi understand that she wasn't going to magically get over Spencer if she learned to conjugate the verb *essere* or perform a perfect "side basic." She wasn't going to get over him *ever*.

"So don't tell me to move on. Because you don't get it. You don't understand! Not until you've lived through it!"

And, before Gabi could offer any words in her defense, Anna turned and strode across the deck, heading for the gate at the side of the house. Thankfully, it wasn't locked. She couldn't have faced pushing her way back through all those people inside.

You couldn't face having to turn around and see Gabi standing there, silent tears stinging her eyes, a little voice inside her head goaded, but Anna drowned it out by wrenching the gate open and slamming it shut behind her hard enough to make the latch rattle. And then she marched to the cul-de-sac where she'd parked her car, climbed in and drove herself home.

Chapter Three

Anna didn't bother turning the lights on when she got back home. She headed straight up the stairs and into the master bedroom. The digital alarm clock on the bedside table blinked the time: 11:36. She turned away from it.

If she didn't look at it, she couldn't see the numbers getting higher and higher, finally reaching that dreaded row of zeros. And if she couldn't see them, it wasn't real. Midnight was a threshold she didn't want to cross. Not just this particular midnight, which loomed over her like a threatening shadow, but every midnight. Every day without him was one too many.

Anna had developed little rituals to help her get through the days and nights, and she needed one of those now. She walked over to Spencer's built-in wardrobe. After dropping her handbag on the floor, she curled her fingers round the handles and eased the doors open. All his suits and shirts were still hanging there, just where he'd left them. She knew it was a horrible cliché, but she couldn't bring herself to throw them into a bin bag or take them down to the charity shop.

She sighed and pulled the sleeve of the nearest shirt toward her, held it up to her face and breathed in. His scent was no longer there, even though she refused to wash any of them, but she pretended it was. Every time she did this, she tried to recall it precisely, but it was getting harder and harder to do.

Spencer would have laughed at her for being so sentimental, but then Spencer had laughed at everything, made a joke of everything. It had charmed and infuriated her in equal measures. He'd even done it the first time she'd told him she loved him.

That frosty November evening nine years earlier had been magical. They'd been out to dinner in central London to celebrate their two-month anniversary, but instead of catching the Tube back to Charing Cross, they'd opted to wander beside the Thames, strolling along the Victoria Embankment, with its sturdy stone walls, globe-like lamps decorated with ugly, bulbous-headed Victorian fish and wooden benches with strange mythical creatures woven into the wrought-iron supports. The lights of the Festival Hall and the Southbank Centre had twinkled across the water at them, and the London Eye, glowing bluish white, had kept watch.

Spencer had pulled her into his arms and kissed her, before holding her face between his palms, looking deep into her eyes and saying, so simply, so seriously, "I love you." Then his face had broken into a huge grin. "I'm sorry," he'd said, laughing, "I just couldn't hold it in any longer."

She'd felt dizzy and breathless. Spencer had a way of doing that to her, of making her question if up was down and down was up; he was the magnet to her compass needle. "I love you too," she'd whispered back, and his smile had grown even wider, but then the edges of his mouth had turned downward. "I beg your pardon?" he'd said, mischief twinkling in his eyes. "I don't think I quite heard you."

She'd laughed softly, then had cleared her throat and tried again, louder this time. "I love you too."

Spencer had cupped a hand to his ear. "Nope! Still can't hear you." She'd punched him playfully on the arm. He'd kept moving closer and closer until their lips had almost touched, then he'd suddenly let go of her and had leapt onto one of the benches facing the river, feet planted wide, arms outstretched. "When you love someone," he'd shouted, "you don't say it quietly, you proclaim it from the rooftops! Like this . . ." And he'd bellowed to the seagulls sitting on the ropes of lights between the lampposts. "I love you, Anna Mason! I've loved you since the day I met you and I always will!"

He'd held out his hand to her and she'd taken it, let him help her up onto the bench so she'd been standing beside him, trying not to let the heels of her boots get stuck between the wooden slats. He'd grinned at her, waiting for her to follow suit, and she'd almost yelled her own declaration of love into the night air, but something had stopped her. Instead, she'd turned to face him. Sometimes, Spencer needed to know that his way wasn't the only way.

"You heard, you idiot," she'd mumbled into his ear, and then she'd kissed him just as softly and just as sweetly as he'd kissed her.

After that, it had become their "thing"—if she said "I love you" first, he always responded with "I beg your pardon?" and then she'd cap it off by whispering, "You heard, idiot." She'd imagined them saying it to each other well into their eighties . . .

A sob escaped her lips and she sank to the floor of the wardrobe, taking both shirt and hanger with her, and then she buried her face in the blue-and-white striped cotton and cried until there were no tears left.

How was it possible to *ache* for someone this way? Not just metaphorically, but literally? Now she understood why people talked about having a broken heart, because she knew it was entirely possible for it to throb in pain along with every single beat.

She lost track of time, curled up on the wardrobe floor with Spencer's shirt clutched to her chest. Eventually, though, she blinked, regained the sense of where and who she was. The ache didn't stop, though. It never stopped.

She reached out to retrieve her bag from the bedroom floor and then returned to the wardrobe. Once she was huddled with her back against the wall, she pulled her phone out and pressed a button to wake it up.

Eleven fifty-six. It was almost midnight.

Anna closed her eyes and tried to stop time through the sheer strength of her will. Four minutes. Probably less than that—three and a bit—was all she had left of this year before it slid away, taking another piece of Spencer with it.

It didn't work. When she opened her eyes again, another minute had evaporated. She stared at the phone as an inner battle began to rage. There was another ritual, you see. One that was even less healthy. In the sane part of her head, she knew that. That was why she'd banned herself from doing it. She *was* trying, even if Gabi didn't think she was.

Put the phone down, she told herself. *You promised yourself you wouldn't do this again, remember?* It had been months since she'd been this weak.

But she didn't put the phone down. Slowly, deliberately, she pressed the screen and pulled up her contacts and then, just as slowly, just as deliberately, she located Spencer's name and hit "call."

Even before it connected, she could hear the message—hear his voice—in her head: *Hey! This is Spencer. I'm off having fun without you right now, but if you really have to leave a dull and boring message, you know what to do . . .*

Oh, how she longed to do just that, to pour it all out to him, but she didn't. It wasn't enough. She wanted to talk to him, yes, but she didn't want an empty, one-sided conversation. She wanted to hear his voice, his real voice, not a tinny recording from years ago. She wanted him to talk back to her. And then she could finally say what she should have said to him that last evening before he'd walked out the front door to go to the corner shop, something more meaningful than, "Can you grab a pint of milk while you're there?"

Her thumb hovered above the "end call" button. In all the times she'd dialed his number just to hear his voicemail greeting, she'd never once left that message because, even though Gabi might tell her she was stuck in the past, she really wasn't. She wasn't kidding herself. This was just an echo of him, nothing more. She knew she couldn't bring him back.

But it seemed that if she was going to fall from grace this evening, she was going to do it spectacularly. Maybe it was because she saw the time at the top of the phone change to a row of perfect nothingness that she did it. Maybe it was all the swelling emotions inside her from that evening clamoring to be let out. Who knew? All Anna understood was that all the words she thought she'd have a lifetime to say were stuck in the logjam of her throat and then, suddenly, three escaped. They would have to be enough.

"I love you . . ." she whispered in a voice that was raw with tears.

There was a heartbeat of silence, then another.

And then the reply came.

"I beg your pardon?"

Chapter Four

Sometimes, waking up is like emerging from a gentle, white fog. Slowly, the mist clears, and one finds oneself refreshed and ready to face the morning, seeing and thinking clearly. Unfortunately for Anna, waking up the following day was more like the aftermath of being buried alive in an avalanche. Her sleep had been blessedly blank and white, but it felt as if something heavy was sitting on her chest, pinning her to the bed, and she couldn't quite make sense of her surroundings. She lay there, unable to move, unable to think. Eventually, she began to punch herself free.

The first step was to get her eyelids open. She blinked a few times and just about managed, even though one eye was being more cooperative than the other, and turned to focus on the clock, but where she'd expected to see a digital display, there was now an old-fashioned alarm clock with bells on the top and little brass feet.

Even though the thick curtains were drawn, only barely emitting light, she realized the window was in the wrong place. It should have been on the right side of the room, but it was clearly on the left.

She sat up in bed, frowning, and then—finally—it all began to fall into place. She wasn't in her bedroom, but the spare room. She rubbed a hand over her gritty eyes and her stomach lurched.

Oh, God. Last night . . . The phone call.

She didn't even remember hearing Spencer's voicemail greeting, she realized, only what had come afterward—the voice, the one that had spoken where there should have been only emptiness and silence.

When she'd heard it, she'd immediately thrown the phone into the far reaches of the wardrobe, then had half crawled, half scrabbled her way across the bedroom floor until she'd reached the opposite wall, where she'd sat with her back pressed up against it, her knees pulled up against her body, staring at the open wardrobe as if a ghostly apparition might emerge at any second. At some point, she'd stopped shaking enough to stand up, stumble from the room and make it across the hallway, where she'd collapsed into this bed and, if the bedclothes were anything to go by, had slept fitfully and frantically.

She'd had all sorts of strange dreams after Spencer had died, ones where they'd been living their normal lives, and they had seemed so real that waking up again had been like being back in those first awful days after the accident. And then there were the nightmares . . .

But the dreams weren't always bad. Sometimes, in that twilight between sleeping and waking, she'd imagine him there in the bed beside her, warm and solid and alive. Once or twice she was sure she'd felt his breath on her back, his fingers brushing her thigh, but when she'd woken up properly his side of the bed had been cool and unwrinkled. She'd assumed it was her subconscious refusing to accept the truth, trying to fill the gaping hole he'd left behind.

Had last night been something like that? She'd been upset leaving the party. It could have triggered something . . .

Anna pondered the idea as she shifted position, realizing she'd got distracted and hadn't actually registered the time on the alarm clock. She turned her head to take another look.

Eleven thirty-two? She sprang out of bed.

She was supposed to be having a New Year's Day lunch with Spencer's parents at half past twelve, and it was a forty-five-minute drive to Epsom—at the very least. That meant she had to get into the car, well, now!

But one quick glance in the mirror confirmed that plan was a bust before it had even got underway. She was still wearing the same wrinkled black dress from the night before, her tights had a ladder that started under her heel and disappeared up under her hemline and her hair looked as if she'd been caught in a hurricane.

There was no time to analyze what had happened last night now. She had to get herself in the shower and dressed in a presentable manner in under fifteen minutes, and then, even if she flirted with the speed limit all the way to Epsom, she was still going to be cutting it really fine.

Spencer's mum was a stickler about punctuality, and Anna always made sure to turn up to their fortnightly Sunday lunches on the dot of half past twelve, even if they never ate until one. While Spencer had been famously late for everything, and Anna couldn't remember one family function she'd been to with him where they hadn't arrived at least half an hour after they were supposed to, Gayle seemed to hold her daughter-in-law to a different standard.

Maybe that was because the lunches had started not long after Spencer had died, a way to support each other through that awful time, to laugh and cry and remember him, and the tradition had just kept going, no one brave enough to suggest otherwise. Being late would have seemed disrespectful.

By noon, Anna had got a grip of herself and made it into her car. By twenty past, she was joining the M25 and putting her foot down. It was raining hard, that horrible, cold, icy stuff that would have been sleet if the temperature had been a degree or two cooler. She put the windshield wipers on max and forced herself to overtake a few cars and trucks instead of hugging the slow lane, as she usually would have done in such weather. However, the journey was a familiar one, and it wasn't long before she was driving mostly on automatic pilot, allowing her thoughts to wander.

What had *really* happened last night?

There really were only two possibilities: either she'd heard the voice on the phone—Spencer's voice?—for real, or she'd *thought* she'd heard it. Neither scenario calmed her down much—option one was just too "out there" to consider, and option two meant she was starting off the New Year by having a nervous breakdown.

Because he hadn't just said any old words, had he? He'd said, "I beg your pardon?" *Their* words, their thing.

Had she just wanted to hear it come back to her so badly that she'd imagined it? It had to be that. She'd been running off emotion last night, even before she'd got home and ended up curled up on the floor of her dead husband's wardrobe. Look at how she'd spoken to Gabi . . .

Oh, God. Gabi!

She'd forgotten to call her last night to apologize. She was a horrible, horrible friend!

Anna was usually a very careful driver, so much so that

Spencer had taken to calling her "Grandma" when she'd got behind the wheel, but she swerved onto the hard shoulder and brought the car to a stop. This *was* an emergency. Her handbag was on the passenger seat, and she delved into it with her left hand and started rummaging around. It was only when her fingers reached the lining at the bottom that she realized her mistake.

Her phone was still sitting in the bottom of the wardrobe, where she'd thrown it after the call. As bad as she felt about Gabi, there was nothing she could do about it now. It would have to wait until she got home later that afternoon.

Anna squinted at the road ahead, indicated and pulled back into the traffic. The voice—his voice—replayed itself inside her head as she did so.

I beg your pardon?

Just what Spencer would have said, but it hadn't been filled with barely contained laughter or the husky softness she would have expected. He'd sounded so serious, so sad. As if he'd been aching every bit as badly as she had at their separation.

That made sense, in a weird way. But also, it didn't. Why, if she'd invented it, hadn't she imagined Spencer's usual cheeky tone? That was what she'd been yearning to hear, after all, his very *Spencerness*, captured in an inflection, a nuance, to hear the smile in his words. Why had she made him sound so mournful?

Spencer would have laughed at her for letting her imagination run away with her, but was it really so ridiculous? They'd always said their love was special. Once, when they'd been at a dinner party and one of his friends had said he'd want his wife to move on and marry again if something happened to him, Spencer had quipped that he wasn't that generous, that he'd find a way to come back because Anna was his and always would be his. What if he'd found a way to do that? No one *really* knew what happened after you'd died, did they? It was the one area where science could never prod its curious fingers. What if something beautiful, something *impossible*, had occurred?

No, she told herself. *Just no.*

It couldn't be true. Because what was she going to do if it was? March into her in-laws' house for lunch and calmly announce that she'd had a chat with their dearly departed son the night before? It sounded ridiculous. It *was* ridiculous.

Okay, good. Anna released a shaky breath. Putting it in context like that helped. So what if it hadn't all been a dream? That didn't mean all of it had been real either. It was probably a mixture of reality, imagination and emotion—that was what she was going to tell herself if she started freaking out about it again. And she would keep telling herself that all the way through lunch that afternoon.

Chapter Five

What I could really do with, more than anything else, Anna thought, as she arrived at Spencer's parents' house and killed the engine, *is a hug, plain and simple.* She wished she were pulling up to her own parents' house, that it was her mother who would dry her hands on a tea towel and come running to the front door to greet her, but that wasn't possible. Not unless she wanted to jump on a plane and travel almost three thousand miles.

Her parents had moved to Canada not long after she and Spencer had married. Anna's mother worked as a conference center manager for an international chain of hotels, and the kind of position she'd been working toward her whole career had come up. The only snag? It was in Nova Scotia. Anna's father had just retired from being a civil engineer, and their only child was settled, so they had taken the leap. The plan was to move back to the UK when her mum retired. Anna visited, of course, and they had Skype calls regularly, but it wasn't quite the same. You couldn't hug a screen.

Anna ran from her car and rang the Barrys' front doorbell. Quarter past one. She'd never been this late before.

Gayle answered. She smiled at Anna, but there was a stiffness in her posture as she leaned in and kissed her briefly on the cheek. No hug was forthcoming. "You're running a bit late," she said, taking in Anna's woolly sweater and jeans, which were definitely not as smart as her usual family lunch attire, but Anna had barely had time to find anything clean, let alone iron anything.

"Um . . . yes. Traffic was a bit bad." She nodded toward the rain, still falling in large, icy drops beyond the overhang of the porch.

"Well, we managed to hold off a bit," Gayle said, opening the door wide. "But you're here in the nick of time—we were just about to sit down." And she led the way through the house to the large dining room that overlooked the garden. Spencer's older brother, Scott, was already there, helping to carry covered dishes in from the kitchen. Anna always felt a little jab in her ribs every time she saw him. He looked so much like his younger sibling. Both boys had inherited their mother's fair hair and blue eyes, although Spencer had always looked the more boyish. Scott's features were sharper, his expression naturally more somber.

He and his wife had announced just before Christmas that she was expecting their first child at the end of May. Teresa gave Anna a little nod as she arrived from the kitchen, carrying a dish full of stuffing balls. Anna couldn't help looking at her stomach, trying to work out if there were the beginnings of a bump there under her loose top. While she was overjoyed for the couple, she felt a little flush of envy every time she thought about it.

She tried to help but was shooed away, so she slid into her normally assigned seat at the bottom of the table. Spencer's dad, Richard, winked at Anna, making her feel slightly less as if she had her tail between her legs for being late. Spencer had taken after his father, a man who had, apparently, been telling "dad jokes" well before he'd actually become a dad. Anna gave him a conspiratorial smile back and felt her shoulder muscles unclench.

When lunch was over, they retired to the living room. This

was Anna's favorite part of the afternoon. The tradition had started right after Spencer had died. To while away the hours doing something other than drinking endless cups of tea, they'd looked through the photo albums together, trying to pick a few for the upcoming funeral.

It hadn't been an easy job to narrow it down to just a couple. With his mischievous blue eyes and boyish grin, Spencer had been very photogenic. And even after the funeral, they'd kept going with it. It had been comforting to see him smiling back from the pages at them, just being *Spencer*. It still was.

Gayle went to the special shelf on the bookcase that contained the large albums, all arranged in date order, and pulled one from the left-hand end.

Toddler pics? Again? It seemed an awfully long time since they'd looked at anything from the other end of the shelf, from any of the albums Anna might have a chance of featuring in, and she really could do with seeing some solid evidence of her time together with Spencer today, because everything seemed to be upside down and back-to-front. An anchor of some sort might have been helpful.

She nodded along as usual anyway as Gayle leafed through the album, making the appropriate noises at the right times, and it wasn't hard to do because she *did* love seeing all these favorite pictures of her husband—the one of him on top of a lion in Trafalgar Square, or the one of him with the snowman he'd built in the back garden.

Anna looked over at her mother-in-law, with her perfectly coiffed, Mary Berry–style hairdo, her erect posture and precise movements. Her fierce loyalty and protectiveness toward her family were truly admirable, but they came with a downside.

Gayle was the sort of mother who believed no woman was good enough for her baby boys, and it had taken a while for Anna not to feel like an outsider at family gatherings.

But after Spencer had died, that had changed. Gayle had clung to her, opened her arms and welcomed Anna into the family in a way she never had before. They were united in their loss, their grief. She'd *needed* Anna. Both Scott and Richard didn't do emotion, one buttoning down hard, the other finding safety in humor when things got too much, so Anna had been the one person Gayle had been able to talk to. They'd cried and laughed and remembered together.

Anna's parents had come to stay as soon as they could after Spencer had died. They'd even offered to move back to England permanently, but Anna had refused, telling them they couldn't put their lives on hold indefinitely for her. However, once they'd actually left, she'd realized how much it had helped having someone else in the house. She knew one or both of them would have dropped everything again if she'd told them she was feeling lonely, but that wouldn't have been fair on them. So having this new, closer connection with Gayle had meant everything.

Once the photo albums were put away, a conversation began about how they'd all spent New Year's Eve, but nobody lingered on their tales, because it was glaringly obvious that someone was missing from all of them. To make up for that, Scott relayed a story about the millennium New Year, when they'd had a big reunion with Gayle's side of the family. Anna had heard the anecdote countless times before, but it still made her smile. Fifteen-year-old Spencer had crept out of a long and boring dinner and lit five hundred pounds' worth of fireworks meant for midnight while the rest of the family were still enjoying their desserts. He was lucky he hadn't blown himself to kingdom come.

Anna glanced across the table and saw Gayle smiling widely, but her eyes were glittering, and she kept looking down at her dinner as the others laughed and delved into the memory in greater detail. She suspected her mother-in-law was thinking exactly the same thing as her: that it seemed so unfair. Everyone had always joked that Spencer's reckless side would be his undoing, so it seemed wrong that he'd been minding his own business, sensibly walking across the road, when the end had come. It made his death even harder to bear.

When there was a gap in the conversation, Anna said, "What about that night when Spencer stayed in and missed going up to London with everyone because Lewis was sick? He wasn't always impossible."

"God, I loved that dog," Richard chipped in, smiling. "Only one in this household who took me seriously!"

Gayle turned to face Anna. "Did Spencer tell you about that?"

"No."

"But you weren't on the scene then, were you?"

Anna took a moment before she answered. She didn't want to contradict her mother-in-law, but she wasn't going to lie. "We'd only just got together. It was all very new."

Gayle frowned. "I don't think you were." And she went on to supplant Anna's story with one of her own.

Anna stayed quiet. She knew she was right, because that had been her and Spencer's first New Year's Eve together. They'd spent it here in this house, cuddled up on the sofa with the sickly dog. Even if her mother-in-law didn't remember, why had she pressed the point, and—to be honest—been a little snippy? Was this punishment for holding up lunch?

However, if Gayle was annoyed, she showed none of it as she recounted an incident from when Spencer had still been in primary school. In fact, her usually prickly demeanor melted away and she laughed and gesticulated as she told how Spencer had hidden behind the sofa so he could stay up to ring in the New Year with the family. They'd found him asleep there in the morning, after a great deal of panic about his empty bed. This memory was safe territory for Gayle. No danger of anyone not born a Barry accidentally trespassing in it.

Anna nodded and smiled along—she couldn't do anything else, having no personal knowledge of the incident—but as she sat there, she realized this hadn't been the first time that Gayle had been a little "off" with her in recent months. She hadn't thought anything of it at first. Her mother-in-law had never been an easy person to get along with, so she'd merely assumed it was just Gayle being Gayle. Maybe she was being uncharitable, but now she was starting to think otherwise.

Chapter Six

Anna felt a little nervous as she walked up the path to Gabi's block of flats. She'd stopped off at a service station on the way back from Gayle and Richard's, where she'd picked up a bottle of red wine and a large Toblerone. She balanced them in one hand while she pressed the intercom with the other.

"Hello?"

"It's me," Anna said, her voice less confident than she wanted it to sound. "Can I come in?"

Usually, the buzzer would have sounded immediately, but today there was thick silence. After a few seconds, however, the door hummed and clicked. Anna stepped inside the communal hallway and began to climb the stairs to the first floor.

Gabi opened her front door, smile noticeably absent, and allowed Anna to walk past her into the living room. Anna perched on the edge of the sofa and looked around the room she knew so well. While she went for clean lines and neutral tones, Gabi's decorating style was more colorful and eclectic.

What always stood out to Anna was the number of photograph frames cramming every single surface, all of Gabi's family back in Brazil. Not only were there plenty of pictures of her parents and siblings—two brothers and three sisters—but there were snaps of uncles and aunties, nieces and nephews too. From what Gabi had told Anna, they were a large, close-knit family, always in each other's business but always there when they needed each other. Being an only child, Anna had often wished for a family like that.

She and Gabi had met in their early twenties when Gabi had moved from São Paulo to London for university, and they'd instantly hit it off. However, it was after Anna's parents had left for Canada that they'd really become close, bonding over both having their family thousands of miles away. Gabi had become the sister Anna had never had, which was why she was determined to fix this.

She placed the chocolate and the bottle of wine on the coffee table. Gabi sat down on the armchair across the room, back straight, arms folded.

"I'm so sorry, Gabi. I was a total bitch last night."

"Yes, you were."

Anna swallowed. "Did you get home okay?"

Gabi raised an eyebrow and shot Anna a look that said, *Seriously?*

Anna buried her face in her hands. "I know, I know . . . I don't know what I was thinking! I was just . . ." She looked up again. "You know I would never do anything to hurt you on purpose, don't you? Because you're the best friend anyone could ever have. You try to help me, put up with all my crap, and this is how I treat you. I don't blame you if you don't want to speak to me at the moment. I don't blame you if you don't want to speak to me ever again!"

Gabi's expression softened a little. "There you go, being all dramatic again."

Anna paused for a few moments and thought hard. There was really only one thing she had left to say. "I'm so sorry. Can you forgive me?"

Gabi sighed. "Maybe. But things need to change." She tucked one leg up underneath herself and reached for the Toblerone. "*You* need to change."

"I'm okay," Anna said, mostly on reflex.

"No. You're not. You walk around like a zombie most of the time and when you do connect with the world around you—with the *people* around you—you go crazy!" She shook her head. "It is not healthy, Anna."

Anna wanted to disagree, but the events of the previous night loomed between them as evidence. "I don't know what came over me."

Gabi sighed again, and it struck Anna that Gabi did that a lot when she talked to her these days. She hadn't realized she'd become the sort of friend who was hard work, but she obviously had. Maybe she hadn't realized that because, as Gabi had so eloquently put it, she was a zombie.

And that was exactly what it felt like: as if a piece of her had died with Spencer and she'd been shuffling through life—sleepwalking—ever since.

"I understand that some days are good, and some days are bad," Gabi said gently. "And that Christmas and New Year are hard for you, but . . ."

"I know," Anna said again. It was all she could say. Last night was a mirror held up in front of her, one she couldn't look away from, and she didn't much like what she saw.

Gabi shifted, sat up a little straighter. "So . . . What are you going to do?"

"I don't know," Anna replied slowly, and she really didn't. She'd done it all. Grief counseling? Tick. Self-help books and support groups? Tick. Nothing seemed to work. "I wish I did."

Gabi didn't say anything; she just smiled.

"What?" Anna said, slightly scared of the answer to her question.

"How about salsa?"

"Really?" she replied, hoping that Gabi was just pulling her leg. The determined pair of eyes that sat above the troublesome smirk said otherwise.

"Really. If you go to salsa, we won't talk about New Year's Eve again."

Anna hesitated. Gabi was still sitting with her arms folded, watching her. Waiting. Anna swallowed.

"It will be fun," Gabi added, without smiling this time.

"You really think I need to—"

"Yes. I do." Gabi's answer was hard, but her eyes gave her away. Behind the determined stare, Anna could detect quiet pleading. Gabi was worried about her. Really worried. That was why she was clinging on to this idea as if it was a lifeline. It wasn't about the dancing or the classes. Her friend was just desperate to know there was hope, that Anna could find some way to be happy again.

She nodded. "Okay." She'd do just about anything for Gabi. Even salsa.

Gabi jumped off the armchair, squealing, and ran across and dived on Anna, wrapping her in a hug. "I will ask Jeremy about—"

Anna pushed Gabi back enough to look her in the face without going cross-eyed. "Hold on! No one said anything about Jeremy!"

Gabi tipped her head to one side and gave Anna an exasperated look. "But Jeremy is very nice—and very hot!"

"You go salsa dancing with him, then!"

"No one is asking you to marry him. It's just dancing. Think of him as . . . What is the word? Training wheels! You can take them off when you are ready for more."

Anna folded her arms. "I said yes to salsa, not to Jeremy. And if you're going to make me salsa at all, then *you* are going to be my partner."

"Oh, yes?" Gabi held out her hands and beckoned to Anna with her fingertips. "Show me!"

Reluctantly, Anna got off the sofa and joined her friend. Gabi wouldn't let her sit back down until they'd tried a few steps of what *seemed* like salsa, but it all got out of hand when Gabi tried to dip Anna and lost her balance. They ended up on the floor in a heap, giggling.

"It's good to hear you laugh," Gabi said.

Anna sighed. "I know."

They pushed themselves onto all fours and then crawled back onto the sofa. "I'm going to get glasses," Gabi said, nodding at the wine. "Do you want to sleep here tonight?"

Anna crawled over to Gabi's end of the sofa and gave her a big, fat, squishy kiss on the cheek. "I love you, you know that?"

Gabi gave her a squeeze back then shoved her off so she could stand up. "I know. It's hard not to."

Anna gratefully accepted the large glass of red wine Gabi handed her a minute or so later, and the duvet and pillows that were thrown at her when they'd polished the bottle off so she could nest down on the sofa. Gabi even produced a pair of freshly laundered, brushed cotton pajamas for Anna to wear.

"Thank you," Anna said as she took them and held them to her chest.

"They are too small for me now. You can have them if you want."

"Not for the pajamas, you doofus—although they're lovely—I meant for everything."

"I just want you to be happy."

Anna nodded. She knew that. But it was safer not to reply in words, because she also knew that what Gabi wished for her just wasn't possible. There was a difference between having a quick giggle over falling over your best friend's two left feet and being truly content and peaceful. Anna wasn't convinced she could ever feel that way again. How was it possible when a huge piece of herself was missing, and always would be?

ANNA RETURNED HOME the following morning and headed straight for the shower, leaving her clothes in a heap on the bathroom floor. It was her first day back at work after the Christmas holidays, and she didn't want to be late, even if it wasn't the most thrilling job in the world.

Before Spencer had died, they'd worked together, but it hadn't always been that way. He'd left university with a degree in computer science and, after a few false starts, had ended up working for a medium-sized video game developer. However, as the popularity of smartphones had risen, Spencer had become obsessed with creating a game app that would go viral. He'd tried all sorts of different things, from racing cars to flying sheep or bubbles that needed popping. He'd earned enough from a couple of them to go part-time, but he'd never quite come up with the big success he'd been looking for.

The problem was that Spencer was a mass of overflowing energy, and he struggled with focusing on one task for a consistent length of time. This became more apparent when he worked whole days at home with no structure. Anna had just accepted that was who Spencer was, but it had frustrated him to no end.

He'd begun a search to find a time management method that worked for his butterfly brain, but nothing had seemed to stick until he'd stumbled upon the concept of "block scheduling," which gave him the structure he needed without pinning him down too hard. However, the only relevant app he could find was not only a bit basic but hot pink. Spencer had ranted at length about that—who on earth made their app all pink with no option to change the color scheme? Anna had finally got fed up and told him to stop moaning and start creating an app of his own. He had the skills to do so, after all.

And Spencer had done just that. He'd teamed up with a couple of other guys he'd known at uni, and together they'd built BlockTime, a stylish, intuitive time management app that (a) wasn't hot pink and (b) integrated seamlessly with existing calendars, to-do lists and other apps. And, thanks to Spencer's attempts to create the next viral game, it was more than a little addictive to use. It had taken time, but eventually it had grown in popularity.

Anna had quit her job as an HR assistant manager and had gone to work for the three guys. At first, she'd just done the admin and kept the books, but as time had gone on, she'd become involved in the design side. She had an eye for that kind of thing, it turned out, and while the "boys" had plenty of innovative ideas, they weren't always very practical. They'd needed someone to keep them grounded, to make sure the app was the kind of thing people would find easy to use, as well as being cool and full of technical wizardry. She'd loved working alongside Spencer, seeing him do what he was good at. When the money had finally started arriving, they hadn't been rich, but they'd been comfortable.

She'd taken time off after he died, of course. But two months had turned into three, and then three into six. Eventually, she'd had to admit that she just couldn't face going back into the office. Vijay and Rhys, the other directors, had understood. She'd inherited Spencer's share in the business and received a monthly cut from that, but other than that she left them to it. At least one thing she didn't have to worry about as a widow was money.

But she'd needed something to fill her days, so she'd applied for an admin job at a successful family-run plumbing business, and she'd now been there more than two years. What with it being winter, pipes freezing and boilers giving out, there was likely to be a lot of paperwork to catch up on after the Christmas break. Today was not the day to be late.

When she emerged from the shower, pink and scrubbed, she wrapped a towel around herself and hurried out onto the landing, but then she hesitated. The next logical place to go was the bedroom. She needed fresh clothes. But she hadn't been in there since she'd fled the house the day before.

Stop being daft, she lectured herself. *There's nothing to be frightened of.*

Before she could talk herself out of it, she walked into her bedroom. Spencer had very helpfully pointed out that one of her weaknesses was bottling everything up until she reached the boiling point, and then, when it exploded out of her, she did and said bizarre things. Was it too much of a stretch to think that she'd *hear* bizarre things as well?

She walked toward the wardrobe, slowly, quietly, almost as

if she was creeping up on it, and then she hooked her fingers around the edge of the half-open door and pulled. Her phone glinted at her from the floor, looking so ordinary, so innocent. She bent down and picked it up.

There. That hadn't been so hard, had it?

And because it hadn't been hard, because it all felt a bit surreal, like something that had happened in a dream, she pressed her thumb to the wake-up button and brought the display to life.

She pulled up her phone history. There, near the top of the list, was a call made at exactly midnight on New Year's Eve. She became aware of a woolly, tangled feeling in her stomach, a strange tightness in her chest. The evidence was there. She'd really dialed. She'd really said, "I love you."

The real question was: what had she heard in the silence that had followed? Nothing? Something? Her imagination going wild?

It had to be that.

She couldn't entertain anything else. She couldn't let herself hope and then let those hopes be dashed again. As low and lifeless as she felt at the moment, it was nothing compared to the first few months after Spencer's death. She didn't want to go hurtling back to that dark place.

Which meant what she did next was important. She was on a threshold. A knife edge. And there was only one possible direction she could let herself fall.

She lifted her thumb and swiped, deleting the log of just that one call. There. Gone. It had never happened.

Chapter Seven

*T*he February night air was cool on Anna's skin as she walked toward home. She'd known that coming out tonight was going to be a mistake, but she'd come anyway, only to be proven right. Instead of feeling buoyant and energized as Gabi had promised, she felt exhausted and flat.

She and Gabi had been going to salsa classes for six weeks now, although, much to Gabi's annoyance, Anna had insisted on going to the Tuesday night class instead of the Wednesday night one she knew Jeremy attended. However, once a month, the salsa school held a "party," an opportunity for students from both classes to mingle and practice their moves in a more informal atmosphere.

Anna had cried off the January salsa party, but Gabi had been determined that neither of them were missing the February one, especially as it had been scheduled to coincide with Valentine's Day. It didn't take a genius to understand there were certain milestone days every year Anna struggled with. She had done her best to reassure Gabi she'd have a much better evening staying home, out of the way of "loved up" couples, and starting the dark drama series that was next on her "to watch" list, but Gabi hadn't taken no for an answer, so off to the civic center they'd trotted.

Gabi's night had gone well—she'd snagged the attention of

Lee, the guy she'd had a crush on since the previous party—but Anna's night had been . . . well, not what she'd expected.

Jeremy had been there. She'd been prepared for that. He'd asked her to dance. She'd expected that too. He'd been charming, making her laugh about carrying on with salsa instead of joining his sister in her latest fitness craze (Burlesquercise), but when the song had finished, he hadn't lingered. In fact, he'd gone straight off and danced with another woman. Anna had got the distinct impression he was just being chivalrous, that she was just one in a long list of wallflowers he'd decided needed rescuing. For some reason that had irritated her.

But what had she been expecting? That with all her joie de vivre and sparkling conversation, a catch like Jeremy had been pining away for her for the last six weeks? That he'd come along that night in the hope of seeing her?

It was fine. She didn't want him to want her. And she certainly didn't want him, nice as he was. However, despite all her breezy inner protestations, as she'd watched him execute moves far above her skill level with a girl with a very swooshy ponytail, she'd been aware of a door slamming shut inside herself. A door she hadn't even known had been open.

That was the moment she'd decided to make her excuses to Gabi and head home.

When Anna walked back inside her house, it seemed empty, even though all her possessions were still exactly where she'd left them. Nothing was missing. Except, maybe, the card that should have been on her mantelpiece, the flowers that should have been in the vase on the dining table. There was no Valentine's fizz in the fridge, and there would be no laughter and warmth between the sheets of her bed when she finally crawled into it later on.

She missed him so much.

Most of all, she missed his touch. Not just the sex—that would be easy to get, if she were so inclined, a physical need to be met like hunger or thirst—but she missed those little moments of contact that only came with familiarity and intimacy. She missed having someone to snuggle up with on the sofa. Someone to kiss her goodbye in the mornings. Someone to fall asleep on during a train journey home after a night out in London. All seemingly tiny, inconsequential things. Except they weren't. It had taken losing them to make her realize how essential they were.

Anna tried to ignore the feeling that she was an empty shell, nothing else inside her but this ache for something she couldn't have. She tried to distract herself by pottering around, slipping off her shoes, hanging up her coat, putting the kettle on to make herself a cup of herbal tea she didn't really want. But the void inside just throbbed.

Eventually, she turned on a single lamp in the living room and sat down in the corner of her sofa. It was so tidy, so neat. That was Anna's natural state. She found it easy to put things away, to keep things ordered, but it wasn't how their home had been when Spencer had been alive.

She reached over to the coffee table and pulled the newspaper out from the shelf underneath, then flapped the pages open and messed them around a bit, before crumpling a section up and letting it slide onto the floor. That was how he'd always left it. It had driven her mad, but now she almost missed the socks down the side of the sofa cushions and the boxers that only made it halfway into the linen basket.

She sank back into the sofa and sighed. Would it ever stop, this feeling? Wasn't time supposed to heal all wounds? In her opinion, time was doing a pretty crappy job. *Buck up, time! Sort yourself out.* After all, it kept marching her steadily away from the last moment she'd seen Spencer living and breathing, whether she wanted it to or not. Surely it owed her a little something in return?

She tucked her legs up under herself and reached for her phone. This was a bad idea, but it had been a difficult night to get through; she was going to allow herself one small concession, one tiny weakness.

She pulled up her messages, found Spencer's name, then scrolled back to February fourteenth, three years earlier. He'd died a little over a month later, but on that Valentine's Day, Spencer had sent her a series of funny little text messages, crammed with emoticons and saucy suggestions about how they should spend the evening together when he got home.

Anna smiled as she reread them, reveling in not just the words but the memories of that night, memories that only two people in this world had been party to, and now she was the sole keeper of. It would be wrong to let them fade and die.

But reading it back, remembering it all, was like picking at a scab. It started with that feeling, that delicious temptation, knowing there was something you wanted to do but shouldn't. Oh, and then the moment came when you let your self-control crash and gave in to it. Bliss. Relief. Everything focused on that moment of instant gratification.

But it didn't stay that way for long. The wound was open again, and it began to sting and seep. There was a price to be paid for that split second of euphoria, and Anna paid it in full as she stared at the bright screen of her mobile, full of Spencer's personality captured in letters and stupid little cartoon faces, and the ache deepened until it was almost unbearable.

But then an idea crept into her head, a magnetic tug pulling her to a destination she didn't want to visit. To take her mind off it, she opened up the photos app on her phone and began scrolling back through the images of them together, lingering on them the way she'd wanted to at her mother-in-law's the previous Sunday (it had been secondary school pictures that day: toothy smiles, trophies and too-big blazers) but eventually she reached the earliest ones, and as many times as she tried to swipe down to reveal more, the pictures bounced back up to the top of the screen, stubbornly refusing to do as she asked.

And the tugging toward that bad idea, that black hole, was still there in the background, whispering to her, hypnotizing her to the point where she numbly opened her contacts and found the favorites. Spencer's name was at the top. She stared at it.

You said you wouldn't do this again, that sensible little voice in her head whispered. *You promised yourself that Valentine's Day would be different from New Year's Eve*, but her finger pressed the screen while the inner voice was still talking, and the phone began dialing his number. Even though her heart was beating double time due to the memory of what had happened last time she'd done this, she held the phone up to her ear.

The ringing on the other end of the line stopped and she held her breath, waiting for what came next. However, instead of Spencer's message, she heard a generic robotic voice instructing her to wait and speak after the tone.

How the heck had that happened? Had she been in such a flap last time that she'd managed to press the wrong button and delete his voicemail greeting? No, that wasn't right. You could do that to your own message but not to someone else's. It didn't make sense.

She pressed the "end call" button in frustration. What had just happened? Had it been a wrong number? Seconds ticked by as she glared at her phone screen, holding her breath, and then she dialed again. This time there was no message at all.

The call connected.

"Hello?"

Anna froze.

Was that him? It had only been one word. She couldn't tell! She couldn't think! Once upon a time, she'd been able to tell his voice from anyone else's, and it cut her to the core that she'd lost that treasured skill and hadn't even realized it. "Spencer?" she said in a croaky voice. "Is that you? Please let it be you." She started to cry. "I have so much I want to say . . ."

For a long time, there was nothing but silence. No voice. Not even the sound of someone breathing—which, in a rather morbid way, made sense—but she felt a presence. Someone was there. Someone was listening.

And so she started to speak. She began to say everything that had been boiling up inside her for two years, ten months and twenty-two days.

"Spencer, it's me . . ." She broke off, unable to carry on because her throat was so tight, and she had to concentrate on getting the next words out. "I love you, Spencer. I know you always laughed at the idea of soul mates, but you were mine. You *are* mine. And I miss you so much . . . Sometimes, I feel as if I'm never going to feel normal again. Strike that, because I feel that way *all* the time. And how could I go back to normal without you, anyway? I'm not sure how I go on living and breathing without you as it is."

A sudden wave of emotion hit her. Not something crashing

over her from the outside, but something rising up from within. "And I'm angry with you for that! I'm cross that you left me here alone, like it's some big joke. Like you're going to jump out from behind a corner and shout, 'Only kidding!' But it's not funny anymore, Spencer! It's just not funny. So stop it, you hear me? Stop it. Because I want you back." She hiccupped in a breath and then let out a sob. Her voice dropped to a whisper. "Please come back."

No reply.

Gluey tears had collected under her lashes and she wiped them away with her hands. "Please talk to me." She waited. Seconds ground past. Still there was no response on the other end of the line, but she could feel him there. She really could.

"Spencer?" she eventually said. It felt as if she was tiptoeing beyond the edges of life, of what was real. Maybe the rules were different there. Maybe she shouldn't take some things for granted. "Can you hear me? Do you even remember me? It's Anna . . ."

Please, she whispered silently, not knowing if she was appealing to Spencer or God, or the night around her. *Please, let there be someone there. I feel so alone.*

She waited for him to say her name, waited for him to say it in that soft, sexy way he always had when he'd picked up one of her calls, as if he had a special smile just for her. *Anna*, he'd say, and he'd load that one word with everything he felt for her. He wouldn't have even needed to tell her he loved her each day, even though he always had. Just hearing her name on his lips would have been enough.

And then it happened. What she'd been waiting for happened.

"Anna?"

Chapter Eight

Anna.

He'd said her name, but it wasn't soft and warm and full of smiles. Just a word repeated because it made no sense to the person speaking it. Anna felt as if someone had tipped a bucket of ice water over her head.

Oh, my God! What am I doing?

She ended the call, dropped the phone, then sprang off the sofa and stood at the opposite side of the room, trembling. She turned so she didn't have to look at the screen and found herself facing a small sideboard. She flung one of the doors open to reveal several dusty bottles of whisky. Spencer's whisky. She pulled out a tumbler and reached for a bottle, bypassing the smooth Highland Park for the Lagavulin. She needed earthy, peaty tones and a fire in the back of her throat. She half filled the glass, knocked it back in one go, then shuddered.

By the time she was at the bottom of her second glass, she wasn't quite as mortified as she had been half an hour earlier. In fact, she was starting to feel much more philosophical about the whole thing. So much so, that she reached over, picked up her phone and dialed the number again.

There was no mechanical voicemail message, just a hesitant silence on the other end of the line.

"I'm sorry. I know . . ." she said, hoping the edges of the

words weren't blurring into each other too much. And then, when all that came back was a soft grunt, she added, "I know you're not him . . . That you're not Spencer . . ." She broke off again to cough back a sob as the truth of that realization hit her a second time, as ridiculous as it was to have even considered it in the first place. "I just wanted to say that I'm sorry. For phoning in the middle of the night—twice now!—and rambling on like I've become unhinged."

Another soft grunt. But there might have been the merest smidge of a smile behind this one.

"I'm not unhinged. I'm just . . . just . . ."

There was a heavy, masculine sigh.

"I don't know what I am," she ended weakly.

For a few seconds it was very quiet, and Anna was half expecting to hear it deaden, for that silence, that gap in a conversation when no one says anything, to become the blankness of no one else being there at all, but then she heard him take a breath, readying himself to speak. "You haven't lost your mind," he said.

His voice was rich and warm and certain. Anna was tempted to believe him, even though she wasn't sure it was the truth. Reality had been a hazy concept for a long time now. "How do you know? After all, I'm talking to a stranger in the middle of the night."

"Life . . . isn't always easy," he replied slowly. It seemed as if he was picking his words carefully, not because he didn't have the conversational skills, quite the reverse. She had a feeling that this man was always careful with his words, always weighed them and used them sparingly. "Things happen . . . Things you couldn't ever have predicted. And when they do, it can throw you, turn you upside down and your life takes a very different path."

Anna held her breath. How did he know? Was there something strange and supernatural going on here after all? It seemed as if he'd peered inside her skull and recited back to her all the things she was thinking and feeling but could never tell anyone.

"And when life changes suddenly and unexpectedly," he continued, "there's a grieving of what was and what never can be again. I would call that being human."

That all sounded very logical, which was very reassuring. He could just be telling her what she wanted to hear, of course, to get the hysterical woman off the phone, but even so, his words had the weight of truth about them. Of experience.

Are you human? she wanted to ask, but she'd already subjected this poor man to a hefty dollop of her stupidity; he probably didn't need more. She swallowed the question and took a different tack. "Thank you," she whispered. "And sorry . . . I won't ring again." And then, because it seemed rude not to, she added, "Good night."

A pause, as if he was considering her words, as simple as they had been. "Good night . . . Anna."

And then he was gone, cut off by the pad of her thumb on the glass of her phone screen. *Good night, Anna.* There had been no smile in that voice just for her. But there had been something. Something she couldn't quite put her finger on.

Didn't matter, though, she thought as she stood up, turned off the living room light and headed up the stairs. She wouldn't be dialing that number ever again.

Chapter Nine

Anna kept her promise to herself—she didn't call Spencer's number again. Or what turned out to be Spencer's *old* number. She did, however, call the mobile phone provider and, after twenty minutes on hold and being rerouted through three different departments, finally the mystery was solved.

She'd been paying for Spencer's mobile with a joint credit card she no longer used except for that bill. The account was still active, but the card had expired last September. She'd found an urgent email buried under five hundred other unopened messages in her inbox, warning her Spencer's account would be closed in sixty days if a new payment source was not provided. When that hadn't happened, his number had been reassigned.

It was *her* fault that tiny but vital connection to Spencer had been lost. Nothing spooky or supernatural. No act of God or fate or whatever it was that was laughing at her from above the clouds as it toyed with her life. Her own stupid fault. She wished she could rewind time and go back and read the buried email alert before it was too late, to get her lethargic backside into gear and call the phone company.

But she supposed if she'd had the power to do that, she'd have skipped over those inconsequential things and would have gone back to the day Spencer had died. Instead of yelling down at him to get a two-pint carton of milk when he went to the shop, she would have run down the stairs, stopped him as he was opening the door, pinned him against the wall and kissed him senseless. Thirty seconds was all it would have taken, and then that drunk driver would have been further down the road or all the way around the corner. None of this would have happened and she wouldn't be living this nightmare.

That thought plagued her more and more as the next few weeks ticked past, leading up to March twenty-third, the third anniversary of his death. The Barry family had forgone their scheduled Sunday lunch two days earlier and were meeting up to mark the occasion, so Anna had taken the day off work. About eleven in the morning she climbed into her car and headed out of London.

She glanced up at the sky as the houses and shops melted into woods and farmland. It was gray and moody, threatening rain. Disappointing, but fitting. She had mixed feelings about the day ahead. The last two years, she'd met up with Spencer's family and they'd all just assumed they would do the same today, but now she was thinking about it, she wondered if she'd have been better off spending the day on her own. A day to be quiet and reflect might have been just what she needed.

She sighed. It was too late to change plans now, anyhow. It would be insensitive—if not downright rude—to call and say she wasn't coming.

Her phone was sitting in a mount on the dashboard and she glanced at it. What she really wanted to do was call her mum and get some emotional support before she arrived at her destination. It would be early in Nova Scotia—not long past breakfast time—and her mother might well be up and driving to work in the nearby city of Halifax.

But Anna had to walk a fine line with her parents. It might be different if they didn't live on another continent, but they did, and she had to deal with that. Even though it had been three years, she knew they'd drop everything to come and visit if they felt she was struggling, but that just didn't seem fair. They had their own lives, and she didn't want her mother to jeopardize a job she adored.

In the end, she gave in and made the call. She could edit what she said, after all, and skirt around the really dark stuff that went on in her head, as she usually did.

"Hello, darling," her mum said, and Anna could hear the dull rumble of traffic in the background. "I suspected I might hear from you this morning, but I was going to call later if I didn't." She sighed. "I've been thinking a lot about Spencer myself in the last few days. You know how much your father and I adored him. I can hardly believe it's been three years . . ."

Anna sucked in a breath and blinked furiously, caught off guard by her mother's words.

"How are you doing?" her mum asked softly.

"I'm . . . managing," Anna lied, but then compensated with a bit of truth. "But I'm not really looking forward to today."

"Another trip to the crematorium and one of Gayle's buffets?"

Anna grimaced. "No, thank goodness. I couldn't have faced sandwiches and finger food again this year. Maybe that's just as well. I'm starting to find going to Gayle and Richard's a little—I don't know—claustrophobic."

"Really? How so?"

Anna frowned as she concentrated on overtaking a car that was going half the speed of all the other traffic. "I'm not sure how to put it into words. You know how important it is to me to keep that connection with Spencer's family, but sometimes I find Gayle a little bit distant. Maybe it's just me . . ."

She trailed off to consider this. She *had* been out of sorts, ever since New Year's Eve. That night, that *call*, had done it. Maybe she was just being oversensitive?

"I get what you're saying about Gayle," her mum said. "She's always struck me as a little . . . structured."

Anna chuckled softly. That was certainly one word for it.

"I thought she was that type from the first time we all had dinner together, but my heart really went out to her after Spencer passed away." She paused for a moment and sighed. "I can't even imagine how I'd react if I lost you, and I couldn't judge her if she was being a bit, well, controlling, in those months after he died. People deal with things in their own unique ways."

"Yes," Anna replied thoughtfully as she turned onto the A21 and headed toward the coast. "Being in control . . . I suppose that is Gayle's way of dealing with things. She likes her routines, her rituals." But so did Anna, so maybe she shouldn't judge her mother-in-law for that. "Anyway, no mini Scotch eggs and fondant fancies today, thank goodness. She suggested doing something different."

"*Gayle* did? You do surprise me! But maybe it's healthy that she's decided to plan something different this year? It shows that perhaps she's beginning to move on."

"Yes," Anna replied softly. She supposed that made sense, even though she didn't think she'd seen much evidence of that in their fortnightly lunches, but maybe she should give Gayle the benefit of the doubt? She hadn't always been quite this *structured*, after all. In the years before Spencer had died, she'd always been reserved, a little bit starchy, but she'd seemed softer, more ready to show her emotions. Anna had always thought she'd got on fine with her mother-in-law.

"So, what are you doing today instead?" her mum asked.

Anna brightened. "We're going to Camber Sands," she said, smiling to herself.

"In March?"

Anna laughed. "Yes, in March." She didn't mind what month it was. "It was one of Spencer's favorite places. The Barrys used to rent a cottage right on the beach almost every year when he was a kid. His dog, Lewis, used to love it there, ran round like an idiot on the sand all day long. We rented a place there for our first anniversary, a little wooden bungalow on the road just behind the dunes. Do you remember? The website pictures made it look like shabby chic, but it turned out to be just plain shabby."

Her mother laughed. "Oh, yes! Didn't the electricity cut out?"

"The first time we tried to boil the kettle. We had to light candles and wait until the owner came the next morning to show us how to deal with the temperamental fuse box."

She and Spencer hadn't cared. Not only had the candlelight made everything more romantic, but Anna had been secretly pleased. They'd never forget that anniversary now. They had another anecdote to file away under "Anna and Spencer's marriage," one they'd share with their friends, and years later with their children and then their grandchildren when they took them to the beach. This was gold in the treasure chest of her soul.

But now Spencer was gone, those shiny moments she'd collected and cherished were all she had left. Only sometimes they felt like arrows in her heart instead of riches. Sometimes they were both at the same time. It was all very confusing.

Her mother must have guessed her thoughts, because she said,

"I know it's hard, darling. Especially as you didn't have a proper chance to say goodbye to Spencer . . ."

Anna's breath hitched and tears stung the backs of her eyes.

"But maybe today will be a good day to try and do that? Not forget him, of course, but find a way to, you know . . ." Anna's shoulders slumped, and she mouthed the next words along with her mother. ". . . *move on*."

Her mother was almost as bad as Gabi, suggesting projects to fire her passion, different support groups and self-help books. "I suppose so," she said. It was just that nothing seemed to excite her anymore; nothing seemed to light her passion. It was very hard to move forward when you felt like a flat tire.

"Listen . . . I'm just pulling into the hotel parking lot, so I've got to go, darling, but I want you to know I'll be thinking of you all day. Call me again if you need me."

"I will," Anna said hoarsely. "Thank you, Mum."

"Nonsense. It's what I'm here for."

"I know. But I appreciate it anyway." Anna heard her mother's engine cut out. "I'd better let you go . . . Love you, Mum."

"Love you too . . ." And then her mother was gone. Anna concentrated on the road again, chewing over what her mother had said. It made her think of that stupid phone call on New Year's Eve. That's what she'd been hoping for, she realized now, a chance to talk to Spencer, to say all those things she wished she'd said to him but never had. And then that hope had been snatched away again when she'd realized it was just her imagination conjuring up things she wanted to be true.

And she was sad it wasn't true, even if it had been a ridiculous idea. Even if it had been just that one time, it might have been enough. A chance to say a proper goodbye. Their *last* goodbye.

Because she needed to do that. Or at least start to do that. Her mother and Gabi were right. She needed to learn to live without Spencer, no matter how nonsensical the idea seemed.

As she drove, she pictured herself standing on the dunes at Camber Sands, looking out across a beautifully ruffled sea, the wind rustling the long, waxy grass, the pale sun low in a slate-blue sky. She imagined herself breathing out. That was all she was asking for today. Not complete peace and healing. Just some space to close her eyes, think of Spencer and breathe out. All the way.

Chapter Ten

Anna pulled into a near-deserted parking lot an hour or so later. She turned off her engine and opened the car door, glimpsing flat gray sea between the Marina Cafe, public toilets and other low buildings. The moment her head rose above the level of the open door, the wind whipped her hair in front of her face. She left it there, too busy thinking about the last moments of the journey itself to bother pushing it out of the way.

On the drive down the narrow, dead-end road that led to the beach, she'd passed her and Spencer's bungalow, and even though it had been remodeled and extended, she'd recognized it straightaway.

This had been a good choice for today. The whole place was full of memories of Spencer; even this parking lot nestled in a gap in the dunes, with its ever-present drifts of sand that curled and swirled in the breeze. In her mind, she could see him at the pay-and-display meter, swearing colorfully as it refused his fifty-pence piece over and over. And there near the café was the sandy slope he'd carried her up from the beach because she'd just dried her feet off from paddling and hadn't wanted to get them gritty again.

She sighed. She couldn't wait to just start wandering around, letting those happier moments come back to her. She needed them.

She turned as another vehicle arrived—Gayle and Richard's ancient but pristine Rover, with Scott and Teresa in the back. It pulled into a space on the opposite side of the parking lot, near the café. Anna locked her car and began to walk in that direction.

Gayle emerged from the Rover in a smart black dress with matching jacket, her hairdo defying the blustery weather—how did she manage that? Shellac?—and supervised with military efficiency as Richard removed a canvas shopper from the trunk and donned Wellingtons.

"Hi," Anna said as she strolled over.

"Oh, hello," Gayle said, smiling slightly. "You're here." And then she took in Anna's jeans, dark-green sweater and her usual black coat. Her eyebrows lifted an infinitesimal amount. Anna had gone for comfort over style, but even if she'd decided to dress more smartly, she wouldn't have chosen all black for today. She didn't want to dress up like it was his funeral all over again.

The others emerged from the car and greeted her, all three of them giving her a hug and kissing her on the cheek. Richard and Scott wore dark suits, and Teresa a demure charcoal dress similar to their mother-in-law's. None of them looked as if they were ready for a day at the beach. Had someone forgotten to give Anna the memo? What was the deal here, anyway?

"Have you got the bag, Richard?" Gayle asked.

"Roger that," Richard replied, holding it slightly higher for his wife's inspection.

She nodded, then turned and set off in the direction of dunes that rose from the far edge of the parking lot, undeterred by her unsuitable footwear. "Right," she said. "Come on. First stop is 'our' picnic spot in the dunes."

Oh, Anna thought. There was a plan. Of course there was. One, obviously, that she'd had no part in putting together and hadn't been consulted about. Well, Anna had a plan of her own, one that was just as important. She stood taller and pulled her coat tightly around herself. "Actually . . . Gayle?" she called out.

Gayle turned around, her expression a mixture of bafflement and irritation.

"Before we head off, could we just backtrack to the bungalow—the little yellow one—along the road? It's just that Spencer and I—"

"Maybe later," Gayle said, turning and continuing in the direction she'd been going, and then added over her shoulder, "If we've got time . . . We don't want supper this evening to be too late, do we?"

"Supper?" Anna echoed.

"Back at our house. I've got sandwiches and vol-au-vents ready. Richard sent you an email about it, remember?"

Anna's mouth fell open, but she had nothing to say. She did remember getting an email, but to be honest, she'd just skimmed it for where and when to meet. Richard had a tendency to waffle on somewhat.

Maybe she couldn't be cross about that, but she was more than a little irritated at being dismissed and overruled. Gayle seemed to be forgetting that this day was for all of them to remember Spencer, not just her. Anna was just trying to work out how to say that without seeming too bitchy, when what her mother had said to her on the phone came back to her. Being in control was Gayle's way of coping. This wasn't personal—she had to remember that.

Anna stood there for a moment, irritation and compassion

warring for the upper hand inside her, then her shoulders sagged. Okay, despite being royally ticked off by Gayle's imperious attitude, she'd hold fire for now. But make no mistake, she'd be visiting that yellow bungalow later on that afternoon, come hell or high water, and Gayle would just have to deal with it.

Anna blew out a breath that did little to calm her jagged emotions, dug her fists into her pockets and trailed behind the tight-knit group heading up the large dune that constantly threatened to swallow up the eastern boundary of the parking lot.

ANNA MOVED THROUGH the next hour or so as if she was outside herself, as if she were watching a film of the proceedings and the camera had pulled back for a long shot. It was the only way she could cope. Gayle had cast herself as chief mourner, even though every single person there ached just as hard as she did. Anna was relegated to loyal sidekick, having to stand next to Gayle as she gave a speech at the family's favorite picnic spot, as they wrote messages to Spencer on scraps of paper, then rolled them up and stuck them in a bottle, which was then buried in the sand at a location Gayle had chosen.

Anna would have liked a little more than the two minutes Gayle had allotted to work out what she'd wanted to write because when she'd stared at the blank strip of faux parchment (Gayle never did anything by halves), she just couldn't make her brain work. She'd kept staring at it up until the last ten seconds, and then she'd scribbled *I love you* and stuffed the paper in the bottle. Heartfelt. True. But not very eloquent. Also, not the "goodbye" she'd been revving up to. How could she rush that?

And then they were hurried on to the next place of significance to everyone but Anna and Teresa, now almost six months pregnant, who was waddling up and down the dunes without a squeak of protest. It would make Anna look bad if she said anything.

She tuned out her mother-in-law's voice, let it become part of the background noise, like the squawking of the seagulls, as she tried to find that still place in her heart where she could talk to Spencer, tell him what she'd wanted to say today. She'd just about gained the right amount of focus to start when Gayle clapped her hands and announced, "Well, I think it's time we got to the most important part of the afternoon, the reason we chose to come here this year . . . Richard, have you got the bag?"

Richard, who'd hardly said a word since they'd arrived, nodded. Anna's attention was drawn once again to the canvas shopper he was carrying. He'd been lugging it around all over the dunes. What exactly was inside it?

He held the bag up to Gayle and she reached in and reverently pulled out a small pewter urn. The kind with a lid. The kind used for . . .

But, no. That couldn't be right.

"We'll walk out to the shore now the tide's out," Gayle announced, "and then Richard and Scott can scatter the ashes in the sea."

Ashes?

She can't have just said that, Anna thought, even though the urn in Gayle's grip was evidence to the contrary, but she hardly had time to process that before Gayle added, "We're all agreed this is the right place?" There were murmurs and nods of agreement as Gayle looked from person to person. "This is where he would have chosen if it had been up to him." And then she shifted her gaze to Anna.

"Ashes?" Anna echoed weakly. It was the only word going round her head at that moment.

Gayle nodded.

"*Spencer's* ashes?"

Teresa shot a nervous look at her mother-in-law and then her husband. Scott was busy studying an abandoned plastic spade half-buried in the sand and didn't seem inclined to glance up.

Gayle stood a little straighter. "Yes."

"But Spencer's ashes are in the garden of remembrance at the crematorium!"

Gayle's stare didn't waver. "Your half of them are. Our half are here . . ." She patted the urn in her hands gently. "And we're going to scatter them in my son's happy place, the place where he had the most joy."

Their half?

Anna stood openmouthed as the rest of the family headed down the side of the dune that led to the beach. They were carrying a piece of her husband with them. A piece that she'd never known existed!

She dug back in her memory to that foggy time after Spencer's accident, a period when she'd hardly been functioning. Richard and Scott had stepped in and done a lot of what had been needed: meeting with the funeral directors, dealing with probate. It was possible that they could have kept half of the ashes for themselves without telling her, but why would they do that? Why hide it from her?

But maybe they *had* consulted her. They could have asked if it was a good idea to have circus performers and pink-spotted elephants at the funeral, and she probably would have nodded and said, *Fine . . . Whatever you want . . .*

The rest of the group had descended the far side of the dune and were already out of sight. Anna started to run after them, but now the sand had been disturbed, the top layer kept sliding over the layer underneath, taking her with it. It was like running up a "down" escalator. She forced herself to stand still for a moment, caught her breath, then chose a different path and planted purposeful feet, one in front of the other, until she made it to the top.

When she crested the dune, she found Teresa waiting for her and they fell into step together, eyes fixed on the other three members of the Barry family, who were now some distance away. Camber Sands was one of those shallow beaches perfect for families on summer holidays, because at low tide the sea retreated almost to the horizon, leaving pools of seawater to be warmed by the sun for children to paddle in. On a day like today, though, it was a long and blustery walk to the waves.

"You didn't know?" Teresa asked as they trailed behind the others. Anna shook her head. "Cow," Teresa muttered.

Anna shot her a surprised look. She'd never once seen or heard any hint that her sister-in-law did anything but toe the party line, but the response resonated with her. It resonated quite a lot, actually.

Gayle *was* being a cow today, and Anna had put up with all of it, ignoring all the little digs and snubs, because she was trying to be the daughter-in-law Spencer would want her to be— kind and supportive, making allowances for the other woman's pain—but it had become startlingly clear in the last half hour just how much of a one-way street that was.

Spencer had adored his mum, but he hadn't been blind to her faults, and if there was one thing he'd prefer his wife to be, rather than a doting daughter-in-law, it was someone who had a backbone. He'd always encouraged her to stand up for herself, to be more assertive.

Spurred on by that thought, she marched toward the small cluster of people where the shallow beach met the waves. The furnace of her rage roared brighter with every step. Teresa plodded along behind her, doing her best to keep up.

Anna's first urge was to stride up to Gayle and let it rip, but then she thought about how both Spencer and Gabi had always said that she bottled everything up until she couldn't hold it in any longer and then it all came pouring out in an unintelligible eruption, "unintelligible" being the operative word. She couldn't have that. She needed Gayle to get this, to understand that it was not okay to have excluded her from today's plans so completely.

When she reached her in-laws, Anna fixed Gayle with a steady stare and opened her mouth to begin. At the very same moment, Richard unscrewed the lid of the urn and Anna choked back the words, hit by a pain in her chest that was as powerful as it was unexpected.

A high-pitched wailing pierced the bluster of the wind around them, not a cry of despair but something primal and raw.

Anna guessed that she must have lost her internal battle after all, that the moment the lid had come off the urn, the boiling emotions she'd been trying to keep at bay had overtaken her like a tidal wave. She clapped a hand over her mouth as Gayle crumpled beside her, dropping to the wrinkled wet sand, and Anna realized it wasn't her making the noise after all. It was her mother-in-law, her perfectly put together mother-in-law.

The sand and saltwater were making an awful mess of Gayle's smart outfit, but she didn't seem to notice. She was too busy trying to grab a breath between the heaving sobs, supporting herself with one palm splayed against the damp sand, her fingertips digging in so deep they disappeared.

Anna wanted to grab Gayle by the arm and force her to stand up again, to make her stop that horrible noise. *No*, she wanted to scream. *This was not your moment. This was not your husband. He was mine! And I was his happy place, not this soggy, dirty beach. I was what brought him the most joy!*

Both Richard and Scott attempted to help Gayle up, but she batted their hands away, and her raw sobbing continued. Anna stared down at Spencer's mother, and words from that strange late-night phone call on Valentine's Day drifted into her mind.

When life changes suddenly and unexpectedly, there's a grieving of what was and what can never be again. I would call that being human . . .

Yes, Anna reminded herself, finding steadiness—strength— from those words in what was otherwise a day full of vertiginous twists and turns. They grounded her, brought her back to what was real and true. *Whatever Gayle has done today, she is human. And she deserves my compassion.*

Slowly, carefully, she got down on her knees beside Gayle, put an arm around her shoulder and drew her close.

Chapter Eleven

Anna followed Gayle and Richard's Rover back from Camber Sands to their house, sitting stiff and tight-lipped behind the wheel of her car. Her anger had been quenched briefly when Gayle had broken down on the beach—no one could have remained unmoved by that gut-wrenching sorrow—but it had begun to grow again as she'd stood by helplessly while Richard and Scott had scattered Spencer, or what was left of him, onto the waves.

She guessed it was supposed to have been a dramatic send-off, but the tide or the currents must have been doing something strange because the tiny little pieces of her husband had floated in a grayish-white scum on top of the silt-laden water and lapped around their ankles. It had been horrible. She couldn't have thought of a worse ending to an already unbearable day.

She'd been so bewildered that she hadn't even remembered about the little yellow bungalow until she was halfway back to Gayle and Richard's. The whole journey back, the words she'd collected to say to her mother-in-law circled in her head, and now she felt like one of those unexploded Second World War bombs. The tiniest touch, the slightest wrong move and— *boom!*—she would detonate.

She pulled into the drive behind Richard and Gayle. Getting out of the car was an effort, and not just because she was stiff from driving; she felt utterly exhausted and her body was rigid with tension. The front door of the house was open, Gayle standing beside it, ready to shoo her guests inside. Anna approached the threshold but stopped before stepping over it.

"Anna?" There was a whiff of irritation in her mother-in-law's tone and Anna felt her blood pressure rise. She couldn't look at Gayle. She couldn't even look at the hallway through the open door. She was only just about holding on to her last shreds of self-control.

If she went in there and had to make polite conversation after all that had happened that afternoon, that bomb inside her *would* go off. She was just so angry. Horribly, horribly angry. But having a meltdown over cucumber sandwiches and tea cakes wasn't going to help anyone this afternoon.

"I'm sorry . . ." she muttered. "I think . . . I think I've got a migraine coming." And before Gayle could say anything else, Anna ran back to her car, jumped inside and reversed out of the drive.

She knew Gayle would be staring after her as she drove away. *What about the finger sandwiches, Anna? What about the vol-au-vents?* But Anna didn't care about the sodding vol-au-vents.

She drove home with her fingers tight round the steering wheel, jaw clenched, resisting the urge to use the accelerator to vent her anger. *Hold on*, she told herself. *Just a little longer, then you can close your front door behind you, sink against it, and let it all out.*

Almost an hour and a half later, thanks to a snarl-up around junction five, Anna hauled herself from her car and stared at her house. Just the sight of it almost brought tears of relief to her eyes. The walk to her front door seemed to go in slow motion, but she finally put the key in the lock, opened the door and then banged it closed behind her.

Thank God.

She sank against the back of the door and waited for the emotions to start flowing . . .

But nothing spilled out, nothing exploded. There was no pounding of fists on the tiled floor of her hallway or shouts of rage echoing up the stairwell. She opened her mouth, giving permission for the howl of fury she'd been keeping inside all the way back from the beach to emerge, but all she could hear was her own shallow breathing. She closed her eyes, giving tears a chance to gather behind her lids, but when she opened them again, they were as dry as Gayle's pork and sage stuffing.

She let out a growl of frustration and made her way upstairs to her bedroom, where she lay down on the unmade bed and pulled the duvet up over her head. Damned if she did, damned if she didn't. It was all too much.

But the usual comfort of her blank, white cocoon didn't help her today. Even so, she closed her eyes and breathed in and out, at a total loss for anything else to do.

One moment, that was all she had wanted.

One moment to be still today, to remember him in the way she wanted to, so she could start doing what everyone was always telling her she needed to and move forward. But it seemed she wasn't allowed that.

As much as the focus was always on Spencer when she visited his family, she couldn't talk freely to Gayle, even though she wished she could, and she didn't want to worry her own parents. Gabi tried, God bless her, she really did, but she only wanted to hear good and positive and healthy things, and the truth was, some days Anna was anything *but* those things. Sometimes she *needed* to be despondent and negative and toxic. It was the only way to let the poison out.

She lay under the duvet in a half trance, letting her thoughts wander, like a bird hopping from branch to branch in search of a roost. They came to rest in an unexpected place.

There had been one person who'd listened, a *someone* who'd seemed to actually understand.

But this person was also a *no one*, an anonymous voice at the end of a phone line, completely unconnected from her life, from all the emotional baggage anyone who'd known her or Spencer came with.

Things happen . . . , he'd said. *Things that turn you upside down and your life takes a very different path.*

Spencer's number had been assigned to him, the *no one*. She really wanted to call that number again, she discovered, which was more than a little surprising. Maybe it was because, in her mind, he was still part of that connection to Spencer.

But phoning again would be completely weird. This time she'd be ringing to speak to *him* and not the ghost of a long-dead husband. This man. This stranger.

This kindred spirit.

That thought stuck in her head for the rest of the evening. She stayed in bed, reading, moping, staring at the ceiling. After a few hours, she took a bath and got into her pj's, then returned to bed to read and mope and stare at the ceiling some more.

Eventually, she could avoid the urge no longer. She pulled her phone off the bedside table and pressed the entry near the top of her "recents" list, the number still labeled as "Spencer." Her heart thudded as she waited for it to connect. She closed her eyes and prayed hard she wouldn't hear the robotic voicemail message, and it seemed, for once, her prayers were to be answered. The ringing stopped, and shortly afterward, a deep male voice said, "Yes?"

"It's me again," Anna replied, then blew a breath out to steady herself. "It's Anna."

Chapter Twelve

Anna."

There wasn't a hint of surprise in his tone. There wasn't a hint of much, actually.

Instead of apologizing and hanging up like any sensible person would have done, she asked, "Do you remember me?"

A pause followed, one she couldn't interpret, then he said, "Yes. I remember you."

A bald statement of fact. No joke that strange women who phoned at random times of day or night might be hard to forget. That was the sort of thing Spencer would have said, but this man wasn't Spencer. She needed to remember that.

Her throat dried. Where were words when you needed them? She'd had thousands waiting and ready to go, but now they'd all run scurrying into the shadows.

"I wondered if you'd phone again," he said.

"Really? You were expecting me to?" Until tonight she'd had no intention of doing so. How had he known?

"More pondering the probability."

And then it went silent again. She'd called him to talk, after all, but now she couldn't think of a single thing to say.

And he clearly didn't have anything to say to her.

Just like that, she knew she'd made a horrible mistake. Her words were clanging nails dropping on concrete. This wasn't the lovely, warm, intimate bubble of conversation she'd imagined it would be. It wasn't the place where she could spill her soul and find healing.

Oh, Anna. What have you done? It's time to apologize for disturbing this man and put the phone down. Once again, you've conjured something from your imagination that isn't there.

A terrible sense of loss came with this epiphany. However, there was one thing she needed to know before she pulled the phone away from her ear and ended the call. "When we talked before . . . How did you know?"

"How did I know what?"

"About the exploding . . . About the keeping it all in and then . . . just . . ." She made a gesture with her hand, her fingers springing apart from a closed fist, and realized she was making no sense again. *Good one, Anna. Should have hung up when you had the chance.* From the silence on the other end of the line, she guessed he was thinking the same thing.

He breathed out, long and hard. "I just know."

That was enough, just those three words. He'd said everything he needed to say, everything *she* needed him to say.

He got it.

Not because someone had told him, but because he'd lived it too. Anna choked back a sob. "Th-thank you," she sputtered as hot tears streamed silently down her cheeks.

More silence followed, but this time it was warm. Open. Giving her space, giving her permission. Anna started crying so hard she thought she'd run out of breath. She lost all sense of where she was, of time passing.

Eventually, she sat up, letting the duvet fall away from her face, and reached for a tissue from the box on the bedside table.

The nose blow that followed was not very ladylike or demure. "Sorry," she whispered again, although she wasn't quite sure if it was the gurgling snotty noise or the crying in general that she was apologizing for.

"You didn't find Spencer?" he asked.

Anna frowned, confused. "What?"

"You were angry with him for leaving."

It all came back then, how she'd rambled on the last time she'd called. Oh, God . . . What a fool she'd made of herself. He deserved some kind of explanation. "I am. I was . . . He's not coming back. I know that now."

There was a soft exhalation at the other end of the line, not so much a sigh but a gesture of recognition. "Are you better off without him?"

One corner of her mouth curled up in a twisted kind of smile. Even though he was wrong, that Spencer hadn't left her of his own free will, she liked the way this man phrased it; he didn't *tell* her she was better off but asked for her opinion on the matter. "No," she said truthfully. "I'm definitely not better off without him."

Another breath . . . sigh . . . Whatever it was. He understood this too.

"Will it always hurt this much?" she asked.

"Probably."

She almost laughed. God, it was refreshing not to be given a platitude or a proverb.

"He died," she said softly, not aware she was ready to tell this story until the words left her mouth. "He was thirty-one, and he died."

"Yet you phoned him," he said, clearly perplexed.

"Yes. Stupid, isn't it? Wanting to talk to someone who'll never be able to hear you again, who'll never be able to talk back."

He let out a hollow laugh. "No."

Anna closed her eyes as more tears surged down her face. Oh, the relief . . . "You have no idea how lovely it is to be able to say all of this, to be honest, and for someone else to understand."

"Then tell me more."

Her eyes snapped open again. "Oh, I don't think I should . . . I mean, I've invaded enough of your time already. You must have other things—"

"I don't," he said, cutting her off. "Not right now."

"But why would—?"

"Because I wish I'd had someone." There was a pause, a moment of heaviness. "Someone I didn't know. Someone who wouldn't judge me . . . I won't judge you, Anna."

No, he wouldn't. She knew that already. She'd known that before she'd picked up the phone this evening, hadn't she?

So Anna talked. She told him about the day Spencer died, the darkness afterward. She told him about the horrible time she'd had at the beach with Spencer's family that day. And he listened. He didn't say anything, didn't comment, until she finally ran out of steam. "Sorry," she said again when she'd run out of words.

"Why do you keep apologizing?"

"Because . . . because normal people don't do things like this," she replied.

"Maybe they should."

"Because I'm bothering you?"

"You're not."

She wrinkled her nose. "I'm not?"

"I'd have told you if you were, and then I'd have hung up."

Anna couldn't help laughing softly. She didn't know much about this man, but she knew enough from his direct, no-nonsense answers that this was the truth, and for some reason that made it funny.

"You know my life story," she mused, "and I know nothing about you."

"Nope."

She smiled again. "Apart from the fact you're not fazed by strange women phoning you up and pouring their life stories out to you. Is it a specialty of yours?"

There was a little huff that might have accompanied a smile. "I have to admit that you're the first."

For some reason that warmed her. She sighed. "I should probably stop tying up your phone line. Someone else might be trying to get through." She imagined friends, a wife, even, getting frustrated with an electronic voice apologetically telling them this person was busy.

"I doubt it," he said in that same blunt tone. "This is a new phone number and I haven't given it to anyone else yet."

"Oh." Anna shifted and reached behind her so she could readjust the pillows and lean back against the headboard. "But it's been almost four months since I first called. I'm the only person you've talked to in all that time?"

"You're the only human being I've talked to, full stop."

"You speak to *non*–human beings?" she blurted out, aware it was the most ridiculous response she could have offered. However, picking up the phone and dialing his number this evening had also been pretty ridiculous, so at least she was being consistent.

And then it occurred to her what he'd just said: he hadn't talked to another soul in almost four months. That just wasn't normal. Why hadn't he? She'd been so focused on what she needed from him, she hadn't even stopped to consider the truth of what she'd just told him—that she knew nothing about him. He could be in prison, in solitary confinement. That would be a very good reason not to have much social contact, wouldn't it? He could be dangerous or psychologically disturbed. Or both. And here she was chatting away to him, telling him everything about herself.

He made a noise that *might* have been a laugh if it hadn't been filled with such heaviness. "I talk to the dog sometimes. I have to, otherwise my vocal cords might atrophy."

Atrophy. That was a good word, wasn't it? A clever word. This man had education, so maybe he wasn't a psychopathic, stalking axe murderer behind bars after all. And he had a dog. That had to say something about the kind of person he was, didn't it?

"Why don't you talk to anyone?"

"My choice. I live in the middle of nowhere. Don't get many visitors."

Anna frowned. Was he a liar too? "And yet you still get a decent mobile phone reception?"

"It's weak, but I have a booster that amplifies the signal. When we had a storm just before Christmas and the landline went down for the fourth time in as many months, I decided I needed a backup."

"Hence, the new phone and the new phone number," Anna said, sighing. "I bet you weren't expecting this to happen when you got it."

"No." Again, no sense of irritation or weariness in his tone. She would have been on the verge of concluding that he was a bit strange *not* to mind her weird phone calls out of the blue, but now she knew just a little bit more about him, she wondered if maybe he was lonely. That would explain things.

And she did know a bit about him now. She crossed "dangerous" and "psychotic" off her mental list and added some new qualities: patient, calm and . . . kind. Yes, despite his bluntness and offhand demeanor, he'd been very kind to listen to her.

However, it struck her that there was one important bit of information she didn't have about him. "I don't know your name."

"It's Brody."

That fitted the deep gravel of his voice somehow. She tried to picture him and came up with salt-and-pepper hair, maybe a beard. She got the sense he was older than she was, but it was hard to tell from his voice alone. He also sounded weary, as if he'd lived through a lot.

"Brody," she repeated quietly, and then, because her manners hadn't deserted her completely, she added, "It's very nice to meet you."

He laughed then, a proper deep rumble. "Surprisingly, I'm going to say 'likewise.'"

There was nothing much left to say now. The bomb was no longer ticking away inside her. He'd defused it cleanly and effortlessly while they'd been talking, and she hadn't even noticed. No explosion was imminent.

So that was that, then. It was time to go. The only problem was she didn't know how to end a conversation like this. "Well," she began but was quickly drowned out by the insistent barking of a dog in the background on the other end of the line.

"Hang on a sec," Brody muttered, and she could hear him putting the phone down and moving away, then muttering something along the lines of "Calm down! It's only an owl."

A few moments later he was back, sounding marginally more ruffled than he usually did, which was kind of reassuring. "Sorry about that."

"It's okay," Anna replied. It had made her smile. She liked dogs. She and Spencer had talked about getting one not long before he died but had decided it wasn't the best timing as Anna had just come off the Pill and they were going to start trying for a baby. Another thing that had been stolen from her. But she wasn't going to think about that right now. "Anyway, I just wanted to say—"

More barking.

"Lewis!" he shouted. "Quiet."

There was such authority in his tone that the dog instantly fell silent.

"You have a dog called Lewis?" Anna asked, her voice raspy.

She heard movement and faint panting, and then he said, "Daft animal," under his breath and she could picture the dog sitting at his knee and looking up at him with complete adoration as he scratched it between its ears. "Yes," he replied.

It was a sign.

Not from her deceased husband or anything stupid like that, but it was a sign. Why else would this man have not only her husband's phone number but also a dog with exactly the same name as his favorite pet? This was another connection that couldn't be ignored.

"Can I call you again?" she blurted out.

He took a moment to reply. "If you need to."

"Thank you," she said quietly.

"Goodb—"

She jumped in before he could finish. "Is it okay if we don't say that word? I know it sounds strange, but I've had too much of 'goodbye' today. Can we say something else or just hang up?"

He must have got used to her strange ways by now because he just said, "Fine," not sounding offended in the slightest. Thank goodness. "Sleep well, Anna."

She used all her determination to press her thumb onto her phone screen and make him disappear. After staring at her mobile for a few seconds then, thoroughly exhausted, she turned out the light. She turned onto her back and lay staring at the ceiling, and for the first time that day, Anna breathed out. All the way.

Chapter Thirteen

Brody stared at his shiny new phone. It was silent now, but the echo of Anna's last words was still ringing in his ears. Lewis was nudging at his hand, asking for attention, but Brody kept his gaze on the screen. He didn't actually expect it to jump into life again, but he kept looking at the display of recent calls. There were only four, all from the same number.

Each entry was just a row of digits. Eleven to be exact. That was all that was left of her after she'd hung up. It seemed a little impersonal after the conversation they'd had.

He pressed "Add new contact." All the while he was typing her name into the correct field, he told himself he didn't really need to do this because she was the only person likely to call him in the foreseeable future—and that was only a vague possibility—but he carried on anyway until he was finished.

There was an icon next to her name, a lifeless little gray silhouette of a woman's head on a paler background. It seemed too bland, so he pulled up the library of pictures that were preloaded onto the phone and chose one: an arching stalk of lily of the valley. For some reason, it seemed the most fitting.

She'd sounded young, more than a little fragile. Lost.

Brody knew what it was like to feel lost. He knew it very well. Maybe that was why he'd kept listening instead of hanging up.

He stuffed his phone in his jeans pocket, then went and fetched

Lewis, let him out of the back door of the cottage one last time before they both settled down for the night—Lewis in his bed in the kitchen near the oil-fired AGA, and Brody upstairs in one of the low-ceilinged, black-beamed bedrooms. He lay in his bed and stared at the misty, moon-soaked clouds through the open curtains, thinking about the conversation he'd had with Anna.

She was still in the awful, early stages, when everything was raw and all-consuming, when you got stuck in an endless, grinding loop of hurt and sorrow. And regret. *Don't forget about the regret*, he reminded himself. It might seem the most benign item on the list, but Brody knew it was the heavyweight. Regret would knock you to the floor with a single punch if you let it.

Did I lie to her? he wondered as he shifted, trying to get comfortable. Would it have made a difference if he'd had someone to talk to, some faceless person who hadn't known him, who hadn't been tainted by the knowledge of what had happened? Logically, it seemed possible, but he doubted it. He doubted it very much.

There was a faint scratching at the door, then it was nosed open by a naughty but rather hopeful terrier. Emboldened by the lack of a reprimand, the animal trotted over to the edge of the bed. A second later, the mattress dipped, and Brody felt the damp touch of a nose on his hand. Lewis collapsed on top of the duvet beside him and let out a long doggy sigh of contentment.

He usually kept his phone in his study, but it lay on the dark wood of the old and rickety bedside table. He drifted off to sleep, half wondering if it would make another sound that night, but when he woke again the next morning, only four calls remained in the log. He shooed Lewis off the bed and dragged himself up.

He caught sight of his distorted reflection in a wardrobe mirror that was cloudy and dappled with age. When had he last had a shave? Last week? The one before? Whenever it was, he looked a state. Maybe he'd do it when he came back from his run. Although he didn't know why he was thinking of bothering with shaving. There was no one here to impress. Only Lewis, and being a shaggy kind of dog, he'd probably prefer Brody the way he was.

He looked more like his father now he was getting older. There were a few specks of gray at his temples, which was expected, he supposed, given that on his last birthday he'd become officially middle-aged. Forty hadn't been a shock, though. He'd felt older than that for years now. Much older.

The lanes that crisscrossed this part of the moor were still sleepy with mist when he set out. The nearest village was five miles away, and the nearest town more like thirty, which was exactly why he'd chosen this spot for his home. Most likely, the only living things he'd see on his route were some cows and a few crows.

He checked his watch as he began to run. The grocery delivery was due at eight, so he'd make sure he was back at least ten minutes before that. He turned and vaulted over a farm gate, which was no problem, thanks to his long legs, and powered up the edge of a muddy field toward the top of a steep hill.

When he returned to the cottage, dripping with sweat, the pleasant sting of lactic acid in his muscles, Lewis came bounding into the yard to greet him. However, something else was also in his yard—a van with *Hexworthy Organics* emblazoned on its side in large green letters, its engine idling.

Crap. It was early.

Lewis, the traitor, went running off, tail wagging, to greet the driver, but Brody cut round the back of the outbuildings that were part of his property. Talking to the man wasn't necessary: he always left a note with his order for the driver to leave every-thing in the small and very ancient conservatory that served as a mudroom. He wouldn't quibble about substitutions. He'd take whatever they brought.

He entered his garden and slipped back into the house through the French doors that led from the patio into his living room and then slipped into the study next door. This guy must be new, because he was pounding on the front door, yelling, "Hello?" Lewis was barking along, just for the sheer joy of joining in. Stupid dog.

Read your clipboard, mate, Brody thought. *All the relevant infor-mation is on there, and then you can sling your hook and leave me alone.*

What Brody could really do with was a shower, but the stairs could be seen through the glazed portion of the front door, so he sat down in his desk chair and waited, staring at a patch of chipped paint on the windowsill until the knocking stopped and he heard the rumble of an engine pulling out of the yard and disappearing down the lane.

Chapter Fourteen

Exactly a week later, Brody's phone rang again. He was sitting in his small study, a fire tickling the logs in the grate. The room was crammed with shelves of books of all shapes and sizes. In the corner was a rather ancient high-backed armchair, left behind by the previous owners—as was much of the furniture in the house. At the time, it had seemed the easiest option. In front of the window was an old wooden desk, the kind with a green leather top. There wasn't much on it but a fine layer of dust and his mobile phone.

Its usually blank and lifeless screen lit up just after ten that evening, vibrating softly on the leather surface of the desk. Lewis raised his head from his paws as Brody stood up to fetch it and replaced it again when his master was once again seated in the armchair next to the fire.

"Brody?" she said, sounding for all the world as if she expected to be talking to herself, or an empty room.

"I'm here."

He heard Anna's sigh of relief. "I hoped you would be."

He smiled, surprised at how pleased he was to hear her voice again.

She inhaled, held her breath for a second, then said, "I have a question I'd like to ask you. I've tried asking other people, but I suspect they're telling me what they think I want to hear, rather than giving me an honest answer."

He settled into his chair, staring at the windows of his study, the night so dark it seemed as if someone had painted them black from the outside. "Fire away."

"Do you believe in soul mates? You know, one person for life . . . forever?"

He pondered her question for a moment. "Not really."

"Thank you," she said. "I needed to hear you say that before I could be really sure about what I thought. Everyone has given me tips on how to wrap my head around grief, told me how I should be feeling, but it's made it difficult to pin down what I really think about things. Important things."

Brody nodded. Oh, those well-meaning souls . . . He knew the sort well. "And what *do* you think, Anna?"

"That Spencer was my soul mate."

"How did you know?" It wasn't a question filled with judgment or scorn. He genuinely wanted to hear her answer.

"I just did," she said wistfully, "right from the very first time I met him."

"You fell in love at first sight?" Okay, now he was skeptical.

"If that's what you want to call it. Although, I didn't think of it that way at the time. I wouldn't let myself. I mean, it's stupid, right? Fairy-tale stuff?"

Brody gave her a grunt in lieu of a proper answer. It communicated his position just as effectively.

"Seeing him for the first time was like running into a brick wall at full speed. I mean, physically—I actually lost my balance—and then I started getting all breathless and the soles of my feet began to burn. I tried to act normally, to say hello, and I just couldn't do it." She laughed softly. "But neither could he . . . That was when I knew that was it. This was *him*."

Brody frowned. "Sounds to me like you're talking about physical attraction."

Anna let out a laugh. "I should have guessed that you're a cynic."

"Yes, I am," he said. "And proud of it."

She sighed.

"Okay," he said. "Prove me wrong. What was it about him that convinced you he was . . ." He paused slightly, finding it harder than he would have expected to say the next words. ". . . the One? What made you the perfect match?"

Anna went silent for a while. He could almost hear her thinking. "I suppose, on paper, it shouldn't have worked. We're very different. I'm shy, but he was a complete extrovert, full of beans and always coming up with crazy plans and schemes. Spencer was a dreamer, and that's what I loved about him: his imagination, his passion. That, and the fact that while other people might have thought I was black-and-white compared to his Technicolor, he didn't. He believed in me in a way no one else ever had."

"I can see why you—or anyone—would be won over by that kind of support."

"It was more than just 'support,'" she replied. "It meant everything to me. When you're shy, it's easy for people not to see you. They think they do, but they don't."

"And Spencer saw things other people missed?"

"Exactly. Other people called him a high-flyer, but he said he could only fly so high because I grounded him, because I was his anchor. That's what I mean when I say we were soul mates," she said, and Brody imagined her giving a tiny shrug. "We just fit together. It was easy . . . Effortless. And we made each other better. It wasn't until I met Spencer that I really realized who *I* was."

"No one should need someone else to tell them who they are, Anna."

"It wasn't that," she replied, a hint of defensiveness in her tone. "He just loved me for who I was, let me be *me*." She sighed. "And now he's not here anymore. Losing him has changed me fundamentally. I won't ever be the same."

He nodded. "You're right. You probably won't."

And then he regretted being so blunt. He'd spent too long in his own company, had forgotten that other human beings didn't always appreciate such a straightforward approach.

But all Anna said, with a smile in her voice, was, "Gee, Brody! Thanks for the pep talk!" He found himself laughing, and she joined in with him. When they both had fallen quiet again, she said. "I have another question . . ."

Brody braced himself. He wasn't used to having deep, meaningful conversations late into the night, not unless you counted the odd philosophical debate with his furry companion.

"Why did you call your dog Lewis?"

Brody smiled. It was as if she'd read his mind. "After C. S. Lewis, the author of the Narnia books."

"Oh . . . I loved those as a child. It took me years before I could stop checking the backs of wardrobes just to see if there were fir trees and snow there."

"Me too." He liked that they had that in common. "Why do you ask? About Lewis?"

"When he was younger, Spencer also had a dog called Lewis. I was curious to know if you'd named him for the same reason."

"And how did the other Lewis get his name?"

Anna chuckled again. "After Lewis Hamilton. Spencer worshipped that man."

Brody shrugged to himself. Not a bad choice. "I suppose he's very good at Formula One, but worship might be taking it a bit too far."

"That's what I thought," she said cheerfully, then sobered slightly. "The year Spencer died, I'd planned a surprise for his birthday. I'd booked for him to drive a high-performance car at Brands Hatch, but he never got to do it. The company was wonderful about it, though. They gave me a voucher to use another time, no expiry date or anything."

"Did you use it?"

She sighed again. "I've been meaning to give it to my brother-in-law, but I keep forgetting. I think it's sitting in a drawer somewhere . . . That's the funny thing about the future, isn't it? We have all these plans, some small, some grand, but things don't always work out the way we expect them to."

"No," Brody replied thoughtfully. No, they really didn't. Ten years ago, if you'd asked him what his life would be like now, he'd have said he'd still be happily married to Katri.

"I imagined my life—mine and Spencer's, really—like a giant calendar stretching into the future, reaching through the decades. I'd penciled in plenty of future events. You know the sort of thing . . . In three years, we'll definitely have a baby. In five years, hopefully, a second. Ten years after that I'll be moaning about ferrying them round to all their activities, and ten years after that I'll be attending my first university graduation.

"I kept filling in the pages of my imaginary calendar, not even realizing I was doing it, because they were just wisps of hopes and dreams I was jotting down. I saw us growing old together, becoming grandparents, our hair going white, always griping that we couldn't remember where we'd left our reading glasses, even though they were on top of our heads . . ." She tailed off and made a noise that was half-sob, half-chuckle. "I thought I'd be the sort of grandma who wore knitted cardigans and slippers and smelled vaguely of peppermints."

Brody smiled at the picture she'd painted.

"But now I might never get to be a grandmother. Or even a mother."

He felt a stab of pain on her behalf.

"And then one day I woke up and all the pages in my calendar were gone. Ripped out."

He nodded to himself. "And then you don't know what to do, where to start." At least, that was how he'd felt in the beginning. Those paths were clearer in his imagination now. It didn't mean he had any more ability to travel down them, however.

"Exactly. And now every day I wake up and all I have are blank pages. It's like a fog I can't see through, stretching on for the rest of my life."

Brody didn't say anything. He didn't have any answers and he wouldn't insult her with platitudes.

"I know that I need to start putting something in there," Anna continued, "that I need to start dreaming again, hoping again. But how do I do that without him?"

He could hear the tears in her voice and it almost broke his heart. He wanted to give her a step-by-step plan, a bulleted list of how to climb out of that hole, but he wasn't sure he had anything helpful to give her.

"So I just keep traveling through the nothingness," Anna said, sounding even wearier than she had before. "Waiting for the fog to clear, for inspiration to strike, but it never does."

Brody knew all about inspiration, about its stubborn refusal to arrive on time, if at all. "Do you think you'll get married again?" he asked, needing to take his mind off the current subject.

"Yes . . . No . . . I mean . . ." She let out a huff of exasperation. "I don't know what I mean! I don't want to be lonely, so getting marr—" She broke off and tried again. "So not being *alone* sounds good. I'm just not sure I can ever see myself with someone else."

He absorbed her words for a moment. "You feel guilty for even thinking someone could fill their shoes."

"Yes," Anna said, sounding quietly relieved. "You've felt that way too?"

"Yes," he replied. Such a small word for all it encompassed.

"What happened to—?"

Anna's voice was drowned out by Lewis, who suddenly leapt to his feet, ran to the French doors in the living room and started barking at the blackness outside. "Sorry," Brody muttered as he ran after him, grabbing him by the collar and leading him back to the study. "He's been a bit of a nightmare since he heard that owl outside last week. Every time there's the slightest noise, he's off, just in case it's come back."

Brody had just about got his dog back to the study, but Lewis wriggled, pulling his collar out of Brody's grasp, and raced back to the French doors, making twice as much noise as before.

Anna laughed softly. Brody had to stick a finger in his free ear so he could hear her properly. "I'd better let you go and sort him out," she said. "Thank you, Brody, for listening. I'm so glad you picked up when I called."

Brody nodded to himself. "So am I," he admitted, before ending the call to go and deal with his dog. He opened the doors to let Lewis run around the garden. Hopefully, it would confirm the owl was long gone.

When Lewis finally trotted back inside, panting, Brody didn't scold him. Instead, he gave him a treat, reached down and scratched his head. "Good boy," he said softly. "Excellent timing." Because he'd had a nasty feeling Anna had been about to ask him a question he didn't want to answer. There were some things he'd really rather she didn't know about him.

Chapter Fifteen

*B*rody opened the door to his study just before dawn and flicked on the light. He walked over to the desk and took a moment to look out over his garden through the window. There was only just enough light to differentiate the edges of the bushes and the trees from the receding night.

Before he could talk himself out of it, he pulled a notebook from a stack crammed into one of the shelves and leafed through it to see if there were any empty pages. There were. Lots of them. Only a few at the front had been filled. As he glanced at them, he noticed how much his handwriting had changed in the years since he'd last used it. The scrawl in these pages wasn't that of a schoolboy, although it had something of that innocence, that optimism. These days, he printed carefully, making deep black scratches in the paper.

Okay, he thought to himself. *It's just words. Nothing to be scared of. Once upon a time, you used to be good at this.*

Years ago, a little voice in his head whispered. *And how many times have you tried since then? How many times have you walked away leaving nothing but a blank page? Plenty,* he told himself. But he hadn't pulled a notebook off this shelf in at least five years, possibly more. It might be different this time.

He sat down and picked up a fountain pen from a pot on the windowsill. He had to shake it a few times before it would make a mark on the paper, but he eventually got the ink flowing. He lifted the pen, letting the nib hover just above the creamy paper, and exhaled.

And that was how he sat, staring at a spotless page of empty lines, for a good ten minutes. When he couldn't take it anymore, he stood up, threw the pen down and stormed out of the room.

He tugged on a fleece and headed out the back door. Lewis followed behind and immediately disappeared down the garden, running after an unseen quarry with glee. Brody shook his head then entered one of the small outbuildings in his yard. It was pretty rough-looking, with no plaster on the walls, and a rumpled and crumbling concrete floor, but it had electricity and everything else he needed. He flicked on the light and the old oil-filled heater sitting on the floor, then pulled a tarp off a long workbench.

Underneath were tools and some partially carved wooden shapes: rings, chunky blocks, a few other irregular pieces. He picked up one of the rings. It was still rough in places where the grain had fought being shaped. He reached for a piece of sandpaper and gently, rhythmically, rubbed the possible splinters away, using finer and finer grades of paper until the object was smooth and shiny, ready for paint.

He worked on five rings, each progressively smaller than the last, and when that was done, he began painting them in colors so bright they jarred with the muted greens, soft grays and cool browns of the moor outside.

Leaving them to dry, he hauled a large box from under the workbench and placed it on top. It was full of similar wooden shapes in bright colors. He stared at the assortment of handmade toys for a moment and began pulling them out one by one, assessing them. Most went back in the box once it was empty. One or two remained on the workbench. Not quite perfect. He'd see to them later.

Once all the acceptable pieces had been loaded back in the box, he looked at it and sighed. Moji had left a message on his voicemail last week, saying she was desperate for stacking rings and building blocks. According to her, there'd been a bit of a baby boom in Totnes. Her children's book and toy shop was crying out for more stock.

He would make one of his semi-regular deliveries today, more to help Moji out than because he needed the money his hobby brought in. In the days when he'd earned plenty, he'd invested well, and he lived frugally now. Still, a little extra spending money wouldn't hurt.

However, the thought of leaving Dartmoor, of driving into town, even one as quaint and friendly as Totnes, filled Brody's stomach with ice. He ignored the sensation, opened the workshop door and whistled for Lewis, who came running immediately, ears raised, eyes aglow with anticipation.

The dog raced for the car the second Brody reached for his keys. Brody followed him, trudging toward his ancient Land Rover with his box full of hope and joy. At least *one* of them was looking forward to this trip.

THE SUN WAS still low on the horizon, coloring it with broad streaks of lemon and peach, when Brody pulled into the public parking lot behind the High Street in Totnes. Since the place was virtually empty, he chose a space close to the exit. He turned the engine off and sat there, staring straight ahead. Lewis, who had been curled up in the back, jumped through to the passenger seat, looked at him and woofed.

Brody looked back at him. "I know," he said wearily. "Give me a minute."

He'd caught a segment on television a few months ago, something about well-being and mental health. What had the slick-looking, white-smiled TV doctor said about calming yourself down in stressful situations? Something about breathing? The need for mental preparation? He'd been determined not to pay attention to the segment, but it seemed as if some of the information must have sunk in anyway.

And as he sat there *not* remembering, he was aware of his heart pumping, rapidly but not uncontrollably, in his chest. The bottom half of his lungs seemed to be closed for business, causing him to suck air in through his nostrils and release it again unwillingly. His hands, which gripped the steering wheel, were starting to get clammy.

But he couldn't stay here like this, frozen, all day. The shops would be opening soon and he wanted to be driving back toward the moor, foot pressing pleasingly on the accelerator, when that moment came.

He glanced across at Lewis. "Just do it, right?"

Lewis cocked his head and barked joyfully. Brody swore he'd never met a dog so unfailingly enthusiastic and optimistic. It was almost sickening.

He took a deep breath and opened the car door. The first thing that struck him was the noise, even though it was early and hardly any cars or people were about. There was a hum in the air, the particular collective reverberation of people living and working in close proximity. When his home had been in the city, he wouldn't even have noticed the sounds—just part of the wallpaper of life—but compared to his cottage on the moor, even the rumble of a distant car a few streets away seemed noticeable and loud.

Had he really lived in London for all those years? It seemed like a different person who'd done that.

He quickly retrieved the box full of toys from the trunk and, taking Lewis with him on his lead, navigated the narrow back streets and alleyways, ending up at the rear of a shop near the bottom of the narrow, steep High Street.

He placed his cargo down by the back door and slipped an envelope with an inventory and prices for each item inside. He was just about to walk away when he paused and glanced at the door. Speaking with Anna had made him realize what a hermit he'd become. Instead of retracing his steps, he picked the box up again, making sure it was secure in his left arm, and rapped on the wood with his free hand.

A few moments later, the door opened, and Moji appeared. "Brody! To what do I owe this pleasure?"

He'd known Moji for close to two decades. Long ago, in that other life, she'd owned a children's bookshop in South London, but then, when her husband had divorced her and flown back to Nigeria, she'd moved down here, along with her eldest daughter. It had been on Moji's recommendation he'd looked in this area for somewhere quieter six years ago, when the city had become unbearable.

She was petite and round, and she had to reach up to put her arms around him so she could pull him into a hug and press a kiss on his stubbly cheek. Brody let her, but it had been a

long time since he'd touched another human being and it felt
strange. He wasn't sure it was an entirely pleasurable experience
anymore, which seemed odd, seeing as he'd always considered
himself a tactile sort of person.

Moji released him and for some reason, Brody thought of
Anna, of what she'd said about her husband. She hadn't got used
to the lack of these basic human things yet, the way you do when
you lose someone. That hunger for connection still burned inside of her. He suspected that was what had prompted her to call
her husband's number in the first place. It was probably why she
kept calling Brody. It wasn't him she wanted, really, just what he
represented. A tenuous bond to what she'd lost.

He suddenly wished very hard that the hunger never left her.
Not the tearing pain that came with it; one could always dispense
with that. But it occurred to Brody that maybe the yearning was
supposed to evolve into something more positive: passion, drive.
Living. Not this awful blank numbness.

Lewis was looking up at Moji adoringly. She bent down to
give him a tickle under the chin, then straightened with her
usual self-contained grace and looked at Brody expectantly. He
realized he hadn't answered her question as to why he'd knocked
on the door instead of leaving the box as he usually did. He
shrugged. "Seemed ages since I've seen you."

And it had been ages. Maybe six months. He only made these
trips every five or six weeks and had got into the habit of sneak-
ing in and out of town before anyone would be about.

"Let me make you a cup of tea," she said.

"Well, I . . ."

"Go on, now you're here! Only a quick one." She retreated
inside before he had a chance to argue.

Brody swallowed, then followed her into the small shop, glancing nervously at the partially glazed front door. The sign hanging there read OPEN, meaning the opposite word was visible from the street. He was grateful for that.

There wasn't room for both of them in her tiny kitchen, which he expected had once literally been a broom cupboard, so he waited in the shadows at the back of the shop while Moji made the drinks. When she was finished, she handed him a strong tea in a mug that said *Booksellers Believe in Them Shelves*. He couldn't help smiling as he took it.

Moji settled herself onto one of two stools behind the counter and motioned for him to take the other one. "Those stacking rings have been selling like hotcakes," she said. "And the pull-along trains too. Are there any more in that box?"

"Three of the rings, one train, but I can make more if you want."

Moji took the train out of the box and handled it, running her fingers over the silky painted wood. "Such beautiful workmanship. You have a real gift." She then glanced up to the shelf behind the till and Brody knew what was coming next. "I don't suppose . . ."

He shook his head. Moji was talking about the unpainted, unvarnished figure of a willowy wood elf he'd done last summer, carving on a whim, letting his fingers create without thought. This is what he'd come up with. The delicate figure had flowing skirts and a faraway look in her eyes. She was completely different to anything else he'd ever made, and for some reason that had bothered him, but he'd known that Moji would like her, and for Moji's friendship (and her lack of judgment about his peculiar ways) he'd made a gift of the elf to her.

"Lots of people come in wanting to buy her, but I just can't bear to part with her. However, if you could make me another one . . . Or maybe even three?" she said, smiling widely with a naughty glint in her eyes.

Brody chuckled. One of the things he liked about Moji was her tenacity. "She's one-of-a-kind," he told her. "Like you."

She punched him on the arm. "Oh, you old charmer," she said, laughing.

But just then the shop door rattled. Brody stood up, almost sending his stool flying. A middle-aged woman with pasty skin and frizzy hair had her nose pressed up against the window, eyes shielded by her hand. She tried the locked door again.

"Some people!" Moji said, smiling good-naturedly all the same. She headed for the shop door. It was a journey of ten steps, maximum, even with Moji's tiny legs.

"What are you doing?" Brody asked, gripping his mug tightly and taking a step back, closer to the wall.

"I'm going to let her in. It's only Alison Shaw. She told me last week that she was expecting another grandchild imminently and he must have arrived."

"But you're not open yet."

"It's only another ten minutes and she's one of my best customers."

Brody put his mug of tea down on the desk, even though he'd only taken a couple of sips from it and it was still blissfully hot. Lewis, who'd been sitting patiently beside the kitchen-slash-cupboard in case biscuits might appear, cocked his head to one side and his tufty little eyebrows lifted in surprise. "I'll be off then," Brody said firmly. "I don't want to get in the way of—"

"Nonsense! Alison would love to meet you. She nearly always

buys those sorting cubes you make when each grandchild gets a little older, really raves about them . . ." Moji closed the distance to the door.

That was Brody's cue. By the time she'd flipped the sign over so *OPEN* faced the street outside, he was in the backyard, a confused-looking and biscuit-deprived Lewis trailing dejectedly beside him.

But Brody didn't hurry back to his car. He couldn't. His lungs had given up completely now.

The yard around him became distant and rather fuzzy, as if he was viewing it through a dirty telescope from far away, and the sounds that had been so invasive when he'd first got out of his car were drowned out by the rushing noise in his ears.

Oh, God. This was it. The moment he was going to die. He reached out to the brick wall for support and dropped into a crouching position, head bent toward his knees.

Moji was only a short distance away inside the shop. He could hear her chatting to the woman about her daughter-in-law's water birth and might have been able to call out to her, but the thought of opening his mouth and firing words from it only made his head spin faster and his heart pound harder.

He had to get up. He had to get to his car. He had to . . .

Something warm and rough touched him and he flinched before looking down to find Lewis sitting neatly beside him, quietly licking his hand.

It pulled him back into the moment. Something shifted inside him. The rushing in his ears remained, along with a vague sense of being off-balance—like one might experience on a cross-Channel ferry—as he tried to place one foot in front of the other, but he could move again. That was something.

It seemed to take hours instead of minutes to get back to the parking lot. A woman with a stroller scowled at him from the other side of the road, obviously thinking it was a little early for him to have staggered out of the pub.

When he got to his Land Rover, he climbed inside. The lack of power door locks meant he had to reach over to press the buttons down on the passenger side and both the back doors one by one. That done, he sat with his elbows on the steering wheel, rested his head in hands and tried to get the world to stop shaking.

Chapter Sixteen

Anna sat at one end of a long table in the upstairs room of a funky bar in Covent Garden. It was decked out like a nineteenth-century gentlemen's club, complete with wood paneling, richly upholstered chaise longues and a stuffed stag's head above the fireplace. On the table in front of her was a large balloon glass full of wonderfully aromatic alcohol, finished off with a giant ball of ice and a sprig of rosemary. She was joined by eight other people, each with an identical glass, and the tenth seat, beside her, was empty.

As she listened to a smartly dressed man with a waxed moustache detail the history of gin, she surreptitiously checked her phone.

There was a text from Gabi. *Be with you in 2 mins!*

Gabi had messaged earlier to say she was going to miss the beginning of the gin-tasting class but that she would definitely make it before the end.

Anna sighed. This was yet another activity Gabi had talked Anna into not long after the New Year's Eve debacle—just in case salsa had proved to be a flop—but there had been a three-month waiting list, and now the actual day had come, Gabi's photo assignment for the day was running late, and Anna was sitting here on her own.

A short while later, a rather hot and flustered-looking Gabi slid onto the empty chair beside Anna. She leaned over and whispered, "I will tell you all about my nightmare photoshoot later . . . You won't believe what the client . . ." She trailed off as she noticed the gin expert pause and glance disapprovingly in her direction.

Sorry! she mouthed back at him and mimed zipping her lips shut.

Tom Collins (not his real name, Anna suspected) gave Gabi a disapproving look then turned to the rest of the group and resumed his lecture. Anna dipped her head to hide a smile. The man obviously took his gin very seriously. Anna and Gabi sat and listened attentively while "Tom" explained the difference between London and New Western dry gins.

"When I booked this session, I thought we'd be doing a lot more tasting and a lot less listening," Gabi muttered under her breath.

"Shh," Anna replied, not taking her eyes off their instructor. "It's educational."

"Finally!" Gabi said, as they were presented with a new combination of gin, tonic and botanicals to sample.

Anna took a demure sip. She wasn't sure if she could discern all the notes of the different botanicals in this one, as Tom had said they would, although she could definitely detect a hint of cinnamon. She wasn't sure what arrowroot tasted like, so she had no idea if she could identify that.

During the time they were supposed to be discussing the gin with each other, Gabi leaned in and said, "We were shooting a burger cookbook today. Five burgers! And I hate doing burgers."

"Why?" Anna asked. "They're not difficult to cook, are they?"

"No . . ." Gabi glanced at the instructor, who was chatting seriously with a group at the other end of the long table. "But each bit—meat, bun, lettuce, tomato and other ingredients—have to be picked and styled individually, even the way the mustard drips and the cheese melts, and then it is a race to get the shot before the bun goes soggy. We were just about to do the last dish of the day when the client decided he did not want the brioche bun he'd picked. He wanted sesame seed instead!"

"Not good?"

"No. Not good. I had to go shopping, and they were out of stock at the local supermarket, so I had to spend forty minutes gluing sesame seeds onto a plain bun. With tweezers, Anna! This is why I *need* gin tonight . . ." She sighed dramatically and flipped her long hair over her shoulder. "Sometimes I think I need a less stressful career, one where I can work with food, but I don't have to deal with *people*."

Anna smiled. "No, you don't. You love your job, and not everyone has that. You're very lucky." She thought for a moment. "I don't feel that way about my job at all."

"I guess you're right." Gabi nodded grudgingly. "About my job *and* your job. You never talk about it. Nothing good, nothing bad. That says something."

Anna frowned. Did it? When she'd applied for the position at Sundridge Plumbing and Heating, it had just been a way to cover the bills. Everything had seemed dull and pointless at that time, so why should her job be any different?

"It's not like when you worked with BlockTime," Gabi said. "You never *stopped* talking about work then."

Anna shrugged. "It was a start-up, so it was an exciting time, and it's hard to get fired up about invoices and plumbing bookings in the same way."

Gabi looked thoughtful. "Why don't you go back?"

"To BlockTime?" Anna shook her head. "I don't think so."

"Why? You loved working with Vijay and Rhys."

And Spencer, Anna silently added. *What I really loved was working with Spencer.*

"I know . . . But the reason I didn't go back after it all happened was that it was just too painful, Gabs. I tried for about two days, remember? But all I could see was the empty chair at Spencer's desk, his mug, unwashed and gathering dust, next to the kettle. It was too much. I couldn't do it."

Gabi reached over and rubbed Anna's shoulder. "I understand, but maybe it is time to get a different job now, one that you *do* find exciting."

They were prevented from discussing it any further because Tom Collins launched into his spiel about the final gin on the tasting menu. Baskerville Gin was made in Dartmoor with spring water from the national park and flavored with gorse flowers and hawthorn berries. Anna sipped it gingerly when given the go-ahead. It was complex, with bold, clear flavors and an underlying earthiness. For some reason, it reminded her of Brody.

And thinking of Brody took her back to the conversation they'd had last week about her blank, looming future, how she'd told him that she needed to start dreaming again. Isn't that what Gabi was talking about too?

"I think it's more than just finding a new job. I struggle to get excited about *anything*."

"This is why I suggest all the classes," Gabi said seriously. "I hope you will find something that makes you feel . . ." She broke off, searching for the right words. "That makes you *feel*. Life is nothing without passion, Anna."

"I think I'm starting to get that now."

"Hallelujah!" Gabi threw her hands up in the air. "What made you understand this finally?"

Anna was about to tell Gabi about the conversation she'd had with Brody, but then she stopped herself. Gabi didn't know about Brody yet, and Anna wasn't sure she wanted to tell her. Because telling her about him would mean telling Gabi how she met him, and Anna just *knew* that Gabi would give her one of her trademark *Seriously?* looks when she heard the whole story.

Besides, how did she tell her best friend that she'd tried talking to her about the same things she shared with Brody, but that Gabi just hadn't been able to listen? Not in the way Anna had needed her to. That would only hurt her feelings, and she'd been trying so hard. And it wasn't Gabi's fault—she just hadn't been through anything similar like Brody had.

They paused their conversation as the class came to an end, then took their drinks and moved to a quieter corner of the room. "Okay," Gabi said as they sat down. "Do you still want to go to salsa, or do we need to find a new activity?"

"I'm happy to keep going with salsa," Anna replied. "I wouldn't want to deprive you and Lee of the chance to see each other."

Gabi smiled, and her face glowed. Things had been going well with Lee in the last month or so. Very well, seeing as they were now official. Anna was so pleased for her—it was about time Gabi had someone who showered her with attention like this. She was crossing her fingers that this guy didn't turn out like all the others. However, Lee's job as a police officer made his social life challenging, and Gabi's wasn't much better. He and Gabi had to take the chance to meet up whenever they could.

"How about lettering? Like the pretty bullet journals on Instagram? I saw an advert for a class in the art supplies shop when I was picking up new paintbrushes for work. You were always good at design."

It was the sort of thing Anna would have been interested in, once upon a time. She weighed the idea up in her mind, tried to get excited about it, but it was like attempting to start a car with a flat battery—there were a couple of hopeful flickers and then, well, everything flatlined.

"I think, just like with the job, trying yet another class isn't going to solve anything."

"But—"

"Not that I don't appreciate your input," Anna added hastily, "or that I don't enjoy most of them. It's just that I think it's deeper than that. I need to find a sense of purpose to life again."

"That's why it is good to do classes," Gabi replied. "To help you find that spark."

"Yes and no," Anna said. How did she explain this? "It's a bit of a catch-twenty-two situation. The classes are all well and good, but without that spark inside to start off with, there's nothing to ignite, nothing to fan into flame. The activities just become something else to cross off on a tick list." She sighed. "You were right—I *am* a zombie. Something's dead inside, Gabi—there is no life, no passion—and I don't know how to get it back again."

Gabi swirled the gin around her glass and stared into it for a moment. "Maybe it's like this . . ."

"Like gin?" Anna asked.

"No, like gin *tasting*. We live our lives . . . We try one thing, we try another thing, until we find out what works for us." She took a sip and then looked back up at Anna. "What do you *want* your life to be, Anna? If you could choose? What would you do next?"

Anna blinked and looked back at Gabi. If only she knew the answer to that question.

Chapter Seventeen

Anna grimaced as she knocked on Gayle and Richard's front door. It had been almost a month since the Camber Sands outing, and she hadn't attended the Barry family lunch the fortnight before, due to an actual migraine this time, not just a fake one. In that time, she hadn't called Gayle, and Gayle hadn't called her. Mind you, they'd never spent much time talking on the phone, so nothing had really changed there.

Her mother-in-law answered the door. She gave Anna a lavender-scented kiss on the cheek as usual, but the memory of that blustery, gray day at the beach loomed between them as Gayle ushered her inside. Anna quickly joined Scott and Teresa in the dining room to help set the table. Scott pulled a chair out for his wife, raising his eyebrows.

Teresa rolled her eyes. "I'm not sitting down," she said, answering his unspoken request. "I'm fine."

Scott scowled until Teresa went over and thanked him by kissing him softly on the cheek. His hand drifted possessively toward her protruding stomach and he rubbed it gently, which earned him a glowing smile from his wife.

It was touching that the pregnancy was bringing this protective side out in Scott, but Anna had to turn away and busy herself with the large canteen of cutlery inherited from Gayle's mother. Is that what Spencer would have been like with her, with their baby? She wished she'd had a chance to find out. But not wanting to put a damper on the afternoon, she sucked in a breath and hurriedly swiped at her eyes.

Lunch continued as countless other lunches before it had, with the polite passing of covered vegetable dishes, the obligatory compliments to the cook and exclamations on how crispy the roast potatoes were. Richard, as always, filling a moment of silence with, "Well, this is keeping us all quiet!" as he grinned broadly round the table. They all knew which parts they were supposed to play, which lines were theirs. In some ways, this made it easier. Anna discovered she could park the irritation she'd been feeling on the drive there and just skate over the top of it.

As Teresa passed her the custard jug for dessert, Gayle coughed gently. "Is that okay with you too, Anna?"

Anna looked at Gayle, the jug warm in her hands. She must have drifted off and missed something. And she obviously hadn't heard Gayle correctly. For a moment, it had very much sounded as if her mother-in-law had asked her opinion on something.

"Um . . . Could you run that past me again?" Gayle was not looking impressed. "Sorry . . . Got distracted by your yummy-looking apple pie."

Gayle gave her a curt nod, mollified, and carried on. "It's been three years now," she said, keeping direct eye contact with Anna, just to make sure she continued to pay attention. "And our regular family lunches have been lovely, but I feel that it's time to have them once a month rather than every fortnight."

Everyone else looked at Anna, waiting for her response. Was this a trick question? Was there some horrible catch she hadn't spotted? Changing Sunday lunches to once a month felt like being let out on parole early. There was only one possible response. "That's fine by me."

"Since this is the third Sunday of the month," Gayle said, "why don't we just continue in that pattern?"

Scott pulled out his phone to look at his calendar. "So the next one will be in May, on the . . ."

"On the sixteenth," Gayle finished for him. "And June's really should be on the twentieth, but Richard and I wanted to talk to you all about that."

The atmosphere grew solemn. Anna blobbed a bit of custard on her pie and placed the jug back on the table. No one else was picking up their forks and spoons, so she followed suit, and hoped it all wouldn't be cold before Gayle had finished.

"It would have been Spencer's thirty-fifth birthday on the twenty-eighth, so I propose we move June's lunch to the following Sunday, but instead of having it here, we'll go out— somewhere Spencer liked to eat."

"What was the name of that restaurant near you, Anna?" Richard asked. "The very smart Indian place we went to for his thirtieth?"

"The Cinnamon Café," Anna replied. "But the prices are more upmarket gastropub than cheap and cheerful local take-away."

Richard waved her concerns away with a brush of his hand. "Don't worry about that," he said, smiling. "Gayle and I would like to treat you all."

There were murmurs of thanks from around the table, and Anna breathed a sigh of relief. Last year Gayle had insisted on doing a "nice" roast, incorporating all of Spencer's favorites, the crowning glory of the menu being Spencer's favorite black cherry cheesecake. Yuck. He'd always asked for it when they went round to his parents because Anna refused to serve it at her dinner table. Even the smell of all that fake cherry flavoring made her want to gag. Stifling the urge to vomit definitely wasn't the way she most wanted to remember her husband.

And since the suggestion was to meet up the day before his birthday, it meant Anna would have the actual day to herself. Her spirits lifted. What about going back to Camber Sands? She could wander around the way she'd wanted to. She might even stay a night or two at a bed-and-breakfast.

Her luck continued after dinner. When Gayle reached for the pale blue photo album that Anna recognized as the one containing Spencer's baby pictures, Richard peered around the edge of his Sunday paper and said, "Didn't we look at that one last time?"

Gayle's fingertips were already on the spine of the album, but as she hesitated, Richard rose and chose a volume from the other end of the shelf. A wedding album. Anna's heart did a little leap. "How about this one?" he said, handing it to Gayle, then returned to his paper, giving Anna a treasonous wink as he passed her. Anna could have kissed him.

Gayle didn't move for a moment but then she turned and came to join Anna on the sofa, laying the album down on the glass and wood coffee table as they always did, then opened the cover.

The first group of pictures were of Anna on her own and with her bridesmaids, but Gayle flipped through that section of the album swiftly until she found the photos of Spencer and his best man. She took a long time looking at each shot, drinking it in, and then she carried on to those taken after the ceremony. She paused at one of Anna's favorites: a close-up of both of them, so similar to many others taken that day, except that Spencer had an extra twinkle in his eyes and one corner of his mouth lifted slightly in mischief. Gayle let out a little sigh. "He looks so handsome, doesn't he?" she said, almost reverently.

"Yes," Anna replied. He really did. Tears threatened, but she blinked rapidly, refusing to allow them to form.

She glanced across at Gayle and, seeing a similar sheen in her eyes, debated whether to reach out and touch the other woman's arm, but she must have dithered too long, because Gayle seemed to inwardly shake herself, regaining her composure. She turned the page, and the moment was gone.

"I think it's time for a cup of tea," Gayle said when they'd finished. She rose to replace the album on the shelf. "Would anyone else like one?"

Anna slumped onto the sofa and let out a long sigh once Gayle had swept from the room. Richard rustled his paper and lowered the top edge so he could look at Anna. "You mustn't mind her," he said in a low voice. "She doesn't mean to be so . . . you know."

Anna nodded. This was about as eloquent as Richard got.

"She found the anniversary very hard," he added. "You wouldn't know it to look at her, and she'd deny it if you asked, but she's struggling."

Anna stood up, went over to Richard and gave him a hug. They stayed like that for a few seconds, him reaching up with his paper on his lap, her bending down over him, and then he patted her on the back, and she gave him a quick kiss on the cheek.

She exhaled as she stood up again. *Come on, Anna. Stop being so petty. Yes, she's a bit of a nightmare, but it's not because she hates you. She's hurting. Just like you are.*

Anna was pretty sure she was never going to get an apology

from Gayle for the ashes, but maybe she could broker a truce, allowing the current chilly awkwardness to defrost a little. Rather than sitting back down, she went into the kitchen to see if she could be of any help.

When she entered, Gayle was standing with her arms braced on the counter, looking out of the window. There were no cups and saucers out, and the kettle was silent, no steam wafting up from its spout. Gayle turned, looking mildly surprised to see her. Anna thought her mother-in-law looked as if she'd aged ten years during the walk down the hall to the kitchen.

"Don't worry about tea for me," Anna said, deciding this wasn't the time to bring anything up. "I think I'm going to head off shortly."

Gayle just nodded, then walked over to the freezer, where she removed a plastic container from a drawer and handed it to Anna. "You'd better take these, then," she said, as Anna looked on, confused. "From after Camber Sands. We had quite a lot left over."

Anna looked down. Inside the box, misty with frozen air, were twelve perfect vol-au-vents. The dig was as effective as if Gayle had prodded her in the chest with one of her perfectly manicured fingernails.

Gayle turned and busied herself putting a few things away from the dishwasher. "You were quite rude, I thought," she said, when she stood again, "to leave without having supper with us. We were all finding it difficult that day, not just you—and the very least you could have done if you were going to speed off like that was come in and say a proper goodbye to everyone."

Anna was speechless.

Gayle put the mug she was holding in the cupboard, then

turned to face her. "In difficult times, family really should stick together."

Oh, *now* Anna was family? It hadn't felt that way at Camber Sands, not one bit.

"I think you owe me an apology," Gayle added.

Anna felt as if she'd been punched in the head. Gayle wanted an apology? From her? In what alternate universe was the woman living? She opened her mouth to tell Gayle exactly what she could do with her fricking apology, but then Richard's words came back to her.

She's struggling . . .

She looked back at Gayle. That tightness around the jaw, that determination, it was all Spencer. Mother and son had always looked like each other, but Anna had never seen it as clearly as she did at that moment. Her anger crumbled like the dry pastry inside the Tupperware box she was holding.

"I am sorry the day ended badly," she said, and that was as much of an apology as Gayle was going to get, because it was the truth. "I found it difficult too . . ." she added but trailed off again as she saw the steely look in her mother-in-law's eyes. There was no point. Not today. Gayle's guard was up as high as it would go.

She hugged the chilly plastic box to herself. "Thank you for the vol-au-vents," she said, then gave Gayle a quick kiss and walked away.

Chapter Eighteen

"Do you like vol-au-vents?"

Brody was once again sitting in the armchair in his study. Lewis warmed his feet, and his mobile phone was alive and making noise, but this time there was also a tumbler of good single malt beside him on the occasional table with barley twist legs. He frowned. Had Anna just said what he thought she'd said?

"Brody?"

He decided to run with it, even though it was a totally bizarre way to start a conversation. "What kind of vol-au-vents?"

She gave an exasperated sigh. "I don't know! Does it matter?"

"Tinned salmon, definitely no. Egg mayonnaise, not if you paid me. Prawn cocktail? Maybe. So I'd say it matters."

"I was talking about vol-au-vents more as a general principle. As a concept."

Vol-au-vents as a *concept*. This was something new to Brody. Thinking deeply and abstractly about flaky, retro party food was not something he'd ever imagined himself doing, but he found he was relishing the prospect because he was thinking about something new, something different from the same old things that ran around the worn track inside his head day after day.

"No," he said thoughtfully, firmly. "I'm not sure I do like vol-au-vents."

"Thank you!" Anna said, and the relief and validation in her tone had him imagining her collapsing back into an armchair, argument won, even though he had no idea what the battle had been about or who she was having it with.

He tried to imagine what she looked like as he talked to her. It was strange just to hear a voice and have no visual to go with it. He pictured Anna with long hair with a bit of a wave, delicate features. Large eyes. He probably imagined her that way because the first time he'd spoken to her, she'd sounded childlike. Not innocent or immature—she'd experienced too much for that—but in the sense that she'd sounded lost.

"So what's with this sudden obsession with canapés?" he asked, one corner of his mouth kicking up in a smile. "If you want to get started on sausage rolls, I have quite strong opinions about those."

Anna laughed. Brody had forgotten how good it felt to make someone do that. The air around him felt warmer. "Really? Sausage rolls?" she said.

"I've become quite fussy about sausages in general, not just those wrapped in pastry," he said, aware how much of an old codger that made him sound but somehow not minding. "Maybe it's living in the country. There are some great farm shops nearby." Ones that delivered and let you pay online, thankfully, but he didn't tell her that.

"Where are you?"

"Devon."

"Oh, Devon is lovely," she said wistfully. "I once had a holiday there, a really good holiday . . ." She broke off, and Brody guessed she was thinking about her husband. He waited, not minding, wondering if the recollection made her happy or sad.

Holidays were simultaneously the best and the worst memories, he'd found, packed as they were with new places and new experiences, which made them richer and more colorful than everyday life.

Anna sighed again, and when she spoke it was clear she'd pulled the plug on whatever mental slideshow she'd been watching. "I'm not a country girl," she said ruefully. "I can only just tell one end of a cow from the other. I live in—"

"Don't tell me!"

"Oh . . ." She sounded puzzled. "Why not?"

"Because I'm a stranger, really. Would you tell a random stranger where you live?" He realized he'd be worried about her if she did.

"Well, no . . . But—"

"I'm thinking about your safety. I could be a deranged, axe-murdering stalker and you'd never know."

Anna laughed again. This time it was deeper, more from her belly. He was starting to find that sound a little addictive. "Are you?" she asked, trying to sound serious—and failing.

"No," Brody replied, trying not to smile, because he had a valid point to make. He also failed miserably. "But I would say that, wouldn't I? Especially if I was a deranged, axe-murdering stalker."

"Brody, you seem to forget who keeps phoning whom out of the blue. If anything, *I'm* the one to worry about."

There was that.

"Anyway," she continued, "I live in London. In the suburbs. With almost nine million people in this city, I don't think it's too perilous for me to reveal that."

"No," he replied. "But maybe we should consider that, technically, we *are* strangers. We've only talked a handful of times. Just for now, maybe we should stick to the basics: general locations, first names only."

Anna was silent for a moment. "Okay. I suppose that's sensible."

He was telling himself he was suggesting all this secrecy, this anonymity, to protect Anna, but was that the whole truth? Wasn't there a little bit of him that was eager to protect himself as well? If she didn't know exactly where he lived, she could only ever exist at the end of the phone line, and that was a very safe distance indeed. Had his need for isolation become that complete?

"Anyway," Anna said, with the tone of someone switching tack, "about the vol-au-vents. I suppose I ought to explain . . ." And she launched into a story about her husband's family that had him wincing and smiling in equal measure.

When she'd finished her tale, he sighed and said, "You know what your problem is?"

"Please, do enlighten me," she said in a smooth tone that only just hid her sarcasm.

"You let your mother-in-law have all the power."

Anna's voice shifted up an octave. "*What?* No, I don't! I don't let her have anything. She stole it. She *hijacked* it!"

"Nope," Brody said, still smiling. "You gave it to her. And you're still giving it to her, every time you interact with her."

"No, I'm not!" He almost expected steam to wisp out of his phone as she fumed for a few silent seconds, but then she added, "Am I . . . ?"

"I think you might be."

"How?" she almost wailed.

He took a sip of his whisky and thought about the best way to put it. "When something big happens, something devastating, you can't process anything else because of the shock of it—your brain just goes into shutdown, only doing what's absolutely necessary to keep you functioning."

Anna made a noise of recognition. "That sounds about right."

"So you just react to everything that's happening around you. No planning, no proactive choices, just reacting. And it's easy to get stuck in that loop." He should know. He'd spent a few years in that place. "If you want to take back control, you need to stop reacting. To her."

"Well, that's very easy to say, but how do I actually do that?"

Brody's mouth twisted. "Damned if I know. She's your mother-in-law. You'll have to work that one out on your own, just like I had to with mine."

Anna didn't reply straightaway and, at first, he thought she was considering her advice, but when she spoke again, it was obvious her thoughts had led her down another path. "Are you married?" she asked, her tone wary.

Brody knew what she was asking: Should they be talking like this? It was innocent, to be sure, but there was something about the easy intimacy they'd fallen into so quickly that would have rung alarm bells for him once upon a time.

"No. I'm not married. Not anymore."

"Oh." She fell silent again. "I knew there was a reason you understood. You've lost someone too."

The obvious answer was yes, he did. He had. But Brody didn't want to give the obvious answer, so he stayed silent.

"Was it a 'her' or a 'him'—the person you lost?"

He hadn't planned on telling her anything, but then he heard himself say, "Her."

There was a pause as she absorbed that fact. "How long ago?"

"Nine years." His mouth just kept moving, despite himself. It was most strange. He put his glass down decisively. "Listen, Anna . . . I probably ought to go. Lewis is asking for a walk before we settle down for the night." He glanced down at Lewis, who was snoring gently at his feet and hadn't even lifted an ear at the mention of his name. All the warmth that had gathered while he'd been talking about stupid things like sausage rolls and vol-au-vents drained away, leaving him more than a little disgusted with himself.

"Oh, okay . . ." Her tone was confused, and rightly so, but he wouldn't let himself register the tinge of disappointment in it.

"Goodb—"

"Don't say that word," she said quickly. "Remember?"

"I do now," he said, but her answer gave him hope he hadn't just ruined the chance of her calling back ever again. He had the feeling that the day she said it to him, he'd never hear from her again. He was glad that day wasn't today.

"Say something else," she added softly.

He thought for a moment. "Till next time."

From the way she breathed, he could tell she was smiling. "Till next time," she echoed, and then she was gone. The study didn't seem as cozy after that.

He reached down and rubbed Lewis's belly. The dog opened one eye and yawned. "Come on," he said. "Don't make me a worse liar than I already am. It's time for you to go down the garden."

He followed his dog out into the yard and stared up at the night sky. Thanks to his remote location, he often was able to see more stars than he could count, yet tonight there was nothing but thick gray clouds. It seemed fitting. She was so honest, so open with him, and he was giving her the impression he was being the same with her, but he wasn't. He really wasn't.

Chapter Nineteen

Gabi and Anna arrived at the civic center just as their salsa class started. There were about a hundred people in the hall, most arranged into large circles with women on the outside, men on the inside, and a few stragglers, like the two of them, were shrugging off jackets or changing shoes. Gabi spotted Lee across the room and waved wildly, before blowing him a kiss.

She turned to Anna, who was changing her sneakers for shoes with a low heel. "Thank you for doing this—for swapping to the Wednesday night class. With Lee's new shift change, we lost two more nights when we could see each other."

Anna looked up at her as she fastened the buckle on one of her shoes. "You know I was happy to do it." She looked down again and tried to stifle a fluttering in her stomach. She'd told the truth—she was happy to do this for Gabi, but that didn't mean she wasn't a little nervous for herself.

Because Wednesday nights didn't just mean Wednesday nights, did they? They meant Jeremy. A picture of him at the Valentine's event popped into her head, and even though that had been months ago, her stomach did a little roll. It was most disconcerting.

Anna noticed their teacher scowling in their direction. "We'd better get a move on," she said and dragged Gabi into the beginners' circle alongside her.

To begin with, most of Anna's attention was taken up with mastering a couple of new steps, but then she caught Jeremy's eye across the room. He nodded and smiled. Her *Not Spencer* alarm remained silent, which was reassuring, so Anna nodded and smiled back.

But maybe she shouldn't be scared if her little internal alarm did trip. Hadn't she said to Brody that she didn't want to be alone for the rest of her life? The journey had to start somewhere. There would be no possibility of that if she ran a mile in the other direction every time she clapped eyes on anyone remotely suitable.

She had to give herself permission, she realized, to be *open* to the possibility of a new relationship—even love—in the future, no matter if it seemed nonsensical in the present. Spencer wouldn't have wanted her to wither and shrivel without him. Yet, all she'd done since his death was hibernate. Anna let that thought sit in the back of her mind while the class continued.

When nine o'clock rolled around, they thanked their teachers and Anna went to get her coat and shoes.

"Lee and I are going to the Three Compasses," Gabi said, appearing beside her. "Want to come?"

The pub along the road was a regular haunt for some of the salsa students after class. Gabi had gone there on a Tuesday sometimes, but Anna had always made an excuse and headed home. It was clear from the way Gabi didn't wait for an answer but busied herself putting on her jacket that she expected Anna to do the same tonight too.

Anna laced her sneakers and straightened. "Actually, I think I will. Just a quick one—and then I'll head off and leave you two to have some time together."

Gabi rewarded her with a dazzling smile. "Great! I'll go and get Lee." She returned a short while later with her boyfriend, hanging on to his arm so tightly that Anna wasn't sure there was a millimeter of space between their bodies. It gave her a little pang to watch them. She and Spencer had been just the same, even after they'd been married a few years.

Despite the fact that the southeast of England had been experiencing a bit of a heat wave for early May, great purple clouds loomed on the horizon and it had been drizzling steadily most of the evening. Anna observed Gabi and Lee, practically Velcroed together, as they hurried the short distance to the Three Compasses, her presence alongside them almost forgotten.

They were just at the door to the pub when Gabi stopped suddenly. "Oh, no," she said, looking down at her torso and feeling around her shoulders with her hands. "I think I left my scarf at the civic center." She looked at Lee in horror. "It's my favorite one, the one you bought me from Camden Market!"

Lee's serious police officer side snapped to attention. "Where did you last see it?"

"On one of the gray plastic chairs near the door," Gabi said, her brow furrowing.

"You two go ahead," Lee said. "I'll go back and find it."

"My hero," Gabi said softly, and he winked, saluted her, and jogged away.

Anna noticed him smile at a couple of girls heading for the pub, and when she turned to look at Gabi, she saw Gabi had noticed it too. "It's okay," she said to Anna, as they pushed the ornately engraved glazed Victorian doors open and entered the pub. "It's just how Lee is."

"I know . . ." Anna said. Lee certainly was a notorious flirt.

Gabi looked serious. "I know he gives it all that South London, cheeky chappy banter, but you don't need to worry. He told me he's a one-man woman now."

Anna chuckled. "Don't you mean a one-woman man?"

Gabi made a face. "Yes. That! What I'm trying to say is that he has told me that I've got nothing to worry about. He's all mine."

"I'm glad," Anna said. She so wanted this one to work out for Gabi.

When their drinks arrived, they moved away from the bar and found a little table in easy view of the door so Lee would find them when he returned. Indeed, it wasn't long before the ornate doors swung open and he appeared, triumphant, waving Gabi's scarf. He came over to the table and claimed a kiss as a reward as he looped it round his girlfriend's neck, then reached for his waiting beer.

"I ran into a few waifs and strays when I went back," he said, after taking a long sip. "Told 'em they could come and join us. Hope you don't mind." The pub door opened again and a dozen or so people trailed in, all members of the salsa class. There was Big John, the girl with the ponytail and . . . Jeremy.

There wasn't enough room for the whole group to sit down, so someone suggested the pub garden. The ground was wet, but it had just about stopped raining and the clouds must have rolled off in another direction because all Anna could see was a dusky-blue sky.

When they got outside, Anna expected the rest of the group to split into smaller huddles of conversation. This would have allowed her to employ her usual tactic of hovering on the fringes, but Jeremy began to tell a story about how he'd accidentally got roped into taking part in a flamenco show when on holiday in Spain and everyone gathered around to listen. It seemed that, just like someone else Anna used to know, he could hold the attention of a group easily, charming them, entertaining them.

She laughed along with the others as he described his efforts in his mostly forgotten schoolboy Spanish to tell the dancers they should pick someone else from the audience. It felt safe to allow herself to relax a little because he was talking to the whole group, and she didn't feel singled out, the sole focus of his attention. Be *open*, she reminded herself. That's all for now.

There was a brief moment where his gaze landed on Anna, just as she'd been staring at his face, trying to work out what exactly it was that made the arrangement of his features pleasing. Their eyes met and locked, just for a second. Despite her not having heard a peep from her *Not Spencer* alarm all night, it now started pulsing like a heartbeat.

Shut up, she told it. *There's nothing to get your knickers in a twist about. I'm not going to leap on the man. I'm just admiring him. From afar.*

And that was okay, she realized. To appreciate a nice-looking man.

She was still young, and it was only natural. To be honest, it was quite a relief to know that this vital part of her hadn't withered and died with Spencer, as she'd assumed it had. Those needs and desires were still there, waiting for her to have need of them.

And, in the spirit of embracing new experiences, when the salsa crew did inevitably splinter into different groups, Anna didn't slink away when Jeremy came over to say hello. They were right in the middle of a conversation about old Hitchcock movies when the heavens opened. The umbrellas listing through the central holes of each picnic table were hanging limply, leaving them with no shelter from the fat drops of rain that seemed to target them like tiny bombs.

Most of the group ran back inside, including Lee and Gabi, but Anna and Jeremy were further away from the back door of the pub, so they ran from table to table, trying to find an umbrella that worked. The first one wouldn't open and the second wouldn't stay up. By the time they'd huddled under umbrella number three the rain was hitting Anna's scalp and running through her hair and down her forehead. Both she and Jeremy were drenched.

"It would have been safer to make a dash for the lounge bar," Anna said as she pushed a few damp strands off her forehead.

Jeremy smiled down at her. "Where would have been the fun in that?"

Anna shook her head and shrugged, smiling back. "Where indeed?"

And then, suddenly, the air thickened around them and it all didn't seem so funny anymore. Anna swallowed and glanced back toward the pub.

"I think it's easing—" she began.

At exactly the same time he said, "There's something—"

They both fell silent.

"Anna," he began again. "Would you like to have dinner with me sometime?"

No frills. No beating around the bush. Anna liked that approach, or she would have if her mind hadn't been full of blaring sirens and flashing lights. The little alarm was making up for lost time. Her hand shook as she hitched her handbag strap over her shoulder. That fight-or-flight feeling was back again in full force, and since she wasn't about to punch Jeremy on the nose, that left only one option.

Not Spencer.

I know, shut up, okay. I know. I'm dealing with it.

"I'm sorry . . ." she began.

"I don't think I'm reading this wrong, am I?" he said softly, plainly. Not in an accusing way but in a curious, slightly confused way. "I mean, just then . . ."

Anna might be a coward but she wasn't cruel enough to lie to him about that. She shook her head. "No," she whispered. "You weren't imagining it."

"But . . . ?"

"You are nice," she said forlornly. "You're the first person I even . . ." She trailed off, obviously not as brave as she wanted to be. She looked down at her feet for a moment. "It still doesn't mean that I'm ready," she added, looking back up at him. "Not yet."

"I see," he said gently. There was a warmth in his eyes that made her want to cry.

"I'm so sorry," she said.

He nodded, not in agreement that she had something to apologize for but merely to signal her message had been received and understood. "It's okay. I can't pretend I can understand what you've been through, but I do understand why you might be hesitant."

"Thank you," she replied quietly.

He nodded again, then turned and strode across the pub garden, turning the collar of his jacket up as he went. When he reached the back door, he gave her a nod and then disappeared inside. She stared after him, hugging herself, and the rain stopped as suddenly as it had begun.

Moments later, Gabi appeared. "Was that Jeremy? You were out here together alone?" she asked, not doing a very good job at hiding her glee as she looked over her shoulder.

"Yes," Anna said, staring blankly in the same direction. For some reason, she felt hollow.

"And?"

Anna turned and headed to the gate that led directly onto the street. "And nothing."

Chapter Twenty

Brody pulled into the parking lot of the big supermarket in Totnes. It was seven-thirty on a Monday morning, probably one of the quietest times of the week to go grocery shopping. However, he wasn't here to go grocery shopping. Not exactly.

He ignored the neat rows of parking bays nearer the store where the majority of spaces were filled and pulled his Land Rover into the middle of a row of empty bays at the far end. He turned the engine off and sat there, taking stock.

His breathing was even. No headaches or tingling. His pulse was faster than normal, considering he was a pretty fit guy, but it wasn't hammering. *This is good*, he told himself. *This is okay*.

He glanced at the book lying on the passenger seat. *Panic Attacks and Agoraphobia: A Practical Guide*. It had taken him a week to order it after the incident at Moji's shop, another two before he'd opened the cover, and he'd been reading it on and off for the last month or so.

The early chapters on self-care hadn't seemed very useful, so he'd skipped over them. He ate well, looked after himself, ran at least four times a week. Nothing new to learn there. He'd also skipped over the following few chapters of psychobabble, suggesting things like journaling. What was he? A thirteen-year-old girl? Besides, every time he picked up a pen, it was the same.

His brain emptied and all he could do was stare at the blank page. Hardly a therapeutic pursuit.

What had caught his interest was the section full of practical tips and exercises. "Systematic desensitization" was where he'd eventually landed. He could see the sense in that: expose yourself to a situation that has caused panic before—but do it in a smaller way, tackle the situation in bite-sized pieces—and gradually you should be able to defuse some of those panic attack triggers.

This supermarket had seemed the obvious place. He'd had his very first attack here, right in the middle of the fresh produce section. At the time, he'd thought he was dying. He'd been sure he was either having a heart attack or a stroke, that something inside his brain had just popped, ripping through his consciousness, erasing neurons left and right, doing untold damage. Other shoppers had frowned and tutted, assuming he was under the influence of something other than his own brokenness.

While he wasn't exactly whooping for joy inside his head at being back here, he did feel a tinge of excitement mixed in with the trepidation. The local farm shops he used provided excellent quality meat, fresh produce and a few grocery extras, but if he wanted something a little more exotic, he was out of luck. And he'd been hankering for Thai green curry for months now. He had all the right herbs and spices. The only thing missing was fish sauce, and his last bottle had run out almost a year ago. And the more he'd thought about it, the more Thai green curry had been all he'd been able to think about.

His plan was simple: three easy steps. A few techniques from the book combined with a bit of stern self-talk should power him through it. It wasn't as if he was trying to do a full shop,

cramming a shopping cart with items and staying inside the supermarket for up to an hour. Just one bottle of fish sauce. Five
minutes, in and out. He could manage that.

Because what was he going to do if he couldn't? If he couldn't
turn the tide? Live his life like a hermit, growing older and griz-
zlier and more eccentric in his windswept little cottage on the
moor?

Up until now, he hadn't thought much about the future, not
long term, anyway. Not in the sense of years and decades instead
of days and months. But listening to Anna talk about her future,
full of pages yet unwritten, had made him think about his own.

When he imagined the book of his life, he couldn't see blank
pages ready for the touch of a pen. It was slammed shut. Locked.
Hidden away in a dusty drawer and forgotten about. It made him
feel like a coward.

So here he was. Day one. Step one. He had to do it.

His pulse kicked up a notch just thinking about it, then settled
into a steady trot, but he didn't let it deter him. He took a deep
breath and reached for the car door handle.

The first half of the walk across the parking lot was okay. He
used his imagination to paint over the top of what was there and
turn it into a place that held no fear for him. The low-budget
shrubs and spindly trees between the rows of vehicles became
gorse and bracken. Scattered cars among the empty spaces became weather-hewn boulders. The sound of the traffic, only
twenty feet away on the main road that ran past the supermarket, became the rushing of the wind between the rocky tors of
the moor.

However, as he got closer to the store, it became harder and
harder to keep the images in place. It was the noises that really

threw him: shopping cart wheels rattling, car doors slamming, bored children whining from their metal carts. He wasn't used to it anymore.

By the time he got to the entrance, not so much a door but a large rectangular hole, he needed to stop, close his eyes, and breathe. Other shoppers wandered past him; he could feel the breeze from their movement, but he tried to ignore them, concentrating instead on counting to three as he breathed. *In, two, three . . . Out, two, three . . .*

He opened his eyes, keeping the rhythm going in his head. He was on the edge of the cliff of his panic now. This was what he was supposed to be doing, wasn't it? Pushing himself, bringing himself closer to the edge than was comfortable without toppling over it.

He'd been keeping his focus blurred, trained on nothing in particular, but now he lifted his head and chose something random to home in on—a display stand, full of DVDs of last summer's blockbuster action hit. He counted the slots, the individual cases, and when his head was full of numbers instead of the whispering panic, he began to move toward it. It felt as if he were edging his way along a tightrope, strung from the edge of his cliff toward the horizon, suspended over thin air.

What must have only been a few seconds later, he reached out to grip the cardboard edge of the stand. He was teetering on his cliff again now, so close to plummeting over the edge. Even though his eyes were fixed on the DVD display, all of his senses seemed hyper-sharp. He could hear the shopping cart wheels rumbling in the aisle next door. His skin prickled and his breath caught in his throat. Even though the aisles were almost empty, just a few determined early birds come to get their shopping before the morning rush, he felt as if he was in the midst of a jam-packed, crowded city.

On his cliff, he could feel air, cold and beckoning, beneath his toes. He could sense pebbles and scree skittering down the face of the rocks as the cliff below them started to crumble.

Push through, he told himself. *It's a supermarket, for God's sake, full of carrots and celery, currant buns and tins of soup, not a war zone. Keep going. Just keep walking. Get what you need.*

He put the DVD back, fumbling to get it into the cardboard slot, and then made his way to the end of the aisle at the back of the shop. From there, he moved along the ends of the rows, stepping-stone to stepping-stone, scanning the lengths of the shelves for a hint of any Asian foodstuffs—coconut milk, noodles, dark shiny bottles of soy sauce—but he couldn't see anything like it. When he got to the place he'd always found them before, the shelf was full of baked beans and cups of instant noodles. It seemed as if someone had moved every single flipping thing in the supermarket around just to confound him.

He stared at a can of spaghetti hoops with miniature frankfurters, and his hand shot out to grip the shelf, squeezing it so hard the metal edges dug into his fingers.

Focus, Brody. Focus.

He couldn't even pick out single items on the shelves now. All the colors and shapes were blurring together. He stumbled blindly down one aisle and into the next, only pausing when his chest felt so tight that he had to stand still to draw breath. By some bizarre, God-given stroke of luck, he found himself staring at a small glass bottle full of sour brown liquid, a curving dragon emblazoned across the label.

Fish sauce.

He grabbed it off the shelf and hugged it to his chest, closing his eyes with sheer relief. He couldn't imagine feeling any more triumphant than if he'd climbed Everest in a single leap. But just as he was about to open his eyes and head for the bank of tills at the front of the shop, there was an almighty crash behind him. The bottle slipped through his sweaty fingers, and he only just managed to catch it again before it smashed onto the floor.

"Sorry, love," a woman said cheerily, from a few feet away. "These shopping carts have a mind of their own!" And she began picking up the cans of bamboo shoots and water chestnuts she'd just knocked off the shelf.

Brody hardly noticed her. He certainly didn't respond. Everything around him was melting into itself, simultaneously shooting away and becoming distant while feeling so close his skin crawled and he was sure he would suffocate.

He turned and started running. He ran down the aisle toward the tills but didn't stop when he got there. He just sprinted straight through, the bottle of fish sauce still clutched in his fist, and kept going toward the natural light and fresh air of the gaping entrance.

He was almost there when a security guard spun around to watch him.

"He didn't pay for that!" a voice behind him yelled.

"Hey!" the security guard shouted and began to pound after him.

As he ran, Brody fumbled into his back pocket and pulled out a twenty-pound note. He threw it in the direction of the security guard. "Sorry!" he yelled over his shoulder. "Can't stop . . . ! Emergency."

The perplexed guard bent down and scooped up the crumpled

note, then stared after Brody. But Brody didn't notice. He was too busy sprinting across the unforgiving pavement of the parking lot, which seemed to be expanding and stretching, like distances did in nightmares when something was chasing you. All he could think about was getting back to his car, throwing himself inside and locking the door.

Chapter Twenty-One

*B*rody sat in his armchair, staring at the fire burning in the grate and listened to Anna. When they'd first started talking, the calls had been more sporadic, but that had been close to two months ago, and in recent weeks they'd become more regular and more frequent.

"I've been trying to push myself to go out of my comfort zone, be a bit more sociable. You know, just being open to things," she said. "People tell me it would be good for me."

It seemed he and Anna had similar goals at the moment. Brody's mind flashed back to the feeling of terror as he'd sprinted across Morrisons parking lot in Totnes earlier that week, and he felt his chest and face flush. He hoped she was having more success.

This evening, he'd made that stupid Thai curry, with his twenty-pound bottle of fish sauce. It had smelled amazing while it had been cooking, but when he'd sat down at his kitchen table, bowl piled with fluffy Jasmine rice and the fragrant sauce, he'd raised his fork but hadn't been able to take a bite. It was tainted now. The flavor would forever remind him of his failure.

Another thing to cross off his list of experiences. Another thing to avoid. It struck him that while Anna's world was expanding, his was continuing to shrink to practically nothing. "How's that going for you?" He hadn't meant his reply to have a cynical, slightly sarcastic edge, but it had come out like that anyway.

"Ugh!" was Anna's only reply. There was a vague rustling in the background, and he imagined her sitting at the kitchen table and planting her head on its flat surface, feeling the cool of the wood against her forehead.

"That good, huh?"

There was more shuffling, and he sensed she'd adjusted her position so she could talk again. "It's not terrible," she said. "Not really. It's just . . ." She broke off while she searched for the right word. "Different. And different is hard work. Sometimes exhausting, sometimes overwhelming. You know what I mean?"

Unfortunately, he probably knew that better than she did. "Yes."

He could hear the smile of relief in her voice when she answered. "I knew you would."

He loved that sound. That slight change in her tone when she'd managed to express something she needed to, the joy at both having released it and having had it accepted and comprehended. And he loved that he was part of that process, even if all he did was sit and listen. But in his shrinking universe, the fact that he could do *anything* positive, especially for someone else, was a rare blessing.

"My friend Gabriela has a new boyfriend," she continued. "And she's at that stage where everything he does is amazing, where every thought he has is an Einstein-worthy expression of wisdom."

Brody let out a gruff laugh. "I can see what you mean about exhausting!"

Anna laughed too and the remnants of the jittery feeling that had niggled at him since he'd recalled the supermarket incident melted away.

"But that's how it's supposed to be, isn't it?" she added. "At the beginning? You're supposed to feel that way. And I'd be sad for Gabi if she didn't, but . . . I'm going to sound like a horrible friend if I say this, but you've already listened to me rant and rave and cry, so you might as well hear this." She shifted position, preparing herself. "That's also part of the problem: they're just so . . . so . . ."

"Sickening?" Brody suggested, making Anna chuckle.

"No," she said. "I shouldn't laugh. Told you I was awful. They're just so *loved up*. And I'm happy for her, I really am, because she deserves this but . . ."

"It reminds you of what's missing," Brody finished for her.

"Yes," she whispered.

For more than a minute they stayed like that, listening to each other's silence on the other end of the line.

"And I know people do go on to marry again after the death of a spouse," Anna finally said, "but it doesn't seem real to me. It's something I know logically, like a date learned in history class or the principle of gravity, but it doesn't make it make sense here . . ." Brody heard a faint thumping sound, like a hand or a loose fist meeting clothing. ". . . in my heart. Because how could it ever be the same again? Do you feel that way too?"

Brody looked down at Lewis, who was napping in front of the fire, as usual, and he stalled by taking a sip of his whisky. "I understand what you mean" was all he was able to say. Now was not the time to explain.

"How about you? Will you ever get married again?"

He reached for the tumbler of whisky on the table beside him, held its comforting weight between his hands. "I don't think so," he said. Definitely not at the moment. Finding a new life partner wasn't exactly a breeze when every time you came into contact with new people your knees turned to jelly, and you wanted to vomit.

"Do you get lonely? I do . . . Even though I can't envision anyone else in my life, I find I don't like having no one."

Brody exhaled. Until Anna had started calling him, he hadn't even considered whether he was lonely or not, but now he wondered. Was he?

He thought about how sometimes he'd come into his study in the evenings and stare at the phone lying on the desk, about the hollow sensation that followed when it stayed blank and silent, and he couldn't share the things he'd stored away to tell her that day.

But maybe it wasn't supposed to be like this. You weren't supposed to have only one person in the whole world to share things with, were you? Did that mean he was lonely?

"Maybe I do . . . Occasionally. But I'm not sure marriage is the solution. I wasn't a brilliant husband the first time around."

"It wasn't happy then, your marriage?"

"At first it was," he said. "But then . . . Things happen . . . Life happens . . . And sometimes it changes you as a couple. Sometimes you just don't fit together the way you used to afterward. Sometimes you just can't work through it."

Anna let out a heavy breath. "I don't know whether that's easier or harder," she said. "Losing them when it's great or losing them when it's falling apart and you never have that chance to put it back together again."

Losing them . . . He was glad she'd phrased it that way, because it meant he didn't have to lie to her about Katri. "I don't know either," he said, staring out the window. There were no street-lights this far out into the countryside, no light on in the yard, and the blackness of the night was complete. "But the past is the past. I suppose all you can do is try to move forward, work out what to do with the rest of your life."

"Everyone seems to think that enough time will pass and sud-denly it'll be easy," she said. "As if there's an expiry date on love."

"For some people there is," he said, staring grimly into the dancing flames in his fireplace. "Maybe you were just very lucky." He knocked back another slug of whisky, enough this time to scald the back of his throat. "And maybe, if you do want to have another relationship again someday, you should just ad-mit you need a bit more time. No one's going to judge you for that."

"It doesn't always feel that way," she replied mournfully. "Es-pecially not when there are . . . possibilities . . . out there, should I choose to pursue them."

"Possibilities?" he echoed, his voice low and rough.

"Men," she replied simply.

Brody's pulse kicked. For once, it had nothing to do with panic, and everything to do with the thought of Anna. And *pos-sibilities*.

"Someone asked me to dinner last week," she said so softly he almost didn't catch it.

Brody stayed still, stayed quiet. He really didn't know how to react to that.

"I say I want to move on, that I want to stop feeling this mis-erable, but do I want to? Really?"

"Only you can answer that," he said as he ran a fingertip

around the rim of his tumbler. He'd read enough books on grief that he was an expert on it—inside his head, anyway. When it came to practical steps, he wasn't doing quite so well. But that didn't mean some of what he'd learned wouldn't help Anna. "It isn't that black and white, is it? Emotions . . . Life . . . They're complicated. Grief has different stages, and the path is different for everyone. There shouldn't be any judgment about which route you take or how long it takes you to get there."

"I suppose so," Anna replied, sounding tired.

"And, sometimes, even when we truly want something," he added, the image of the supermarket entrance front and center in his imagination, "we find ways to sabotage ourselves."

"Do you think that's what I do? Sabotage myself?"

"I don't know," Brody said carefully. "I suppose you'll only really know when you go on the date itself."

"Oh, I'm not going on the date," Anna said in a rush of nervous laughter. "I said no."

Brody felt a flush of relief. He stopped messing around with his glass and drank the remaining sliver of whisky, reminding himself as he did so that he had no right to feel territorial about Anna. She was a friend, a voice on the end of the phone, that was all.

You're just invested in knowing she's finding happiness, a little voice inside his head said in a soothing tone, and Brody decided to agree with it. He was just feeling protective about someone he cared about. Nothing more, nothing less. And he did care about Anna. How could he not? She was his only regular human contact at the moment, unless you counted Moji, and he'd only seen her twice in the last six months.

"Who is he? The man who asked you out?"

"Oh, just a guy at salsa class . . ."

"You do salsa?" Brody's eyebrows shot up. He'd imagined Anna curled up in a window seat reading a book, or taking long walks in a country park, not doing salsa dancing.

Anna gave a soft laugh. "Gabi talked me into it months ago. She's one of those people who think I should immerse myself in new experiences. This one seems to have stuck. Although . . . I have to say, most evenings, I'd rather be curled up in front of the fire with a good book."

Brody smiled triumphantly to himself. "Why did you say no?" He'd decided not to pry, but the question had come out before he'd been able to stop himself.

She sighed. "I don't know, really . . ."

That wasn't what Brody wanted to hear, he discovered. He wanted her to say Salsa Guy was ugly or unbearably dull or had an extremely bad case of halitosis.

"Jeremy's nice," she continued wistfully.

Jeremy? Good grief.

"He's great company, confident and funny . . . and he's a great dancer."

Good for sodding Jeremy, Brody wanted to say, but he kept his mouth firmly closed. She'd turned him down, after all. There must be *something* wrong with the guy.

"But . . ."

"But what?" he asked casually.

"He's not Spencer," she finally said with both weariness and conviction. "He's just not Spencer."

And neither are you, Brody told himself. *Don't go all stupid. You've been starved of good conversation for too long. Of course, you're going to get attached. It's just a fact of human psychology.*

"Brody?"

She pulled him out of his thoughts and into the present. "Mm-hmm?"

"Do you think we could FaceTime or Skype sometime? I'd really like to talk to you face-to-face."

Brody sat there, stunned. He hadn't been expecting her to ask that, which was probably strange, seeing as it was a fairly normal way to communicate these days. "Um . . . I don't have those apps on my phone."

"But you could download them, right?" She paused for a moment and then added, "If you wanted to."

"I don't know," he replied, answering both questions at once, even if he was the only one aware of that. "My phone is pretty basic. And the signal here isn't very good." He was making excuses now. Why?

"Oh, okay," Anna replied. "It was just a thought. We can chat about it another time. Anyway . . . I'd better go now. It's almost one, and I've got to be up at seven. Until next time, Brody. Thanks for the chat—as always."

"Night, Anna. And, as always, no problem. You don't have to thank me. I enjoy talking to you."

He could hear her smiling before she responded. "I enjoy talking to you too."

And then she was gone, leaving him feeling warm inside but also pondering why his initial reaction to video calling with Anna had been to resist the idea. He stood up, collected his glass and laid his mobile phone back in its place on the desk. It wasn't that he didn't want to see her face, that was for certain, so what was it?

Lewis, who had looked as if you could drive a tractor trailer past him and he wouldn't have stirred only moments before, leapt to his feet, looking hopeful. He blinked at Brody.

"Come on, young man," Brody said, as he headed out the study, turning the light out behind him. "One last run down the garden for you."

As he waited at the back door, Brody stared into the night sky. He and Anna's relationship had started off as voices only and that was what he was comfortable with, he realized, so why shouldn't it continue that way? It was probably sensible too, given the boundaries they'd put on not knowing more about each other than first names and general locations.

Yes, sensible, he told himself as Lewis trotted back up the lawn and ran past his legs into the warm house. *Very sensible. Not cowardly at all.*

ANNA STARED AT her phone as the screen went dark. The thought she might be able to FaceTime with Brody at some point buoyed her up. He always made her feel better about things and it would be nice to see his smile one day and not just hear it.

She sighed, playing back their conversation as she stuffed her feet back into the slippers that were sitting on the carpet in front of the sofa.

She hadn't realized it, but up until now, she'd been feeling guilty about turning Jeremy down. However, after talking to Brody, she felt much better about her decision. She wasn't being selfish. She was doing the right thing. For Jeremy too.

She yawned and covered her mouth with her hand, closing her eyes tight, and when she'd finished, she stretched, easing the kinks from her shoulders and back, from where she'd been curled up in the corner of her large squishy sofa. As she'd said to Brody, it was late, and she did feel tired, but now that she thought about it, she wasn't sure she was sleepy. She always felt very peaceful, very relaxed, after talking to Brody, but she often felt energized too.

She picked up her phone again to check that her alarm for the morning was set and spotted the Facebook icon on her home screen. She avoided social media these days, but now and again she'd hop on to put little blue thumbs-up signs on posts from people she knew, that she hadn't talked to in a while, and hadn't seen for even longer. She opened the app and scrolled down her feed, slowing for pet pictures and caustic cartoons, but easing past smiling couples and pictures of babies a little faster.

That's why she didn't do this more often. Because what did she have to put up there? A lovely house, to be sure, but where were the people? Where were the smiles? She couldn't imagine Gayle posing for a selfie with her after a Sunday lunch.

She was about to zip past a photo of a newborn baby, wrapped tight in a cream blanket, face pink and scrunched, when something made her pause, possibly the flicker of recognition of the name at the top of the post, even though she hadn't consciously read it.

Oh, my goodness! It couldn't be . . . She clicked on the photograph to enlarge it.

It certainly was. The picture had been uploaded by Scott Barry, and the caption underneath read: *Taking our little man home from the hospital.* It had been posted earlier in the week. But that was almost two weeks early! She'd only seen Scott and Teresa for May's family lunch the Sunday before and there'd been no sign that Teresa was about to go into labor the next day, not that Anna really knew what the signs were.

Anna let the phone drop into her lap. And four days ago? Why hadn't anyone called her? Why hadn't anyone let her know?

She picked her phone up again and stared at the picture of the baby.

Spencer. They'd called him Spencer.

A lump rose in her throat and she began to cry big, fat, gluey tears. She wiped them away, desperate to focus on the picture, desperate to see a likeness, but this baby's face was so fresh, so new, that it hardly had a hint of its own identity, let alone a similarity to someone else's.

What was she going to do about this? It was obvious that, in the mad rush of labor, delivery, and sleepless nights, Scott and Teresa hadn't got around to letting people know. Or they hadn't got around to letting *her* know.

She sat with the feeling that suspicion produced for a few seconds, a low drag in the pit of her stomach, then told herself to stop being silly. They were busy and sleep-deprived, that was all. They probably thought they had told her.

But that meant they might be wondering why she hadn't made contact to congratulate them. Anna frowned. She wasn't sure how to handle that. Leaving a comment that hinted at their omission might seem like a dig, but she also didn't want to say nothing. That would also be rude. They might think she was jealous.

Oh . . . Maybe that's why they hadn't told her.

It got awkward sometimes with Scott and Teresa when something was said or done to highlight the fact that they still had what she'd lost, but she wouldn't have thought that would mean they wouldn't tell her about the baby being born, especially with the name they'd given him. She hoped they didn't think she was jealous, even though she was, just a little bit.

She closed her eyes and hugged the phone to her chest. *More than just a little bit, Anna. Stop kidding yourself.* She wanted what they had so much that sometimes it became an actual physical pain, but that didn't mean she couldn't celebrate their happiness too.

Wiping another stray tear away, she woke her phone up. She wouldn't leave a comment on the Facebook post—that seemed too casual, too impersonal. Phoning in the middle of the night was also not a good idea. She'd text. Hopefully, that would hit the right note.

She typed quickly, congratulating her sister-in-law on the birth of her lovely baby son, and letting her know that she'd love to come and see him for herself over the weekend. If they felt up to visitors, of course.

Chapter Twenty-Two

hank you so much! They're gorgeous." Teresa lifted the pair of dungarees Anna had bought from the wrapping paper, letting them dangle. "They're impossibly huge, though!"

Anna thought they looked impossibly small, but she nodded in agreement anyway. All her attention was taken up with the warm bundle of pinkness in her arms. The baby was looking at her, his grayish-blue eyes intently staring at her face, and his little mouth making different shapes. She wasn't sure if he was testing it out, finding out what it could do, or whether it was purely involuntary. It was fascinating.

"Are you okay with him?" Teresa asked. "I can take him back if you're not."

Anna smiled wryly and looked across the room to her sister-in-law. "Are you sure *you're* okay that I've got him?" she asked. "I'm a total newbie at this."

Teresa nodded. "To be honest, it's a bit of a relief. He's lovely and, on one hand, I can't get enough of him, but on the other . . . Let's just say I now know how dairy cows feel. The boy is perpetually hungry!"

"How much did he weigh when he was born?" Anna asked, jiggling the baby slightly because he'd started to wriggle.

"Not even three kilos," Teresa replied, looking incredulous.

"Which was a bit of a shock, given how long it took him to arrive! I'd thought a small one would pop out more easily."

"You had a long labor?"

"Didn't Gayle tell you all this when she phoned?"

"Um . . . Not really." Anna concentrated on making eye contact with the baby, avoiding her sister-in-law's gaze.

"I'm flabbergasted," Teresa said, flopping back even further into the pillows of the armchair. "Richard keeps joking she's stopping people in the street to give them a blow-by-blow account of the delivery, followed by a complete rundown of his vital statistics."

Anna made a noncommittal noise and concentrated on making expressive faces at her nephew.

"What?" Teresa said, her tone full of suspicion. "Anna?"

"Erm, well . . . She didn't actually call," Anna said, wincing slightly, but quickly added, "or if she did, I must have missed it."

Teresa frowned. "That's odd. Scott and I were exhausted, so he asked his mum and dad if they could share the news."

Anna tried to make her smile look sincere. "It probably was a mix-up due to all the excitement."

Teresa pressed her lips together. "You don't think she, you know . . . did it on purpose?"

Teresa had Anna's full attention now, even as the baby began to fidget harder in her arms. "No." She shook her head slowly, ignoring the sinking sensation in her stomach. "What reason could she possibly have not to tell me?"

As if he was taking this literally, little Spencer, who had been squirming harder and harder, opened his mouth and let out an ear-piercing cry. Anna looked nervously across at Teresa. Her sister-in-law unbuttoned her shirt and held out her arms, a weary look on her face. "I told you . . . Dairy cow!" The baby settled into a steady sucking rhythm and Teresa relaxed and smiled across at Anna. "That's me, then. I'll be stuck here for the next half an hour—if I'm lucky!"

"Since Scott has escaped to Sainsbury's, do you want me to make your cup of tea?"

Teresa smiled at her. "Thought you'd never ask!"

Anna smiled back and went to make the hot drinks, and when she returned to the living room, she said, "It's not just me then. You find her—Gayle—difficult too?"

Teresa sighed before glancing down to check on her son. "I put up with it for Scott's sake. She's intense, I know, but she's basically harmless. I just try to let it all slide off."

Anna sat down on the sofa and clasped her hands in her lap. "But how do you do that?" She'd managed to keep her cool at the one family lunch she'd been to since the vol-au-vent incident, but she'd discovered that "not reacting" was a lot tougher than it sounded.

Teresa thought for a moment, idly stroking the downy hair on the top of the baby's head. "The way I look at it, without Gayle, Scott wouldn't be my Scott. He's much more like her than his dad, but it's watered-down in him. He's quietly determined, not noisily pushy, but that's where he gets his drive from."

Anna sipped her tea. "I suppose you're right. I always thought Spencer was just like his dad: laid-back, full of fun, but he had that drive too, and that's what prompted him to take a risk and follow his dreams."

It occurred to Anna that if Spencer had been just like his father, he'd have been happy to potter around in a middle-management job until his retirement, just as Richard had done. Maybe that ambition, that creativity, was his mother's gift, even though she was struggling very hard to see where it came from. Was Gayle a dreamer too? It hardly seemed possible.

Teresa lifted the dozy baby so his chin was resting on her shoulder, then she rubbed him firmly on his back. After a few moments, he let out a gurgling belch. "I wonder what this little man will be like. Whether he'll be like me or like Scott? Or just a mixture of all of us in his heritage, combined to a secret recipe that is uniquely him." She looked down at her son with such love that tears almost sprang to Anna's eyes. "It's all in there," Teresa added. "All those things have already been planted, but it's going to take years to see them come to fruition, for them to work their way out."

That was a beautiful thing, Anna decided, to watch a person unfold like that.

Teresa caught Anna's eye. There was a huskiness in her tone when she said, "A lot of the time I find myself hoping that he's just like his uncle."

Anna didn't say anything. She just gave a watery smile to her sister-in-law, and then she went across the room to give her a hug. Just in case the moment was getting too girly and emotional, little Spencer responded by doing the manliest thing he could think of and let out a giant fart. Anna caught Teresa's eye and they both burst out laughing.

Teresa lifted him and undid a couple of snaps so she could peek inside his onesie to see what the damage was. "Oh, crap," she said. "Literally. It's exploded right out of the diaper, and it's probably gone halfway up his back." She pulled a face. I haven't got used to that bit yet," she said, standing up and giving her son a disgusted look. "I'd better change him. Third time today, and it's not even noon yet!"

Just as Anna had sat back down again, the doorbell rang. "Get that, would you, please?" Teresa said as she headed up the stairs. "It might be another flower delivery."

But when Anna opened the door, instead of finding a bouquet, she came face-to-face with her mother-in-law. "Oh! It's you," Gayle said, echoing perfectly what Anna was thinking. "Where's Teresa? Where's the baby?"

And hello to you too, Anna thought, as Gayle hurried past her, but she held her tongue, reminding herself of what Teresa had just said. Maybe, if she squinted and tipped her head in the right way, she would be able to see that little speck of Spencer in Gayle. It might prevent Anna from throttling her.

Richard trailed in behind, as always, laden with bags. He gave Anna a one-armed hug, careful not to bash her with what was obviously a prize haul from John Lewis's baby department. "I think what you meant to say, my darling," he called after his wife, "is, 'Anna! What a marvelous surprise!'"

"Oh, yes. Of course," Gayle said absentmindedly as she made her way into the living room. Richard and Anna followed.

"I dropped in for a visit," Anna explained. "Teresa's just gone to change his diaper."

As if on cue, her sister-in-law came back down the stairs. "All nice and fresh for Grandma," she said, and handed the baby over to Gayle, who had spun around and stretched out her arms as soon as she'd heard Teresa's voice.

Gayle's face lit up as she cradled her grandson in the crook of her arm. "He's grown so much!" she said, turning to exclaim to Richard.

"We only saw him yesterday. How on earth can you tell if he's grown at all?"

But his wife had already focused her attention back to the baby in her arms. She walked into the living room and sat down in the corner of the sofa. "He looks so much like Spencer," she said, almost whispering.

Richard gave one of his weary, well-worn huffs that seemed to be his main method of dealing with his wife when she was being a little exasperating. "That's because he *is* Spencer."

"No," Gayle said, tickling the baby under his chin so he opened his mouth and his eyes wide, "I meant *my* Spencer."

Richard shot a look at Anna. "Don't you mean 'our Spencer'?"

Then Gayle did the most bizarre thing. She took her eyes off the baby for a few seconds and giggled. Actually giggled. "Oh, silly me. Of course I meant *our* Spencer." She smiled at her husband, not minding his dig at all, and then things went even further into strange territory, because she turned that smile on Anna, clearly including her in the joke. "But he does look like him, don't you think?"

There was such hope in her eyes that Anna dutifully walked across the room and inspected her nephew yet again. She supposed he looked as much like Spencer as any baby could. He had the blond hair (albeit the merest hint of peach fuzz), the blue eyes, and he certainly knew how to make himself heard and command the attention in any room he was in. "I suppose he does."

Gayle smiled again. Anna was starting to think that the baby was a magical being, a changeling. His presence seemed to have wrought an amazing transformation on his grandmother. Anna smiled back at Gayle and it felt good. Hopeful.

She couldn't wait to tell Brody. Gabi was very loyal, but Gayle had now become enemy number one in Gabi's eyes since the vol-au-vents incident. It would take a while for her to warm up to the idea that reestablishing a closer relationship with Gayle could be a good thing.

But Brody . . . Brody would see it straightaway. He would celebrate quietly with her. Quietly, because she couldn't imagine him doing anything noisily or hastily. He always seemed so self-contained, so steady.

Not for the first time recently she wondered who he was when he wasn't her shoulder to cry on, what he did for a job, for example. She knew he liked the outdoors and lived in a remote area, so maybe he did something like farming or forestry?

Anna watched while Gayle alternately fussed over little Spencer and instructed Teresa on the finer points of using both the top-of-the-line breast pump and the video baby monitor she'd brought with her, but after a while Anna checked her watch. "I'm going to head off," she said. She'd been here a couple of hours and it was probably time to reduce the crowd Teresa had to deal with.

"Well, it's been lovely to see you," Richard said. Gayle even looked up from fussing over Spencer and agreed, smiling. Wonders would never cease.

Teresa showed Anna to the door and they hugged. "Don't be a stranger," Teresa said as they pulled away from each other

"I won't."

"I've always felt that, in family terms, our husbands were the main events in the Barry family," Teresa added. "So we 'also-rans' have to stick together." She gave Anna another squeeze. And as Anna started to head toward her car, she called out, "See you next Sunday?"

Anna stopped and turned, frowning.

Teresa elaborated. "Lunch at Gayle and Richard's."

"Didn't we say we were only doing lunch once a month from now on? And the next one isn't until the day before Spencer's birthday. That's weeks away."

Teresa looked uncomfortable. "Well, yes . . . But I thought we'd kind of reverted to the old pattern anyway." Anna's frown deepened, and taking it in, Teresa carried on talking. "I mean, I just assumed you couldn't make it the time before last."

"The time before last?" Anna asked, her voice thin.

Teresa looked sheepish. She glanced back toward the living room, where they could hear Gayle's over-loud baby talk continuing. "We went over for lunch on the third."

Anna went cold. "Are you telling me that family lunches have been continuing every fortnight without me?"

"No. I mean, I don't know . . . It was just that one time. Maybe Gayle invited us because she was taking pity on me, because I was heavily pregnant, and she was saving me from cooking?"

"But didn't you say you're going next week too?"

Teresa sighed. "Well, you know she wants as much 'baby time' as possible." She looked down for a moment, studying the paving stones of her driveway, before meeting Anna's gaze again. "I don't think this has been engineered, Anna, honestly I don't."

Anna nodded and smiled, but her jaw felt tight and she knew the warmth hadn't reached her eyes. She turned and walked toward the street, where her car was parked.

WHEN BRODY STARED at the notebook on his desk early on Sunday morning, everything inside him said, *Run!* He wanted to shoot out the back door of his cottage, across the yard and into the safety of his workshop. He wanted to feel a chisel in his hand, lose himself in the mindless shaping of wood.

But Brody didn't run. Instead, he pulled out his desk chair and sat down. He sat there for a minute or so and then, when he was ready, he opened the notebook lying on the desk, picked up his fountain pen and pressed the nib against the page.

Write, he told himself. *Write something. Write anything!*

The nib began to move. A word began to form.

Pain.

Brody wasn't sure where it had come from, but it had come. Not a word he wanted to read, particularly. Not a word he really wanted to think about. But it was a word, so both triumph and discomfort swirled within him. He made the pen move again.

Grief . . . Guilt . . . RAGE.

Brody stared at what he'd just written. He did feel angry, he realized, but he didn't know who with. He tried again.

I'm sorry, I'm sorry, I'm sorry . . .

The heart-thumping feeling became even more dramatic. Was he getting enough oxygen? He wasn't sure he was getting enough oxygen. He closed his eyes and took a deep breath. "Come on," he said out loud. "Enough of this. Write a bloody sentence!"

He began to write again. Or, at least, that was what he'd intended to do, but it seemed his subconscious had other plans. His pen began to sketch a man. He was standing alone, and as Brody let his imagination take over, the landscape around him began to form. There were mountains behind him, stark and jagged, and at his feet was the edge of a gaping chasm. The man was looking into the gash in the earth, Brody realized. He'd been looking into it for so long he'd forgotten he could do anything else.

The anger in Brody's chest began to swell and his pen moved faster and faster, filling in the outlines, bringing shadows and darkness to the scene. He kept going until the fire inside him dwindled and when he looked again, he discovered the man had gone.

Logic told him that he was still there on the page, that he'd just covered the figure in dark ink during his shading frenzy, but in his mind he knew differently. He knew exactly where the man was.

The man was at the bottom of the chasm.

Chapter Twenty-Three

The sun beat down on Anna's shoulders as she slid a small case into the trunk of her car, smiling to herself. Tomorrow would have been Spencer's thirty-fifth birthday, and this evening she'd be installed in a bungalow in Camber Sands for two whole nights. Their bungalow. She was almost disappointed it had been renovated by the new owners. The details on the website she'd booked through cited features like a tumble dryer, Wi-Fi and a log burner. She doubted that this time the electricity would cut out or that the plumbing would creak. Still, it would be a chance to remember Spencer in her own way, free from any interference, and it looked like the weather was going to be glorious. She couldn't have planned it better.

Just one more hurdle to get through before that was possible: the special Barry Sunday lunch Gayle had planned. Anna was still reeling from the news that Teresa and Scott had been going to lunch with her in-laws fortnightly, as if nothing had changed, but she wasn't going to think about that today. She wasn't even going to mention it, because she was dreaming of warm night breezes, cool water lapping at her bare toes and silky sand rumpled and creased by an outgoing tide.

One lunch was all she had to get through and at least it was at the Cinnamon Café instead of at Gayle and Richard's. *This is just the prologue*, she told herself as she pulled into the restaurant's parking lot and found a space next to Scott and Teresa's car. *The main event is later. Let everything slide off you for the next hour or two, the way Teresa does, and then you'll be on your way.*

To be honest, the change of location was a breath of fresh air. Anna hadn't realized how stale they'd all been getting at Gayle and Richard's Sunday after Sunday, how stuck in a rut they'd become. When she greeted her in-laws, they were led to a circular table—no possibility of them taking their usual seats—and the excellent, innovative Indian cuisine they ordered seemed to put them all into a good mood, even Gayle, and if that hadn't done the trick, she could always have cooed over her new grandson, who was sleeping soundly in his pram next to the table.

When coffee was served, Anna began counting the seconds until she could walk out of the restaurant door. All she could think about was the overnight case sitting inside the trunk of her car, which was probably why she missed Gayle putting a large gold-embossed folder on the table, until she coughed to get everyone's attention.

"I decided to get a little gift for you all to mark what would have been Spencer's birthday, something special." Gayle patted the folder, then opened it and passed large cards to both Scott and Anna. Anna recognized the thick white card and gold scrolling as the sort of thing professional photographers used for protecting prints and enlargements. Had Gayle got them all a photo of Spencer? Goodness. That was actually very thoughtful of her. "Thank you so much," she said with real warmth as she opened the card to reveal the picture. She could take this with her to Camber Sands this afternoon and stand it on the mantelpiece.

Gayle seemed very pleased with the praise and puffed up a little.

"The man I got to do it even used his computer to do some tidying up. It was so clever! Richard and I have had one blown up to go in the living room, with a lovely frame."

Anna looked down at her gift and felt stupidly proud when she realized Gayle had chosen a solo shot of Spencer from their wedding album. However, as she continued to study the picture on the table in front of her, a cold feeling crept into her stomach. She knew every photograph in her wedding album intimately, so of course she recognized this particular shot. But there was something different, something off.

Little Spencer started to stir, and Teresa stood and picked him up, rocking him, while she and Gayle began a discussion about whether the two brothers had looked more like each other when they were younger or as they'd grown older. Anna cocked her head to one side, squinting slightly. What was it that wasn't quite right . . . ? Was there something missing? It was like trying to thread a needle without her reading glasses on.

And then it hit her.

It was her.

She was the thing that was missing from the photograph.

She jumped to her feet, spilling milky coffee not only all down her cream blouse but also over her dead husband's smiling face.

This hadn't been a solo portrait of Spencer on their wedding day, one taken with his best man before the service. It had been one of her and Spencer together *after* the ceremony. Look, there was the proof: a couple of pastel flakes of confetti still resting on his shoulder.

"Tidying up," Gayle had said. *Photoshopping* is what she'd meant.

She'd had Anna airbrushed out of the picture.

ANNA SLAMMED HER front door behind her and marched up the stairs. She wasn't heading to Camber Sands. Not yet, anyway. There were a couple of things she needed to do first after that horrendous bloody lunch.

She walked into her bedroom, stripped off her coffee-stained blouse and threw it on the floor then went to the wardrobe. Not hers but Spencer's. She opened the door and slid the first shirt her fingers found off its hanger. It was the one she'd bought him a few summers ago, white collarless linen. She pulled it on over her bra, then turned and headed back downstairs.

This was all Gayle's fault! That woman had spoiled everything. Yet again.

And there was no way Anna was going to another Sunday lunch, not in the history of this universe. Which was just as well, seeing as she probably wasn't welcome at Gayle and Richard's anymore, anyway.

She was about to head out back to her car, where her suitcase waited for her, but as she strode across the hall, she turned on her heel and changed direction, making a beeline for the kitchen. She opened the freezer and crouched down so she could pull out the bottom drawer, where all the items past their best-before dates and crusty with frost ended up. Her fingers closed around a medium-sized Tupperware box and she pulled it out. The contents rustled and rattled slightly. The sound both infuriated and thrilled her.

She stood up and looked around. No, this wasn't the right place.

Taking the box, she left the kitchen and headed across the hallway into her open-plan living and dining room. She walked to the bay window that overlooked the street, then turned her back to it. From here, there was a good long stretch of space all the way to the French windows that led out onto the garden. Perfect.

She peeled back the lid of the box, reached inside and lifted out one of the dozen vol-au-vents inside. It started to crumble immediately. Even though the cold burned her fingertips, she held it for a few moments, focusing intently on a spot at the other end of the room, before lifting her arm and hurling it with all her might.

For a few heart-stopping seconds it flew through the air and then—*bam!*—it hit the window, and the frozen flaky pastry exploded, shattering into what seemed like a million tiny pieces. Anna almost let out a gurgle of joyous laughter, then she picked up another vol-au-vent and threw it after the first.

This one didn't disintegrate quite so dramatically, but it felt just as satisfying, especially the dull thud as the frozen filling hit the floor. That was it. She couldn't stop after that. She had to keep going and going until the box was empty and the far end of the living room looked as if there'd been a massacre at a 1970s dinner party.

Anna dropped the empty plastic box and let it fall to the floor. She didn't even think about getting the Hoover or a dustpan and brush as she smiled and turned to head outside. She got in her car, backed carefully out of her driveway, then pointed her car in the direction of Camber Sands and put her foot on the gas.

Chapter Twenty-Four

The only sound was the night air whispering in the dune grass and the dull thump of a bass beat from the pub further along the bay. The water was so flat, the night air so still, that it might be a mile away. Possibly more. Anna only caught snatches of the music as the faint breeze shifted and circled around the dunes beyond her little yellow bungalow.

Only a feeble glow from a table lamp illuminated the living room as she sat at a little metal bistro set in the garden, her fingers wrapped around the stem of a wineglass. It was past midnight and there was a chill in the air, so she'd wrapped a chunky cardigan over the top of her pajamas and had pulled a pair of socks onto her feet.

Up above, the stars glittered. Away from the light pollution of the London suburbs, they seem to have multiplied tenfold. It was breathtaking. For the first time in years, and definitely in three years, three months and four days, Anna felt still inside. She felt quiet. It was pure bliss.

It was also odd, given the day she'd had, but there you go. Life was funny like that sometimes.

Her phone was sitting on the table in front of her. She woke it up and glanced at the time. Would he still be up? Should she even try? Her thumb hovered above the phone for a few seconds.

She was going to press it anyway, so she didn't know what she was waiting for. He was always there when she needed him.

When the call connected, she didn't bother with pleasantries. "You know you said, 'don't react' when it came to my mother-in-law?"

Brody answered her question with a wary, "Yes?"

"I had an epic fail."

"Oh."

Yes, *oh*.

Along with *Oh, my God! What did you do?* and *What were you thinking?*, these were the questions she'd asked herself a hundred times over since she'd left the Cinnamon Café earlier that day. But Brody remained silent, giving her time and space, as always, letting her reveal things at her own pace.

She started at the beginning, filling him in on the whole awkward afternoon, how she'd been doing so well, keeping her cool and saying nothing, and then she got to the subject of Spencer's portrait. "And as I was staring at the photo, it suddenly struck me—like a baseball bat to the side of the head—what she'd done. She'd erased me, Brody! She'd wished me away."

For months now, she had been trying to pin a label to that feeling she always got when she was with Gayle, that niggly little sensation that had always bothered her, the feeling that Gayle wanted to keep her close yet push her away at the same time, and suddenly all the pieces fell into the right place and she knew what she was dealing with.

"She's jealous. She resents me because Spencer can't be all hers. Because he was mine too, and she just can't stand it."

"So, you *reacted*."

Anna hid her face in her hands, feeling heat flush through her body just at the memory. "Yes," she said, and the word was muffled through her fingers. "I definitely reacted."

Again, Brody didn't push. He just waited until she was ready to say more. She let her hands drop and carried on talking. "She lit my fuse and I went off. I spilt coffee all over myself and over her glossy eight-by-ten tidied-up photo—she'll never forgive me for that alone!—and then I stood up and told her that what she'd done wasn't okay, that it really wasn't okay." Anna chewed on the side of her bottom lip for a moment. "Okay, maybe 'told' is downplaying it a little. I think I might have shouted it."

"Really? In the middle of a restaurant?"

"Don't you dare laugh at me! This isn't funny!"

"No," he replied, but she could still hear it in his voice. He was only just holding back a chuckle, she suspected.

"And, of course, everyone else in the place was looking on as if I was being totally irrational—even Scott and Teresa, because they didn't know, they didn't realize. They recognized it was a wedding picture, but not what Gayle had done . . . And why would she do that, by the way?" Anna knew she was jumping around all over the place, not finishing one thought before she started on another, but she just couldn't get her brain to sit still. "*Why?* There were plenty of lovely pictures of him on his own, taken the very same day."

"Why do *you* think she did it? Do you have any ideas?"

Anna stared at the shadowy humps of the sand dunes beyond the garden. "Because it was perfect, that's what she said. It was the perfect one. And Gayle is all about perfection, all about control." She let out yet another heavy sigh. "And I'm just so *over* being controlled by her. I couldn't do it anymore. So, when she gave

me one of her looks and said I was being insensitive, I lost it." She
winced again, remembering the shocked looks on the rest of the
family's faces.

"She knew what she'd done, Brody. She knew what I was
talking about. I could see it in her eyes. But she didn't even have
the grace to look guilty. So I told her that she was a coldhearted,
manipulative bitch and that I was glad Spencer was dead because
it meant I'd never have to see her again."

Anna swallowed. She'd felt wonderful at the time, slightly
euphoric, even. But now, when she thought about it, she just
felt sick. "I went too far, didn't I? This is my problem. It's always
been my problem. I get so worked up and I can't think straight,
and I say things I never should say, that I don't even really mean."

"You didn't mean she was a coldhearted manipulative bitch?"
The smile was back in Brody's voice, but Anna ignored it.

"Oh, yes. I meant that."

He finally cracked and stifled a laugh.

"But I shouldn't have said that I was glad Spencer was dead.
I could never be glad about that." She trailed off, her thoughts
taking a more morbid turn.

"Anna?"

"Yes?" she replied softly.

"How do you feel now?"

Anna shifted on the metal chair, hugging her cardigan around
herself. "Weird. I thought I'd be upset, and I am . . . There are
moments when I get all fired up and angry again when I think
about it, when I turn it all over in my head, but in my heart . . ."
She placed a palm against her chest and waited, allowing herself to feel the beat beneath her hand, the steady pulse of life.
"I feel . . . better. Free. But that could just be the eye of the

hurricane, couldn't it? It could just be that I've got no energy left to feel anything else. It might all start up again with raging force in the morning."

"Maybe," he replied, not sounding worried about the prospect of that at all, which somehow made Anna feel better, and allowed her to relish the calm, even if it wasn't going to last.

"What are you going to do now?"

That was a very good question. She felt like anything was possible. She felt like a racehorse at the track, a creature that had been primed and trained, all amped up and ready to go, and finally the switch had been pulled and the gate had been opened. It was time to run. Forward.

"I don't know," she replied honestly. "I'm at Camber Sands. I came to get away, clear my head, which is probably a good thing . . . I've had texts from my sister-in-law, but I'm not ready to read them yet, let alone answer them. Maybe tomorrow." She breathed out, and with it the last bit of tension drained from her limbs. Suddenly, after being so wired and unable to settle, she was ready for a long, deep sleep. "Thank you, Brody. Yet again. For listening."

There was no smile this time in his voice when he replied. His tone was thick, gravelly. "Anytime. Always."

Anna yawned. She needed to get to bed but, at the same time, she didn't want to end the call either. "I think I'm having what's called a post-adrenaline crash, or something like that." She yawned again, and this time her eyelids became heavy. "This is going to sound a bit strange, but what the heck, seeing as I'm so far past my own boundaries today, I have no idea what I'm doing . . . Would you mind if I didn't hang up, if I just carried my phone around with me for a bit, but didn't actually say anything?"

He took a moment to reply. "If that's what you want."

"Thank you, Brody. Until next time . . ."

Anna tucked her phone into one of her cardigan pockets, then jammed her hand into the other pocket and pulled out a piece of paper. She unfolded it and read it yet again. This was exactly what she needed to do to commemorate her husband's birthday. It was a bit last minute—so not her—but so very Spencer. She hoped they'd have space tomorrow, because he'd have loved to see her do this. It was the perfect way to remember him.

Yawning again, she stood and went back inside, closing the patio doors behind her. Before getting into the soft double bed, she pulled her phone out of her cardigan pocket and looked for somewhere to put it. The pillow next to hers always seemed empty these days, so she put it there to fill the space, then curled into the duvet and fell into a deep and restful sleep.

BRODY'S CHISEL SUNK into the wood he was holding in his left hand and he began deftly shaping the block, referring to a rough sketch in a notebook laid on the workbench. It had been weeks since he'd sat at his desk, held a pen in his hand and waited for words to come, but that was what he'd done when he'd got up before dawn this morning. He'd had a dream last night, the details of which were lost in his subconscious, but he'd woken energized. Inspired. He'd really thought today might have been the day. He'd been wrong.

Or sort of wrong.

Like before, he'd started with a word—the one Anna had described the way she'd felt last night: "free." And then he'd allowed his imagination off the leash in a way he'd hadn't done in years, too afraid it would head back to that same awful destination.

Other words had come: "brave," "strong," "good" . . . And, like last time, when his rusty brain had run out of words, his pen had continued making marks on the creamy paper of his notebook. Brody was no great artist, but he had enough skill to sketch an idea and the end result be recognizable as something, even if it was just a wisp of an idea caught from a dream he couldn't remember.

He'd drawn a woman. Well, an elf, really. Similar to the one Moji had in her shop, so he'd decided that maybe his subconscious wanted to make another one. He'd give it to Moji and she could sell it. It was the least he could do after all her kindness to him over the years.

When he'd finished sketching, he'd headed out to the workshop to get started. Lewis had followed him, slightly perplexed and wondering where breakfast was, and now here they both were, under the harsh glare of the fluorescent tubes until dawn broke properly, Lewis in his bed in the corner and Brody leaning over the workbench, trying to see if he could make this glimmer of inspiration come to life.

Brody hummed while he worked. He tried not to make many decisions or pay too much attention to what he was doing, just in case he jinxed this almost forgotten feeling of creative flow. He didn't even glance at his notebook much. The image seemed stuck in his mind, so there was no real need.

But when he'd come close to finishing, when the major features—limbs and body, clothes and face—were just about there, only needing a little refinement, Brody realized he'd taken a wrong turn somewhere. The little figure, maybe only ten inches tall, was close to the sketch he'd drawn earlier that morning, but there were significant differences too.

She wasn't an elf, for one thing. She wore a dress, but it was plain and simple, no fluted sleeves or Celtic knotwork. Her hair was long but remained above her shoulder blades rather than skimming the backs of her thighs. He guessed, if he were able to lift her hair, that he'd find that her ears weren't pointed but small and rounded.

His creation was human. Or maybe only half human, because there was something otherworldly about her too, something different.

Who was she?

The answer came in a flash from his dream, an image that fired across the synapses in his brain and stung them into life, like an electric shock from a defibrillator. He suddenly knew exactly who she was. His whole body grew hot and his skin shrank until it was three sizes too small.

It had been one of *those* dreams, or at least he assumed it had, the tiny portion he could remember was him and her between the pure white sheets of a rumpled bed. He remembered the sensation of skin touching skin, the thrill of being near her. Or who he imagined her to be.

Anna . . .

If there were any steamy details to the dream, they were lost to him. What he did remember was her laughter, the way she'd looked at him. Her eyes had been full of fun and teasing, but also something else. Something deeper. He'd felt known. Accepted.

He put the figure down, even though there were still a few small finishing touches that needed to be attended to. His chest hurt and he pressed a palm against it, sure another panic attack was about to descend on him, but was surprised to find his heartbeat sound and steady. This wasn't his nervous system misfiring, telling him peril was lurking nearby when it was doing nothing of the sort. This was something far more dangerous.

It was want.

Need.

For something he couldn't have. For something he'd promised himself he'd never look for again, because, after the mistakes he'd made, he really didn't deserve it. And even if he had been so foolhardy as to open his heart again, it would be a very, very bad idea. Not just for him but for the poor woman he dragged into the pit with him. He would never want to do that to someone he truly cared about.

He realized he'd been avoiding looking at his creation and he forced himself to focus on her. He took in the large eyes, the faraway look that made her seem sad, but also the hint of a smile in her expression, not even fully formed enough yet to play on her lips, but it was there, waiting to burst forth. *You aren't real*, he told the figure silently. *You're just a figment of my warped imagination. Nothing but my subconscious playing a vicious prank on me.*

It didn't matter. He wasn't keeping her. She was for Moji, anyway. But after he picked the figure up, intending to complete it, he paused. She wasn't the elf Moji had asked for, and he'd done too much to make any changes now.

He stared at her for a few seconds, then put her up on the shelf that held some of his tools above the workbench, and picked up another block of wood. He pulled his notebook closer and focused on the drawing. This time he was sticking to the plan.

Chapter Twenty-Five

The crash helmet fit snugly over her ears and went some way to drowning out the rumble of engines and the squeal of tires. Anna stood at the edge of Brands Hatch racetrack, shaking. She'd turned up two hours ago with Spencer's voucher, hoping there'd be an open slot today, and had finally got the word someone else had canceled and she could have her go. The wait hadn't helped her nerves much, though. Gabi would probably love this, but now the moment was upon her, Anna was definitely having second thoughts.

A sports car shot past at a dizzying speed. She clasped her hands together, closed her eyes and prayed. *Please let me live through this . . .*

"Anna Barry?" someone called.

Anna opened her eyes to find a guy who hardly looked old enough to have passed his driving test standing in front of her. "Yes?" she said, wishing she had a bottle of water (or possibly something stronger) with her. Suddenly, her throat was very dry.

"Your turn," he said, gesturing to the sleek gunmetal Aston Martin idling a few feet away. "Hop in."

We have a deal, God, remember? Anna added silently as she slid into the supple leather of the driver's seat. *You make sure I get around this track in one piece and I'll . . . I'll . . . Well, no time to work that one out now. Let's just say I'll owe you one.*

She closed the door, did up her seat belt and then when Ade, the teenage driving instructor, was in the passenger seat, she pressed gingerly on the accelerator and pulled away.

Ade let her get away with twenty miles an hour for approximately ten seconds, then ordered her to put her foot down. There were other vehicles on the track, and it wasn't safe for her to be crawling along like a pedal car, apparently.

Oh, how Spencer would have laughed if he could have seen her now.

Anna gritted her teeth, gripped the steering wheel. Ade sat in the passenger seat with a huge smirk on his face, like this was some big joke. Just like Spencer would have done. But for some reason Anna didn't find it endearing, she just found it hugely irritating.

Without even trying, she discovered she was going faster.

"Better!" Ade said, looking unbearably smug. "Now, ease off the gas coming into this bend . . ."

Anna didn't have much time to think about anything else for the next ten minutes. It took all her concentration to follow Ade's instructions and navigate the hairpin bends the track was famous for. He would tell her when to hug the white line at the edge of the track, when to put her foot on the throttle, always urging her to go faster than she was comfortable with.

The worst thing was *not braking* going into the bends. Every time Anna's heart was in her mouth and she was desperate to close her eyes, despite the fact she knew it was the stupidest thing she could have done . . . and accelerating out of the turns was even worse! It seemed her whole body and brain were a bundle of overstimulated nerves, and all her emotions, dampened down and numbed for so long, were suddenly turned up to the max. That might have been a good thing if the overriding emotion she felt hadn't been sheer terror. She couldn't have been happier when they pulled back into the pit after her three laps.

Thank God for that. Literally. She opened the door and reached for the strap of her helmet.

"Not yet," Ade shouted from the other side of the car.

"What?" Anna yelled back.

Ade circled the car and came toward her. "You haven't finished yet," he said.

"I haven't?"

He gave her that cocky smile again and Anna's blood pressure reached a new peak for that day. "Nope. Your experience includes a high-speed passenger lap."

Anna began shaking her head. "I . . . I don't think . . ."

"You've already paid for it," Ade replied, not smiling now, and his eyes glittered with challenge.

Anna started to feel a little queasy. It was the sort of look Spencer would have given her in a situation like this, full of boyish arrogance, so sure he was right about everything. She couldn't help thinking about what he'd have done if he'd got to use this voucher as planned. She could imagine him diving out of the driving seat and jumping into the passenger side, banging on the dashboard to make Ade hurry up and get on with it.

You're going to make me do this, aren't you? she said to someone.

Whether it was Spencer, God or her conscience, she wasn't sure, but it didn't mean the answer didn't come back just as clearly.

Yes.

She set her chin and looked at Ade as she tightened her helmet back up. "Let's do this."

THREE MINUTES, THAT was all it took to do one complete circuit of the racetrack, and Anna was sure she was going to be reunited with Spencer every second of it. "Oh, God . . . ! I don't want to die!" she wailed as they took another corner at what seemed like two hundred miles an hour, even though Ade had patiently explained while zooming through the chicane that the turns came too quickly for the car to reach its maximum speed. But as they accelerated into yet another bend, Anna decided she wasn't quite sure she believed him.

She was doing her best not to shout out or brace herself against any part of the car's interior because she'd already worked out that Ade took it as a sign to stamp his foot down. When she got out of this car and got the use of her legs back, she was going to kick his butt, she really was. Let's see who'd be smirking then!

The g-force as they went into the turn threw her against the car door, making her head bounce around like a puppet's, and she'd barely got her breath back when Ade began to accelerate along one of the straighter patches. Pavement and greenery streaked past the window in a blur. She glanced across at him and he was laughing, actually laughing.

Only one more turn, he mouthed at her as she closed her eyes and began to pray again. She could already feel the car surge forward as he floored it.

It was worse with her eyes closed, she discovered, like being locked in a washing machine on the spin cycle, so she quickly opened them again, only to discover they were hurtling toward a safety barrier. The back wheels skidded, and she flung her arms out and gripped onto the dashboard. She didn't care if Ade saw her fear anymore, because they couldn't possibly go any faster than they already were.

Much to her relief, she saw the spectator stands looming ahead, meaning they were about to pass the finish line. She almost wept with relief, only to scream loudly when Ade didn't bring the car smoothly to a halt but executed a perfect handbrake turn that left her stomach in the top of her skull.

The world kept moving, even though the car had stopped, but Anna didn't care. She scrabbled at the door handle, managing to catch it on the fourth try, and practically tumbled from the car and onto the pavement.

She bent over, bracing her hands on her knees and gulping in great lungfuls of air. And then, very strangely, she began to laugh. And once she'd started, she couldn't stop. It might have been endorphins or adrenaline or just plain old insanity, but she crumpled like a rag doll and sat on the track, laughing until she almost couldn't breathe anymore.

Ade came around to help her up, his smirk finally gone.

It took two attempts to get Anna to her feet because she was giggling so hard, but when he managed to do it, their eyes met. He gave her a nod, and that little gesture *might* have contained a hint of approval. "You're not dead, then," he said.

"No," she replied. "I'm not. I'm very much alive."

Ade just grinned at her.

Anna sobered and narrowed her eyes. "No thanks to you," she told him, but instead of belting him round the chops as she'd planned to, she planted a big wet smacker on his cheek and walked away.

Chapter Twenty-Six

Brody stood in his garden, the scents and sounds of twilight all around him. Now and again a bat flittered between the nearby trees and the eaves of his outbuildings. It was past nine o'clock but, this far south in June, the sun still glowed behind the trees down the valley.

His phone rang and he pulled it from his jeans pocket. He no longer kept it on his desk until late in the evening, when he'd retire to his study to read and wait for it to light up. He'd got into the habit of keeping it on him. Just in case. And here was his reward. He smiled as he lifted it to his ear.

"I did it, Brody! I actually did it!"

Brody smiled. Whatever it was that she'd done, whatever she was celebrating, he was glad she was sharing it with him. And by the sound of her voice, he was the first person she'd shared it with. A little flame of hope flickered inside his chest, but he snuffed it out. It meant something, but it didn't mean that.

"What did you do?" he asked, but before her answer came, a thought flashed across his brain. "You used the voucher. You went to the racetrack?"

Anna gasped. "How did you know?"

"I just   did. You had fun, then?"

"No! I thought I was going to die!" Anna erupted into

laughter. Laughter with a slightly hysterical edge, it had to be said. "But I suppose, in a strange way, I did enjoy it. Not the actual experience maybe, but the feeling afterward."

"Which was?"

"I feel energized. I feel . . . awake."

He knew she was telling the truth, could hear it in the buoyancy of her tone, the lightness. Such a difference from the first time he'd heard her voice. It made his chest ache. He wished more than anything else in the world he'd been there to see it today, to see her climb from the car, a look of joy and exhilaration on her face. He was so proud of her.

If they had been proper friends, the kind that met up and saw each other face-to-face once in a while, he would have suggested going out to celebrate. He was on the verge of asking her anyway, but then he sobered.

No. She had other friends for that. Better friends for that.

Friends? Come on! Tell the truth. At least to yourself. You want more than that.

No point, he replied to himself firmly. *If I can't even manage "friends," what's the point in taking it any further?*

As Anna began to describe in detail her experiences at the racetrack, Brody wandered back into the house, paying more attention to her words than he did to where he was going. He ended up in his study. Leaving the light off, he eased himself into his armchair and looked up at the bookshelf. The little wooden figure that should have been an elf sat in front of the top row of paperbacks. It hadn't seemed right to leave her in the dark and cobwebby workshop.

She wasn't looking down on him, keeping him company. Instead, she looked off into the lavender twilight, staring into her distant future. A future full of fresh territory, fresh challenges. That was where she belonged.

Anna was moving on.

That was good. It was what she needed, what he wished for her, but he couldn't help feeling that, at the same time, she was moving *away* too. Oh, she'd probably still call for the next few months, possibly even the next year or two. She'd still tell him about her life, but that didn't mean the distance between them wouldn't increase. It didn't mean it wouldn't grow into a chasm.

Because there she was, blossoming. Becoming.

Whereas he was stuck in this damn chair. And it wasn't even a particularly nice armchair. A spring had broken at the back of the seat and the arms were becoming threadbare.

"Did this happen to you?" she asked. "At some point in your journey out of grief, did you . . . I don't know how to put it . . . Did you suddenly feel as if there might be hope, that life might be okay again one day? Not the same, of course, but just better than it had been?"

Brody crafted his answer carefully. "There certainly have been times where I've felt lighter than others." He wasn't going to admit to her he'd been feeling hollow and empty for so long, he'd kind of got used to it.

"And was it, you know, a *moment*, like I had, or was it a slower process?"

"It was less . . ." Brody fidgeted in his chair. ". . . dramatic." And then, before she could probe any further, he headed her off at the pass. "So, what do you think is going to come out of this 'moment'? What is going to change going forward?"

She sighed. "I don't know. All I know is that sometimes I feel happy and scared, hopeful and overwhelmed all at once. There *might* be light in my future instead of just darkness, but for some reason I find that slightly terrifying too."

Brody smiled. She'd put it so well. "Isn't that what life is about?"

"I suppose it is . . ." She paused, and he could tell she was thinking about something. "You're right—I *should* make some changes going forward, and as we've been talking I've realized one of those things is my job. Gabi said something a couple of months ago about me not loving it and I didn't really take on board what she was saying."

"You're going to look for a new job?"

"Yes," she said, sounding very certain.

"What kind of job?"

She laughed. "That's the whole problem! I think I've worked out that I don't want my current job, but I have no idea what I want to do instead. I suppose I'm just going to have a look at what's available and see if anything sparks my interest."

"It's a start."

"Yes," she said again, still sounding so sure and confident—so different to how she'd come across when he'd first heard her voice on the other end of the line on New Year's Eve.

When they finally ended their conversation, Brody couldn't stop thinking about that, about how much Anna had changed, how much progress she'd made.

Whereas, all you're doing is treading water, the little goading voice in his head said. *Stagnating. You're all full of good advice when it comes to Anna but where is all that wisdom when it comes to your own life?*

He glanced across at the book sitting on his desk, the one about panic and agoraphobia. He'd been trying to do everything it said for a couple of months now and it really wasn't working, was it? Maybe this wasn't something he could do on his own. But he supposed he'd got so used to doing *everything* on his own, that it hadn't occurred to him to try a different route.

So what are you going to do, huh? Are you going to be brave, like Anna is being brave, or are you going to sit there and fester in that armchair until you become part of it?

That, thought Brody, was a very good question.

Part 2

Chapter Twenty-Seven

As summer ebbed away slowly, blessing the beginning of September with warm days and crisp skies, Anna pondered her conversations with both Brody and Gabi. What *did* she want her life to be like? She turned the idea over and over in her head, looking at it from every angle, but got no closer to an answer.

There was an ache beginning inside her, a yearning for something more, but when it came to nailing down specifics, she just couldn't create a picture in her mind. And with no vision of her future to guide her, she found herself stalled.

She signed up to a few job search websites. Some of the positions listed seemed interesting, but she never quite got to the point of filling in an online application. She didn't want to set off down the wrong path; there was no point swapping one unfulfilling job for another. Until she decided what she wanted to do next, she might as well stay put at Sundridge Plumbing and Heating.

Maybe she just wasn't ready for that level of change? It had been almost three months since she'd been to the racetrack, and she couldn't evade the feeling that since that day everything had turned upside down, even though on the surface life seemed pretty much the same. It was as if her mind and emotions had been shaken up and jumbled about like the flakes in a snow globe and she was still waiting for everything to settle and return to normal.

But that wasn't an entirely bad thing. There were good signs, shoots of spring after her long emotional winter, things she'd forgotten had once been part of her life. She found herself laughing more, but also crying more too. Sometimes, with sheer frustration, when it came to thinking about her mother-in-law.

Gayle. What was she going to do about Gayle?

Teresa kept trying to broker a truce, but Anna wasn't ready to say sorry. She knew her behavior had not been good, but she also knew that if she went and groveled to Gayle, her mother-in-law would stiffly accept her apology, then refuse to take any responsibility for all the terrible things *she'd* done. Anna's outburst at the Cinnamon Café hadn't happened in a vacuum.

There were other reasons too . . . Anna could see now that she'd tethered herself too strongly to the past, but now she had begun to let some of these things go, she felt cast adrift.

And that was the problem with Gayle. She was still firmly camped in that dark place Anna was so desperately trying to get away from. Anna sometimes wondered if that was why she kept putting off getting in touch. It was all so new, so fresh, this feeling of freedom. Maybe she was scared of losing it, scared Gayle would suck her back into being that way too?

Her one constant in this sea of internal change was Brody. They spoke at least four or five times a week now. Despite a few further requests from Anna, they still hadn't FaceTimed. It wasn't that Brody had ever squashed the idea completely, more that it never seemed to come to fruition. Maybe he wasn't very good with technology. Maybe there was something about his appearance he felt self-conscious about, who knew? She'd decided to stop pushing and let him come around to the idea at his own pace.

However, they had managed to extend their communication methods to include picture messages. Brody had sent her a picture of a rocky tor bathed in dawn light only that morning. No words—they saved those for their late-night phone calls—but while the sun was up they sent each other pictures snapped with their phones, little snippets of their daily lives.

Brody often sent her images of beautiful sunrises and sunsets, misty moors, rabbits on his lawn. Anna was having to up her photography game quite a bit to make London seem as picturesque, but she was starting to get the hang of it, especially as Gabi had shared some tips about framing and lighting.

On the walk home from work, one day in early September, she stopped, noticing the way the early evening sun was highlighting the rough sandstone bricks of a converted warehouse. She zoomed in and took an angled, almost abstract picture of an area of light and shadow, including the corner of a cast-iron window. She shared the image with Brody instantly, hoping he would see the same stark beauty in the shapes.

When she reached home and collapsed onto her sofa, she checked her messages and was rewarded with a reply—a picture of a colorful pheasant in a leafy lane. She smiled as her stomach rumbled. What was she going to have for dinner? Pasta again? Or something from the selection of ready meals stacked up in her freezer? It was all she'd had the energy to cook for . . . well, years now, even though, once upon a time, she'd been a keen cook.

Salsa was providing some much-needed exercise in her routine, but it occurred to her that she'd feel even less sluggish if she started paying attention to the quality of what she was putting into her body too? *Make the effort, Anna. Go on.* A nice homemade Thai curry would be a good start. She hadn't had one of those in ages.

Despite the fact she was tempted to lie down on the sofa and close her eyes, she pushed herself up and walked to the small supermarket a short distance away, grabbed a few items, and then headed back home, where she began assembling and preparing ingredients. She chopped a stick of lemongrass and added it to the finely sliced shallots that were sweating gently in a pan on her stove.

Just as she added a dollop of green curry paste, her phone rang. She turned the heat down and jogged back to the living room to fetch it, wooden spatula still in her other hand. It was her mum. At least *she* wanted to video call.

Her mother's face appeared on the screen. "Hello, darling," she said, smiling.

Anna walked back to the kitchen and balanced her phone on the shelf to the left of the cooker hood so she could dump the chicken into the pan while she was talking. "Hi, Mum. What's up?"

"Nothing especially. I was just thinking about you. How are you doing?"

Anna picked up her phone and angled it to take in the pan on the stove. "Wish you could smell as well as see . . . I'm cooking a Thai dish. I'm quite excited about it, actually."

She placed the phone back on her shelf and discovered her mother looking at her from over the top of her glasses. "I asked *how* you were doing. Not *what* you were doing."

"Oh. You know . . ." Anna turned away, reaching for some chopped lime leaves to throw into the pan. She knew the script to this bit: *I'm okay, getting better slowly, taking things day by day . . .*

She opened her mouth to recite it, but then she frowned and pinned her bottom lip with her teeth for a moment. "Actually, Mum, I'm beginning to think I turned a corner this summer."

"I'm so pleased to hear that, especially after that business with Gayle on Spencer's birthday. I must admit, I was a little worried that might set you back."

"Yes, even despite that. In fact, maybe because of that." She'd already told her mum about the visit to Brands Hatch but she began to delve into more detail, explaining just how it had shaken something loose for her. Up until that point, she hadn't wanted to admit to her mother how much she'd been struggling.

Her mother listened carefully and when Anna had finished, she said, "I'm so glad you felt you could talk to me about this, sweetheart. I wish you had sooner."

Anna nodded as she concentrated on her cooking. "I know. Me too."

"What do you think has helped? Was there something in particular?"

Anna stopped stirring, realizing she still wasn't being entirely honest with her mother. There was a big part of the picture she was still skirting around—Brody. He was the catalyst for all this change.

For the first time since she'd started speaking to him, it felt strange—maybe even a little wrong—that she hadn't shared this information with her mother. She stared at the chicken as she pushed it round the pan with a spatula, letting her thoughts gather, and then the story of calling Spencer's phone on New Year's Eve began to spill out, ending with her telling her mum all about the solid shoulder she'd been crying on for a good few months now. "I think it made a difference," she said. "Having someone to talk to who not only could empathize but who'd also experienced the same thing."

As the words left her mouth, she realized she still wasn't clear on the details of Brody's loss, even though she'd asked him about it a handful of times. Reviewing the conversations they'd had over the last couple of months, she noticed a pattern—every time she asked him a more personal question, he sidestepped it, but he did it so neatly, deflecting the conversations back in her direction, that she'd never spotted the trend until that moment. What was up with that? She made a mental note to pin him down properly when they next spoke.

"I'm glad you found someone you could talk to," her mother said. "But didn't the grief support group help with that?"

Anna shook her head. "It's not the same. It felt so forced, sitting in that dingy room, spilling everything out to strangers."

"But this man on the phone, he was a stranger too, wasn't he?"

"Yes, he was," Anna said, "At first . . ."

"So how is that different?"

"I don't know if can explain it, because I'm not really sure I can pin it down myself. Maybe it's the fact it was just an anonymous voice, no expectations, no judgment. All I know is that it helped. *He* helped." As Anna stirred her curry mixture, she was overcome by a sudden conviction. "Everyone who's lost someone should have the opportunity to talk like that, Mum. Not counseling or therapy, although those things are good—but with someone who gets it because they've walked that path."

Her mother smiled the very same smile she used to smile when Anna brought home her nearly always glowing school reports. "Well, that sounds like a great idea!"

Anna squinted at her mother. "What idea?"

"Setting up something for widows and widowers to talk to each other. I've been saying for ages that you needed a project to work on, something to feel excited about."

Anna nodded slowly. Her mother *had* been saying that. For months, if not years, just as Gabi had. But she hadn't been ready to listen to them, had she? It had taken ages for her to relent to any of Gabi's suggestions for evening classes, and even longer before she'd found a class she enjoyed. But here she was now, nine months of salsa under her belt, and actually looking forward to it each week. Maybe there was something in what her mother was suggesting too?

"I wouldn't know where to start," she confessed.

"No, me neither. I mean, you found this Brody by accident. How would anyone else do it? You can't just start at the top of the phone book and begin dialing random numbers—if anyone *had* phone books anymore!"

Her mother was smiling now, and Anna smiled back. The idea was wonderful, but there were other things she needed to focus on at present. "Anyway, Mum, what I'm really trying to get across is that I'm ready to make some changes to my life." She took a deep breath. "And that includes starting to date . . ."

"Oh!" She'd obviously caught her mum off guard with that one. "Oh, Anna . . . I think that's . . . Well, it's a big step. But it's wonderful!"

"I have to admit, I'm terrified."

"Of course! But if you think you're ready . . . Is it this Brody chap?"

Anna blinked. *Brody?* "Um. No. He . . ." Her brain tangled around that idea. That was clearly impossible, because . . . because . . . "No, it's not Brody, Mum. He's just a friend." But even as her mouth said the word "friend," she realized that was a pale and faint description for what Brody had come to mean to her. She shook her head, unable to process that thought right then. "His name is Jeremy. He's from salsa. He's asked me out before—a few months ago—and classes have just started up again after the summer break. He's still single, and I *think* he's still interested." She'd had a brief conversation with him after class, and although she was out of practice at this sort of thing, she thought she was reading things correctly.

"Oh, well, do keep me updated on—"

Anna became aware of an acrid smell from the frying pan. She looked down and swore. "I'd better go, Mum! I'm burning the dinner!"

"Of course, of course," she replied. "Love you, darling! Now go and save that delicious curry!"

Anna said a hasty goodbye, then turned her attention to her dinner. Was the chicken charred? She inspected it with her spatula, turning different bits over. Maybe a little. But not so badly she needed to abandon the dish. So what if it was a little smokier than normal?

She tipped the can of coconut milk into the pan and stirred. As she put the rice on, her thoughts returned to her conversation with her mother. How wonderful it would be if everyone could find their own Brody. But how would you do it?

She glanced across to her phone still sitting on the shelf, and reached for it, intending to use the timer function to make sure she didn't burn the rice as well, but when she saw row upon row of colorful icons, she froze.

An app.

She shook her head as she picked up the phone and set the

timer going, then she put the phone back on the shelf and looked at it, watching the numbers counting down to when her dinner would be ready.

Was that even possible? Just the thought made something surge inside her chest. She didn't know. However, she knew a couple of people who might.

Chapter Twenty-Eight

*B*rody drove into his yard, climbed from his Land Rover and slammed the door, aware that Lewis was probably sitting on the other side of the back door waiting for him, wondering where he'd been. Brody had driven all the way to the outskirts of Dartmouth that morning, but he hadn't been able to take Lewis with him. Therapists (or whatever the official title was) didn't appreciate furry, four-legged chaperones for their appointments, he'd discovered.

He'd looked the guy up on the internet a couple of months ago, not long after Anna had told him about going to the racetrack. This had been his sixth session. He had no idea if it was working yet. Especially as the only place he'd been, other than out on the moor or on his own land, was to Ibrahim's office for his sessions, and just driving in the direction of any town got him all stressed out anyway.

He unlocked the back door and was greeted by a slightly frantic and pleased-to-see-him Lewis, before the dog bounded past him, running off to the other side of the yard, where he started barking in the direction of the footpath that ran down the side of the property. It wasn't a territorial kind of bark, but a *look at this!* kind of bark.

At the very same moment, Brody saw a flash of color in his peripheral vision. He turned to see a woman in brightly colored walking gear, and beside her, a man in darker, more muted colors.

"Oh, hello!" the woman called out. "Thank goodness! I think we're a little lost . . ." And she made to clamber over the dry-stone wall that acted as a boundary between the footpath and his garden. Brody started to back away, even as the woman made eye contact and waved a badly folded map at him. "I don't suppose you know the way to Hexworthy, do you?" she said loudly, completely ignoring the fact she'd just hopped onto his property uninvited. She was middle-aged, and what his mother would have called a "jolly hockey sticks" type. "We're booked at a B and B in the village . . ." She broke off to look at her partner in crime.

"The Sheep Dip Bed-and-Breakfast," he supplied.

"The Sheep Dip Bed-and-Breakfast," she repeated, as if her companion hadn't just said exactly the same thing, and turned her hopeful gaze back to Brody.

Brody just stared at her, frozen to the spot. His heart began to pound, and his fingers went numb and tingly.

Remember what Ibrahim said, he told himself raggedly inside his head. *You are okay. You are not having a stroke. Just the same non-dangerous symptoms you get every time you have a panic attack. Don't fight it, just . . . notice. Accept.*

Ibrahim had suggested keeping a record of when and where he had his most anxious moments: what triggered them, how long they lasted and how bad they were on a scale of one to ten.

Six, Brody thought, matter-of-factly in the corner of his brain that seemed to be functioning almost normally. *Although it could peak at an eight or nine if she keeps striding toward me that way.*

From talking to Ibrahim, he'd worked out that it was other

people—strangers, more specifically—that triggered most of his panic attacks, and the more of them there were around, the more severe the episode, especially if he was in a confined space, like a shop, or even an outside area without many exits. He needed to know that he could get away, that he could escape.

Not for the first time, Brody chided himself for not planting a hedge or getting a fence, but hardly anyone used this old foot-path. These were the first walkers he'd seen in months.

There was nothing he could do about that now. His only options were (a) turn on his heels and run, which would make him seem incredibly rude, or (b) talk to the woman. And since his feet seemed to be cemented to the dusty ground, it appeared option (a) was more wishful thinking than anything else.

Concentrate, Brody! What was the first technique Ibrahim said to employ?

Breathe.

He needed to breathe.

The thought came cleanly and smoothly into his head like magic. As if it belonged there. He dug his feet even harder into the cobblestones and lifted his head, stared the woman in the face, all the while inhaling as evenly as he could, then letting the air out slowly again.

Hockey Sticks slowed a little to let Wiry Man catch up, so they approached him together, then thrust the map out at him. "Would you be able to point out where we are?"

Brody nodded. He was so familiar with his little corner of the moor that it didn't take more than a second before he jabbed a finger at the map.

The woman squinted at where he'd pointed and looked back up at him. "Is it far?" She tipped her head up to look at the sky, which was taking on a golden tinge as the sun threatened to set behind one of the tors on the horizon. "We'd like to get there by dark, if possible."

"Five . . ." he managed to utter, but it sounded as if he was talking with a tablespoon of gravel in his mouth. He held up his hand so she could count his fingers.

"Five miles?"

He nodded vigorously and pointed to the lane that headed west and down into a little wooded valley.

"Well . . . Thank you," Hockey Sticks said, even though her face suggested she wasn't sure her thanks were welcome. She was mostly right, not because Brody had lost the ability or will to be helpful, but because he was counting down the seconds until the pair disappeared from view and he could implode or lie on the floor or whatever else his body felt like doing to compensate for dealing with their intrusion.

Lewis was sitting beside him, looking hopefully up at the woman, tail wagging so hard it was flinging up a little cloud of dust and dirt. She bent down to stroke his head quickly, then she and her partner were off with a jaunty wave.

When they turned the corner into the lane, Brody let out the breath he'd been holding and supported himself by resting his hands on his knees. He was feeling more than a little shaky and his pulse was still galloping.

But you did it, the usually unhelpful and accusative voice in his head said. *You didn't make a fool of yourself in front of them—well, not much. You didn't vomit. You even spoke!*

I did, he thought, as he dragged in a couple of deep breaths. *I did all of that.*

Chapter Twenty-Nine

*I*t was a warm night for September, so when Brody let Lewis out for his last run down the garden for the evening, he didn't stay at the back door as usual but stepped out onto his patio.

As he waited for his dog, he dialed Anna's number. If she hadn't already called him by this point in the evening, he'd got into the habit of phoning her instead.

"Hey," she said softly when she answered, and he could tell she was smiling, as pleased to hear his voice as he was hers. "I was just about to call you, but you beat me to it!"

Brody began to pace lazily back and forth as they filled each other in on their days. Anna had met her sister-in-law and baby nephew during her lunch break. "Teresa mentioned Gayle again," she said wearily. "I understand it's awkward for her and Scott. I have to keep making sure there's no chance of Gayle and Richard popping round every time I go to visit them. It can't be fun for them being piggy in the middle."

"I know you've said you're not ready but hear me out. Let me side with Teresa for a second, play devil's advocate . . . Because it might not be a bad idea to meet Gayle and discuss how you feel, so you can move forward without all the animosity."

"I know it might be helpful and, even if just for Spencer's sake, I can't ignore her forever . . ."

"But not yet?"

"No. I'm just still so angry with her. I can't seem to get past it—and this isn't me, Brody. I'm not that person. I'm *not* the person who simmers with resentment, who holds grudges."

Lewis was sniffing around some bushes further down the lawn. Brody strolled out onto the damp grass, feeling the whisper of cool night air on his face. He'd been where Anna was at one point, so stuck in his anger that he'd ended up pushing everyone away. He didn't want her to end up like that. How could he explain it to her?

Open up. Tell her the truth. Tell her something real about yourself.

Brody swallowed. It wasn't that he didn't want to share things with Anna. He thought about it all the time, like when he'd met the hikers the other day, or only this morning, when he felt triumphant after writing a full paragraph in his notebook.

He turned back to face his cottage, his gaze drawn to the glow of warmth from his study window. It made him think of the little "not elf" sitting hidden out of sight on a high shelf.

"Grief is a funny thing," he began slowly. "People think of it as sadness, but it's much more complex than that. It has so many layers, so many tangled emotions—including anger."

"I know that," Anna said. "They mention anger in every grief book out there, how you might be angry with the person for abandoning you, even if it wasn't their fault or their choice."

"It goes deeper than that." Brody took in a deep breath. It was now or never, and he was about to jump off into the deep end. "Sometimes you get angry with other people instead. For me, it was with my parents. They tried to be there for me, but I was just so stubborn that I perceived it as meddling, and I got cross with them, and then it just . . . snowballed . . . until we couldn't talk without me feeling a fiery ball of rage in the pit of my stomach."

Anna made a sound of recognition.

"Yes, I had reason to be irritated with them at times," Brody continued. "They *were* meddling and occasionally being a little judgmental, but the fury I felt was out of balance with what they actually said and did, which was really them just trying to help the only way they knew how. It became easier to be angry with them than to be sad about what had happened. I couldn't see it at the time. I truly believed I was justified in taking the stance I did, but looking back, I can see that I blew it all out of proportion. Does that make sense?"

"Maybe," Anna replied warily.

And here was the six million-dollar question. "Do you think there is any possibility you're doing the same thing with Gayle?"

The silence that followed was taut. Brody could sense her struggling with what he'd said, but he trusted her to see the truth.

"Maybe," she said again. "But it doesn't make it any easier to deal with. I still feel what I feel. And I know she won't apologize to me for her part in the way things are between us, that I'll have to be the bigger person and take responsibility for it all, and the idea of giving her a free pass just smarts, so at the moment it's easier to leave things as they are. Gabi has said that maybe it's a good idea for me to have a break from all the lunches and photo albums, and I'm inclined to agree."

Brody felt his throat tighten. This was how it started. But to explain fully how dangerous it was just to put things off, to believe the opportunities for healing and reconciliation wouldn't diminish as time went on, he was going to have to be more specific, and that meant telling Anna things he didn't want to tell her. Things he didn't want to tell anyone because he felt too guilty and ashamed.

He ran a hand through his hair and turned and strode further down the lawn into the darkness. He could hear the gurgle of the stream that ran down the boundary at the bottom of his garden. Sometimes, he sensed that Anna had him on a pedestal, that she thought he was wise and sensible and . . . good. If he told her everything—not just about the state of his life now, but about what happened nine years ago—that pedestal would be smashed and broken. She would never see him in the same way again. Worst-case scenario, he could lose her friendship forever. The thought terrified him.

But it would be worth it if he could help her, if he could prevent her from screwing up her relationships with bitterness and misplaced blame, the way he had. He was just working out where to begin when she spoke. "And talking of moving on, I had an interesting chat with my mum the other week. I've been meaning to mention it. I told her how much our conversations have helped me and she suggested setting up something similar to help other people who've lost someone."

Brody wasn't sure whether to be relieved or frustrated he had a stay of execution. He'd come back to this later in the conversation. "What sort of something?" he said, frowning. Anna wasn't going to suggest adding more people into their conversations, was she? He didn't much like that idea.

"I'm not sure yet," she said, "but some way to connect other people so they can talk with each other like we have."

"Other people? Talking to each other?"

"Something like that. I need to get it straight in my head before I get going with it. I'll keep you posted as I work it all out." She paused and took a breath before carrying on. "And talking of moving on, on finding healing after loss, there's another big step I've decided to take."

Brody was so relieved at the thought he was still going to have Anna all to himself that he said, almost absentmindedly, "Oh, yes?"

"I'm going to ask Jeremy if he'd like to have dinner with me."

Brody recoiled from her words as he would from a punch. "Uh . . ." was all he managed to say. He hadn't been expecting that. She'd hardly mentioned the guy in the last couple of months; he'd been lulled into a false sense of security.

Her voice wavered. "You don't think it's a good idea?"

No, he bloody well didn't think it was a good idea! But he wasn't going to tell Anna that, he realized almost instantly. How could he? Why would he? What was he going to say: *Give Mr. Slick the elbow and have dinner with me instead*? Especially with everything he'd just been about to reveal to her.

"Brody . . . ?"

She was waiting for his answer, yet he couldn't say what he wanted to say. He didn't need a million reasons why he couldn't ask her to dinner. Five were enough.

First, they lived hundreds of miles apart. Second and third, he didn't know her full name or her address, but those were tiny hurdles compared to the fourth reason: even if he knew these things, it wouldn't do him any good. What was he going to do? Travel to London on a packed train, meet her in a café or a swish restaurant? How exactly would that go?

And if that wasn't enough, the last reason knocked the rest down like a bowling ball hitting wooden pins. He'd be a ball and chain around this amazing woman's leg. Instead of letting her reach her full potential, he'd drag her back into the shadowy valley of guilt and grief with him, back into everything she was escaping from. He couldn't do that to her.

He cleared his throat and answered her. "No."

"No, you don't think I should ask him?"

"I meant, 'No, it's not a bad idea.'" He paused briefly, caught off guard by the tightening in his chest. "I think you should ask him. Go for it."

He could tell a smile was blooming on her face as she exhaled softly. It only made the crushing sensation around his rib cage worse.

"Okay, then," she said, sounding more certain. Sounding happy.

Brody wanted to punch something.

"I'll tell you how it goes—if I work up the courage!" she added.

He kicked an exposed root with his boot, then closed his eyes and let his head fall back. "You do that."

Chapter Thirty

Anna sat at a table in a nice little Italian restaurant, knotting and unknotting a thick linen napkin as she watched the large clock behind the bar. She'd got here deliberately early, knowing she'd need some time to center herself before Jeremy arrived. Not for the first time that evening, she made herself breathe out slowly.

La Cucina wasn't in the town center. That had felt too public—which was ridiculous, seeing as a restaurant, by definition, is a public space—so she'd chosen a small, family-run establishment in the middle of a little parade of shops in a residential area.

So here she was, ready for her first "first date" in well over a decade. It all felt very strange. Anna glanced at the clock again. Ten minutes.

The waiter approached. "Is there anything else you would like, madam? An aperitif? Some olives for the table?"

"No. No, thank you," Anna replied, so he busied himself straightening the cutlery and filling her glass with water, even though it didn't need topping up. He'd been like this since the moment she stepped in the door, always bustling, fussing over little details. It was as if someone had set him on a gentle mode of fast-forward. She supposed he thought it made him appear attentive and efficient but, frankly, he was starting to tire her out. It made her jitters twice as bad.

She was on the verge of ordering a cocktail, just to make him

go away, when her phone buzzed. She fished it out of her handbag, and when she opened up her messages, she saw the text was
from Gabi.

Good luck!!! xxxx, it said with a row of hearts and flowers and
champagne glass emojis following in procession afterward.

Another one popped up as she was reading: *Just relax*

Easier said than done, thought Anna.

Gabi finished off in a manner that was so typically Gabi that
Anna had to smile, even while her heart galloped: *And don't
forget to kiss him at the end of the night! (That's an order!)*

Anna closed her eyes and did the long, slow breathing out
thing. Oh, Lord. She couldn't even *think* about that. Dealing
with the beginning of the night was hard enough.

And as if fate knew her level of jitteriness was maxed out, Jeremy chose that moment to walk through the door. Anna resisted
the urge to slide under the table and hide, but instead stood and
smiled as he walked toward her. He always looked good, but he
looked particularly handsome tonight, in a nice shirt and jeans.
Thankfully, Jeremy's effortless, easygoing charm papered over
the cracks of her nervousness, and by the time the waiter had
come to take their orders and had retreated again, she was feeling
on much more of an even keel.

Jeremy took a sip of his wine and sat back in his chair, looking at Anna with a thoughtful expression. "I must admit, I was
surprised when you called."

Anna laughed nervously. "Me too."

"I'm glad you did."

Anna didn't reply with words but with a smile that started
off small and just grew bigger and bigger, seemingly of its own
accord.

Jeremy sat back in his chair and regarded her thoughtfully. "Back in the summer, you told me you weren't ready."

Anna nodded. "I know."

"But you are now?"

Anna could see the questions in his eyes, but they didn't annoy her like those of her friends and family did. These questions belonged there. He had a right to them after all the mixed signals she'd been giving him. If Anna was a traffic light, she'd been flickering between amber and red where Jeremy was concerned. "I am."

"What changed?"

Anna put down her knife and fork. "I have," she said simply, realizing that this was the truth. She no longer felt like a zombie stumbling through life in a haze.

"I want you to know I'm not just after a fling. I'm looking for something more serious."

Anna sighed. "You might have already guessed this, but you're the first person I've dated since Spencer passed away. It all feels a bit new and a bit strange . . ."

She looked up and he didn't seem fazed or perplexed, just accepting. It gave her the courage to carry on. She needed to be honest with him from the start, give him a chance to back out if they weren't on the same page. "I'm not sure I can promise you forever, Jeremy, especially not on a first date. I'm not even sure I believe in *forever* anymore. I mean, the 'till death do us part' bit still looms over that concept like a large black thundercloud."

"I'm not asking for that," he said, his eyes crinkling as he gave her a gentle smile. "Just that you're willing to see where this goes. And I know this isn't easy for you, that we might have to take things step by step."

Anna understood what he was asking for. A green light. Not to the end of a road that stretched out forever, but he was looking for a sign. Something. She reckoned she was ready for *something*. "Yes," she said. "I'd like to see where this goes too."

It felt strange walking down the road with a man, a man who wasn't Spencer. Strange, but not awful.

Anna had deliberately left her car at home, partly because she'd wanted the fresh air on the twenty-minute walk to La Cucina to clear her head before the date, and partly because she suspected a couple of glasses of wine might bolster her courage. She'd been intending to call a cab at the end of the evening, but Jeremy had suggested walking her back and they'd been having such a good time she hadn't been ready to end the evening yet. However, as she got closer to home, she started to wonder if this had been a mistake.

What is he expecting? she thought as they turned into her road.

She wasn't ready to ask him inside her house. Not even a little bit. Not even for "coffee" that actually *meant* coffee. It would be too weird. This was the house she and Spencer had planned to build a life in, and she couldn't imagine another masculine presence inside it. *Baby steps*, she told herself. *Baby steps*.

And those baby steps eventually brought her right outside her house. Anna opened the gate and glanced at Jeremy as he released her hand and let her walk up the path in front of him. She couldn't read his expression, couldn't get any hint of what he thought the next five minutes—or longer—might hold. It unnerved her and her heart began to thud. When she got to the front door, she stopped and turned. Her voice came out thin, her tone patchy. "It was a lovely evening."

He stepped in closer, until their faces were only centimeters apart. "It still is."

Not Spencer! Her little internal alarm squawked. It was the first time she'd heard it that evening, but even now it was weak and half-hearted. Instead of reacting to it as she normally did, she turned and faced it. Replied to it.

No, he's not Spencer, she told it, both firmly and gently, like a primary teacher explaining a basic rule to a new batch of rosy-cheeked four-year-olds. *But maybe that's okay. Maybe I just need to jump over this hurdle and it won't be such a big thing going forward.*

And just to prove it she leaned in and kissed Jeremy. As soon as her lips touched his, his arms came around her, pulling her closer, deepening the kiss a little. It was strange—he kissed differently from how Spencer had kissed. It wasn't all tingling skin and fireworks like it had been with her husband, but it wasn't horrible either. It was a nice kiss, a perfectly fine kiss.

When he pulled away, he said, "Would you like to do dinner again—next Saturday, if that's not too soon?"

Anna nodded again, and then realized that talking might help her seem less of a wet lettuce, and added, "Next Saturday it is." They kissed again, and then he turned and walked down the path.

She watched him for a moment, then slipped inside, closing the door softly behind herself. She shrugged off her jacket and dropped it on the chair in the hallway then went into the living room and sat down in the corner of the big sofa and stared straight ahead.

Did I just do that? Did I actually just kiss another man?

It all seemed a bit unreal.

Are you okay with this? she silently whispered into the air, once again wishing more than anything that Spencer could answer her. She was pretty sure, logically speaking, he'd want her to be happy, to take life by the horns the way he had always done, but thinking it in her head and feeling it in her heart were two completely different things.

She reached over and turned on a lamp and as she did so, she realized she was sitting in the spot she always nestled in when she phoned Brody. Instinctively, she reached into her bag and pulled her mobile out, preparing to dial his number.

A missed call? From Brody? Anna blinked and checked the time. The call log said it had gone unanswered at ten thirty-eight. About five minutes ago—about the time she'd been standing on her front doorstep kissing Jeremy. She prepared to hit the button to call him back, but then hesitated.

It was a reflex now, she realized, to reach for her phone and call Brody any time anything significant happened in her life, good or bad, but even though she'd glibly told him that she'd give him all the gory details of her date, she wasn't sure she wanted to.

Why? Why was this weird?

She closed her eyes and exhaled. The truth was that she didn't know why she was feeling this way, she just was, and it was merely the last stop on a roller coaster of emotions she'd experienced that evening. Maybe she should just let herself calm down and tell him about it tomorrow?

Chapter Thirty-One

The following evening, Anna wrapped herself in a warm cardigan and sat at the table and chairs on her patio. The sky was a deep indigo, a shade so rich she wished she could reach out and touch it. This had been a favorite spot of hers and Spencer's. In the summer, they'd had long, lazy evening meals out here, laughing and talking, wishing on stars and building dreams for the future.

Those same stars twinkled back at her now, but she refused to tip her head back and study them the way she'd once loved to do. She hadn't quite forgiven them yet for not doing their jobs, for not holding on to those promises and wishes she'd given them for safekeeping, but she was coming around to it. Slowly.

She glanced down at the phone in her hand. She needed advice about something she'd been putting off thinking about, but now time was running out and she needed to make a decision. On any other day, she'd have dialed Brody instantly, but she felt bad for not calling him back last night. It was strange. It felt as if something had changed in their relationship, and she didn't know what.

She was on the verge of putting her phone back in her pocket when she stopped herself being so stupid. Instead, she rang his number and waited for him to pick up. He always picked up, she realized. He was always there when she needed him.

"So sorry I didn't call back last night! I was out, and I had my phone on silent."

"It's okay," he said, sounding as grave and unreadable, as he often did. "Did you have a good evening?"

She swallowed. "Yes. I, er . . . I went on a date." She paused, grimacing slightly as she added, "With Jeremy."

A silence fell thick and hard. Eventually, he asked, "How did it go?"

"Well—I think . . ." Anna closed her eyes. She wished she hadn't started this now. Her weirdness about this was obviously giving the whole conversation a funny vibe. Better to move on to another subject. "How are you? Is everything okay?"

"Yes. Why?"

"I just wondered if something was up, if you'd wanted to talk about something in particular last night."

All Anna could hear for a few seconds was the distant noise of traffic on the main road a few streets away from her, the wail of a neighbor's cat.

"No. Not really." He paused again.

Anna frowned. She'd had the strangest feeling for a while now that Brody's *nothing* was actually *something*, filling the spaces in their conversations he often left empty. What wasn't he telling her?

"I just wanted to talk to you . . . Hear your voice."

There was an honesty about the way he said those words that brought a lump to her throat and she instantly hated herself for having doubted him. "Brody . . . I think that's the sweetest thing you've ever said to me."

"It's true," he said, a puzzling hint of resignation in his tone.

She looked down at her feet. She could hardly see the details of her shoes now. They were just blurry gray shapes in the darkness. All the awkwardness she'd been feeling earlier drained away. They were back in their bubble, a unit of two. "I don't know what I'd do without you," she replied. "You're one of my best friends."

There was a slight noise at the other end of the line. She hoped it was him huffing slightly as he smiled. At least, that's what it sounded like. "Good" was all he said. But for Anna, it was enough. She smiled too.

"Oh! I almost forgot! I need to ask your advice about something. Again. Sorry!"

She heard his soft laughter properly this time. "Don't apologize. The only other person who gets the benefit of my advice is Lewis, and I'm not sure he's very appreciative. What's happened?"

"You know I said Teresa had invited me to her birthday party in a couple of weeks?"

"Mm-hmm . . ."

"Well, I was chatting to her about it earlier today. I had assumed it was going to be mostly friends—especially as she said she wanted to make up for the wild bash she should have had when she turned thirty but didn't because she was too depressed about it. Well, it turns out I was wrong. It's going to be a *family* party, everyone from all generations invited, and that means—"

"Ah. I see . . . Gayle."

"Exactly," Anna replied. "I'm dreading it. I haven't seen her since the day I called her a cold-hearted bitch. But I can't *not* go. I can't punish Teresa for what Gayle did, especially as she and I have been getting along so well recently."

Ever since she'd visited when Little Spencer (as everyone now called him) had been born, something had shifted in her relationship with Teresa. They'd always liked each other, but now they had a bond. Teresa felt like . . . well, family.

"I think you've answered your own question," Brody said.

Anna sighed and brought her feet up onto the seat, tucking one under the other. "I know. But what am I going to do about Gayle?"

"Do you have to do *anything* about her?"

Anna pinned the corner of her lip with her teeth. Did she? The idea that she might not was oddly liberating. "You're saying, just go—no apologies, no explanations—and ignore her?"

"I was thinking just be cordial, but it's up to you."

"*Don't react*, in other words?"

He laughed. "Bingo."

She slumped forward onto the table, supporting her head with one hand. "Why do family gatherings have to be so exhausting? I'm already dreading Christmas, even though it's still more than three months away, and don't even get me started about New Year's Eve!"

"Which is worse, do you think?" Brody mused. "Christmas or New Year?"

There was a heartbeat while they both pondered the answer. "New Year," they both said at exactly the same time, which made them both laugh. Anna hugged her knees and glanced up at the stars. It was starting to get a little bit chilly now, but she didn't want to go inside. As she watched one star, trying to work out if it was winking a pale green color or whether it was just her imagination, a thought came to her. "Then why don't we *not* do New Year's Eve this year," she said.

"Hah! That sounds like a marvelous idea."

Anna unraveled the concept a little further. "And why don't we *not* do New Year's Eve together?"

"Spend all evening on the phone?"

That was what she'd been going to suggest, but she suddenly realized there was a better option, an option she instantly knew she wanted more than anything. "No. Let's do it in person."

There was a stunned silence for a few seconds. "What?"

Anna held her breath for a moment then said, "Brody, I think it's time we should meet."

Chapter Thirty-Two

You want to meet up on New Year's Eve? Face-to-face?" Brody said, sounding more than a little stunned.

Okay, Anna thought. Even though New Year's Eve was still more than three months away, and the idea had just popped into her head and she'd run with it, she hadn't expected this reaction. She'd thought Brody would be excited about the idea, even though up until that moment their relationship had been exclusively, well . . . audio.

"What . . . what about Jeremy?"

"What about him?"

"Won't you want to spend New Year's Eve with him?"

Oh. She supposed that was an option. One that hadn't even been on her radar, apparently. "I don't know," she answered. "I don't even know if there will *be* a Jeremy in a few months' time."

More silence.

"Really?" he said, obviously skeptical.

"Yes, really. We've been on one date, and if there's one thing I've learned in recent years, it's not to trust what the future might bring."

"But you're making plans with me," he said in a low voice.

"Yes," she said. "That's different."

"Why?"

Anna stared up at the twinkling stars. "Because I know you."

He went quiet again, but this time it was one of those full silences. She could tell he was thinking carefully about what she'd suggested. And the more she thought about it, even though her suggestion had been a bit out-of-the-blue and random, it seemed like the perfect plan. It would save both of them from being miserable and lonely and give them something to look forward to over Christmas, which was never easy after you'd lost someone special.

"So, what do you think? Shall we do it?"

He cleared his throat. "Why on earth would you want to spend New Year's Eve with me?"

She wasn't sure if she should be insulted that he hadn't jumped at the idea, or sad that he didn't dare believe she meant it. "Because I would like to look you in the eyes and say thank you, for all you've done for me."

He made a dismissive noise. "I haven't done anything, really. It's you . . . It's all you."

"No, Brody. It's you too. You listened when no one else would, when no one else *could* . . . Not in the way I needed them to. And you haven't been afraid to tell me the truth when I needed to hear it." She looked helplessly up at the stars, as if maybe they could help her convince him. "I wouldn't have made it through this year without you . . ."

She trailed off, suddenly wondering if she was reading more into this relationship than there was, but then she thought about how he'd said that he'd called just to hear her voice and it made her feel even more confused.

"I would love to spend New Year's Eve with you, Anna. I just . . . can't."

Anna waited, sensing there was more to come. An explanation of some sort, at the very least, but when the silence stretched on longer than she could bear, she said, "Brody . . . ?"

She heard him exhale heavily.

"Are you okay? Is everything all right?"

She could almost hear him wrestling inwardly with his answer. *Tell me*, she urged him silently. *Tell me what it is. Trust me like I trust you.*

She heard the kind of intake of breath that only occurs when someone is about to say something. Something big.

And then he let the air out again.

"It's nothing for you to worry about." There was a finality in his tone that told her it would do her no good broaching this topic again this evening. But she wanted to meet Brody. She wanted to see his smile, not just hear it. She wanted to give him a hug and thank him for his friendship.

It had saved her.

For too long she'd been the leach in their relationship, sucking the strength and wisdom out of him because she'd been desperate and grieving. Okay, she was still grieving. But she was no longer desperate, she realized. Somehow, her mourning had entered a new phase, and it was time to stop feeling that she and her pain were the center of the universe and to start looking outward again. She closed her eyes with shame at how utterly self-absorbed she'd been.

Was she doing it again now? Was she just thinking about what she wanted and not taking his feelings into account?

Maybe, she had to admit.

Perhaps she needed to back off the idea for now. But that didn't mean she and Brody couldn't find some other way to connect further, did it? "Okay," she said, her mouth forming the beginning of her sentence before her brain had fully formulated her thought. "Well, we've been virtually anonymous to each other for the five or six months we've been talking on a regular basis. I'm pretty sure you're not an axe-wielding serial killer by now—"

He let out a huff of laughter, and it was as if, in the last few minutes, Anna had developed superhero-like sensitive hearing where he was concerned. She heard the mirth but, underneath it, she also heard what he was desperately trying to keep hidden— relief. He was glad she hadn't kept pushing that they meet.

"So, I'm going to tell you my last name," she finished. "And where I live."

The silence at the other end of the line changed. As if he was no longer smiling to himself. As if he was frowning. Wary.

Why?

"My name is Anna Barry and I live in southeast London. Bromley to be exact. Well, not actually in Bromley town center, more Sundridge Park . . ." She was babbling now. "And I'm going to send you a picture . . ."

Was she? Where had that come from?

But the moment she'd said it, she knew it was the right decision. If Brody couldn't—or wouldn't—FaceTime, this was the next best thing. She wanted to have a mental image of him when she talked to him, not this fuzzy, shifting idea in her head made up entirely from her imagination, and she wanted him to be able to picture her too. She wanted him to know who she was on the outside the way he knew her on the inside.

She switched her phone to speaker and navigated to where her photos were stored and chose one to text him. Was it weird that in all the time they'd been communicating, they hadn't once sent a written message? It had always been talking. Voices.

"Anna? You really don't need to . . ."

Anna wasn't listening. She was too busy scrolling down her photo library, trying to find the right one to send to him. The nicest pictures of her were way at the top, quite a few of them with Spencer, and her vanity almost made her want to select one of those, but she paused before she tapped the screen. No. This wasn't like choosing a picture for an Instagram-perfect display that bore no resemblance at all to real life. This was Brody. She needed to find one that showed who she was now, wrinkles and all, one that was honest.

"I'm going to have to hang up," she told him. "I can't work out how to do this without cutting you off. Phone me back when you've got it."

She ended the call before he could protest and chose a photo of herself taken sometime in the last year. She wasn't being cute or sexy (not that she was sure that she knew *how* to take a selfie that was cute and sexy). It was a snap Gabi had taken during a walk in the fields around Farnborough one Saturday morning in February. She'd called Anna's name and had taken the photograph the moment Anna had turned her head. She was staring straight at the camera, a half smile on her lips and weariness in her eyes that said *You're really doing that now?* It was very her. All the better for having been caught in the moment.

She tapped her phone to select it and then, before she could talk herself out of it, she pressed "send" and it was gone. She held her breath and waited.

It took a long time for Brody to reply. So long, in fact, that it got too chilly to stay outside and she had to scurry back indoors to the warmth of her kitchen. She turned off the bright overhead lights and made do with just the one from under the cooker hood, put her phone on the table, sat down and waited.

What was holding him up? She wasn't that ugly, was she?

She knew she wasn't. Okay, she wasn't stunning, and she didn't have the sparkle that Gabi did around her eyes that made Anna think of the word "pretty," but she didn't have a bad bone structure. She could look nice on a night out if she made the effort.

Her phone binged and vibrated against the tabletop. She snatched it up. She had a text from him. A picture!

It took a few moments before her brain made sense of the image on the screen, all shaggy gray hair and large, soulful eyes filled with mischief. She tapped to enlarge it and then she let out a half-frustrated, half-amused sigh. She shook her head, picked up her phone and dialed his number. "I take it that is Lewis," she said when he answered.

"He's much more handsome than I am," Brody said gravely.

"He *is* handsome," Anna had to agree, with his wavy, silvery fur. "What kind of dog is he, anyway?"

"Cairn terrier. Think Toto in *The Wizard of Oz*."

Oh, yes. Anna could picture that. And, from what she knew of Lewis, he was just as spirited and naughty. "Tell me," she said, smiling as she asked the question, "are your eyebrows also that fluffy?"

There was a heartbeat of silence before he answered. "Fluffier."

Well, that might explain the lack of a photo. Maybe she'd been right about him being self-conscious about the way he looked. Oh, Lord. She was pushing again, wasn't she? A whole lifetime of being a meek little mouse, and now that she'd finally found her assertive side, it was starting to run away with her. "I didn't mean you had to send one back," she added quickly. "I'm sorry if you felt steamrolled into something . . ."

"It's okay," he said, a bit more seriously. "I'm not sure I've got a photo of myself on this phone anyway. I'm not big on taking pictures of myself. Maybe another time."

"Maybe," Anna echoed, not quite sure if this was a legitimate excuse or whether he was fobbing her off again. Brody was all arm's length facts and hidden motives this evening.

"But I can tell you my name. I'm Brody Smith. I live in a lane that doesn't actually have a name and is probably too insignificant to have a road number either, but the nearest village is Hexworthy."

"Thank you, Brody Smith."

"It was nothing," he replied, but he was wrong.

This evening, Brody had changed from being a voice on the end of the phone into a real person. Oh, she knew he'd always been real, but somehow, there was a part of her that hadn't thought of him that way. He'd been like something out of a dream. Or a fairy tale. A rather gruff and opinionated fairy godmother, maybe. But somehow, by revealing his last name and as much of an address as he had, he had solidified into something from this world. If she wanted, she could get in her car and drive to that place.

Not that she would, of course. Not without him saying she could first. That would be a bit too much like stalking. It was enough to know it was possible for now.

Chapter Thirty-Three

Lewis barked at Brody then went to sit by the back door. Brody was still staring at his phone after ending his call with Anna, and hardly noticed. Lewis barked again. "Sorry, mate," Brody muttered and went over to let him out.

Lewis immediately ran into the middle of the courtyard and instead of doing what Brody had assumed he'd wanted to do, he just started barking, and then the noise changed into what could only be described as a long, mournful howling, as he sat on his hindquarters and looked up at the moon.

It was a rather spectacular moon, large and full. Almost within reach, it felt like.

"Stupid dog," Brody muttered. "What do you think you are, a wolf? Just because it looks close, because it feels like you can get to it, it doesn't mean you can."

But Lewis ignored him and kept going. *Well*, Brody thought, as he shrugged and headed back into the kitchen, *at least he wasn't disturbing the neighbors*, since they didn't have any.

Even with all that baying, Anna's voice was still in his ears, like the echo of a song heard after the radio has been turned off. He drew his phone away from his ear and stared at it intently before switching to his messages app, looking at Anna's photo. She was wearing a thick gray scarf and a purple beanie with a paler crocheted flower on one side. The sun was low and slanting, highlighting the out of focus frosty fields in the background, but it was the foreground Brody was interested in.

God, she was beautiful.

He couldn't stop looking at her eyes. He'd been right about them. They were large and open, wistful. But he saw other things there too, things he'd known about her even without seeing this photograph: determination, courage, compassion.

The rest of her face came into focus.

If he'd been a stranger, if he'd just seen this as a profile picture on Facebook, he would have probably thought it was a nice enough face but wouldn't have given it more than a passing glance. It was interesting more than traditionally pretty.

But he wasn't a stranger, and he couldn't seem to maintain that kind of detachment for too long. He stared at the photo, drinking it in, God help him.

You're a sad case, Brody Smith. A really sad case.

Half in love with a girl you've never met, never even seen, and she sends you a picture and then, well . . .

You need to get out more, mate.

He exhaled loudly and forced himself to put the phone to sleep. He didn't, however, manage to make himself put it back down on the desk. Instead, he tucked it into his back pocket.

He'd chickened out of sending her a picture in return. What had he been so afraid of?

No, I mean, really . . . Maybe you should take a good look?

There was a mirror in his hallway. Not because he actually used it much, but because the previous owners had left it, and mirrors seemed to belong in hallways. He marched himself off to it and stood in front of it, feet planted wide.

This is the face of a coward, he told himself. *Are you really so vain*

*that you couldn't have held the phone up and taken a picture, right
then and there? Afraid she'd see the gray in your stubble, the hardness
in your jaw?*

No, he wasn't afraid of those things.

*Afraid she'll be able to see why you lock yourself away like this?
Afraid that if she ever found out, she'd never speak to you again?*

That was more honest. Stupid, but honest. His logical mind
knew this, but he still wasn't any closer to taking the picture
than he had been twenty minutes ago.

And, God . . . How he wanted to meet her! But it was a bad
idea, on so many levels. *Never going to happen, mate. Stop kidding
yourself.* A friend, she'd said. Nothing more. That would have to
be enough.

He'd been okay for a long time in this cottage, insulated from
the world outside—comfortably numb, as a well-known song
suggested—but it was no longer the sanctuary it had once been.
In fact, he was starting to find it a little claustrophobic.

Lewis was still howling outside, and as Brody listened to the
sound, it seemed to reverberate inside his chest, building up to a
sense of longing that was almost unbearable. He lifted his phone
out of his back pocket and stared at the picture of Anna once
again. The ache intensified. It was a knife in his chest, and someone was twisting it.

You might as well go outside and cry for the moon with the dog, he
told himself. *It'll do you just as much good.*

IF IT HAD been Gabi who'd been speaking to Brody, she would
have Googled him the moment she was in possession of a sur-
name, but Anna lasted six days before she cracked and decided
to type Brody's name into the search box on Facebook. She did

it early one morning when there was no chance of him ringing her. Because that would be awkward.

Not that they'd agreed *not* to do this. They hadn't even discussed it with each other. *He's probably looked you up already*, she told herself flatly. *Nothing to get all silly about.*

But . . .

Stuff it. Her fingers moved quickly on her laptop keyboard, and she pressed "enter" before she could talk herself out of it.

The results were much more plentiful than she'd anticipated. Crap. While Brody wasn't a terribly common name, Smith was. Obviously. Well, the only thing to do was to go through the list. She knew a bit of information that would help her narrow it down: his location (Devon) and his age (older than her but not geriatric), and so she began to trail through them.

There was a Brody Smith who was a researcher at Stanford.

A travel writer based in New Zealand who spent six months of the year sailing around the South Pacific on his boat.

An up-and-coming sixteen-year-old actor, who already had a legion of besotted teenage girls following his every move on social media.

Anna looked through them all but nothing matched. Her curiosity had been fanned fully into flame at that point, so she switched to Google. It was much the same story there. So many Brody Smiths! And that didn't even include the ones who also had middle names. There was a Brody Michael Smith, a Brody Alexander Smith, even a Brody Zephaniah Smith.

She clicked on Brody Zephaniah Smith, just because it was an unusual name, and discovered he'd been a fire-and-brimstone preacher from the 1920s, now sadly deceased. After that, she decided to switch to a search page of images for the same name rather than text because then she could filter out the sepia and black-and-white photos that were part of people's family history records, or Brodys who were too old or too young to match the one she was searching for.

She looked at the top row of results and clicked on the first color thumbnail she saw, but it turned out to be a website for a children's author called Brody Alexander (no Smith attached at the end—Google must have glitched). Had she heard of him? She clicked on "About" on the author's website and had a read. Nope. He lived in London and he was married.

Before she closed the page down, she glanced at the black-and-white photo beside the biography. Not bad. Dark hair. A bit rougher around the edges than you'd expect a children's author to look. Younger than she was looking for, possibly the same as her, early thirties, so that was all wrong too. He was looking into the camera and not exactly smiling, but there was a hint of it in his eyes. Anna looked more closely. There was something there, something that made her stomach flip a little. Could it be . . . ?

She studied the photograph for a good ten seconds, all the while feeling slightly breathless, but then she clicked the X at the corner of the web page to make it disappear.

No. It wasn't right. His expression had been too . . . youthful, too fresh and unsullied by the darkness that life could bring. It wasn't him. It wasn't her Brody.

Because her Brody had a secret.

She was more certain of it every time they spoke. It was something to do with his wife, she was sure, something about his grief and loss. She'd tried probing a few times, but as she'd already discovered, he was very adept at conversational sleight of hand. She supposed she could try harder, but when it came down to it, she discovered she didn't want to. If it was too painful to talk about, she should let him be. If anyone understood that, it was her.

Anna sighed and flapped her laptop closed. She was just going to have to be patient with him the way he'd been patient with her. And in the meantime, she'd just have to do her best not to be eaten alive by her own curiosity.

Chapter Thirty-Four

*W*hat about this one?" Gabi emerged from the changing room and twirled around, grinning. Anna could hardly see her for a cloud of white tulle and taffeta.

"It's lovely!" she said.

Just like the last three wedding dresses Gabi had tried on. Anna was still a little fuzzy about how they'd ended up in a bridal boutique. They were supposed to be finding Anna a dress for Teresa's party next Saturday. All she remembered was Gabi muttering something about this shop also doing evening wear, and before Anna had known it, they'd been inside the door, and when the sales assistant had assumed they were there to try bridal gowns on, Gabi hadn't corrected her. Instead she'd shushed Anna, who'd been about to explain, smiled widely at the woman, then reached out and grabbed something off the rack.

Anna hadn't minded at first; she'd been going with the flow, but she'd been sitting on this padded bench for almost half an hour now. "Gabs?"

"Yes?" Gabi said, twisting this way then that as she studied herself in a full-length mirror.

"Is there something you're not telling me?"

"Such as?" Gabi rearranged her breasts to get just the right amount of cleavage in the scooping neckline.

"Gabriela!"

Gabi stopped what she was doing and spun round to face Anna. The dress continued to rustle and move for a few seconds afterward.

"Has Lee . . . ? You know . . . ?"

"Proposed? You know I would tell you first if he had!"

"I was starting to wonder whether all of this"—Anna waved her hand to encompass the luxurious fitting room—"Was leading up to something."

Gabi swished her way over to Anna and sat down beside her on the upholstered bench. "No, he hasn't proposed." Normally, Anna would have expected Gabi to deliver news like that with big, sad, puppy-dog eyes, but it looked very much as if she were biting back a smile. "But I think he might!" she added, bouncing up and down slightly.

Anna studied her friend's face. "Really?"

"He texted me last night to say he wants to talk about our relationship—that there is something big he wants to ask me."

"Something big?" Anna said. "He used those precise words?"

Gabi scrunched her nose up. "Let me think . . . He said . . . I don't remember what he said *exactly*. But it has to be something big, don't you think, if he is taking me out to dinner in a really nice restaurant? It has to be more than if I want pizza or Indian next time we get takeaway!"

"Well, yes. It sounds as if it's something more than that, but it could be anything, Gabi. I know you really like him, and you'd really like to settle down, but don't you think you're getting ahead of yourself?"

Gabi looked hurt. "You don't think he'd *want* to propose to me?"

"Oh, Gabi!" Anna pulled her into a large, rustling hug. "*Of course* I think he should want to propose to you! He'd be lucky to have you." Really lucky. "But do you think you're ready? It's still quite soon to be thinking about marriage."

And, she didn't want to add this, she wasn't one hundred percent sure Lee was ready either. Not that he didn't look very invested in Gabi whenever Anna saw them together. It was just a feeling she'd had for a while, fueled by something that had happened at salsa the other week when Gabi had an evening shoot, and hadn't been able to go.

Anna had left the hall just as the social dance part of the evening had started, heading for the ladies' room, when she'd spotted Lee and the girl with the swooshy ponytail together in a corner of the winding corridor. They'd been standing a respectable distance apart, hadn't even been touching, but something about it had made Anna feel uneasy.

She pulled back and made eye contact with her best friend. "This is big, Gabi. *Huge.* We're talking about the rest of your life."

Or his, Anna added silently, unable to stop thinking about her own marriage.

"Didn't you once tell me that you knew you were going to marry Spencer after your third date?"

Ah. There was that. Past Anna had kind of sabotaged Present Anna's very sensible point, hadn't she?

"Is it that you don't think Lee and I are good together?" Gabi asked, brows pinched together.

"No, it's not that . . ." And it really wasn't. "I just don't want you to jump in with both feet and get hurt."

"You did—with Spencer."

"I know," Anna said, her heart sinking like a lead weight. She returned Gabi's anxious gaze. "And look how that turned out."

"But not because he didn't love you enough."

"No," Anna conceded. "Not because of that. But it didn't make it any less painful when it all came to an abrupt end." She paused, finding her throat too tight to continue for a moment. "I just don't want you to have to go through anything even vaguely resembling that."

Gabi kind of wilted at that point and all the fight leeched out of her. She pulled Anna in for a one-armed hug and kissed the side of her head. "I get it now. Thank you. But . . ."

Anna gave her a squeeze and pulled away to look at her. "But . . . ?"

Gabi's expression became determined. "But you can't go through life avoiding love on the off-chance that it all goes horribly wrong at some point."

Can't you? Anna thought. In that moment, it seemed a terrifically good idea. Could she even do it all again? Now she'd paid that price once, she knew just how high and devastating the stakes were, and Anna had never been much of a gambler.

But if she really thought that, what was she doing even dating Jeremy, knowing he was looking for something serious ultimately? There had been one more oh-so-casual dinner last Saturday night and tonight they were due to go out for their third. She'd thought she'd been ready to at least start down that path, but it seemed her true feelings about long-term relationships—the feelings she'd just splurged all over her best friend—were contradicting her.

She rubbed her forehead. The whole subject was starting to give her a headache.

Anna's phone buzzed at that moment, and since Gabi had caught sight of herself in one of the mirrors again and was momentarily distracted by her own loveliness, Anna pulled it out of her pocket. She smiled and tapped on the photograph that had arrived in her messages inbox to enlarge it. It was a picture of Lewis, dripping wet and caked in what looked like peaty, black mud.

Every time she got a message from Brody now, it lifted her. What if she *could* find a way to help other people find their own Brody? She'd been chewing the idea over in her head for the last couple of weeks, ever since she'd had that conversation with her mother, but she hadn't contacted Spencer's former partners, Rhys and Vijay, yet, wanting to have something more concrete than a one-line idea. How would you get people to sign up? How could you protect their privacy and identities? What happened if someone tried to use the app to take advantage of people when they were at their most vulnerable? These were all things she needed to think about, and that wasn't even including whether the technology would fall into place.

"Come on," Gabi said, interrupting Anna's thoughts by grabbing her hand and pulling her to her feet. "Stop mooning over texts from Jeremy and help me out of this thing. You're right— I'm getting ahead of myself. I should probably be looking for something sexy to wear to dinner. I blame my mother. Now I've turned thirty, she's lamenting my status as *solteirona*—a spinster, I suppose, is the closest translation. All of my sisters are married, so I'm the only one left to focus on." She gave Anna a meaningful look. "Let's just say sometimes I'm glad she's five thousand miles away . . . Shall we try the boutique across the street next? I saw a blue dress in the window that would look fabulous on you!"

Anna unlaced the bodice of Gabi's dress, then watched her head back to the dressing room. As she waited for Gabi to reappear in her normal clothes, she wondered why she hadn't corrected her about the sender of the text. She still hadn't told Gabi about Brody. She'd been meaning to, but she'd gradually come to the realization that she didn't want to. It kept that connection private. Intimate.

When they entered the shop across the road, Gabi headed straight to a rack, picked up a cocktail dress, and handed it to Anna, saying, "This is the one!" before picking out a shorter dress in canary yellow for herself.

Before she could argue, Gabi tugged her arm and led her in the direction of the fitting rooms. When they both emerged from their respective cubicles, she smiled at Gabi. "That looks amazing on you!"

"And so does yours! Look . . ." Gabi turned Anna around to gaze in the full-length mirror.

Oh.

Anna stared hard at her reflection. Layers of midnight blue chiffon wrapped around to form a bodice, and then floated to just above the knee. Vertical rows of sequins glinted discreetly from the tiny pleats of the fabric, adding an almost imperceptible shimmer. She didn't quite look like herself. She looked otherworldly, willowy. Like she'd just stepped out of a storybook. How did a dress do that? Maybe it really was worth the eyewatering price tag.

Gabi beamed, pleased with herself. "You said you needed something nice for Teresa's party."

"It's not just nice. It's spectacular! I just don't know about the—"

"Don't think about that. Some things are worth more than money." She grinned cheekily. "Aren't you glad I didn't make you get one from the last shop?"

Anna chuckled. "Definitely. I don't think turning up in a wedding dress would endear me any further to my mother-in-law."

"Hmm. You have a point there."

"I know that Spencer would have hated the idea that there was a rift, but I just can't face her at the moment, Gabs. I just can't." She turned and fiddled with the zip at the back of the dress. She wanted it off now. Somehow, it didn't feel so fairy-tale-ish anymore. "What did I do? What did I do to make her change like that?"

"It's not you, honestly. It's her . . ."

"That's what Teresa says."

"See? We're all on your side."

Anna squeezed her friend and then returned to the fitting room. While she was changing, her phone buzzed in her handbag.

"That man is besotted with you!" Gabi said, as Anna pulled the curtain back and checked her phone. Gabi must have got a glimpse of the screen before Anna had turned round because she said, "Jeremy sent you a picture? Is it . . . *naughty*?"

"No!" Anna exclaimed, reminding herself of a rather prudish fourteen-year-old. Which, unfortunately, might not be far off base. She still didn't feel inclined to do anything more than kiss him at the end of their date tonight.

Just to prove to herself that she wasn't a completely spine-less creature, she picked up the hanger with the blue dress on and took it to the cash register. Behind her, Gabi let out a little whoop. Anna put her phone down on the counter to get her credit card out of her purse. Gabi tried to snatch it up to get a better look, but Anna was too fast for her.

"I didn't know Jeremy had a dog!" Gabi exclaimed as Anna pressed the button to send her phone to sleep, hiding the picture message before she could read more. "Or one that was so . . . scruffy? Is that a word?"

Anna nodded. "It's a word."

In fact, it was a very good word for Lewis in that picture. Brody had sent one of his dog in an old-fashioned claw-foot tub. Lewis was covered in bubbles; obviously the next chapter in the story that had begun with a dip in the bog. "It isn't Jeremy's dog," Anna said, turning away to receive her receipt from the sales assistant.

"Who does it belong to?"

So much for keeping her friendship with Brody private and intimate. Gabi would want to know everything now. Anna tucked her phone back into her bag and removed her credit card from the reader. "He belongs to a friend of mine—Brody."

Gabi frowned. "Brody? Do I know him?"

Anna shook her head. "No."

"The text you got in the wedding shop. That was also from Brody?"

"Yes," Anna said as they exited the boutique.

"I never heard you mention anyone with that name before. Who is he? Why does he send you photographs of his dog?"

"He's just someone I met . . . We talk. That's all."

"One of Spencer's friends?"

"While he wasn't a friend of Spencer's, I suppose you could

say I met him *through* Spencer." She was taking the coward's way out of this conversation, she knew. She'd tell Gabi soon, but on her own terms, when she was ready for the full interrogation.

They started walking back down the High Street. Anna noticed Gabi wasn't looking very happy. While one of her best traits was her fierce loyalty, it did sometimes mean she could get a little territorial about her friends.

"I'm doing what you want me to do," Anna said. "I'm finding new things in my life—new experiences, new friends. I'm trying to move on. Be happy for me."

"I know," Gabi said, and her expression lost some of its hardness. "I am very proud of you."

"Good," Anna said, linking her arm in Gabi's and turning her back in the direction they'd just come from. "Because I haven't maxed out my card completely yet, so we're going to go and get you that killer yellow dress. Teresa said I could bring a plus-one, and we might as well walk in looking spectacular together!"

Chapter Thirty-Five

Anna stepped from the passenger seat of the car and stared up at the imposing facade of the Warlingham Court Hotel. She was very glad she hadn't come alone.

"Nervous?"

She turned to face her "plus-one," who was not wearing a canary-yellow, figure-hugging dress but a well-cut suit and a shirt. A last-minute substitution. "A little," she admitted to Jeremy. "I'm glad you're here."

The yellow dress was currently five miles away in a smart modern-European restaurant. Gabi and Lee were finally having their "talk" tonight. Lee had postponed two other dates already and Gabi was stressed out to the max, desperate to hear what he had to say. When she'd told Anna about the clash of dates and had said she'd put Lee off, Anna had shaken her head. She couldn't put her friend through any more waiting.

However, until that point she hadn't realized how much she'd been relying on the idea of having Gabi beside her as moral support when she saw Gayle this evening. And she didn't want to rope Scott and Teresa in and make them choose sides, so she'd been planning to duck out. However, when she'd mentioned to Jeremy at salsa that she might be free on Saturday after all, and told him the reason, he'd volunteered to come with her instead. Anna had phoned Teresa to make sure this was okay, and Teresa had been, well, strangely excited about the whole idea, so that had been that, and now here they were.

Jeremy smiled at her as he locked the car and offered her his arm, but she shook her head. They'd decided they wouldn't be too touchy-feely this evening. There was no point in adding fuel to the fire; Teresa deserved a fabulous party, not another traumatic chapter in their ongoing family saga.

They walked up to the hotel and entered the lobby, where they found a sign directing them to the relevant function room. The bass of the DJ's throwback nineties playlist could be heard as they turned the corner to where the double doors were open. Scott and Teresa were standing there, smiling and greeting their guests as they arrived.

Teresa grinned widely as she saw Anna and held her arms open. "Glad you could make it," Teresa said, as she kissed Anna on the cheek, then whispered in her ear, "Is this *him*? Salsa guy? Not bad!"

Anna smiled weakly. "Are you sure this is okay? I don't want to make things difficult between you and Gayle."

Teresa waved Anna's concerns away with a sweep of her hand. "This is *my* party," she said, lowering her voice, "not Gayle's, and I say you can bring whomever you'd like. It's been three and a half years, Anna. You're allowed to move on."

Anna nodded, and inside her head, the familiar litany rang: *Three years, six months, nine days* . . . But Teresa was right. Maybe if she and Gayle could coexist this evening, if her mother-in-law could see that it was okay for her—for all of them—not to stay so firmly anchored in the past, then they'd all be happier. Maybe this night could be a turning point, not the disaster Anna had been dreading. "Is she here?"

"Not yet. I'm expecting her around eight-thirty."

"And Little Spencer?"

Teresa nodded toward the function room. "My niece has got him at the moment—he's asleep in his pram, out like a light, but we'll see how long that lasts!"

Anna laughed and wished Teresa luck, then she greeted Scott and introduced Jeremy. As they turned to go through the double doors and into the party itself, Anna felt her stomach flutter.

"What does she look like?" Jeremy said in a low voice as they turned left inside the entrance and headed for the bar area. Anna regretted the "no touching" rule at that moment, because she could have hugged him for reading her so well.

"Tall, early sixties, but looking good for her age. Blond, with one of those blow-dried, swept-back styles that's held together with half a can of hairspray."

"A bit Margaret Thatcher–ish, then?" Jeremy said with more than a glimmer of mischief in his eye. Anna smiled. This man had a talent for making her do that.

"And twice as scary," she replied in a low whisper, "but it's more of a bob than the full-on eighties Maggie crash helmet."

Jeremy nodded. "Got it."

They headed for the bar. "Are you going to confront her this evening?" Jeremy asked, once they had drinks in hand and were making their way to a table. Anna turned and looked at him in horror. "Well, it seems as if you need to have it out with her at some point."

"No, I don't think so. Not yet."

Not because she was scared to, but because Brody's advice still rang true in her ears. "I don't want to give her the satisfaction. I think the best thing I can do is just live my life, do what I think is right. I don't need her permission to do that."

Jeremy nodded toward the dance floor. "Does this life you're going to live include dancing? The kind where we stay two feet away from each other at all times, of course."

"Maybe," she replied, smiling. "In a bit."

As promised, they kept their tour round the dance floor purely platonic, smiling at each other every now and then, but mostly just enjoying moving to the music. *The salsa lessons must have helped*, Anna thought, *because she didn't feel as self-conscious as she used to at events like this.*

They were halfway through dancing to their third song when Anna felt a sudden change in the atmosphere. She looked around, but beyond the dance floor, the rest of the room fell away into shadows. The people sitting around the banquet tables drinking and chatting were little more than dark blurs. A thought dropped into her mind like a pebble hitting a pool of water: someone was watching her. The next realization followed on like a ripple.

Gayle had arrived. The hairs on the back of Anna's neck lifted and she shivered.

Cold? Jeremy mouthed to her.

She shook her head. *Do you mind if we go and sit down for a bit?* she mouthed back, with hand gestures for extra clarity.

He looked slightly perplexed, but he followed her lead as she headed away from the dance floor. Thankfully, in the opposite direction from where she'd felt that . . . presence. It was like being trapped in a bad horror movie.

She tried to chat as much as the music would allow and, when Jeremy went to get a second round of drinks, Anna decided to escape the function room on the pretense of going to the ladies' room. She was halfway down the plush, carpeted corridor before a steely voice rang out behind her.

"How dare you!"

Anna spun around to find Gayle marching up behind her, fire in her eyes.

"How dare you bring that man here! Are you trying to hurt us, to hurt me? Because well done, you've done a marvelous job!"

"Teresa said I could bring a plus-one," Anna said, trying to keep the wobble out of her voice.

"Even if she did, you should have known better! You should have brought someone else—that loud friend of yours. She would have been fine!"

"Her name is Gabriela," Anna said stonily.

"You shouldn't have brought him to our *family* party," Gayle said, and Anna couldn't help noticing a tiny bead of bubbly saliva at the corner of her lips. Good grief. She was actually foaming at the mouth.

A girl in a short silver dress and high heels tottered past on her way to the loos. Anna had to step to the side to make room for her, which gave her some much-needed distance from Gayle.

She looked at her mother-in-law's face. Although, as she'd said to Jeremy, Gayle really did look good for her age, up close Anna could see the fine lines on her skin more clearly, the wrinkles and puffs beneath her eyes, their purple tone cleverly hidden with a good concealer. Gayle looked old, she realized. And not nearly as invincible as she made herself out to be.

"Not everything is about Spencer," Anna said, not aiming to injure but to explain.

Gayle stared at her as if she'd lost her mind. "Of course it is! Because he should be here tonight, like he should be at every family gathering! How could you ever forget that?"

"I *know* he should be here," Anna said, with a softness in her tone she didn't have to fake. This was the one core thing that, deep down, connected her and Gayle. If only they could get back to that place where it meant love and support and togetherness, not competition and accusations. "Do you think I don't wish it was different? I'd much rather Spencer was here."

She felt the truth of that statement like a stab to the chest. If she could pick between the two men—no matter how nice and supportive and good-looking Jeremy was—of course she'd choose Spencer. She would always choose Spencer. Something shifted inside her at the thought.

"Spencer was the love of my life," she said and saw an unexpected warmth flood her mother-in-law's eyes. Maybe there was hope after all? "And nothing will ever change that. But what happened has happened. He's dead, Gayle, no matter how much we wish he weren't. And we've got to find a way to live without him, to move forward."

Anna saw the moment the soft patch in Gayle's armor hardened and turned back to steel. It was just as she'd said the word "dead." She'd been too blunt.

"And you call that 'moving forward'?" Gayle said, her volume rising with every word as she flung an arm in the direction of the function room. "Flaunting yourself with him? You're just throwing it in our faces!"

"I was only dancing," Anna replied, more than a little exasperated. "There was nothing inappropriate going on."

Gayle's face betrayed just what she thought about that.

Anna stared at Gayle, begging her to understand. "Aren't I allowed to be happy?" she asked. Her voice cracked and her eyes filled as she said it, taking her by surprise. She really did want that now, she realized. She wanted it so badly.

Gayle pressed her lips together. Anna knew she had no sensible answer to that, because if she said "yes" Anna had won, and if she said "no" Anna had also won because Gayle would prove herself to be a cold-hearted bitch after all. Instead, master of keeping others in their place, Gayle changed tack and found a more suitable offense. "You're being disloyal," she said flatly.

"To whom?"

Even though she knew exactly where Gayle was going with this, the accusation hit Anna harder than she expected it to. "To Spencer." Gayle must have seen the pain in Anna's eyes because she took the opportunity to dig the knife in a little deeper. "And to the family. You know how much my son cared about his family . . ."

Anna almost laughed. "What? The family that you've been doing your level best to push me out of for the last year? *That* family? Do you think I'm so stupid that I can't tell you don't like me, Gayle? That I don't know you can't stand having me around?" Anna really did laugh then. It was a horrible, tight little noise that got stuck in her throat. "What I don't understand is, if you'd rather I disappeared from your life, why the hell do you care what I do, or who I do it with?"

Gayle's eyes had started to blaze while Anna had been talking and now, like a dragon exhaling flames, she scorched Anna with her fury.

"Because it should have been you!" she screamed at the top

of her lungs, so loud that the sound bounced off the walls and ceiling of the narrow corridor and echoed back to Anna. "It should have been you that went out that night to go to the corner shop! And because of you, because of your laziness, my son is dead!"

Chapter Thirty-Six

Anna sat in bed, her back against the padded headboard, her knees pulled up toward her chest, the duvet tucked under her arms. She'd turned the lights off but had left the shutters open, and the bedroom was illuminated by the glow of the streetlamp across the road.

Thank goodness that girl with the silver dress had emerged from the ladies' toilets immediately after Gayle had dropped her bombshell. Gayle had frozen the moment the words had come out of her mouth, and she'd looked horrified, as had the girl in the silver dress, who'd obviously overheard the entire exchange. Anna had just turned and walked away. She'd gone to find Jeremy, and they'd said a hasty goodbye to Teresa and Scott before leaving.

Anna hugged her knees. She needed to talk. To Brody.

She'd been silent the whole journey home in Jeremy's car, so much so that he'd got worried and had pulled over and had begged her to talk to him. She'd just shaken her head. Her lips had seemed glued shut.

It wouldn't have been a good idea, anyway. She'd been afraid that once the floodgates were open, she'd lose control completely. She didn't want to do that in front of him.

But Brody . . . Brody had already experienced all of that from her. And more. He could take it. And she had no doubt that there wasn't anything she could say or do that would mess things up between them.

She'd ended up leaning over and kissing Jeremy on the cheek, whispering a soft "sorry" before she'd climbed from the car, and now she was sitting in bed, her thumb hovering over her phone screen.

Just as she was about to dial Brody's number, her mobile rang, startling her so much she dropped it onto the duvet and had to scrabble around to pick it up again before her voicemail kicked in. This mind reading was happening more and more when she and Brody spoke; either she'd just be about to call him and her phone would ring, or she'd dial his number and he'd say he'd been about to do the same.

"Hi," she said on an exhale of air that betrayed her relief at hearing his voice.

"Hi," he said back.

Anna hugged the duvet harder. "Do you ever think . . ." She paused, willing herself to go on. After what had been said tonight, she really needed to know the answer to this question. "Do you ever think it should have been you, not them? That you should have been the one who died instead?"

Brody took a few seconds before he answered, and when he did his voice was hoarse. "Yeah . . . A lot."

Anna nodded to herself. She'd known he'd get it. "I used to think that way *all* the time. Until tonight, I didn't realize that I hadn't so much recently."

There was silence again, but this time it was thick. Tense. "What happened at the party this evening, Anna? I haven't heard you talk like this for months." He sounded concerned, maybe even a little scared.

Anna let her phone drop to the duvet and buried her head in her hands. "*She* said it to me—Gayle. Those exact words: that it should have been me." Anna went on to tell him the whole story, finishing with, "And the look in her eyes . . . I know she meant it, Brody, I really do."

Brody swore softly.

"And the weirdest thing is that I'm not even sure I can hate her for it. Because she only said what I've thought a million times myself. For ages, maybe even years, I wished it *had* been me. I longed for it, bargained with God for it, but He didn't take the deal. Is that terrible?" she asked a little desperately. "That I wanted to die? It seems so selfish, so ungrateful . . ."

Brody's voice was thick. "I think, given the circumstances, feeling like that is entirely understandable. In fact, I'd say far more people feel that way than ever let on. I certainly did. If I could have made that trade, I would have done it in a heartbeat."

Anna sobbed with relief, and Brody gave her time, listening patiently as she rode the storm, only speaking again when all that was left were a few waves rustling against the shore.

"You said 'wished,' Anna. Past tense. Not 'wish.' That's good . . . It means you don't feel that way anymore."

Anna lifted her head from her hands. Had she said "wished"? She hadn't even paid attention. She sniffed. "You're right. Most days I don't. Do . . . do you?"

Brody pondered that for a moment. "Not most days," he said, with just a sliver of surprise in his tone. "Not anymore."

They fell silent, but it wasn't like the silence at the end of the line when Anna had first phoned Spencer's number after he died, vacant and cold. It was warm and comforting. It breathed.

"Thank you, Brody." Anna lay back on the pillow, suddenly

exhausted. "Can we do that thing again, where we don't hang up straightaway? While I don't like saying 'goodbye,' I like saying 'good night.' It's nice to think of you here beside me."

There was a strange tone in Brody's voice when he replied. "Sure," he said. "I'd like that too."

Chapter Thirty-Seven

*B*rody woke up feeling unusually energized. For the first time in ages, he'd slept through the night without tossing and turning or spending at least a couple of hours staring at the ceiling in the wee hours in the morning. Maybe it had something to do with the phone on the bedside table next to him. He'd drifted off listening to Anna's soft breathing as she slept.

He practically sprang out of bed, startling Lewis, with the idea of going on an extra-long run, but as he began to get dressed, he realized it wasn't a run he needed; it was something else.

This strange buzzing feeling needed to be let out, but he knew instinctively that a run wouldn't help. It would still be there when he returned, muscles aching, damp with sweat. And he definitely needed to do something to expel this feeling. Not because it was bad, but because that's what you were supposed to do with it.

So that was why, after a strong coffee and a steaming bowl of porridge, he found himself at his desk. His heart was pounding as it always did when he sat there these days, but something was different about that too. It wasn't fear alone that was making his pulse race; there was something else in the mix.

Instead of reaching for pen and paper, he opened a drawer and pulled out his laptop. Initially, he'd abandoned this method of capturing words because it had been too hard, returning to pen and paper, which somehow helped his imagination flow better, but after a while, even that had become stagnant. Holding his breath slightly, he clicked on an icon and opened up his preferred writing software.

New project. New document. New everything. He stared at the blank rectangle on the screen in front of him, waiting for letters and words, sentences and paragraphs. But that white space was no longer an impenetrable fog, because as he waited, it began to clear. He could make out a figure, a child, standing with her hands on her hips and her chin lifted in defiance.

He closed his eyes to shut out the picture, shifted in his seat, readying himself to stand, but as he planted his feet on the floor and twisted to do just that, something in the corner of his eye caught his attention. The elf. Or the "not elf," as he'd begun to think of her. She wasn't looking his way, just staring past him into the distance, but it was as if she'd whispered something to him. Brody sat back down, placed his hands on the keyboard, and his fingers began to move.

Thirty minutes later he was halfway through what might turn into a short story, maybe even a novella. It was rough. No planning had gone into it—he'd just written what he'd seen inside his head, whatever had come out of the fog. It started with the Not Elf sitting in a woodland glade, the sunlight warm about her shoulders, the grass cool and full of daisies. He'd described her in detail, then how she'd woken up from a deep and dreamless sleep. Without a kiss. Without a prince or anyone else to save her, just because she was ready.

He paused, fingers frozen above the keyboard, as the next set of images began to form. He continued to type, describing how she stretched, her muscles stiff and unfamiliar after so long, how she wobbled to her feet like a newborn foal. But as she'd raised herself to full height, something had happened. Strength came, filling her with purpose. She turned and looked at a dark and difficult path that led between the trees. She was about to go somewhere. She was about to leave her sleepy woodland glade.

Brody took his hands from the keyboard and pushed himself back from the desk. The sentence he'd been writing was only half-completed, but he found he didn't want to scoot the chair forward again to finish it. He didn't want to know where this woman who wasn't an elf was going to go.

He spun his chair around and stood up. Time to take a tea break. There was no point pushing himself so hard he just locked up again. Besides, it was always good to leave a chapter or a scene half-done. That way he wasn't starting from nothing the next time he sat down to write. It had been a technique he'd used many a time when this had been his career. Nothing wrong with that. Tomorrow, he could just pick up the threads and carry on.

He made it look casual, even to himself, but he took great care not to make eye contact with the little wooden woman on the other side of the room as he turned and left the study.

Chapter Thirty-Eight

*S*orry, but the person you've called isn't available at the moment . . ."

Anna tapped at her phone screen to end the call. That was the sixth time she'd gone straight through to Gabi's voicemail since getting home from work. It was most frustrating. Did Gabi have a job Anna didn't know about? It wasn't unusual for her to get last-minute bookings, but she wasn't usually incommunicado for forty-eight hours. Anna hadn't talked to her since just before her "big night" with Lee on Saturday, and now it was Monday evening. She was starting to get worried.

Unlike Gabi, Anna hadn't been hopeful that Lee was about to propose, but that didn't mean it was all doom and gloom either. He might have wanted to ask her to go on a fantastic holiday, or move in with him, but as time crept on, Anna was beginning to think this was less and less probable.

Or maybe she was just being paranoid? Lee and Gabi could be snuggled up somewhere in a newly engaged bubble of love, having forgotten the rest of the world existed. She put her phone down on the sofa cushion and stood up, thinking it was about time she started the jambalaya she intended to cook for herself that night.

However, she was only two steps away when her phone rang, and she stopped and twisted to check the caller ID. Gabi! She dived for her phone and brought it up to her ear. "Hey there!" she said a little breathlessly. "What's the news?"

The only reply she got was a sniff. Was Gabi actually crying with joy? It was possible. Gabi was definitely a crier when anything seriously good or seriously bad happened. Spencer had teased her about it mercilessly.

Anna gave her a few moments to collect herself, but when she heard another sniff, she frowned. "Gabi?"

"A-Anna . . ."

Anna went cold. Those were no tears of joy. Gabi sobbed, and it made Anna's chest ache. She almost started crying too. "What is it? What happened? Is everyone okay?"

"No, everybody is not okay!" Gabi said, and Anna was slightly relieved to hear anger slicing through the sadness. "Lee *did* want to talk about our relationship, but not to get more serious. The bastard said he wants to see other people!"

"Where are you?" Anna said, looking for her shoes. If Gabi needed her, she was going to be there for her.

There was another sniff. "I'm standing on your front porch."

Anna ran into her hallway, threw her front door open and enveloped Gabi in a hug. Gabi began to cry noisily. Still holding on to her, Anna led her into the house, kicking the door shut with her foot, then guided her to sit down on one of the chairs around her kitchen table.

"What happened?" Anna asked when the crying subsided. She left one arm over Gabi's shoulder and studied her friend's face as she tried to hold back a fresh round of tears. Oh, how her heart ached for Gabi. She knew just how it felt to have all your hopes and dreams for the future snatched away from you and trampled into the dirt.

"I'm making you hot chocolate," she told Gabi as she reached for a saucepan and dashed milk into it. "And when you're ready, I'm here to listen."

Gabi nodded, her hands clasped together in front of her. She said nothing for a few minutes, but then her eyes became fierce and determined. "It was all going so well," she began. "After all, he took me to Caprice—delicious French food, silly prices . . ."

"Bastard," Anna said emphatically, which made the corner of Gabi's mouth lift just a little. Anna meant it, though. Lee had known what he was going to say to Gabi. Saying it in pretty surroundings didn't make it any better. It smacked of guilt. And cowardice. Anna shook her head gently, more to herself than to Gabi. She'd had a feeling about the guy, hadn't she? She should have seen this coming. She should have been able to protect Gabi from this.

"We ate our meal and were going to share a tiramisu when he said we needed to talk about our relationship." Gabi pressed her lips together and shook her head, warding off more tears. "I put my spoon down and smiled. I tried not to get carried away, like you said, Anna, but I could not stop hoping he was going to pull a little box from his pocket. Then he reached out. He stroked my hand. And he said we should not let things get stagnant . . ."

Gabi carried on speaking, head down, directing her words toward the table. "I was so set on what I thought he was going to say, that nothing he said made sense to me. So I had this big, stupid grin on my face . . . And then, one by one, the words made sense. It was like he poured a bucket of ice water all over me."

Anna left the milk heating on the stove and sat down in the chair opposite Gabi. "And what exactly did he say?"

Gabi met her gaze. "He likes me, and that he thinks I'm great fun but . . ."

"But?"

Gabi's bottom lip quivered. "But apparently, I'm not enough fun on my own . . ."

"So he doesn't want to break up?" Anna asked, just to make sure she was understanding this right.

"No."

"But he wants to see other people as well as you?"

Gabi nodded, looking even more broken.

At that point the milk boiled, foaming over the edge of the saucepan and hitting the stainless-steel stove with a hiss. Anna jumped up, grabbed the pan, and took it off the heat. Then she looked at the mess. "Stuff it," she said, leaving the saucepan on the counter and heading in the direction of the living room. "Forget hot chocolate. There's only one drink for situations like this."

She returned with two glasses of Lagavulin and set one down in front of Gabi.

"Whisky?" Gabi said, frowning.

"You'll thank me later," Anna replied and dropped back into her chair. She and Gabi looked each other in the eye, raised their glasses, swallowed, then grimaced in unison.

Gabi coughed then said something in Portuguese that her mother probably wouldn't have approved of. She closed her eyes and placed a hand at the base of her throat, seemingly concentrating on something. When she opened her eyes again, she handed Anna her glass. "Another."

Anna went to fetch the bottle and placed it on the table between them. "So . . . What did you say to him?"

Gabi knocked back a second whisky and replaced her glass on the table with a satisfying thud. "I told him he could see as many girls as he wanted, but that I was not going to be one of them."

"Good for you! And then what did you do? Did anyone need stitches?"

Gabi shook her head, and then a tiny smile curled her lips, almost in spite of herself. "When I walked out the restaurant, he was *wearing* the tiramisu."

Anna laughed. She raised her glass and toasted Gabi's moxie.

Gabi's smile faded. She stared at her empty glass for a few seconds and then she slumped on the table, her long hair spilling over her arms, and started to cry. Anna got up, went around the table and crouched down beside her, hugging her and rubbing her back. "Do you want to stay here tonight?"

The rustling of the curls on the tabletop told Anna that Gabi was nodding. She started to cry even harder.

Anna kept crouching beside her, kept holding her. It was all she could do. And that made her heart break. If there were something she could do to stop it—invent a pill, perform a challenge set by the gods, step into Gabi's body and take it herself—she would. But she knew she couldn't. Just as Gabi hadn't been able to do it for her.

Anna led Gabi upstairs and showed her to the guest bedroom. She found toiletries and a fresh toothbrush and handed over a spare set of pajamas. Once Gabi was changed and ready, she climbed into bed and lay there on the freshly plumped pillows. She looked utterly exhausted, beyond thought, beyond speech.

Anna knew what this felt like: when you were so wrung out

from all the emotion that all you wanted to do was be by yourself and curl into a little ball. Hide under the duvet and pretend the outside world didn't exist.

Once again, she forgave Gabi for all the "meddling" over the last few years. Watching her best friend go through this for one night was bad enough; it must have been awful for Gabi to have to do it week on week, month on month, year on year. No wonder that sometimes she'd got a little pushy.

Chapter Thirty-Nine

*B*rody sat in his armchair and coughed. That dodgy spring was definitely on its last legs. He could feel it sticking into his left buttock. Terrific. He shifted position and placed a mug on the small table that stood between the chair and the fireplace. It was his usual dram of whisky, but this time he'd added hot water, lemon and a pinch of cinnamon. He'd woken up this morning feeling clammy and feverish, and now his nose had started to run. Even more terrific.

He picked up his phone, pressed a sequence of buttons and called Anna's number.

"Hi," she said, but he could hardly hear her.

"I think there's something wrong with the connection," he told her. "I'll hang up and try again."

"No! Don't do that!" There was some muffled noise, as if she was walking to another place in the house. He heard a door close, and then she continued. "There's nothing wrong with the line. I was just whispering."

"Oh, okay," he said, dropping his volume level and tone to match hers. "And why are we whispering?"

"I've got someone staying with me."

Brody's stomach dropped. He deliberately hadn't asked about this Jeremy guy, even though he was aware she'd been seeing him for a few weeks, but this was a new development.

"Sorry . . ." she added.

Not as sorry as he was.

"She just came out of her room and headed for the bathroom and took me by surprise. I thought she went to sleep hours ago."

"She?"

Anna sighed. "Gabriela. Poor thing. Her boyfriend dumped her a couple of days ago. Or, I suppose, technically, she dumped him, but only because he deserved it. I said she could stay at mine because she says all she does is cry all day when she's on her own." She sighed heavily. "At least when she's here she's only crying *half* the time . . ."

"How long is she staying?" Brody asked.

"I don't know."

"Are you okay with that?" Brody had never been big on having houseguests for an extended period, even back in the days when he'd had friends who'd wanted to stay with him.

"More than okay," Anna said firmly. "Gabi was there for me when Spencer died. She can stay as long as she likes, move in permanently if she really wants to."

Brody brightened at that idea. It'd make it more difficult for Jeremy to get a similar notion.

"She's a total mess," Anna said heavily. "She called in sick for work, which isn't great because she's a freelancer and she had to cancel a job, but she just couldn't face it, so what can you do? I even took Tuesday off as well, but I can't do that every day. So I'm just doing the things she did for me when I was a total mess: snuggling up with her on the sofa to watch comfort movies, buying her a bar of chocolate on the way home, or a copy of her favorite magazine, making her soup and—"

A sneeze caught him by surprise. "Sorry," he said when he'd

wiped his nose. "I hope I didn't deafen you with that one." He'd never been the sort to produce a discreet little snuffle if in public. His sneezes only came out at one volume: loud enough for most of Devon to hear them.

Instead of laughing at his joke, Anna said, "Sounds like you need someone to look after you too."

Would you like the job? The words almost came out of his mouth as fast and loud as the sneeze, but he managed to hold them back. What a stupid thing to ask.

Oh, but if only he could . . . The thought of Anna pottering around in his kitchen making soup or curling up beside him on the sofa while they watched a film together stole his breath away.

Not going to happen, mate. Stop dreaming. Cook your own soup.

"I'm okay," he finally said in answer to her question. "I'm old enough and ugly enough to take care of myself."

Anna made a thoughtful noise. "I think that's Gabi's problem," she mused. "She's in a mess because she misjudged her ex, but then she's beating herself up about being a mess, which makes her even more of a mess . . . It's a vicious cycle. What she really needs is to be kind to herself. But we both know how difficult that can be."

Brody grunted in acknowledgment.

"So, in the meantime, I'm going to step in and do it for her. We all need that, I've realized: to be kind to ourselves . . ." She drifted off for a moment. "For a long time, I wasn't at all. I think I actually hated myself. Although I'm not sure what for . . . Being alive when Spencer was dead, maybe? Who knows?"

Brody grunted again. He knew all about this too, the self-hatred, the guilt.

"Uh-oh," Anna suddenly said. He could hear her moving

again, and she lowered her voice. "Gabi's come back out of the bathroom. Oh, God. I can hear her crying," Anna said, no longer bothering to whisper. "I'd better go."

Brody nodded. This was how it always was with Anna and him. He'd feel that bond, that connection. It would feel all-encompassing, as if it was the only thing in the world, and then something would happen to bring him back down to reality with a bump, to remind him that he was only a tiny part of her life. "Until next time," he said gruffly.

"Yes," Anna replied, with a softness in her tone that tore his insides a little more raggedly, and then she was gone.

Chapter Forty

While she'd been talking to Brody, Anna had crept downstairs and into the living room, where she'd sat on the arm of the sofa. The light from the hall had allowed her to see just enough so she didn't bump into the furniture.

"Anna?"

Anna shot off the sofa, heart pounding, and found Gabi standing in the doorway to the living room, half-asleep and fully bedraggled. "You scared the life out of me!"

Gabi rubbed a hand across her eyes. "I heard you talking . . ."

"Sorry. I was on the phone. I was trying not to disturb you." She met Gabi in the doorway then led the way back up the stairs. Gabi followed mutely behind her, but as she stopped at the door to the guest bedroom she yawned and asked, "Who were you talking to?"

"Just . . . a friend."

"Not Jeremy?"

Anna shook her head. "No, not Jeremy."

"A friend?" Gabi said again with more than a dollop of disbelief in her tone. "No one talks that long on the phone anymore, not unless it's your significant other. Even we text each other more than we talk to each other."

"Well, I do. I talk on the phone to . . . people. Sometimes."

Gabi stared back at her. "Was it that guy . . . Brett?"

"Brody . . ."

"Tell me how you met him," Gabi asked, frowning. "You said 'through Spencer,' but *how* through Spencer?"

This was it, then. Anna had a choice to make; either she kept being evasive, fudging the issue, and risk hurting Gabi when she was already feeling so low, or . . .

"Okay," she said. "I'll tell you about him, but we might as well get comfy if we're going to do it." She gestured for Gabi to go inside the bedroom and they both climbed onto the bed, Gabi under the duvet, Anna on top of it, where she sat up against the pillows with her legs crossed.

She began her story with her exit from the party on New Year's Eve all those months ago and ended with the pictures and messages that pinged between his phone and hers on a regular basis now. Gabi listened to it all, without comment or interruption, which, in itself, should have been a warning signal.

Anna finished talking and glanced across at her best friend, who was propped up on pillows, her arms folded across her chest. She didn't look very happy. "Are you in love with this man?" Gabi asked.

"What? No!" Anna paused before she said more. "No," she said again, more calmly this time. "I'm not in love with him. He's just someone who understands."

Gabi gave Anna a look that said, *What am I? Chopped liver?*

Anna leaned over and hugged Gabi with one arm. "You know I appreciate everything you've done for me, and no one could ever replace you, it's just . . . He lost someone himself, that's all. He knows what it's like."

Gabi pulled away and made herself comfortable, turning onto her side to face Anna. "Who did he lose?"

"His wife." Gabi just looked at her and waited for more information to be forthcoming. Anna thought hard, trying to remember the detail of that conversation they'd had a while ago,
and it only highlighted the fact that Gabi had a point. Even
though Brody knew every intimate detail about Spencer's death
and its aftermath, Anna was still a little fuzzy on his history.
Something dramatic always seemed to be happening in her life
at the moment, and she realized she'd got sidetracked from her
mission to dig deeper into the mystery that was Brody. "We
don't talk about her much—everyone deals with grief in their
own way—but he has mentioned her. He told me they'd been
having problems before she . . ."

What was the phrase Brody had used? He hadn't said, "died."
Passed on? No. Left him? Not that either.

"What do you actually know about this man?"

"I know his name is Brody Smith, that he lives near Hexworthy on Dartmoor, and that he has a dog called Lewis."

Gabi's eyes widened. "Lewis?" she repeated slowly. "Like
Spencer's dog Lewis?"

"Yes."

"That's weird, isn't it?"

"Not really," Anna said. "It's just a coincidence."

"Really?" Gabi plucked her phone out of her dressing gown
pocket and pulled up Facebook. "Do you remember what is on
Spencer's page?" she said as she scrolled through the posts.

Of course Anna remembered what was on Spencer's page.
There were hundreds of posts from three years ago, outpourings
of support and sympathy, exclamations of shock and sadness at
the news. It had been comforting at the time to know that he'd

been so loved, so she'd kept his profile active, and had never quite got around to deleting it.

Gabi's eyes lit up. "Aha!" She turned the phone around and thrust it at Anna, a triumphant expression on her face. "Look!"

There was a picture of Spencer, arms tight around his beloved dog's neck. Both of them seemed to have been grinning at the camera. She remembered him scanning that picture in. The caption read: *Five years since we lost our Lewis. Miss you, mate.*

She looked back at Gabi. "What are you trying to say?"

"That this man may not be who he says he is. Remember all those episodes of *Catfish* we watched together?"

Anna nodded. Gabi had become obsessed with the show after a dodgy internet dating experience. She'd made Anna sit though hours watching the two presenters, Nev and Max, helping people uncover the true identities of their online loves. Hardly anyone had been who they'd said they were.

"Well? Have you done a reverse image search?"

"No . . ."

Gabi let out an exasperated sigh. "That is beginner stuff, Anna! Basics!"

"He's never sent me a picture," she explained.

Gabi buried her face in the duvet and let out a strangled sound.

"What's this all got to do with Spencer's dog, anyway?" Anna asked, sitting up a little straighter and folding her arms.

Gabi lifted her head and sighed. "This is what happens when you watch *Catfish* and you are in a happy relationship, Anna!" She tapped her temple with a finger. "You didn't pay attention, because you didn't think it would happen to you."

Anna blinked. Obviously not.

Gabi sat up too, all traces of sleepiness gone. "He could look you up, find your page, which leads into Spencer's page—which you made fully public, remember, so anyone could post? All he had to do was what I did, and he would find lots of little details to trick you."

Anna shook her head. "No. No way."

Gabi gave her a pitying look. "That's what every person on that show always thought."

Anna racked her brains. She didn't know how she was sure Brody was ~~okay, she just was. All~~ those hours they'd talked, the details they'd shared . . . She frowned. Well, okay, the details *she'd* shared, but still.

And then it struck her. "He didn't know my last name until recently! I'd wanted to tell him before that, but he wouldn't let me. He can't have looked me or Spencer up on Facebook without knowing that!"

Gabi pursed her lips. Despite Anna's protestations, she didn't look convinced in the slightest. "*May*-be," she said. "But I am sure there are ways, if someone knows what he's doing."

Anna stared across the room. "I know you're just looking out for me, but it's okay, really," she said. "A couple of weeks ago, I asked to meet up with him and he said no. He wouldn't have done that if he had dubious intentions, would he?"

"Oh, my God! You were going to meet him?"

"Yes," Anna said, getting irritated despite herself. Gabi was missing the point.

"Anna . . ." Gabi said, as if she was explaining something to someone who was very, very simple. "Seriously?"

Anna hung on to the one detail that was solid, that proved her case. "He said 'no.' But even so, I still would like to meet him. Someday."

Gabi searched her face. "You're really serious about this, aren't you?"

"Yes."

"Even though this means you . . . What did Spencer used to say? That you have 'lost the plot'?"

"Yes." That was what Spencer always used to say, and this was much more like the pre–Lee breakup Gabi. Anna almost hugged her, welcoming this version of her best friend back.

"Please tell me you've done some research of your own."

Anna colored. "A little."

"Hallelujah! What did you find out?"

"Not much. I couldn't find any social media accounts that matched what I know about him. Perhaps he doesn't have any?"

Gabi shook her head again and muttered something about newbie mistakes. "Red flag, Anna. Nev and Max would be ashamed of you!" She reached over to grab her phone off the bedside table. "What is his last name?"

"Smith."

"Smith?" she said, raising an eyebrow at Anna.

Anna looked over Gabi's shoulder as she searched Facebook, Twitter and Instagram. When she'd finished, she waved her phone at Anna. "This is suspicious. I don't like it, Anna. I don't like it. Everybody has some kind of online stuff these days, so it's weird that he does not. What is Brody Smith not telling you—if his name really is Brody Smith?"

Nothing, Anna wanted to say, and she was about to when she remembered the feeling that had been creeping up on her recently. Brody was holding something back. She knew that as clearly and certainly as she knew that he was a good, decent man, and not a scammer or a pervert.

"Just promise me—if you ever, ever think about meeting him, you'll find out more," Gabi said earnestly.

Anna swallowed. "Of course."

However, she thought as she eased herself off the bed and said good night to Gabi. It really was a moot point. She wasn't going to have to worry about the ethics of it, because, as much as she wanted to meet Brody, he obviously didn't want to meet her.

Chapter Forty-One

A couple of days later, Brody stood at the back door to Moji's shop, his arms full. He felt a quiver, a flash of something across his consciousness, and his stomach dropped. He closed his eyes and felt the solid reality of the cardboard box he was holding, the weight of its contents. He breathed in and out, then opened his eyelids.

Okay. He was going to do this. This was a concrete opportunity to put into practice the things he'd only been working on in private up until this point. He'd laid his foundation: exercise, nutrition, better sleep. He'd rehearsed the techniques Ibrahim had introduced him to. They'd both agreed the next step was to use them in a real-life situation, and waiting for the next pair of hikers to appear on his doorstep was not really an option.

They'd kept the toolbox of techniques simple. First was breathing. Second, counting. He'd practiced this lots recently, counting birds, trees, clouds. He'd even mentally prepared for being in the town, adding cars of a particular color or a certain breed of dogs to his list, anything to distract himself from the mounting physical sensations. The more attention he paid to them, the more he was likely to tip himself over the edge.

The third technique was one he found harder to do, but which Ibrahim had suggested keeping in reserve, a last resort, if you like. It involved stepping outside of himself, outside of his symptoms, and analyzing the panic as if it was an external thing, not something happening to him right then and there.

Moji's shop was a good a place as any to start, partly because it had been a challenging situation in the past, and partly because Moji's presence would help, but mostly because he'd been working all hours making wooden toys recently. Something was driving him, some lost creative urge.

Right. He balanced the box in one arm and reached out to knock on the glass. A couple of seconds later, Moji appeared. She beamed when she saw him, then unlocked the door and let him inside. He followed her through to the main area of the shop.

"Cuppa?" she said, waving an empty mug at him with a slogan across the front that read *Toy Shop Owners Do It for Fun.*

"Please."

Once tea was made, Moji set to work unpacking the box. She exclaimed and commented over every set of stacking rings and every pull-along dog (one of which looked remarkably like Lewis) or set of train tracks. However, when she got to the bottom of the box, she really started to gush. "Oh, wow! You made her for me!" she said, unraveling an elegant elfin figure from the roll of bubble wrap. "She's even prettier than the first!"

The new elf was indeed beautiful, even if Brody did say so himself. She had long limbs, pointed ears, and gently waving tresses. She clasped a longbow loosely, and there was a look of focus, of determination, on her finely featured face.

"What am I going to do now?" Moji said, laughing. "I don't want to sell this one either!"

Brody smiled, but as she reached into the box to fetch the last item, he grew serious again. Moji looked up at him, a smile on her lips and a question in her eyes. "You made me more than one?" She was still smiling as she started to unroll the protective layer of plastic bubbles.

"Oh!" Moji exclaimed again as she turned the little wooden figure over in her hands, inspecting it from every angle. "This one is different," she said, looking up at him.

Different, she certainly was, Brody thought. She was his Not Elf. He'd taken her down from the bookshelf in his study. While it had been nice to see her sitting there every evening, keeping him company, he thought it was probably better that he didn't get too attached to her.

"Are you sure—?" Moji began to say, but at that moment the shop door opened and the old-fashioned bell above it jangled.

Brody froze. The hairs on his arms and on the back of his neck lifted. Ice cubes tumbled into his stomach and swirled around there. He began to breathe—in for three, hold for three, out for three. It was an exercise he'd repeated multiple times a day over the last few weeks and, as he began to feel the oxygen reach his bloodstream, muscle memory took over and he realized he had space in his brain for more than just the processing of oxygen.

He looked over to the shop door, where a woman in a chunky sweater and jeans was standing. She didn't even make eye contact with him, just nodded at Moji and then began to browse in the books section.

He hadn't tumbled into a full-on panic attack yet, and if he didn't want to, he needed to find something to count . . .

But he couldn't find anything suitable in Moji's shop. It was crammed to the rafters with all sorts of different toys and objects, but he couldn't find a pattern in any of them. No terriers or red cars here. The woman moved closer, only six feet away now.

He couldn't get enough distance, not mentally, not physically. There was no room to pull back the lens from close-up into panorama and observe himself. Breath became harder to find. He started having that weird "everything's not real" feeling, a sign that he was teetering on the edge of that dreaded slippery slope.

No. He closed his eyes. No! He did not want this to happen. He did not want to fail his first time out. Not when he'd tried so hard. He searched his memory desperately for anything else, but the only other technique he could remember was visualization, and he'd been pretty sure that wasn't going to work for him.

He'd once had a special, secret place like the one Ibrahim had suggested inside his imagination, a place that had always made him feel at peace and alive, but it was gone now. Bulldozed. He tried to go back there with Ibrahim's help, but it had been worse than he'd remembered: barren trees and scorched earth. He'd still recognized some of the landmarks, though. He realized he could have persisted walking through that once gentle meadow with the copse at the end if he'd wanted to, but the air had been thick with fear because he'd known what lay at the end of the path he was treading.

The pond. He couldn't even think about the pond. So he'd run away from that place, locked the gate on it in his imagination. Buried the key.

The woman came to ask Moji a question. Brody didn't hear what. It sounded as if she were talking underwater. Moji laid the wooden figure she'd been holding on the counter and went over to help the woman find the particular book she was looking for.

His Not Elf.

Anna.

He thought about Anna. He thought about the photograph on

his phone, about the expression in her eyes, at once curious and open. She'd been outside when it had been taken. There'd been blurry woodland in the background. He imagined her some-where else near woodland—on his terrace overlooking his gar-den, sitting at the little table and chairs. She wore the gray scarf from her photo and the purple hat with the flower on it. Her breath was coming in pure white clouds as she stared into the distance, and he realized she was looking out for someone, wait-ing. And then she turned and smiled at him.

Brody's heart rate slowed, settled into a steady thump.

Even though she hadn't been smiling in the photo she'd sent, he could see it so clearly in his imagination. The way her mouth curled and creased felt real, felt true. She was looking at him as the sun rose behind her head, its pale golden rays making the frost on the twisted, barren wisteria that clung to the side of the house sparkle.

"Are you okay, Brody?"

He turned to find Moji looking at him. The shop was empty, the memory of the bell over the door an echo in his ears. He was still breathing methodically and slowly, his unconscious brain counting beats of three even as his imagination had drifted else-where. "Yes," he said, a smile threatening to curve his lips. "Yes, I think I am."

Moji looked at the Not Elf. Brody was holding it tightly in both hands. "Are you sure she's supposed to be in the box?" Moji asked. "I mean, I'll take her. She's lovely. But she's not the usual sort of thing you bring me."

"No," he said, staring down at the determined chin, the far-away eyes. "You're right. It was a mistake. She shouldn't have been in there."

Chapter Forty-Two

Anna leaned back in her office chair at Sundridge Plumbing and Heating and rubbed her temples with the tips of her fingers. She'd just got off the phone with a customer, irate because their hot and cold tap labels were on the wrong way around. Not ideal, obviously, but you'd have thought from the fuss they made that raw sewage was pumping through their otherwise perfectly installed new bathroom.

Her mobile buzzed on the desk, a message from Gabi. *Meet me outside the Book Corner at noon.*

Hmm. That was a bit cryptic. And not the sort of message she'd become used to receiving from her best friend since the split with Lee. They usually alternated between ranting about Lee or crying about Lee and who he might be seeing now (there were rumors about Miss Ponytail, apparently).

Ok, Anna had texted back, ready for anything to get her out of the office for a bit. *Why?*

I will tell you when you get here had been Gabi's mysterious reply.

Which is why Anna took an early lunch break and found herself standing outside a bookshop in Bromley High Street one drizzly October day.

"Please don't be angry with me," Gabi said when she arrived and opened the door so they could both go inside out of the rain.

"Why would I be angry with you?" Anna asked as she folded up her umbrella.

Gabi glanced around the shop then motioned for Anna to join her behind one of the bookshelves further to the back of the shop. "I have been digging," she said, looking very serious.

"Digging?"

Gabi nodded. "Concerning your mystery man."

"My mystery . . . ?" Anna stopped. She frowned. "Brody?"

"Sorry," Gabi replied, looking torn. "I wasn't going to, but once I got the idea, I couldn't stop myself. I have too much free time now—especially early in the morning, when I can't sleep."

Anna looked back at Gabi and then she sighed and nodded. Gabi seemed to have two states of being since she'd split up with Lee—sad and floppy, or intense and hyper. "And?"

Gabi led Anna even further into the depths of the shop, where they were surrounded by the bright colors and illustrated characters of the children's section, and pulled a book from the shelf. "Here," she said, handing it to Anna. "This is him."

Anna looked at the hardback titled *The Moon Dragon*. "Gabi," she said slowly, starting to fear for her friend's sanity. "This is not Brody. It's a book."

"*By* him," Gabi said, her eyes boring into Anna's, waiting for Anna to catch her meaning.

Anna laughed. "No," she said. "No, it really isn't." She handed the book back to Gabi. "Brody Alexander," she said. "Not Brody Smith. The same results clogged up the page when I Googled too. It's not him."

"It's the same person. His full name is Brody *Alexander* Smith."

Anna shook her head gently. "But I looked at his website. It said he lives in London. He's married . . ."

Gabi looked at her meaningfully, then opened the cover and flipped to the copyright page. She tapped the creamy paper with a fingernail. "This was published in 2008. Maybe the website has not been updated? Maybe he did live in London at one time—and you said he'd lost his . . ."

"Wife," Anna finished for her. She tugged the book back out of Gabi's fingers. There was that same black-and-white author photo she'd seen on the internet inside the jacket. Her heart stuttered. This was Brody?

"That's why Brody Alexander was high up when we Googled Brody Smith," Gabi explained, her eyes shining with triumph and accomplishment. She'd always fancied herself as a bit of an amateur detective. "I read some online articles about him. One of them said what his real name was, and that he uses a different one for his books."

Anna was still staring at the photo. It wasn't at all what she imagined when she'd pictured him. Not at all. But in a strange way, the face was right—perfect—for the voice on the other end of the phone line, a voice she was so familiar with she could replay snatches of their conversations in her head, should she wish to.

"Maybe I should say 'used' a different name," Gabi added. "He hasn't written for a very long time. His fans are still waiting for the sixth and final book in this series."

Anna looked up at Gabi. None of this made any sense. Brody had never talked about writing, about doing anything much creative, apart from the woodworking he did, which had seemed to Anna like a bit of an old man's hobby. But what had he said once . . . ? Something about having made enough money from a career he'd walked away from to have bought his cottage . . . ? Anna's skin began to tingle.

This was his secret? Why had he kept this from her?

"There is something else . . ." Gabi said hesitantly. "One website also said *why* he has not written a new book for almost ten years, about why he may have disappeared. There was an accident—"

"I don't want to know!" Anna blurted out so loudly that a couple of other customers turned around and frowned at her. "I don't want to know," she repeated more quietly, making sure Gabi met her gaze and knew how serious she was about this. She'd decided not to snoop and, despite the fact she was suddenly desperate to know all the things Brody hadn't told her, she couldn't quite bring herself to go there. If he wanted her to know, he'd tell her. And he'd do that one day soon, surely.

"But—"

"No," Anna whispered harshly and put a finger over Gabi's lips. "All I want you to tell me is this: Do you think he is who he says he is? Is he telling me the truth about himself?"

Gabi nodded. "Yes. I think so."

"Then that's all I need to know," Anna said calmly, even though her insides were anything but.

Gabi exhaled, looking unconvinced. "Okay. If that's what you want."

"It's what I want," Anna said and tucked the book she was holding back onto the shelf where it belonged. "Now let's grab lunch before I have to head back to the office," she said and led Gabi out of the shop.

Later, however, when she'd finished work, she found herself walking past the bookshop again. Then she found herself going inside. By the time she headed home, there was a hardback book nestled in the bottom of her shopping bag.

ANNA SAT IN the sprawling café of Tullet's Garden Center, just a stone's throw away from where Scott and Teresa lived near Westerham, a pleasant commuter village near the M25. She and Teresa had organized a catch-up the Saturday after the party. *Has it only been a week?* Anna thought incredulously. It truly felt more like a month since she'd walked out of the Warlingham Court Hotel with Jeremy hot on her heels.

Teresa was off buying a couple of cappuccinos and Anna had bagged a table and was minding her nephew.

"He's just so deliciously chubby," she told Teresa when she returned with a tray and two mugs of steaming coffee, and then quickly added, "Sorry! Hope that's not the baby version of fat shaming!"

Teresa laughed. "He's almost five months now. He's supposed to be chubby." She reached for her cappuccino and took a sip. "And talking of delicious men, how is it going with the one you brought to my party?"

"Good," she said. "It's all very casual at the moment, though. Nothing too serious."

"Why not? Isn't he as delicious as he seems?"

"No, he is del—I mean, lovely. Charming, polite, interesting . . ."

Teresa smiled at her. "You deserve someone lovely. You really do."

"I know," Anna replied, and realized she actually believed that. "But . . ."

"But . . . ?" Teresa said, frowning. "Do I detect a bit of hesitation? Because I had a quick chat with him at the bar when he came to get a round of drinks. He seems perfect for you."

Anna sighed. "I know. He's lovely. I *should* be crazy about him."

"You just need to give yourself time. Dating someone new was always going to be a big step after Spencer. You guys were just so disgustingly in love."

"Maybe that's it," she said, nodding. "Maybe I'm overthinking things."

Little Spencer began to fuss and wriggle, so Teresa took him from Anna, strapped him into his pram and stood up so she could rock it backward and forward. "And he looked after you, took you home without a fuss, after what happened with Gayle last Saturday night. Patient and understanding are not qualities to be sniffed at."

Anna's eyes widened. "You heard about that?"

"My friend Megan—she was wearing that spectacular silver dress—told me about a fight she'd overheard in the corridor. She'd had a few martinis by then, so it wasn't completely clear who she was talking about at the time, but the penny finally dropped. I would have called you earlier if I'd worked it out sooner."

Anna sipped her cappuccino and gave a one-shouldered shrug. "There was no need. You didn't do anything."

"I'm surprised you didn't tell me yourself."

"I did think about it. I just thought maybe that you'd . . ."

Teresa's expression grew even more serious. "That I'd go along with Gayle for a quiet life?"

Anna nodded silently, feeling slightly ashamed, and looked down into her coffee.

"Oh, Anna . . ." Teresa leaned over, still pushing the pram back and forth, and rubbed Anna's arm. "I must admit that has mostly been my strategy for dealing with Gayle since I got serious with Scott, but I've come around to the fact that my strategy needs some drastic revision. I don't think we can let her get away with this stuff anymore. It's not good for her and it's certainly not good for us. What do you think we should do? Call a family meeting or something?"

Anna shook her head and swallowed. "I don't think I'm ready to talk to her yet." She wasn't sure if she would dissolve into tears or have another outburst, and neither option was desirable.

"Do you want me to say something? Because I will!"

Anna smiled. She didn't doubt that. "Not on my behalf. As much as Gayle is not my favorite person at the moment, she's already lost one son. I don't want her to cut you and Scott out too. Besides, I'm hanging on to the hope that this little man is softening her up a little."

Teresa raised an eyebrow and Anna laughed.

"Well, maybe only on Tuesdays and Thursdays."

Little Spencer began to grizzle, and Teresa sighed. "I think I'd better get him in the car and see if a drive will put him to sleep for a bit." She picked up her handbag and slung it over the handlebar of the pram. Anna walked beside her as they headed through the sprawling garden center and out to the parking lot.

"Listen," Teresa said, as they reached her car. "Christmas is still weeks away, but you know how much of a planner I am, so humor me . . . Would you like to spend the day with me and Scott and this little monster? I can put Gayle and Richard off until Boxing Day."

Anna stepped in and gave Teresa a hug. "Thank you," she said quietly, "that's a really lovely thought, but I've actually just booked a flight to Canada. I haven't seen my parents for about eighteen months and I just feel I could do with getting away."

Teresa nodded. "That sounds like an amazing idea. Just remember . . . If plans fall through, you know where to come."

Chapter Forty-Three

Anna yawned. It was late. She checked the clock on her bedside table. It seemed that, while she'd been reading, Monday night had slipped into Tuesday morning. She put the book she'd been holding down on the bed. She really should turn out the light if she was going to make it to work on time.

A fortnight or so after her breakup with Lee, Gabi was still at a loss as to what to do with herself. She'd called round just after Anna had got in from work the day before, bearing a bottle of wine and insisting they have a girls' movie night. They'd started with *Green Card*, then had gone on to *Moonstruck*. Even though Anna had been ready to call it a day after the second film, Gabi had pleaded with her to squeeze just one more in as she'd found *Sleepless in Seattle* on Netflix. Anna hadn't had the heart to say no.

Gabi was currently sprawled across the bed in Anna's spare room, snoring softly, but Anna had come up to bed and hadn't been able to resist picking up the book on her bedside table before she'd closed her eyes. Two hours later, she was still reading.

It was Brody's book. Or, to be more accurate, it was the fourth book in Brody's children's series. Anna had already read the first three. In just over a week. The lady in the bookshop was starting to recognize her. The last time Anna had gone in, the sales assistant had reached below the counter and produced the book Anna was looking for before she'd had the chance to amble down to the children's section.

"Thank you," Anna had stuttered.

The lady had just smiled. "It happens a lot with this series," she'd explained simply. "Although I must say, you're coming in faster than most. Your little one must be a voracious reader."

Anna had just nodded and tapped her debit card on the machine.

It was hard *not* to read these books voraciously, she'd discovered. They were set in a fictional kingdom where magic and the unexpected were orders of the day. She understood completely why any child would be entranced by them. There were dragons and knights, elves and giants, gorgons and gryphons— along with some fantastical creatures she'd never even heard of and was convinced had come straight from Brody's imagination. These books were full of adventure for the central character, Pip, a poor stable worker's daughter who had dreams of being a knight, but there was also an elegance in the writing, a wistfulness. And wisdom too. Brody didn't talk down to his young audience but credited them with the capability to understand that life had both triumphs and disappointments. No wonder they'd been popular with hundreds of thousands of children and their parents alike.

Anna opened her mouth to yawn and then shut it again, trying to stall it, which only made her want to yawn more desperately. She stared at the cover of the book, which showed a little girl with short blond hair, wielding a sword in the face of a hydra. She still couldn't believe that Brody had written it, that it had all come from his imagination. And there was no doubt it was *her* Brody who had written these words; she could hear his voice in her head as she read each sentence, hear the rhythm and pattern of his speech, certain turns of phrase that were uniquely him.

Why had Pip's adventures been left unfinished? It seemed that the most recently published book had ended on a cliffhanger, with the girl lost and wounded in the Vale of Shadows. It seemed heartless to leave her stuck there, and Brody was anything but heartless.

Why did he stop? Was it to do with his wife's death? Was that why he was hidden away in a cottage in the middle of nowhere? How did it all fit in?

It was a double-edged sword reading these books. On the one hand, she felt that connection to Brody even more strongly. Another layer to him—a really important one—that had previously been invisible to her had been revealed. She felt as if she'd been able to lift the top of his skull and peer inside his head, allowed to see secret things that no one else saw, which was ridiculous, since anyone could walk into a bookshop and read exactly the same words, but somehow this was different. This was her and Brody.

The downside was that now her curiosity about him had more than doubled. The urge to dig for answers about his past was almost overwhelming. She kept finding herself on Google, poised to type his name into the search box, and having to make herself pull her hands away from the keyboard and fold them in her lap.

They'd talked a couple of times since she'd started reading his books, but not since she'd started the third, almost five days ago. She kept meaning to call, but it felt weird having this new information about him, information he wasn't aware she'd found. Their relationship had always been on a "need to know" basis, and she hadn't realized how simple that had made things. They'd been able to talk without the fear of overstepping boundaries, of taking a wrong turn and saying something they'd regret later.

Despite her discomfort, she couldn't put off phoning him forever, because he might guess something was up. *Come on, Anna. Just do it.* Holding her breath, she dialed his number. If he was asleep, she'd just leave a breezy message and try again tomorrow.

However, Brody answered straightaway. Anna had the oddest feeling that he'd been waiting for his phone to ring, that he'd had the same sense that she had, that if they didn't talk tonight, it would feel as if there'd been too much of a gap in the usual rhythm of their conversations.

Anna was desperate to ask him about his books, to find out why he'd stopped writing them, but she knew it wouldn't be the right thing to blurt it all out straightaway. She needed to tread carefully, so instead she just told him been up late reading— without mentioning authors and titles. It turned out that Brody too had been kept up, reading a thriller he'd simply had to get to the end of.

As they talked, Anna couldn't help noticing that the man she was talking to now was very different from the man who had written Pip's story. Something was missing. The man who had written about dragons and magic rivers, about snowflakes that could speak, was a man confident of all the delightful possibilities life could bring, who knew what hope was.

Brody was no longer that man, and she wanted to know why.

She *needed* to know why. It had been more than a month since she'd mentioned the possibility of them meeting each other, but now she just couldn't get it out of her head. Perhaps the questions she wanted to pose should be asked face-to-face? It might make it easier to get him to open up. And if she gave him a month or two to get used to the idea, maybe he'd come around?

"Brody?" she said when there was a lull in their conversation.

"Yes?" He sounded relaxed, confident. It was now or never.

"I know we've discussed this before, but I would really like to meet you in person." Brody didn't reply. Even across the waves that carried their connection, she felt a sudden frostiness in the atmosphere. Why?

"We discussed New Year's Eve and how much we hate it." The silence was thick. She was sure he was going to jump in any second and argue with her, so she just kept going. Words were all she had at this point. "I don't want to go to a New Year's Eve party, Brody. I don't want to mill around with strangers, or even people I know, and make believe that I'm happy and carefree when Big Ben chimes. It's just too exhausting. There's only one thing I want to do this December thirty-first. I want to spend it with you."

Anna's heart pounded. She stared at her phone, willing him to respond and eventually he did. "I'd like that too," he said, and his voice was rough. "I'm just not sure it's possible."

"Why?"

More silence. But it wasn't menacing. The one thing she could tell from his reply was that it wasn't that he didn't *want* to meet her. It was something else. She could sense him struggling with himself, or maybe some unknown enemy. One of his giants. Whatever his reason, it was big.

She pushed aside her curiosity, deciding her key objective should be to make it easier for him to say yes. "I can come to you, or you can come to me. Whatever is easier."

He still didn't respond.

"Or we could go somewhere neutral . . ."

Where? She racked her brains for a good location. Somewhere everyone knew about. Somewhere they could meet on a significant date like New Year's Eve.

The only thing that came to her mind, thanks to the movie marathon earlier, and *Sleepless in Seattle* in particular, was "the top of the Empire State Building." Ridiculous. Meeting up in person seemed a struggle enough as it was without moving it to an entirely different continent.

Maybe it was talking about tall buildings in big cities that jogged her next suggestion free. "The Shard," she said, becoming conscious of the idea the moment she heard herself say it. "The top of the Shard. At eleven o'clock on New Year's Eve."

"Anna . . ."

He was going to turn her down again, and she couldn't bear to hear him do it. Not tonight, anyway. She had to find a way to stall him. "You don't have to say yes now. It's still more than two months away. You don't even have to go at all if you really don't want to. But I'll book two tickets to the observation platform . . ."

Could she do that? Was the Shard even open on New Year's Eve? She had no clue. Well, if it weren't, it would be a "sign," like in *Sleepless in Seattle*, and then she'd never ask Brody to meet her again.

She hurried on before he could shut her down. "If you come, you come. If you don't, you don't. It'll be okay." She had to trust him, that whatever the reason for his reluctance, he'd either get over it or explain it at some point.

He sounded pained when he replied. "You could very well end up standing there waiting all night. You'd be alone at midnight . . ."

The time she might need him the most. Yes, she knew that. It was a risk she was willing to take. "I don't care," she said.

He let out a sigh, so heavy and so bleak that tears sprang to her eyes. Not for herself, but for him. For whatever giant blocked his path and blighted his life. *Think about what brave little Pip would do*, she wanted to tell him. *She's a part of you, and she knows how to fight. She knows how to hope.*

But she couldn't say that. Not yet.

"And if I can't be with you, I'd rather see the New Year in on my own, high above the city, watching the lights sparkle below me."

"Anna . . . Don't . . ."

The disobedient tears lining her lashes fell. "What is it? What's wrong?" she whispered. "Don't you want to meet me?"

His voice was raw when he replied. "I do. More than anything."

Chapter Forty-Four

The weekend before Halloween was gray and drizzly, and Anna holed herself up against the weather. It was the kind of Saturday afternoon that begged big, fluffy socks and an oversized cardigan that reached down to your knees. Anna put on both, then made herself a large mug of hot chocolate and took it into the living room, where she curled up with the fifth, and most recent, book in Brody's series.

When she looked up again, she discovered the rain had cleared but that it was dark outside. How long had she been sitting there? Her hot chocolate was half-drunk and stone-cold. She checked the clock on the mantelpiece. *Six-fifteen!* She was supposed to be leaving the house in just over an hour to meet Jeremy. They were going to see a film that evening at the new cinema down at Bromley South.

She got up and stuck her mug of hot chocolate in the microwave to warm it up. Her mother would be horrified, but her mother didn't need to know, did she? She was about to take it upstairs to her bedroom to sip while she perused her wardrobe, but when she reached the foot of the stairs, she turned and headed back into the living room. She and Jeremy would be sitting in the dark most of the evening, wouldn't they? So she didn't need to go all out on the makeup and a cute sweater and jeans would suffice. That meant she had time for one more chapter . . .

By the time Anna managed to tear herself away from Brody's book, she'd read three more chapters and she was cutting it really, really fine to meet Jeremy on time. She glanced at the clock and then at the book sitting in her lap. She didn't want to go out tonight, she realized. Even though the plan was to see the latest Emily Blunt movie, and she'd been looking forward to it all week. She wanted to stay home and find out what happened to Pip.

Even so, she hauled herself up off the sofa and headed into the hall. It would be rude to bail out on Jeremy this late, so she really didn't have a choice. She ran upstairs and got ready, but as she threaded her favorite earrings into her ears—the final touch—she stopped and looked at herself in the mirror.

There was something missing. But it wasn't an accessory or an extra coat of mascara. It was something else . . .

Where was the fluttering in her stomach? Where were the butterflies that had terrified her so much when she'd first met Jeremy? Now that she thought about it, she hadn't felt them in weeks.

Overthinking it again, Anna . . .

She shook herself, turned away from the mirror and headed downstairs to get her coat.

THE FILM WAS every bit as good as Anna hoped it would be, a well-acted drama with a heart-wrenching love story at its core. When the film ended, she couldn't help shedding a tear. Jeremy reached over and squeezed her hand. "I'm such a sap," she said, smiling as she wiped her eyes with a tissue.

"My sister's the same," Jeremy said. "The happy ending gets her every time."

Anna nodded, still smiling, and looked down. She didn't want to contradict Jeremy, but that wasn't *exactly* why she'd been feeling tearful.

She'd cried for the happy ending, yes, but she'd also cried for what might happen after the credits rolled. It could all get snatched away in a moment, didn't they know that? And then there was a hole in your heart that meant you'd never feel that way again. It was gone and they'd never be able to get it back. For some reason, Anna couldn't stop worrying about them, even though it was completely ridiculous because they were made-up people and would never exist outside of that film.

"I thought they had great chemistry, didn't they?" Jeremy said as he and Anna rode the escalators back to the foyer. "I mean, they really made me believe in them as a couple."

Anna agreed. The casting had been spot-on.

"I must admit, this film wouldn't have been my first choice," Jeremy said, smiling sheepishly. "Not a single car chase! And I don't normally do romantic films, but this didn't seem cheesy in the slightest. It made me think that's what love *should* be like."

Anna nodded. The romantic relationship had been handled really well. Maybe too well, if she couldn't get it out of her head. Because it had reminded her of what she'd had with Spencer, something rare and all-consuming, dizzying and heart-stopping, but at the same time comfortable and . . . easy.

"Fancy a quick drink?" Jeremy said.

"Why not," Anna replied, not quite ready to go home yet. She'd rather she got rid of this weird, shadowy feeling—like an emotional hangover from the movie—before she returned to her house alone.

The recent rain cast a glossy sheen on the night, reflecting

streetlights in puddles, as they walked to a bar just around the corner from the cinema. As they waited for someone to serve them,
Jeremy slid an arm around Anna's waist and pulled her closer, a
casually affectionate gesture that made her stop in her tracks.

It was nice to feel the warmth of his arm around her back, his
hand resting lightly on the top of her hip, but that . . . That was
it. There was no lovely rush of excitement; no sweet ache beginning to build inside. What had the butterflies done? Flown to
warmer climes for the winter?

Jeremy ordered himself a red wine and Anna went along with
his choice, her brain too full to survey the dizzying menu of
cocktails. She stood there next to him, staring at the polished
wood of the bar.

"Is that . . . Is that what you want from a relationship?" she
asked, shifting so his arm fell away and turning to face him.
"What they had in the film?"

He smiled at her. "Well, I'd rather not lose a leg like he did,
but other than that, yes, of course. Isn't that what everybody
wants? Love? Passion?"

She nodded. "I suppose they do but . . ."

"But?" Jeremy's eyebrows lifted. He was still smiling.

Anna swallowed. "I don't know . . . Maybe I'm wrong, but I
not sure it happens twice in one lifetime. I'd hoped it might, but
now . . . I'm really not so sure."

That would explain the lack of butterflies, the lack of any
deeper feelings for Jeremy, despite the fact that Teresa was
right—he was pretty damn near perfect for her. She'd been telling herself it was okay, she was just taking it slowly, but surely
things shouldn't have flatlined already. Six weeks into the relationship with Spencer, she'd been head over heels in love.

Jeremy's expression turned more serious. "What are you saying, Anna?"

That was a very good question. She took a moment to collect her thoughts, to probe if she really could trust this new certainty forming in her heart.

"I think I'm saying that I'm not the right person for you, Jeremy. I thought I could be. I thought I could at least *try*, but . . ." She trailed off and shook her head, aware that the back of her nose had started to prickle.

"You want . . . *that*." She gestured in the direction of the cinema. "The whole deal. And you deserve it! I just . . . I just don't think I have enough left in the tank to do that again, even if I wanted to."

Her *Not Spencer* alarm had been right all along. She should have listened to it.

Not to save herself from pain or to preserve Spencer's memory, but to save Jeremy from having to wear his current expression of disappointment and surprise. He'd begun to invest in her emotionally, she suspected, and it really wasn't fair to let him continue. She likely wouldn't ever be able to give him what he really wanted and needed. It was time to tell him that, to be just as honest with him at the end of their relationship as she had been the first day they'd met. She took a sip of her wine and began what she knew was going to be a really uncomfortable conversation.

When they'd finished talking, Jeremy walked her down the road to the station so she could catch a black cab home. He was solemn, quiet, as they strolled side by side. "I'm so sorry," she said for the thousandth time, and felt fresh tears dampening her lashes.

"It's okay," he said heavily as they stopped on the concourse outside the station. "I don't like it, but I understand." She reached up and hugged him tight. "Sorry," she whispered again. "I hope you find the one you're looking for, I really do . . . She's just not me."

They held on to each other for a few seconds. "Take care of yourself," she whispered, and then they pulled apart.

"Likewise," he said, then nodded her a farewell and turned and walked away down the hill. Anna let out a shuddering breath. She watched him for a moment, then approached the cabby at the front of the taxi line and gave him her address.

When she slammed her front door behind her, the first thing she did—before she even pulled off her coat—was phone Brody.

"Anna?"

"I just ended things with Jeremy," she said, and promptly burst into tears.

Chapter Forty-Five

Brody listened as Anna outlined the events of the evening—the film, the bar, the goodbye. He didn't say much, just let her talk.

"I just feel so awful," she said forlornly. "I thought I was doing the right thing asking him out. I thought I was moving on. I didn't mean to mess him around . . ."

"You didn't," Brody said. "Not from what I can tell. You were honest with him from the start, and no relationship is guaranteed, especially after just a handful of dates. If it didn't feel right, it didn't feel right . . ."

He tried not to notice the sense of lightness in his chest as he said this, tried not to feel pleased at all that bloody perfect Jeremy was out of the picture. He failed miserably.

"And you when you realized how you felt, you were honest with him, told him straightaway."

Anna sighed. "I suppose I did. I just feel so . . ."

"Awful," Brody finished for her and was rewarded with a little huff that he suspected was accompanied by a smile.

"The strangest thing is, I thought I was ready. I thought I *could* find someone new, but it won't ever be the same, now I know I have to factor that in going forward." She exhaled. "But the more I think about it, the more I realize that I'm a tiny bit relieved about that."

"Relieved?"

"Yes. I can say this to you, Brody, because you understand, you know how deep the scars go when you lose someone that way. I'm not sure I *want* to love someone that much again, because how would I cope if it happened a second time?"

He sighed and nodded heavily, even though he knew she couldn't see him. "You're stronger than you think," he told her. "And I'd be here for you." He would always be there for her. "Don't give up, Anna. You deserve to be happy."

There was a muffled rustling noise of fabric against fabric, as if Anna were burrowing down into her sofa. "On the taxi ride home, I was thinking . . . I've decided no more dating for the moment. I'm going to concentrate on other areas of my life instead. Remember I told you I was hatching a plan to help other people like us—widows and widowers?" And she began to fill him in on the idea of using an app to do that, not quite a social network, but a way of connecting strangers who'd lived through similar experiences.

When she finished, he sat there, stunned. There was so much hope in her idea. She'd changed so much during the time he'd really gotten to know her: six months ago, he doubted she would have suggested such a thing. "I think that sounds amazing," he said.

"I thought if anyone would understand my thinking, it would be you, Brody. I'm just pinning down some final details before I go and talk to someone about it, to see if it would be something someone else would be interested in developing."

"Would it help to talk it through with someone?" he asked. "I don't know much about this sort of stuff but I can listen if you need a sounding board." And that was what they did for the next forty-five minutes, until Anna began yawning and they ended the call so she could go to bed.

Brody sat in his chair for at least another half an hour, pondering what she'd said, thinking about how dynamic she seemed compared to him. Even though she felt bad about the whole Jeremy thing, she was still trying new things, doing something with her life. She was making progress.

So are you, a little voice in his head whispered. *In small ways, so are you.*

He'd noted while they'd been talking that she hadn't mentioned meeting up on New Year's Eve again, but he sensed she hadn't dropped the idea. His pulse trotted at the thought. They might not have talked about it during the last week or so, but in that time he also hadn't said "no."

He'd been planning to, but his brain had stalled, and he hadn't been able to think of a good excuse. Not one he could tell Anna, anyway. She was curious, quiet, but full of questions. He'd managed not to reveal anything he didn't want to so far, but if he met her face-to-face it might be a whole lot harder.

That was one excuse for not telling her he wouldn't be going anywhere on New Year's Eve. The other reason, the one he wasn't even sure he wanted to admit to himself, was that, even if he'd been able to continue to dodge her questions, he wanted what she was offering way too much, especially now that he knew the "competition" was no longer in the picture.

To meet her just once, to hold her just once, was all he wanted. He'd be able to walk away not exactly happy but . . . satisfied. It would be enough.

It would have to be.

Liar.

No. Not a liar, he replied to the jeering voice inside his head. *Just a realist.* It was the only way he'd be able to cope.

He was in love with Anna.

How was that for honesty? It had been growing for months, and he'd tried to sidestep that truth, but he could now no longer avoid it. It was pathetic, really. And he'd put himself in this position by isolating himself so completely from the rest of humanity. Of course he was going to form a deep connection with the only person he'd talked to properly for years. He should have seen it coming.

And that person had been Anna. That had been his undoing. When she'd first phoned, he'd thought he was just being kind, helping her out. He'd had no idea that she'd give him far more than he could ever give her. Couldn't she have been some whiny, self-absorbed woman who had irritated him? That might have been preferable. He'd have been able to block her number and forget about her. Damn Anna for being so brave and surprising. He hadn't really stood a chance.

"It's impossible," he said out loud to no one, except maybe Lewis, who had put his head back down on his paws but was still looking at Brody. He sighed again, and his gaze wandered around his study. Eventually, it landed on his Not Elf. After her rescue from Moji's shop, he'd put her back on the bookshelf beside his chair.

Usually, she seemed to be staring far off into the distance but tonight he had the strangest sensation that she was looking right back at him, staring into his eyes. Challenging him.

Why? she was saying to him. *Why is it impossible?*

That was the problem with having a good imagination. She

was a lump of wood, but he couldn't shake the feeling that she was just like the woman who had inspired her creation, full of questions that seemed simple but were actually terrifically complicated to answer.

You know why, he replied. *It just is.*

Chapter Forty-Six

Anna stared up at the tall, wedge-shaped building that sat opposite Bromley South station. It was a bright, crisp autumn day and the sun glinted off the modern tower, making its glazed section almost too bright to look at. She felt a tremor in her stomach. This was where Rhys and Vijay, Spencer's former business partners, now had their offices on the seventeenth floor.

Anna blew out a breath, stuck her hands in her coat pockets and marched herself up to the reception desk on the ground floor of the building. She hadn't seen Spencer's old partners for more than a year now, but she'd emailed them the Monday morning after her brainstorming session with Brody, outlining her idea for the app, asking them if they'd be interested in picking it up and running with it. They'd emailed back and asked for a meeting within forty-eight hours.

There were hugs from Spencer's former partners when she arrived, and genuine smiles, which warmed her more than she cared to admit, followed by offers of coffee and delicious chewy chocolate biscuits, before she was led into a glass-walled meeting room that overlooked Shortlands valley. It seemed as if the whole world was crisp and full of frost-sharpened colors as it spread itself out for her below.

Rhys, a teddy bear of a guy, grinned at her as he leaned back in his fancy chrome and leather chair. "Anna . . . We've missed you!"

"Likewise—it looks like you've got an amazing setup here," she said, smiling as she looked across the modern office space to where a team of what seemed like very young and very edgy employees were all busy "blue sky thinking" or whatever they did in these sort of places. "It's a far cry from where you started."

"From where *we* started." Vijay sat down opposite her and passed her a cup of coffee that smelled rich and fragrant. "Remember those late-night meetings we used to have round your dining room table, dreaming up our plans for world domination?"

Anna laughed. "I definitely remember all the pizza boxes lying around the next morning!"

"We still have those pizza-fueled meetings," Rhys admitted with a grin, "but now I make Vijay clear away the boxes."

Vijay shot Rhys a dirty look then turned his attention back to Anna. "We wouldn't be where we are now without you, Anna."

Anna blushed a little. "Without Spencer, you mean . . ."

Rhys leaned forward and rested his elbows on the desk. "Well, yes. But also because of you."

"Me?"

"I think you're forgetting that one of our most popular features—the completely customizable interface—was your brainchild," Vijay said.

Anna looked at him, confused. She didn't remember having anything to do with that. All she'd done was sit at a desk in the corner and add up the numbers, keep on top of the paperwork.

Vijay's mouth hooked up at one corner as he took in Anna's

consternation. "When we came to you and asked you what you thought of our six brilliant and stylish color schemes, you said you hated every one of them."

"Well, that was more personal taste than a business decision," Anna said uncertainly.

"Yes, but it got us thinking about how different people's tastes are, and how best we could cater to a wide range."

Anna shrugged again. They were giving her more credit than she was due, but she wasn't going to make a fuss about that.

Rhys leaned back again and sipped his mug of coffee. "I can see you're not convinced."

Anna gave him a crooked smile and a half shrug.

"Surely you remember coming up with the name?" he added. "BlockTime wouldn't be BlockTime without you."

"Well, I suppose there is that. But I always thought it was kind of unimaginative and basic. I never really understood why you went with that rather than one of the other ideas."

Vijay gave Rhys a withering look. "This muppet wanted to call it Avocado."

Rhys lifted his chin. "I happen to like avocados."

This remark led to a bickering session about whose proposed name was the stupidest. It made Anna smile because, for all the edgy staff and high-tech office equipment, these were still the same two fellow geeks of Spencer's who'd planned to start a company sitting round her dining table, surrounded by boxes of Meat Feast and Pepperoni Stuffed Crust pizzas.

"So, what are you up to next?" she asked, mostly to distract them.

Vijay turned to her. "More interestingly, what are *you* doing now?"

"Me?" Anna looked between the two men. Rhys nodded. "We like your idea. We think it might have legs—especially if we can forge links with a charity or nonprofit organization that supports people who are grieving. Early days yet, but we're putting out feelers, seeing if there's interest, that kind of thing."

Anna beamed at him. "Oh, I'm so pleased you want to do something with it. Having someone to talk to really kind of saved my life, or at the very least, set it on a healthier track."

"Good," Vijay said. "And we're glad to see you doing so well, but I wasn't kidding when I asked what you were doing now. Where are you working?"

"Oh," Anna said, a little taken aback, but she filled them in on Sundridge Plumbing and Heating, the joys of invoices for taps and bits of piping she still didn't know how to identify. "I think I'm ready to move on, though," she added.

"Yes, do," Vijay said. "Ditch it."

Rhys rolled his eyes. "I thought you said we were going to take this softly-softly."

"Ditch what?" Anna asked.

"Ditch that job and come and work with us again," Vijay said, and he didn't seem to be joking in the slightest.

Anna looked at the surrounding offices through the glass wall of the one she was in. It was no longer the three-person operation it was when she'd been involved. "I know you asked me to stay on after Spencer died, but you're bigger now! I would have no idea how to manage the bookkeeping for this size of operation."

"Forget bookkeeping!" said Vijay, cutting in. "You have Spencer's shares. Technically, you're a partner. Come on board doing something else." He pulled a disbelieving face and added, "You can manage the office if that's really your bag."

Anna looked once again at the team of bright young things buzzing around the open-plan space outside the meeting room. "Don't you have someone to do that?"

Rhys saw where Anna was looking and waved a dismissive arm in the colorful crowd's general direction. "Yeah, but they're creative types, and they're like we were when we started—young and stupid. They think everything we say is gold dust."

"They would've *loved* the name Avocado," Vijay said drily.

Rhys ignored him. "What I'm saying is that we need someone around who'll tell us we need a 'does what it says on the tin' name for a time management app. Someone like you, Anna."

Anna stared back at them. She had the feeling she might cry if they said any more. "You really want me back? Just me? On my own? Even though I walked away three years ago and haven't been involved since?"

Both guys nodded.

"We understood why it was hard," Vijay said, sobering. "We found it difficult too. It was only not wanting to let Spencer down, wanting to make BlockTime a success for him, that kept us going to start off with. Will you think about it? Because the best person to develop your app is you."

Rhys must have seen the look of pure horror on Anna's face because he quickly added, "Not the technical side like Spencer did, of course, but the *heart*. That's why BlockTime worked . . ." And he paused to look across at Vijay, who nodded encouragingly. ". . . because we were all passionate about it."

"And who better to understand what an app for connecting grieving people needs to do than someone who's been through it themselves?" Vijay added. "I'm sure the pair of us would wade in and make all sorts of mistakes."

Anna took a moment to digest that. For so long she'd avoided these two, and any mention of BlockTime, because it had made her think of Spencer and all he'd done, and that had made her think of all she'd lost. But now she was remembering there was joy to be had thinking about all they'd accomplished together too. It was quite a revelation.

"Okay," she said. "I'll think about it."

Chapter Forty-Seven

Brody's phone lit up, Anna's picture in the background behind the button to accept an incoming call. "Anna?" he said as he held the handset up to his ear.

"Brody," she replied. And that was it. No chatter about her day, no random questions from out of the blue. Brody frowned and waited a few more seconds. There was a loud bang in the background.

"Are you okay, Anna? What's that noise?"

"Fireworks," she said, sounding slightly puzzled. "It's Bonfire Night—had you forgotten?"

"I suppose I had. The nearest displays are probably twenty miles away."

Anna harrumphed. "Can't forget round here. They're going off every few seconds." And then she fell silent again. Most odd. It had been a few days since they'd spoken but she'd been so brimming with ideas and energy about this app idea when they last chatted, he presumed she'd been busy.

"Is something wrong?"

"No," she said quietly, and then he heard a gentle huff. Not of exasperation or humor, but as if she were trying to work out how to word what she wanted to say. "But there's something I've been meaning to tell you for a few weeks."

Brody's stomach dropped. Oh, God. She was going to say

New Year's Eve was off. She had something better to do. And someone better to do it with. Even though he hadn't committed to going, and knew he would probably pull out in the end, he didn't want the possibility of it to disappear just yet. "Go on," he said, steeling himself for the worst.

"I know who you are."

Brody frowned harder. "And I know who *you* are . . ."

"I mean that I know who you are in terms of what you do—or what you used to do. I know your full name is Brody *Alexander* Smith."

For a couple of seconds Brody heard nothing but the blood rushing in his ears. "How . . . How did you work that one out?" There was no point in denying it.

"Gabi told me. She did some . . . um . . . investigating. She was worried about me talking to a man I'd never—"

"It's okay," Brody said softly. "I get it."

"It's just . . . I've known for a while, and I wasn't going to say anything, but I felt bad about it, even though it wasn't me who went looking. But then I realized that it's possible we're going to meet soon, that we're going to stand close enough to look into each other's faces. And I realized there'd be this . . . thing . . . between us. A secret. And I didn't want that."

He exhaled and looked at Lewis, who was curled up near his feet. No. Secrets weren't good. They were like walls. Barriers. "Does it matter?" he asked. "What you found out?"

Anna sounded slightly bemused. "What do you mean?"

"I mean . . ." He held his breath slightly, realizing he wasn't sure he wanted the answer to the question he was about to ask. "Does it change anything?"

Once again, Anna confounded him. Despite his reservations,

he'd been expecting a hasty denial—*of course it isn't going to change anything*—but she kept him waiting. His stomach grew icy. How much had Gabi actually told Anna? And what had been the source?

"A little," she said softly.

Brody closed his eyes, tried to breathe evenly.

There was a shyness in her tone when she spoke again. Anna had always said she was shy, but she'd never been that way with him before. The icy feeling started to spread.

"I read your books."

Brody felt as if he'd been punched in the gut, but he had no idea where that reaction had come from. Why did it matter if she had?

"They're beautiful, Brody . . . So full of magic, and not just the spell-casting kind. So full of imagination and depth. I was entranced."

A thousand thoughts and feelings rushed around Brody's head, none of them slow enough for him to tackle and pin down. "Thank you," he managed.

"Why did you stop? Writing, I mean . . ."

Bam! Another punch. And this was territory he really, really didn't want to cover. Especially not with her.

"Gabi said . . ." She paused, then continued nervously. "Gabi said something about an accident."

Brody made a sharp intake of breath.

"Was that how she . . . you know . . . died?"

Brody's voice was barely a croak when he replied, "Who?"

"Your wife."

As much as he didn't want to tell her the truth, he'd heard what she'd said about secrets. He also couldn't lie to her about this, not now she'd asked him directly. "My wife isn't dead," he said slowly. "We're divorced."

"Oh," Anna said loudly and then again more softly. "Then who . . . ?"

Brody's heart thudded.

When she spoke again, she sounded confused, maybe even a little suspicious. "I'm not making it up, am I? You did say you'd lost someone too?"

Brody walked over to the other side of the room to stare out of the blackened window. He couldn't even see the silhouette of the ragged trees that lined his boundary. Darkness began to seep through the panes, filling him. "I did."

There was a moment of pure silence, both where he stood in his study but also at the other end of the line.

Anna whispered, "Who?"

"I . . ."

The wave hammered down on him. Without warning and without mercy. No clues it had been looming. No tingling fingers, no tight chest. *God. Nine years.* He thought he'd outrun it to a certain extent, but here was proof to the contrary: the pain was still as fresh and raw as it had been that day almost a decade ago.

Brody turned and began to run, even though it was a foolish thing to do in his tiny cluttered cottage. He knocked over a lamp in his rush to get to the back door, and it crashed to the floor behind him. He wrenched the door open and ran out into the yard, the frost suspended and waiting in the night air, chilling his face and hands.

"Brody . . . ?" The voice was muffled from where he held the phone against his chest.

He tried to talk, he really did, but no sound would come out. Hardly surprising, since it felt as if someone had launched a wrecking ball into his chest. He dropped the phone and staggered away from it, heaving in rasping breaths that made his entire body shudder. And then he fell to his knees, buried his face in his hands and began to sob.

Chapter Forty-Eight

Thanks for coming over to help," Anna said to Gabi as they walked across the landing and into her bedroom. "I couldn't face doing this on my own."

Gabi sat down on the edge of the bed and bounced a couple of times. "No problem. I have nothing better to do . . ."

"Thanks!"

Gabi rolled her eyes. "You know what I mean."

Anna did know. She remembered feeling the way Gabi did not so long ago. The heaviness. The feeling that everything was too much effort, and there was no point to anything. She was worried about her. It was six weeks since Gabi and Lee had split up and she still wasn't quite her old self. Normal Gabi was bright and bubbly and full of bounce. This Gabi reminded Anna of a half-deflated beach ball. They could both do with the distraction from their thoughts that this chore could bring.

It had been eight days since her last conversation with Brody. Eight days and not a word. Oh, Anna had tried calling. She tried calling a lot. But Brody wasn't picking up. It made her feel sick every time she thought about it.

She walked over to Spencer's wardrobe and opened the doors. Her eyes, as always, were drawn to the neat row of shirts on their hangers. Somehow, they held more meaning for her than any of the other items in the wardrobe. She wasn't exactly sure why, only that when she'd pressed her face against his shoulder and held him tight, his shirts had always smelled so wonderful, of clean, fresh cotton and safety.

Anna still had her hands on the open wardrobe doors. She didn't move. "I've got to do this," she said, fixing her gaze on the shirts. "He doesn't need them anymore."

"That is true." Gabi got up from the edge of the bed, walked toward her and put an arm around her shoulder. "But you don't have to do this if you're not ready."

Anna nodded. "I know. But I've been putting this off for too long. It's time, Gabs. It's just . . ."

"Difficult," Gabi finished for her.

"Yes." Anna replied solemnly. She exhaled. "But I've realized I have to make room in my life for new things, both emotionally and physically. Even if I'm not ready for a new man on my horizon today, I think I want to signal that I'm open to the possibility of him someday—whatever that ends up meaning."

Gabi sighed. "I am sad it didn't work out between you and Jeremy."

Anna nodded. "I'm sad about that too, but it wasn't fair to keep stringing him along."

Gabi looked sheepish. "I was wrong to push you into seeing him. I know that now."

Anna felt a rush of warmth for her friend. She hugged Gabi tightly and kissed her noisily on the cheek. "Not wrong. Maybe just a bit premature." Gabi smiled back at her and then they both turned to consider the open wardrobe. "I don't even know where to start . . . We need a plan."

Gabi put her hands on her hips. "I have a plan, I think . . . We start with one thing—suits or shoes or jackets or shirts . . ."

Anna must have been pulling a face at that word, because Gabi trailed off, swallowed, then carried on. "We start with the group that's easy. We take out all those things, put them on the bed and sort them one by one. You must concentrate, Anna. You need to be 'present,' because otherwise you may feel too sad when it is all gone. You have to make a decision about each thing."

Anna scrunched up her forehead and looked at Gabi. "Where did you get all' of that stuff?"

"Binge-watching *Hoarders* when I can't sleep," she said with a little bit of the old Gabi twinkle in her eye.

Anna laughed and turned back to the wardrobe, scanning the contents. "Let's start with shoes."

And so that is what they did. They pulled out all of Spencer's shoes and boots and trainers and went through them, pair by pair. Some they saved for the charity shop, and some they put into a black bin bag to go out to the dustbin. When both piles were full and there was no more footwear left in the wardrobe, Anna breathed out shakily.

There. She'd done it. And it hadn't been terrible. In fact, there was a sense of peace, of release.

Next, they worked through the trousers, none of which Anna kept, but when it came to tops and sweaters, she saved a few of her favorites: a charcoal cable-knit fisherman's sweater that was way too big for her and a couple of soft hoodies. These were things she'd liked to steal from Spencer when he'd been alive. They made her smile when she picked them up, even if tears welled in her lashes. That was a good sign, wasn't it? If it wasn't exactly a happy feeling, it wasn't all sad either.

As she tied the knot on a full bag, tears began to splash onto her hands. Gabi came over, made her let go and hugged her. "Sorry," Anna croaked when she was able.

"It's nothing, *minha querida*," Gabi replied, and Anna could hear the emotion in her voice. She rubbed Anna's back. "We don't have to put these bags into your car today. We can put them back in the wardrobe . . . Maybe you give yourself time? Get used to it all packed up before you get rid of them?"

Anna sniffed and pulled away to look at Gabi. "Is that what they do on *Hoarders*?"

Gabi laughed loudly. "No! That would be a very bad idea." Her voice softened. "But this is different. You can make up your own rules. You can do what you want."

Anna nodded and tried to suck in a deep breath, but it ended up more like a hiccup. "Okay." She walked over to the wardrobe and stared inside again.

Just as her fingers brushed the shoulders of a few of Spencer's shirts, her mobile buzzed in her back jeans pocket. She quickly pulled the shirts out, threw them on the bed, and grabbed for her phone. It might be . . .

It wasn't.

Her heart sank.

"Brody?" Gabi said drily. Anna had half a mind to think her best friend was getting jealous. She got this pinched little look on her face every time Anna mentioned him.

"No, my mum. Asking what time my flight gets in on the fifteenth of December. I'll go and check the confirmation email when we're finished."

Anna went back to pulling shirts from the wardrobe. When the pile was complete, Gabi said, "But you thought that was Brody?"

Anna glanced over her shoulder to where Gabi was struggling with a black sack as she dragged it back toward the wardrobe and dumped it on the floor. "What makes you say that?"

"Your face. You never do that face when it's anyone else."

"I *might* look that way when you text me," Anna replied. "You wouldn't know, because you're always somewhere else at the time."

"Okay," Gabi said. She pulled her phone out and tapped in a quick message. A split second later, Anna's phone dinged again. She did her best to hide her smile when she saw Gabi's text: **Prove**.

Anna pretended to faint, flopping back onto the bed covered in clothes and hangers. Gabi lay down beside her and they both giggled quietly. "You are silly," Gabi said.

"Only half as silly as you, though," Anna replied and poked her friend gently in the ribs.

"That is true," Gabi said wearily, and they both lay there looking up at the ceiling.

"I'm worried about him," Anna finally said. "Brody."

Gabi pushed herself up on one elbow and looked at Anna. "Why?"

"The last time we spoke, I asked him about that accident you mentioned, and he kind of lost it."

"Lost it?" Gabi said slowly. "How do you mean? Angry? Irrational?"

"I don't know," Anna said, propping herself up to match Gabi's position. "He just . . . He stopped talking, and I could hear him, and then . . . nothing. The phone went dead."

"Did he say sorry?"

"That's just it. That call was more than a week ago, and I've sent messages, tried phoning every day, but he won't answer. I'm scared I've stuck my big fat nose in where it didn't belong and ruined it."

"Maybe you need to back off a little? Give him space?"

"Why do you say that?"

Gabi sighed heavily. "Voice of experience."

Anna waited for Gabi to explain, but Gabi let her body drop back down on the bed and went back to studying the ceiling light. "A coat hanger is sticking into my butt," Gabi mumbled, "but I can't be bothered to move."

Anna poked Gabi again. It was quickly becoming her favorite new method of communication. "What do you mean 'voice of experience'?"

"A little because I see that I was pushy with you sometimes . . ."

Anna squeezed her hand.

"And a little because . . ." Gabi scrunched up her face before she carried on. "Because I phoned Lee."

Anna sprang up to a sitting position and stared at her friend. "You phoned *Lee*?"

Gabi drew a deep breath and opened her eyes again. She nodded. "I was feeling so low. He didn't answer and then . . ." She looked away, color rising in her cheeks. "I did it again."

Anna blinked, too stunned to say anything.

"But I think he changed his number . . . because the next time it was just dead." Gabi's lip wobbled. "I just miss him so much, Anna. I didn't want—" The rest of the sentence was lost as she covered her face with her hands and sobbed.

Anna scooted over and put her arms around Gabi. "I know," she said soothingly as she stroked her friend's hair. "I know . . ."

Gabi cried for a while, then composed herself, wiping her tears away with the heels of her hands. Anna passed her a box of tissues, and when Gabi had produced an elephant-worthy blow, she turned to face Anna.

"Do you think he changed his number because of you?" Anna asked.

Gabi shrugged. "He kept saying he wanted to upgrade—his contract was going to be up soon. Maybe he just got a new phone and got a new number? Or maybe he just didn't want to . . ." She swallowed. ". . . want to speak to me anymore."

Anna put an arm round Gabi and pulled her close. "Who cares why he did it? You don't need him. You deserve better than what he gave you."

"I know . . . I don't want Lee, really. Just being close to someone, not feeling so . . ." Gabi sobbed again.

"So alone?"

Gabi nodded as she wiped her nose yet again.

"I get that."

Gabi reached out and stroked her arm. "You more than anyone else. And I understand in my head I should move on, but my heart feels joined to him, whether I want it or not."

"Like me, you're just not in that place yet. And that's okay. Give yourself some time and space to process it all."

"Like you have."

Anna let out a dry laugh. "Like I'm trying to do."

"You have changed this year," Gabi said, nodding. "You don't see it, but I do. That's why you must give Brody time and space. You just said we can't push these things."

Anna rolled onto her side to face Gabi. "I didn't think I *wasn't* giving him that. I thought I was being a concerned friend." She pulled a tissue out the box in Gabi's hands and used one, suddenly finding herself teary too. "I care about him, Gabs. And I know you think that's ridiculous, seeing as I've never met the man."

"I don't think it's ridiculous."

Anna turned to look at Gabi. This was new . . .

"If you find someone who makes you feel better, even for a minute, then that's special." Gabi gave a hiccupy laugh. "Would you give me his number? I could do with some manly TLC."

Anna laughed as she was supposed to, but it surprised her how territorial she suddenly felt about Brody. "You think I should stop trying to contact him?" she asked quietly, neatly steering the conversation down another avenue.

Gabi nodded. "Yes, for a short time. See what happens."

Anna sighed heavily. "And what if nothing happens?"

Gabi shrugged. "You can't make people do what they don't want to, or aren't ready to do. I've learned this now."

Anna shuffled toward Gabi and kissed her cheek. "I love you," she said, smiling.

Gabi made a disbelieving face, but she smiled back. "It's hard not to. Now . . ." she said, pushing herself up to a sitting position and surveying the tangle of shirts they were lying on. "What are we going to do about this mess?"

"I have a plan," Anna said.

Gabi got to her feet and pulled Anna's arm to help her sit up. "Which is?"

Anna looked around at the clothes strewn everywhere and the piles of black sacks around the room. "Like you said, this is a job one needs to be 'present' for. I vote we leave this for now and open a bottle of something cold, crisp and alcoholic."

"Now *that* is a plan I can support," Gabi replied.

Chapter Forty-Nine

Anna was waiting for the lift in the multistory parking lot. Now it was November, the shopping center was open until nine most nights for Christmas shopping. With her trip to Canada looming, Anna had decided to get a head start. While she was watching the numbers on the display above the lift door count down, her phone rang. She grabbed it out of her handbag but dropped it immediately when she saw the caller ID.

Oh, hell! It seemed to have gotten buried under everything else. She rummaged around in her bag, silently praying it wouldn't go to voicemail before she could get to it. Finally, her stiff and uncooperative fingers grasped it. She pulled it up to her ear. "Brody?" she said breathlessly.

"Anna." He sounded . . . different. Not good. "We need to talk."

"I know," she said, just as the lift pinged and the doors opened in front of her. She'd known they needed to talk for one week and six days now; she was just very glad that Gabi had been right and he'd come around to realizing that on his own.

She squeezed into the lift, which was already filled with people with bulky shopping bags. "Brody . . . Are you okay?"

The lift doors slid closed. Brody said something, but it sounded a bit like he was speaking underwater, and the signal kept cutting out. Damn lift! "I can't hear you," she tried to say clearly but without actually shouting, because it suddenly seemed as if all ears in the confined space were trained on her conversation.

His reply was just garbled rubbish.

"Don't . . . Just don't go anywhere. Okay?" she said more loudly, not caring now who was listening. Let them have their show. "I'll call you back in a minute, I promise. Just please, please pick up when I do."

She started dialing Brody's number the moment the lift doors opened. Seconds later, she was striding across the parking lot, phone pressed to her ear as it continued to ring. What was taking him so long? He must have had the phone in his hand when he'd called her, and she'd hung up less than a minute ago.

It seemed to take an age, but finally she reached her car, unlocked it and slid into the driving seat. She slammed the door closed with her free hand, cutting off the noise of other vehicles and the whirring fans of the air-conditioning units of the shops below the parking lot.

She was staring ahead at a concrete post when he finally answered. "I'm going to tell you about a day in my life from just over nine years ago," he began. "I know you're going to have questions, Anna—you always do—but I'd really appreciate it if you just let me get through it before you ask anything."

"Okay," Anna replied quietly. She became aware of her pulse drumming rhythmically. This was serious. Really serious. Beyond the concrete pillar, the sky was dark and impenetrable.

Brody exhaled. "That day, I traveled with my ex-wife, Katri—she's Finnish—to my parents' house in the Lake District. They'd moved there about five years before. We were living in London at the time, in Richmond . . ."

Not a million miles from here, Anna thought. It was strange to think of Brody living less than twenty miles away at some point in the past, unreal almost.

"It was a long drive, made worse by an accident on the M6, and it took us about seven hours to get there." He paused for a moment, as if readying himself. "Our two-year-old daughter, Lena, was in the car with us."

Brody had a daughter?

Anna's mind reeled. How had she been talking to him all this time without knowing this? But she didn't have time to ponder that question, because Brody carried on, his tone flat like a newsreader's.

"Katri used to get migraines, and all that time stuck in traffic had set one off, so she went to have a lie down as soon as we arrived at my parents' house. They lived in a tiny hamlet, not quite as remote as where I am now, but almost. They've sold the house since, but one of the reasons they bought it was that it had a beautiful garden enclosed with dry stone walls. At the back of the house there was a patio, and then a lawn that sloped gently down to a large pond, maybe thirty feet across. It was beautiful that day," he added wistfully, "full of spring color."

He painted the picture so skilfully that Anna could see it in her head: the climbing roses, the neatly clipped grass, the bright, fresh leaves on the trees.

"Mum put the kettle on, as she always did when we arrived, and she suggested that after being cooped up in the car we went and sat outside and got some fresh air. I took Lena out there, and I sat at one of the large benches that flanked the oak patio table. She started off on my lap, but it wasn't long before she was wriggling. There was a ladybug on the back of the chair at the end of the table and she got up to investigate."

He paused for a moment. Anna could sense him revisiting that memory, letting it play in his head.

"She was fascinated. She put her face right up to it and watched it crawl around. Poor thing only just managed to fly away before she tried to pick it up. Once it was gone, she skipped around the table, singing to herself. She used to do that all the time, just making up the words as she went along. It was the most beautiful and honest creative expression I'd ever heard. And it made me think about Pip, the main character in my novels, and how she'd lost that same kind of innocence and joy, how she'd had to grow up fast and leave her childhood behind.

"I was about to start the last book in the series at that point, but I was stuck, struggling with her character development—what sort of person she'd end up being at the end of her journey. And listening to Lena sing about the 'ladybud' that had flown away, I knew that I couldn't leave her so fiercely independent, almost adult in her thinking. I realized I had to return her to some of that joyful childishness she'd lost. She needed to be just a girl again. She needed to have fun.

"I was lost in thought, just staring out over the garden. I suddenly realized the singing had stopped. I couldn't hear Lena anymore."

Brody paused then, and Anna could hear him dragging in a few ragged breaths, but she kept her promise. She let him talk.

"I stood up and looked around, expecting to see her bending over a flower or grinning at me from under the table, but she was nowhere. I called her name, started to walk down the lawn, looking for a flash of her red T-shirt, which should have stood out wonderfully against all that green, but I couldn't see anything but flowers and grass and shrubs." His voice dropped to a whisper. "And the pond . . ."

Anna clamped her hand over her mouth. She wanted to drop the phone and run away but she made herself sit there. Brody needed her. He needed her to listen to this. *Oh, Anna, be careful what you wish for . . .*

Brody's voice became even tighter. "The pond was covered in duckweed, exactly the same shade of green as the lawn, and to a two-year-old, it might have looked just like grass. I started running, and when I reached the edge of the pond, I could see a hole in the duckweed, ripples in the water . . ."

Anna began to cry. She made sure to do it silently so Brody wouldn't hear her.

"I started grabbing at the water blindly, but the pond was probably three or four feet deep at the edge and got even deeper toward the middle. I couldn't find her, Anna. I couldn't find her, not quickly enough, anyway . . ."

Anna swallowed. She waited until she was sure that Brody had finished his story, or at least as much of it as he could say, before she asked a question. She knew she was probably asking the obvious, but she had to do it. After so many months of mystery, she needed to know for sure. "Did you get her out?"

He cleared his throat and waited a few seconds before carrying on. "Yes. Before the paramedics arrived—my mother had come out with the tea tray just as I pulled Lena out of the pond and laid her on the grass. She dropped the tray, teapot and all, and ran back inside the house to phone them. But it was at least a twenty-minute drive from the nearest town, and I could tell from the looks on their faces when they finally arrived that there was no hope. Even though I'd been doing my best with CPR."

He broke off and all Anna could do was stare at the empty sky beyond the concrete posts of the parking lot. Her vocal cords were frozen shut. Brody had always had the right thing to say when she'd poured her soul out to him, and now she couldn't even say a single word of comfort back to him. Some friend she was.

"Did you know that a child can drown in under a minute?" he asked, but Anna wouldn't have replied if her voice had been working, because it almost seemed as if he was lost in his own words at this point, and he didn't really need her answer. "And that after a certain point, even if they're still alive, their body shuts down, making CPR much less likely to be effective?"

"Oh, Brody," Anna said, her voice finally emerging scratchily from her throat. "I'm so, so sorry."

"We were all numb with grief to start off with. You know what it's like . . ."

Anna nodded, unable to talk without sobbing, so she held it in. Even though she knew Brody couldn't hear her, she felt it important that she agreed, and she hoped he could feel it rather than hear it.

"But after a few months the numbness wore off and I got angry. I blamed my parents—for having the pond, for not having fenced it in to make it safe, even though I knew this was their first grandchild and it probably just hadn't occurred to them. I said horrible things, Anna. I cut them off, refused to speak to them. And that was a despicable thing to do, to blame them, but I was being selfish and pigheaded. What else could I do? I had to blame someone. And I certainly hadn't been able to face laying the blame where I should."

"Brody . . ." Anna said, with a warning tone in her voice. She had a feeling she knew where this was going.

"It was *my* fault."

There. He'd said it. Anna wished she could reach out and touch him.

"I shouldn't have drifted off in my own imaginary world. I should have kept hold of her when she tried to wriggle away. I should have been faster . . . looked harder . . ."

"Oh, Brody," Anna said again. "You know that's not true, don't you?"

"No," he said baldly. "And I'm not the only one who thought so."

"Did your wife blame you too? Is that why she left?"

"At first," Brody said. "While I was still blaming my parents, but later she softened, said it was an accident. She wanted us to go through it together, share our grief, but I couldn't do it. It was as if I had a wall around me. I couldn't let her in. I couldn't let anybody in. It was the only thing holding me together, you see, the only thing keeping me sane."

"I know," Anna said softly. She hadn't had a wall, exactly, but she'd had her own coping mechanism, her numbness, her refusal to engage with the world. She sniffed, and then she sobbed. It had all built up, and now it was coming out noisily. So much for not letting on to Brody.

"Don't cry for me, Anna," he said with so much softness that it only made her cry harder. "I don't deserve it."

Anna grabbed a tissue from a packet in the center console of the car, blew her nose and composed herself. Alongside the aching sadness, his words prompted something hot and fiery inside her. Now she was angry with him too. "After Spencer died, I kept questioning myself, moving all the variables around, as if his death was a game of chess I could win if I could only get the pieces in the right place.

"What if that driver hadn't been drunk that evening? Or hadn't drunk as much? What if I hadn't wanted something from the corner shop, or if I hadn't called Spencer back to ask him to get some milk too? He'd have left thirty seconds earlier. What if he'd crossed the road at a different point? In the end, I had come to one conclusion—this was a game I couldn't win. It was always going to be checkmate because it was an accident—and so was what happened to Lena."

He made a disbelieving noise, but Anna wasn't letting him off with that.

"Like most accidents, there was a multitude of moving parts, just as there was with what happened to me. A handful of circumstances came together, stupid little things that if they'd happened on their own, would have meant nothing. But they did happen together, and it created a perfect storm, for want of a better term. Would you tell me that just because one of those variables was down to me that Spencer's death was my fault?"

"Of course not!"

"Then why won't you accept the same for yourself? If there hadn't been traffic on the motorway, you wouldn't have been as tired. If your wife hadn't had a migraine, then both of you would have been outside with her. You see what I mean?"

"It's not the same!"

Anna closed her eyes and screamed silently inside her head. Stubborn didn't even begin to describe it. She wasn't going to win this argument, not now, not today. "Okay . . . Even if it was your fault, even if maybe you could have stopped it happening, what does that mean? You have to punish yourself forever? What does that accomplish? How does that make anyone, even the people we've lost, any happier?" Her voice grew hoarse again. "How does it make them any more alive?"

Brody remained silent. It seemed she might have finally hit on a nerve.

"You've got to find a way to forgive yourself, Brody."

There was a sarcastic edge to his voice when he replied, "You mean I've got to *be kind* to myself?"

"Yes," she replied simply.

"I can't," he said, his voice stretching so tight that Anna felt her heart begin to crack.

"Can't or won't?" she prodded softly.

Brody didn't give her a reply.

Chapter Fifty

It was the last day of November, and the moors looked magical in the early morning sunshine. Brody had woken up with the urge to go for a long bracing walk, and instead of doing his usual route on the slopes and valleys near his cottage, he'd jumped in his Land Rover and had driven eight miles east to Haytor, a coarse granite outcrop on one of the highest points of Dartmoor. He was ready for a fresh route, a fresh challenge.

He parked the car at the Dartmoor visitor center, took a moment to admire the ancient tor at the top of the hill, and set off, Lewis bounding beside him.

Brody never wore headphones or took music with him when he went for a walk or run. He preferred to keep his senses alert, to take in the environment. The silence allowed his brain to produce its own noise when he needed to think about things.

And since he'd told Anna about Lena almost a fortnight ago, he'd had a lot to think about, good and bad. He'd had a couple of nightmares right afterward, the same as those he'd had for years after Lena had died, but they'd eased off and he hadn't had one in more than a week now. For some strange reason that made him feel optimistic.

Maybe it was because Ibrahim had declared he'd had a bit of a breakthrough. After weeks and months of careful desensitization, teaching his body and mind that a town full of ordinary people was nothing to be terrified of, they'd finally started to agree with him. He'd managed a full trolley shop at the supermarket in Totnes. Not at peak time on a Saturday afternoon, but still. As well as his usual supplies, he'd bought lemongrass, coconut milk and jasmine rice. And, after smiling at the woman at the checkout counter, he'd gone home and cooked himself a Thai green curry. When he'd eaten it, he hadn't been able to help wishing Anna had been sitting across the table from him, sharing not only his meal but his victory.

That evening, he'd felt so invincible that he'd called her and told her he was going to be in London to meet her on New Year's Eve. He'd considered asking her to make the location somewhere less public, somewhere less challenging, but he'd held back. He wasn't ready to tell her about his agoraphobia yet, and he was worried she'd push for an explanation. If she knew what he struggled with, she might call the meeting off, and that was the last thing he wanted.

He *would* tell her at some point. Maybe after Big Ben had chimed at midnight, announcing the New Year. By then his demons would surely have been soundly routed. There was nothing that was going to stop him getting up to the seventy-second floor of the Shard and meeting Anna, from having a proper conversation face-to-face. Absolutely nothing.

Brody reached Haytor and stood, his hands on his hips. The rough grass had been glittering with frost further down the hill but right up here, just covering the rocks and the grassy space at their base, was a light dusting of snow. Brody turned and stared at the village down below. He wasn't ready to go back yet, so he just kept on striding.

And as he walked, his thoughts were not about imaginary characters or tales of faraway lands, but of his own story over the last year. He'd started January in the same dark, unforgiving place he'd been in for the past nine years, both mentally and emotionally. But he was no longer there. As he made his way along the ridge of a hill, miles of countryside stretched before him, he realized he felt lighter inside.

Oh, he knew he still had a way to go, that further progress needed to be made, but for the first time in years, he could see that the prison door in front of him was wide open. All he had to do now was take a step and walk right through it.

The lightness inside spurred him on, and when he reached a small rocky outcrop, he clambered on top of it and yelled for all the world to hear. At first, it was just noise, but then words started forming in his head, and he let them out too. "I'm out of the pit!" he yelled to no one in particular. "I'm *freeeee* . . ."

More words came into his head, and he had to let those ones out too. "I love her," he shouted into the wind, then absorbed the sound of those syllables, their weight and substance, let the certainty come back to him and sink into his bones. And then he turned toward the east, toward the sun—and London—and shouted again. "I love you, Anna Barry!" Lewis barked and ran around madly below him.

It had felt good to say it out loud, even though he didn't know what good it would do him. But letting the words free, so they were no longer trapped inside his head and heart, had seemed like the right thing to do. He could imagine them as a white dove that had been released from the pinnacle of the moors, now rising on thermals and disappearing beyond the horizon. He stood there for a few minutes, watching the sky, before exhaling heavily and making his way off the rocks. Suddenly, he was really hungry.

"I think a massive fry-up is in order," he said to Lewis, who barked his agreement as they set off back in the direction of the Land Rover.

But it seemed his subconscious wasn't finished with him yet. As he navigated through the gorse and jumped over peaty streams, a little voice began to whisper in his ear. A voice he hadn't heard for years.

What about me? she said. *You left me in a dark place too.*

Pip.

Once, he'd heard that little girl speak so clearly that she'd felt real to him. He'd written a handful of books before he'd stumbled across Pip, but she'd definitely been his favorite character: small and thoughtful, bold and resourceful. She'd appeared in his imagination one day, fully formed, with her short, tomboyish blond hair and a determined look in her clear blue eyes. She'd almost felt like another daughter at times.

The resemblance between her and Lena, when she'd come along, had been both unsettling and magical, as if, in some cosmic way, he'd already known his child, the person she would become. For a long time, he'd refused to let himself think about Pip, but he did so now, imagining what the expression on her face would be as she reminded him of her predicament.

Sorry, girl, he replied silently. *I left you camping in that Vale of Shadows, didn't I? I didn't mean to. It was only ever supposed to be a pit stop, but then . . . I just didn't know how to get you out again. I didn't know how to get either of us out.*

Pip tilted her head to one side and raised an eyebrow. *Do you think you could try?*

Brody pondered her question as he turned to come back down the hill toward the parking lot.

Maybe.

Maybe he could.

He'd done a lot of things in the last few months that he'd never thought he'd be able to do again. Maybe there was room for one more impossible thing in his life.

Chapter Fifty-One

Anna's flight got into Halifax airport just after lunchtime on the fifteenth of December. She'd been up since six a.m., and awake for three hours before that, so when she finally collected her suitcase and dragged it blearily through to Arrivals, it took a couple of seconds before she saw her father waiting for her.

"Dad!" she yelled, and almost left her luggage where it was and ran to meet him, but that probably wouldn't have made her popular with airport security, or the passengers groggily following her, so she made herself stay patient and waited until she'd pulled her suitcase through the barriers and could greet him properly. He smiled the whole time he waited for her to make the short journey and wrapped her in a strong, silent male hug the moment she was close enough. Oh, it was good to see him again.

"Where's Mum?" she asked, after kissing him on the cheek.

"Oh, you know," he said. "Cooking . . . Fussing . . . I hope you didn't eat for a least a month before you came because she's determined to fill you up while you're here." He looked her up and down. "You look well."

Anna smiled back at her Dad. She'd learned from an early age that he wasn't one for empty compliments, or empty words of any kind, so when he said something as seemingly throwaway as this, she knew not to dismiss it as small talk. He really meant it.

"Thank you," she said, agreeing to his gesture to take her case as she did so. "I *feel* well."

Her mother was indeed cooking (and fussing) when they arrived at their pretty clapboard house in Chester, only an hour's drive away from the airport. After hugging the life out of her and instructing Anna's dad to deposit the luggage in the spare room, she sat Anna down in the kitchen and plied her with tea and lemon cake while they caught up on each other's news and plans for the Christmas period.

"What about the Barrys?" Anna's mother asked, helping Anna to a second slice of cake. "Have you seen anything of them recently?"

"Well, that's the funny thing," Anna said, her mouth still partly full of crumbs, which couldn't be helped because her mother's lemon cake was notoriously gooey and lovely. "Richard turned up on my doorstep a few days ago."

"He did? What did he have to say for himself?" Anna's mother folded her arms. "I'm surprised that woman let him out of the house! He seems to need her permission to do anything. Talk about henpecked . . . I don't know how he stands it."

Ever since Anna had told her mother about the incident at Teresa's party, Gayle had become "that woman." Anna couldn't help loving her mother for her unswerving loyalty. Her father had returned to the room while they'd been talking, and when he heard the word "henpecked" he winked at Anna, causing her to almost choke on the remaining cake crumbs.

"What did Richard say?" he asked, swiping a slice of cake before her mother could bat his hand away. He was supposed to be watching his cholesterol.

"It was all a bit awkward, but, basically, he said that they'd missed seeing me."

Anna's mother arched her eyebrows. "They?"

"That's what I said to him. I asked why, if both of them wanted to see me, why both of them weren't standing on my doorstep."

"Anna! You didn't leave him standing on the doorstep, did you?"

Anna found herself rolling her eyes like a teenager. "No, Mum. I asked him in, gave him a cup of tea—it's okay, your reputation as a parent who raised me well is still intact."

"Good," she replied, and Anna's father hid a smile.

"He said he knew what Gayle had said to me at the party— Teresa told Scott, and Scott told his dad, I gather—and that he wanted me to know that he didn't agree with what she said and had told her as much."

"Wow," her mother said. "And he's still breathing?"

Anna chuckled. "Looked like it to me. He said he hoped we could—what were his words?—put it all behind us."

"And how did you react to that?"

"I said I missed him too, that I missed being part of the Barry family—because that's true—but I also said that I couldn't just come back and pretend it had never happened, that I wasn't prepared to sweep it all under the rug like I normally do and kowtow to Gayle. He didn't look happy about that, but I think he understood."

"Good girl," her mother said. "You've been far too patient with that woman. So . . . what happens next?"

"I don't know," Anna said, staring out of the window to the pine trees across the road. "I guess I'll work it out when I get back. And talking of work . . . I've decided to take Vijay and Rhys up on their offer to go back to BlockTime. That's another thing I'll have to figure out as I go along, but I'm excited about it. I never really saw myself as a creative person, not compared to Spencer, but the guys made me see that there are different ways of being creative. I'm looking forward to finding out how that applies to me."

Her dad walked past and kissed the top of her head. "I think this is going to be brilliant for you, Anna."

Her mother's eyes sparkled. "I'm so pleased!"

"Thanks for giving me a little nudge in the right direction, Mum."

Her mother looked horrified. "I didn't push, did I?"

"No," Anna said, smiling. Not technically. Her father gave her another wink.

THANKFULLY, ANNA'S MOTHER had been able to schedule quite a few days off work in the lead-up to Christmas, and Anna spent some much-needed time with her parents, allowing them to share some of their favorite haunts in their new neighborhood with her, going out for lovely lunches and long walks, reading books by the fire and eating far too much of her mother's baking. It was just what she needed.

On Christmas morning, Anna woke at five a.m., just as she always had done when she was small, and discovered that Father Christmas (well, actually, just her father) had left a brightly decorated stocking at the foot of her bed. She refrained from rushing into her parents' room and bouncing on their bed as she might have done in earlier years and instead made good headway into the chocolate orange she found inside whilst she read a magazine and waited for them to stir.

As was their family tradition, they had a breakfast of thick bacon sandwiches with a huge pot of tea in the kitchen, then moved to the living room to hand around presents.

Anna perched on a footstool, sipping her large mug of tea. Her mother passed her a large box wrapped in red and silver paper. "Happy Christmas, darling," she said. Anna's eyebrows rose. She had no idea what this was.

She unwrapped it carefully, then lifted the lid of the expensive-looking box. "Oh, my goodness, Mum . . . Dad . . . It's gorgeous!" Inside lay a soft brown leather briefcase, elegant but with the hint of an old-fashioned school satchel about it. She lifted it out of the box and slung it over her shoulder. It was gloriously smooth to the touch and reminded her of the color of chestnuts.

Anna stood up and went and hugged her mother and then her father, bag still swinging at her side. "I love it," she said, stroking it some more. "I'd been looking for something for when I start at BlockTime, but I didn't want a traditional hard briefcase or a messenger bag. How did you know?"

"I saw you eyeing it up when we went to the shopping mall," her mother said, looking very pleased with herself, "and I thought what better present than a smart but very individual bag for a smart but very individual woman about to start a new phase in her career."

Anna hugged the bag to herself without squishing it. Her mother had always been great at her job, always the perfect female role model, and the fact she felt Anna had the potential to follow in her footsteps meant a lot.

She pulled the bag off her shoulder, arranged it at an angle at the bottom of the Christmas tree, and snapped a photo of it, which she then sent straight to Brody, with the caption, *From my Mum and Dad. I'm going to be a proper businesswoman!*

A few minutes later, her phone buzzed in her dressing gown pocket and she pulled it out to find a reply: a picture of a particularly ugly pair of Christmas socks, adorned with a Rudolph with a light-up red nose. *From MY Mum and Dad*, his accompanying message read. *I'm going to look a right plonker!* Anna laughed out loud.

"What's so funny?" her mother asked.

Anna leaned over and showed her the photo. "It's from Brody," she explained, and went on to outline how she'd recently encouraged him to get in touch with his parents after years of a strained relationship. He'd been hesitant but had finally listened to her, and they'd invited him up to Keswick for Christmas. "I hope it's going okay," she said. "This is a huge step for him."

Her mother nodded. "It sounds as if you're as much good for him as he's been for you."

"I'm beginning to think so too. Did I tell you we're meeting on New Year's Eve?"

"At least twice already," her mother said, laughing. "You talk about this Brody *a lot*. Much more than you ever did that Jeremy fellow."

"Do I?" Anna said. "I hadn't realized."

Her mother gave her a knowing look. "And you don't think there might be a spark there between you when you finally meet?"

"Mum . . . You're as bad as Gabi! I've already told you I don't think of him that way." She pulled a brightly wrapped package from underneath the tree and handed it to her mother, shaking her head.

Her mother was planning on serving up a traditional English Christmas lunch, which meant there was plenty of work to be done before the select handful of friends they'd invited turned up later, so as soon as they'd finished dishing out presents and clearing away the wrapping paper, all three of them headed into the kitchen.

Anna began to chop onions for her mother's favorite stuffing recipe—pork with fresh chestnuts—and as her knife hit the chopping board in a repetitive motion, she couldn't help thinking about what her mother had said about Brody, and each time she did, there was a worrying fluttering in her stomach, a tickling she recognized but quickly decided she'd really rather not label.

ANNA WOKE ON Boxing Day to a most spectacular view. Her parents had the large back garden her father had always dreamed about, with woodland beyond, and that morning it was covered in five inches of snow. Unlike London, nowhere near the amount to faze the locals or stop them going about their business, but just enough to make it look as if the whole world was a clumsily iced Christmas cake.

There was a soft knock at her bedroom door, and her mother appeared, carrying a tray. "Thought you might like breakfast in bed," she said as she laid it on the mattress.

Anna pushed herself up to sitting. "Oh, Mum . . . You shouldn't have. Not after all the work you did yesterday."

Her mother shrugged as she poured tea from a teapot. "I don't get the chance to spoil you much, so just let me, okay?"

Anna smiled at her. "Okay," she said, then settled down to eat her breakfast while her mum sat in the armchair near the window. When she was finished, Anna stretched again and prepared to swing her legs around and place her feet on the floor. "I could stay in bed all day if I put my mind to it."

Her mother picked the tray up. "Then why don't you?"

Anna frowned, the soles of her feet only an inch above the thick carpet. "But we're supposed to be going to that open house Barry and Janet are throwing, aren't we?"

"They're our friends, not yours. And they're going to have a houseful anyway. You'll get another chance to meet them before you go home. Besides, I have a feeling you could do with this."

Her mother gave her the firm look she remembered from her teenage years, then exited with the tray before she could argue. Anna dithered for a second, but then caught a glance of the snowy garden and decided that maybe doing what she was told today wouldn't be such a bad idea.

When her parents left the house for lunch with their friends, Anna snuggled down in the duvet and stared out the window, just letting her thoughts wander where they wanted to, until she needed to change position and turned to lie on her back, and then she pulled the duvet up over her head.

It was just as white and calm there as the snowy world outside, but it wasn't like her duvet cocoon at home, she realized. Back there, she'd climbed into bed hoping she would cease to exist, but as she lay there—breathing, relaxing, simply *being*—she didn't feel dead and numb. She felt alive.

She felt like *Anna*.

When she finally had to leave the bed to head to the bathroom and grab a plate of leftovers for lunch, she decided that being alone and chilled out was good but having some company would be even better.

After checking the time, she worked out that it would be midafternoon back home. Her thoughts wandered to Brody. She picked up her phone and dialed his number, hoping fervently that he hadn't been carted off to a buffet lunch with his parents' friends as she almost had been but, thankfully, he picked up.

"Merry Christmas!" Anna said brightly, not so much because she was overexcited about the festive season but because she was really pleased to hear his voice. Brody just grunted, which made Anna laugh.

"How's it going?" she asked him. "Are you wearing the socks?"

That earned her another grunt. "I kind of *had* to put them on this morning . . ." He paused and she stifled a laugh as she imagined him shaking his head in disgruntled disbelief. "This visit is about building bridges, after all, and it's going okay, I suppose. A bit awkward, obviously, because I've kept them at arm's length for so long. I can see they're desperate to rush in, fill in the gap that's been there all these years, but at the same time they're wary, not wanting to push things."

"I'm sure you'll find your way with each other."

"Yes. Yes, I think we will. Eventually . . ."

Anna smiled. "Even though I'm in a different house from the one that I grew up in—in a different country!—I still feel a bit like I'm regressing to my teenage self when I come to stay with my parents. Do you feel that way too?"

Brody laughed drily. "A little. I made the mistake of trying to start a conversation in the middle of the Queen's speech and got a withering look from my father. I kind of liked it, because it was the one moment all day when I felt the years had melted away and we were just ourselves again."

"Better watch yourself," Anna said cheekily. "You don't want your phone privileges taken away!"

"No," Brody said, a real warmth in his tone. "That wouldn't do at all."

She knew he was talking about this . . . *them* . . . and it made her heart feel as light as helium. "No, it really wouldn't."

They sat in comfortable silence for a while and then Brody said, "I'm writing again."

Anna almost leapt out of bed in surprise. Instead she ended up on her knees, almost bouncing on the mattress. "Brody! That's incredible! I'm so proud of you! What brought that on?"

He coughed. Anna could almost imagine him blushing. "I didn't want to say anything at first, just in case it was a fluke, but that was a few weeks ago now I've started, I can hardly stop. It's as if all the words that have been caught behind a dam for the last nine years are suddenly pouring forth at once."

If Anna could have done a somersault right there on the mattress, she would have done. "What are you working on?"

"Well, I don't want to jinx it by saying too much at the moment, but you'll be the first person to hear about it when I'm ready to share."

Anna picked up a pillow and hugged it to herself. "Oh, Brody. I'm so pleased." She sighed. "I wish I could give you a big hug to say well done."

There was a moment of silence. "Well, in five days, you can."

Five days. She could hardly believe it. For so long, New Year's Eve had seemed an eternity away, and now it was practically upon them. "You're definitely going to be there?" she said, feeling an unexpected swoop in her stomach, and another fluttery tickle, which she determinedly ignored. Brody had sometimes seemed a little tense when she'd mentioned their planned meeting.

"I'm coming," he said firmly. "No matter what. I will be waiting for you up there, Anna. You can count on that."

Chapter Fifty-Two

*B*rody closed the hotel room door behind him and slumped against it. He'd made it. He was in London. A place that had once been his home but now, compared to the craggy, misty moor he spent most of his time on, it seemed totally alien. He remained where he was, leaning against the door, overnight bag in hand, and took a moment to catch his breath.

Once he'd collected himself, he stood upright again and walked forward, through a marble-tiled hallway with modern lines and high-end designer fittings. There were a couple of glass ornaments on a sleek console table that he didn't even have a name for. Every object, every detail, oozed luxury.

He almost guffawed at himself as he stepped onto the plush carpet of the living area of his suite. It seemed he could see to the very edges of the city from this height. It stretched out beyond the floor-to-ceiling windows, glittering against a dramatic sunset of purples, grays and pinks.

It would not be an overstatement to say he'd splurged a bit. But it was nothing to do with pampering himself and absolutely everything to do with being practical. At the beginning of December, he'd drawn up a plan with Ibrahim to give himself the best chance of making it through this evening without a major slip. In the run-up to tonight, he'd been to both Totnes and Dartmouth numerous times, and had even fitted in a trip to Exeter. It had been a hard slog, sometimes feeling like one step forward and two steps back, but he thought he was ready. He *hoped* he was ready. While he still wasn't comfortable with large crowds for extended periods of time, he did have a variety of tools to help himself cope with them.

Part of the plan for tonight was to limit the triggers, not deal with packed spaces more than necessary. So, when he'd discovered there was a hotel in the Shard itself, and that it had parking facilities, meaning he'd be able to drive all the way from his front door to the hotel, it had been a no-brainer. It hadn't mattered how much it cost, which was just as well, because availability on New Year's Eve had been slim, so he'd ended up with one of the fancy suites.

He was already in the right building, so no need to deal with taxis or crowded public transport, or even herds of excited revelers in the streets below. And if he felt a panic attack looming, maybe he and Anna could come down here to get away. It would solve a dual purpose, because he had something to give her—if his courage didn't fail him.

In less than seven hours he would meet her, and they would speak face-to-face the way they talked on the phone. He'd be able to see her frown in concentration as she chewed an idea over, or watch her eyes light up in delight. He'd imagined what her smile would look like a thousand times, but tonight he would see it for real, and that meant he didn't really care about the two-thousand-pound price tag for this stupidly ostentatious suite. It was worth every penny.

Don't dream about midnight, though, mate. She's not Cinderella and you're definitely not Prince Charming.

Brody nodded to himself and walked through to the immense

drawing room of his suite, complete with seating area, dining table laid for six, and a telescope on a tripod. He turned right and headed into the bedroom, then sat down on the end of the sumptuously bedecked bed, stared out the window at the darkening sky and wondered what to do next.

ANNA EMERGED FROM London Bridge station along with what seemed like half the city. Everyone was in groups. One such sprawling collection of friends flowed around her on the pavement, as they joked and sang, dawdling along the road in the vague direction of Borough Market. Anna waited until they'd passed and then she looked up. The height of the glass building above her was dizzying. She was still a little jet lagged, thanks to her flight home from Canada only two days earlier. Why else should she feel so jittery this evening?

She checked her watch. Ten-forty. It might take a while to get through security and queue for the lifts. This was it. Time to go inside.

She flashed her ticket at the man in red livery by the door then headed up the stairs to the security area. Once through that, she stood in line for the lift to the thirty-third floor. Everyone was dressed up to the nines and in high spirits. Anna couldn't help being swept along a little with the buzz. She was excited, she realized, more so than nervous, not that it made any difference to her skittering pulse.

One ear-popping ride later, she queued for a second lift to take her all the way to the top. She emerged on the sixty-eighth floor and inhaled deeply as she took in her surroundings. There wasn't much square footage when you were this high up in the needle-like structure of Europe's tallest building. A wide strip of floor ran around a central block that housed stairs and lift shafts, and what little other space existed was filled with people. Some milled around the long bar, others sipped their cocktails and looked out through the overlapping layers of glass and metal to the twinkling city beyond.

Anna turned and faced the stairs. She and Brody had agreed to meet on the top floor of the View from The Shard, where it was open to the air. She buttoned her coat up at the top, took a deep breath and headed up a few short flights of stairs to the seventy-second floor.

It was busy when she arrived up there, but not as crammed as it had been below in the warm. Music played and low lighting in different hues illuminated not just the guests but the large glass panels that rose jaggedly into the sky above their heads, cycling through the colors of the rainbow. She stepped forward and peered around. She'd told him she didn't need a photo, because she already knew what he looked like, but she now realized that relying on the grainy and out-of-date black-and-white photo from his website to make an identification hadn't been the best idea.

While a couple of the men within view might have fitted the bill, they were all with partners or friends. Anna took a deep breath and headed off in a counterclockwise direction. A few moments later, in the opposite corner of the structure to the one she'd entered from, she spotted a lone figure staring out across the city skyline. Although he was less than ten feet from the nearest group of partygoers, he seemed separate, totally self-contained.

It was him.

Anna's heart skipped but she remained where she was, content to study him unobserved for a few moments. He was taller than she'd imagined. Broader too, although not bulky, and he gripped the railing in front of him not so much as if he was resting on it but clinging onto it. It made her feel a bit better that he might be nervous too.

He straightened slightly, as if he'd heard a noise, or had sensed something. Anna held her breath as he turned and looked around. He didn't spot her straightaway. His gaze swept past her, and she could see him scanning the crowd, looking more tense than hopeful.

Now she could see his face properly, she realized he did indeed look very much like the photo on his website. Older, yes. A little more battered around the edges, but pretty much the same. She should have expected that. The Brody she knew would never allow himself to be airbrushed.

What was she doing just standing there? It was stupid. This was the moment she'd been waiting for all year. In a few short seconds, she'd be standing in front of him, and she knew without a doubt that the first thing she was going to do was wrap her arms around him and pull him close. How could she do anything else?

She started walking toward him. He must have sensed the movement out of the corner of his eye because his head turned, and he looked straight at her. Their gazes locked.

Anna stopped, momentarily winded, her smile petrifying on her face. She couldn't quite describe the sensation that had rolled over her the moment they'd made eye contact. It was like . . . It reminded her of . . .

Running into a brick wall at full pelt.

The world shifted beneath her feet, causing her to shoot out a hand to steady herself, inadvertently grabbing onto the arm of a fellow partygoer. She couldn't think straight. Her head was swimming. Only one thing made sense at that moment. Only one person.

Brody.

This was Brody.

Everything she felt for him—all the emotions she now realized she'd wilfully ignored or mislabeled—erupted from deep inside her, leaving her breathless. She'd only experienced this rush once before in her life, and she'd foolishly assumed she'd been safe, that it had been a one-time thing.

This wasn't just Brody. It was *her* Brody.

"Hey," the guy she'd grabbed onto said. "What do you think you're doing?"

Anna snapped her head round to look at him. That was a very good question. She let go of the arm of his suit, shook her head in apology and stepped away. Then Anna did the only possible thing she could do.

She began to run.

Chapter Fifty-Three

*B*rody had arrived the moment the doors of the observation deck opened to the public for the New Year's Eve party. He'd reckoned it would be easier to find a quiet place to wait and let the crowd build around him, rather than having to push through all those people just before he was due to come face-to-face with Anna. He'd hoped it would help to become slowly accustomed to the space, to the rising numbers of bodies, and he'd been right.

Yes, he was still hyper-aware of the people behind him that he couldn't see. Yes, the music was too loud to his ears and the city lights stung his eyes. By his reckoning, he was somewhere between a six and a seven on his panic scale, nine being the point at which he started to slide into the full-blown attack of a ten. He probably would have got to that point already, but there was one thought he clung to as the sea of anxiety churned around him.

Anna.

She was his anchor.

It felt as if he'd been standing in this corner of the observation deck for days, but it must have only been two hours. He checked his watch. Ten-fifty-eight. She would be here at any moment. She might be here already.

Taking a deep breath and keeping one hand on the rail in front of him, he turned, searching the crowd. It was hard to focus, the rising panic making things blurry, but as he began to breathe his familiar counts of three, it slowly became easier to fix on one person at a time.

Movement to his right caught his eye and he turned, looking toward the flash of midnight blue beneath a coat of the same color. His heart almost stopped.

It was her.

He would have recognized her anywhere, even though he only had that one photograph to go on. She started to smile, to lift her hand in a wave, but then she kind of . . . froze. The smile died on her lips. Before he could even make out what was going on, she was running. Running back toward the door she'd just come through, the skirt of her coat flying behind her.

Brody's first instinct was to chase after her. He felt the pull of momentum inside his chest, but his brain hesitated in sending the message to his feet. His hand gripped the railing as if it were welded to it. It took a second or two before he managed to uncurl his stiff fingers and move.

She was out of reach, beyond the sea of people now. There was only one way he'd be able to catch up, and it didn't involve skirting round the edge of the space nervously, one hand steadying himself against the glass and steel.

He had to find out what was wrong. He took a deep breath and plunged through the mass of bodies, not even caring as he bumped against them, as they turned to give him disdainful looks.

Anna had disappeared down the staircase she'd emerged from, the one that read *Emergency Exit and Disabled Only*. He tried to dart after her, but a burly security guard blocked his way and jerked his thumb in the direction of the staircase on the opposite side of the observation deck. He didn't have time to argue, so he dashed through the people again, circling the central block until he reached it.

His feet pounded on the wooden risers edged with metal and he flung himself round each turn in the narrow staircase until he emerged on the sixty-ninth floor, panting and looking around wildly. His face was beginning to tingle, and his hands felt as if someone was jabbing four-inch pins into them, a sure sign that he was over-breathing, that his stress levels were through the roof. Under other circumstances, he might have found that funny, given that this was the highest point in the city and there was no roof above him save the heavens.

Anna must have come down to this level, but because he'd used a different staircase, it was impossible to guess which way she'd gone. The lift shafts and staircases ran up the center of the building, so there was no clear line of sight from one side of the space to the other. Brody swallowed down his panic and did the only thing possible. Somehow, he managed to ignore the throng of strangers jostling against him as he moved through the crowd and completed a full circuit of the floor, but he arrived back where he'd started without even a glimpse of her.

Had she gone down one more level to where the lifts and the toilets were? It was the only place left to look. He headed down yet another staircase to check, thinking as he did so that, with two viewing decks and two different staircases, he and Anna might circle round this place for hours, finding endless ways to evade each other. The most sensible thing would be to go back to where he'd been standing when he'd first seen her. If she was looking for him too now, it was the obvious place for her to go.

He was looking for the "up" staircase to do just that, when he passed the bank of lifts that had brought him up here earlier.

There weren't many people wanting to descend the tower before midnight struck, but a handful were waiting for the next available lift. The doors opened just as he spotted Anna at the back of the group, desperately trying to work her way further forward, and she slid past the bodies and into the lift.

He reached the doors just as they began to slide closed. Their eyes met. She looked as panicked as he felt. Maybe more so. His chest tightened further.

"I'm so sorry, Brody. I—"

The doors cut off whatever she'd been about to say, and Brody was left standing alone in a spartan corridor of polished steel and bare white surfaces.

That was it. He'd been cut free. His anchor was gone. The full storm surge he'd been trying to hold back all evening finally hit him.

Gasping for breath, he clutched at his chest as he stumbled back against the wall and began to slide toward the floor. His vision went blurry and breathing became impossible. He closed his eyes as he heard the lift attendant shout, "Hey! Someone call an ambulance! I think this guy's having a heart attack!"

Chapter Fifty-Four

The lift sped downward, causing Anna's ears to pop, but she hardly took in the journey at all. It was only when a blast of cold air hit her as she stumbled out onto the street that she had any sense of where she was. She was unable to process a single thought, and the adrenaline flooding through her system propelled her forward and away. Fight or flight, they said, and just like last New Year's Eve, flight seemed to be Anna's thing. She was such a coward.

What are you afraid of, then?

The question curled its way into her consciousness but only served to spur her on. She pointed herself toward the crowds and busy traffic of London Bridge Street and staggered along in her heels.

She couldn't think about that. She couldn't think about why she was running or what she had just done. Better to just lurch along numbly in this insulating haze.

She turned the corner onto the main road and was swept along with a group of people at the crossing. She found herself in one of the outlying areas of Borough Market, a kind of glassed-in picnic area on most days, but tonight it had been transformed. People ten years her junior mingled, drinking, talking, laughing.

Anna entered and pushed her way through them until she reached the solid structure of a bar and clung onto it with both hands. "Gin! Double!" she yelled at the bartender. The gin arrived in what looked like a goldfish bowl on a thin glass stalk, but Anna didn't care what kind of glass it was in; it wasn't going to be staying in there long anyway. She downed it and shoved the glass back in the direction of the bartender, who nodded and refilled it as nonchalantly as if she'd been politely asking for a vanilla latte.

She bumped up against something, realized it was a barstool and slid onto it.

No, this was not happening again.

Damn that man for waking her up, for changing her from a sleepwalker into . . . this. This person who could think and *feel*, who had so much more to lose than a semiconscious zombie. It was all his fault.

For a moment, she managed to cobble just enough anger together to justify her actions. But only for a moment. After that, it all began to slide, down and down into a vast black pit that was opening up inside her.

Anna only knew one way to deal with these kinds of feelings. She needed to return to that state, that place—calm and blank and peaceful. But since there were no soft white sheets here, no duvets to be seen, Anna picked up her gin and began to drink.

BRODY CLOSED THE bathroom door, walked over to the toilet and put the lid down. He sat on top of it, resting his elbows on his knees, and his head in his hands. Oh, God. That had been humiliating and embarrassing and terrifying. Basically, his worst fears about a panic attack come to life.

All those people looking at him . . . And he'd had no way to get away from them, paralyzed by his own mind and body.

Thankfully, he'd managed to convince the paramedics he was fine, quietly outlining to them his history as the lift attendant had shooed the gathering crowd back around the corner and out of view. After a few tests and checks, the medical professionals had reluctantly agreed. They'd been really nice about it, actually. Which had only made him feel even more stupid and helpless.

But whatever he'd felt in that moment, it was nothing compared to the stabbing in his chest when he thought of the look in Anna's eyes as the lift doors had closed.

He pulled his phone out of his pocket and rang her number. And then he rang it again, and again, and again. When that failed, he resorted to texting.

Where are you?
Are you okay?
I'm worried about you.
Please call back.

He was behaving like a clingy teenage girl. Also humiliating. But he didn't care. He had to know she was all right. What he felt didn't matter.

He growled with frustration at his blank and silent phone, and was almost tempted to hurl it across the room, but he didn't want to be charged for the fancy TV hidden inside the bathroom mirror, so he stuffed it back in his pocket and strode into his suite.

He kept walking until he reached the corner of the dining area that looked over both the Thames and the city of London. She was out there somewhere amidst all those winking lights, possibly ill, possibly . . . something. He couldn't get his head round it.

Why, after being so insistent that they meet, had she turned tail the moment she'd set eyes on him? It didn't make any sense.

He had to go and find her.

Brody turned and headed across the living area to the glitzy hallway, but the closer he got to the door of his hotel suite, the more the tingling in his fingers and feet got worse. Ibrahim had warned him not to put himself in a panic-inducing situation when his symptoms were already threatening to tip him over the edge.

He made it as far as the door, laid his palm against the polished wood and his heart hiccupped, skipping a beat then doubling up. The air around him began to get fuzzy.

He'd do it, if it were just a case of getting through these symptoms and sensations, if it were just a case of walking through the terror and letting it engulf him. He'd walk a thousand miles in that state to find her, but that was the problem—he didn't think he'd make it a thousand miles. He didn't even think he'd make it fifty feet before his traitorous body hijacked him.

He was useless. Weak.

He dropped his hand and his shoulder sagged as he turned and walked back toward the floor-to-ceiling windows that made up almost half the walls of his suite. He rested his forehead against the glass.

A muffled bang came from somewhere upriver, and from be-hind the buildings to the west, fireworks began to explode. He could just about make out the curve of the top of the London Eye, lighting up with blasts of color. The river below glowed with the reflection of rockets shooting skyward, marking the passage of one year into the next. The city began to celebrate.

Brody didn't think he'd ever felt more lonely.

THE GINS KEPT on coming, causing the bar to grow pleasantly hazy around Anna. Everyone got noisy at some point, counting loudly then cheering and hugging and kissing each other. Anna ignored them all, too intent on shoehorning herself into a state of oblivion. Someone shoved a pint of water her way—possibly the bartender—which she drank enthusiastically, and after that the gins didn't come quite so frequently. And when they did come in the goldfish-bowl glass, they tasted suspiciously like tap water.

The nice bartender with the beard tried to ask her what her name was and if she was all right once or twice, but she rested her forehead on the bar so she didn't have to look at him and waved him away with her hand. That made her giggle. She felt like the Queen. All she needed was a pair of white gloves and she'd be golden.

"Do you have any gloves?" she said, lifting her head and squinting at Mr. Nice Beard.

He shrugged, but then he crouched behind the bar and re-turned a moment later with a pair. Anna put them on. They weren't quite the long, white, satin ones she'd been expecting, more a kind of knitted mulberry, but they certainly were gloves, so she couldn't complain too much. Why had she wanted them again? Had her hands been cold? She laid her head back down on the bar and tried to remember.

She didn't know how long she stayed like that before a crushing headache began to creep up on her. Keeping her right temple in contact with the bar, she flapped a mulberry hand at Nice Beard. "More gin," she mumbled, then giggled again, wondering if the Queen ever said the same thing to the nice, bearded footmen at the palace.

But before the gin came, the headache began to spoil everything, sharpening her thoughts, bringing her closer to consciousness. Dammit.

Without warning, a memory from earlier in the evening assaulted her—the moment Brody had turned and looked at her. The sensation of sprinting into something solid repeated itself, the impact so powerful that Anna nearly toppled off her stool. "No," she whimpered to somebody (she wasn't sure who), "Brody is a friend, that's all. A very good friend."

The someone laughed. They clearly didn't believe her.

"Shut up," she said, opening her eyes and swiveling her head to look around. The laughter only got louder. Harder. But there was no one looking at her, no one taunting her. Only the voice inside her skull. The room began to spin.

She pushed herself up and stared at the bartender. "I don't love him!" she declared emphatically. "I don't."

It didn't matter how much the feelings had whipped and whirled inside her when she'd seen him. It didn't matter how everything she knew about him—his quiet strength, his beautiful imagination, his rough laughter—wound themselves together and stabbed her straight through the heart. She just didn't, and that was that.

Nice Beard raised his eyebrows as he filled another pint glass with water and placed it in front of her.

"I don't," she said again.

He shrugged. "You're not the first person to cry on my bar and say that," he said. "But in my experience, they inevitably do."

Anna shook her head, but it made it hurt all the more. She closed her eyes. "I can't love him like that," she whispered. "He's not Spencer."

She waited for her little alarm to chime in, backing her up, but it was mysteriously silent. "Traitor," she whispered.

"I beg your pardon?" Mr. Nice Beard said.

I beg your pardon.

Anna sat up straight. "Those exact words are what got me into this mess in the first place!" she said vehemently, waving an arm so hard that she started to wobble and had to hold on to her stool.

"I'm calling you a cab," he said.

"Don't need one," Anna said, fumbling around for her hand-bag, which was still slung across her body. "I have my Oyster. Oh. Where is it?"

"I'm calling you a cab," he said again. "Drink your water."

And that is how Anna found herself in the back of a mini-cab. The driver—a woman, surprisingly—had to go around the block twice before Anna managed to tell her where she wanted to go.

"I've been appalling," she wailed at the woman. "I've been awful to him!"

The driver just chuckled. "When it comes to men, that sounds like tit for tat."

"But I need to apologize!"

The woman gave her a look via the rearview mirror. "Happy to oblige," she said drily. "You just need to give me a postcode."

Anna frowned. Where was she going again? What was she supposed to be doing?

Oh, yes. She took a deep breath and told the driver the address.

THE CAB SLOWED and came to a halt. Anna stared out the window. Everything seemed blurry. On automatic, she pulled a wad of notes from her purse and handed them to the driver, and she only partly registered the smile on the woman's face. Tomorrow, she'd probably regret what must have been a ridiculous tip, but right at this moment, all she cared about was getting to her destination, about saying what she needed to say to him.

Anna weaved her way up the path to her front door and, after a couple of attempts, she managed to get the key and lock to cooperate with each other. Once inside, she dumped her bag and coat on the hall floor, then she ran upstairs to her bedroom.

Her breathing was fast and shallow as she opened Spencer's wardrobe. The bottom was filled with black plastic bags and she tore a slit in one at the top of the pile and pulled out a shirt, then buried her face in it and began to cry in loud, juddering sobs.

"I'm sorry," she whispered when she managed to catch her breath. "I'm so sorry, Spencer. I didn't mean to do it. I didn't mean to fall—" She stopped then, refusing to say the words that came next. She would never say them. Instead, she cleared her throat and took a different path, one that led away from that dangerous place.

She started pulling off her dress, all the while saying, "I love you and only you, Spencer. It was always supposed to be that way and it always will be. I promise you that." And then she pulled the shirt over her head and smoothed it down around her torso. "I promise," she whispered again.

Chapter Fifty-Five

*B*rody startled awake. He was lying fully dressed, facedown on top of the duvet on the hotel bed. He rolled over and ran a hand through his hair. He must have fallen asleep waiting for Anna to respond last night.

Since his room had no curtains, only wall-to-wall glass, it was easy to see it was still dark outside. Something buzzed beneath him on the bed. His phone. It must be what had woken him. He grunted and shifted, extracting it from under his left hip, and checked the phone screen. It was—

In an instant, he was sitting on the edge of the bed, his brain suddenly cleared of sleep. *Anna!* With clumsy fingers, he swiped at his screen and held the phone up to his ear.

"Brody?"

"Anna! Where have you been? I've been trying to get in contact all night. Are you okay? What happened?" *Stop,* he told himself. *She can't answer your questions if you won't stop asking them.* He closed his mouth and let her get a word in edgewise.

"Brody . . . About last night . . . I'm so sorry. I just . . ." She let out a heavy breath.

"Are you okay?" Brody asked again. "You're not ill or hurt?"

He heard her swallow. "No."

Was it his imagination, or did he hear a hint of guilt in her tone? "Then what happened?"

"That's just it . . . I don't really know. I just kind of . . . freaked. I don't know why, and I can't even explain it." She paused and let out a nervous laugh. "I mean, you and I both know I can get a little bit . . . weird . . . about New Year's Eve."

Brody didn't say anything. The way she was talking . . . Something wasn't sitting right with him.

"I . . . I would have phoned earlier, but I got a little drunk, and I must have fallen asleep and . . ." She trailed off forlornly and then added quietly, "I just found your messages. I'm so sorry."

"You got drunk?" Brody echoed. "Where? At a bar?"

"Yes, and . . . yes," Anna said, and he could picture her covering her eyes in shame. He wasn't unsympathetic—he knew all about freaking out, after all—but something wasn't adding up here.

"After seeing me? After running away?"

"Yes . . . I don't know what to say, how to explain it . . ." There was a tremble in her voice when she spoke again. "Please, Brody. I know what I did was awful but . . . but can we put it behind us?"

Brody frowned and walked over to the vast windows of his suite's bedroom. She was out there somewhere, and he didn't know where. Why? Why didn't he know that? What was going on with her? "In my experience," he said calmly, "it doesn't work to just sweep everything under the carpet. There was a reason you left last night, Anna. You need to work out what that is and, to be honest, I'd like to know what the reason is too."

Silence.

While he waited for her to answer, his mind went back to that moment when he'd first seen her the night before. The expression on her face—both at that moment and in the lift—haunted him. When he'd finally drifted off to sleep sometime before dawn, it was all he'd been able to dream about. And now it was etched on his memory like the ghost of an image left on an old photographic plate.

That expression told him all he needed to know, he realized. Because he recognized it. He knew the emotion that lay beneath it intimately.

Fear.

But what was she afraid of? He began pacing up along the glass panels that made up one wall of the bedroom, eyes fixed on the city lights outside. Not heights or crowded spaces, otherwise she'd never have suggested this as a location. The only other possible answer he could think of was that she'd been afraid of *him*. Logically, that fit but it didn't mean it made any sense. Did he look like an axe-murdering psychopath after all? He didn't think so. He'd actually *shaved*, for God's sake. It was the most presentable he'd been in years. But then an idea began to creep up on him . . .

"What can I do, Brody?" Anna finally said. "To make things better. I want to make things better. I want things to go back to the way they were."

It didn't escape him that she hadn't answered his question, but maybe it was his turn to lead the way. Over the last year, she'd inspired him to be brave, to work through his fears; maybe he could do the same for her—and there was only one way he could think of. He was going to have to be courageous enough to be honest, like she usually was, right here, in this moment. He stopped pacing, planted his feet and tried to imagine her standing there in the room with him. "I'm not sure I want things to go back to the way they were before, Anna."

She gave a little shocked sob. "Why not? Did I . . . Did I ruin it? Please don't say I did. Brody, you've got to forgive me!"

Of course he was going to forgive her for being afraid; it would be highly hypocritical of him if he didn't, but there was something more here. He stuck his hands in his pockets and walked from the bedroom into the living area, needing more space. He'd told her the truth. After last night, they couldn't stuff their relationship back into the same shape it had been before. It had outgrown that. It had shed that skin. They both had to face that if they were going to go forward.

"I don't want to be just your friend anymore, Anna." He paused, gathering the words he knew he had to say inside his head before he let them out, making sure they were all lined up in the right order, ready to make sense. He was only going to say this once. "I want more than that."

"Brody—"

He cut her off before she could interrupt him further. "I love you." He could hear her breathing, but she didn't say anything. He understood that. He understood how the fear could freeze your thoughts, paralyze your mouth. "And I think the reason you ran away from me last night is that you have feelings for me too."

There. He'd said it. Put it all on the line. Now it was out there. *I jump, you jump. Come on, Anna. Show me how brave you can be . . .*

He could sense her struggling, fighting what he'd said. He sat down on one of the dining chairs and put his phone on the glass-topped table, switching it to speaker, and silently willed her to make the leap with him.

"I can't tell you what you want to hear, Brody. I just can't."

"Why?"

"I can't feel about you the way you want me to."

She was lying. The knowledge made him irritated and elated in equal measures. "Why not?"

"Because you're not Spencer."

He almost laughed out loud. "Bullshit!" She'd always said he never pulled his punches. Seemed he couldn't even stop himself even if he wanted to. "You're scared. I get that."

She made a noncommittal huff.

"And do you want to know *why* I get that?"

He told Anna anyway, whether she wanted to know or not. He began with his first panic attack, how his world had shrunk smaller and smaller until she'd come into his life, how fear had ruled him for years, but also how she'd inspired him to challenge it. Not just that, but to conquer it. He told her about his journey to London to meet her, how he'd had to battle fear a hundred times, how he'd stood on that viewing platform, clenching that damn railing for two hours waiting for her to turn up. How he'd had his worst panic attack yet the moment she'd sped downward in the lift.

"That's everything," he finally said. "Everything I've never told anyone else because I was too ashamed of how weak and broken I felt. Because I was too *scared*."

There was an uncomfortable shuffling on the other end of the line. He might have heard her stifle a sob or wipe her nose too. He really wasn't sure. "Oh, Brody . . ." she said, and her voice was thick with tears. "I . . . I didn't know . . ."

Brody nodded to himself. "I wouldn't have expected you to.

I've done a good job of hiding it from everyone for years. Even myself. But I'm not hiding anymore, Anna, and that's because of you. I don't want to be scared anymore."

The sound at the other end of the phone line didn't change, but he had the oddest feeling she was holding her breath.

"You don't have to be scared either. We can try again . . . Come to the hotel and we'll find somewhere to go out for breakfast, somewhere small and quiet, and we can talk?"

"I can't, Brody. I can't! You know why."

Yes, he did know why. But it wasn't the reason she was giving him; it was the one she refused to admit to herself.

"Please . . ." she whispered, and the tremor in her voice tore his heart. "Please, don't push this. Let's just go back to talking . . . Being friends?"

Brody pushed back in the chair and stood up, leaving the phone on the table. "But I can't do what you want either," he said. "I don't want to lie to you anymore, Anna, and that's what you're asking me to do."

"Then, I can't . . . We can't . . ." She trailed off and he felt the silence turn from jagged and uneven to smooth and gray and flat, like concrete. Before she spoke again, he knew what choice she'd made. "I think you're right," she said finally, and this time her voice didn't waver or tremble. "We can't go back."

"Anna—"

"I think we need to take a break, you and I." The aloofness in her tone cut through him like an icy gust of air.

Brody turned to the window and laid his forehead on its cool surface and closed his eyes. It was no good. He'd hit a brick wall. One he couldn't smash down; one he couldn't climb over or dig under. He'd built an identical wall once upon a time, and it had ruined his marriage, ostracized his family. His wall had stood hard and proud for years, until Anna Barry had come along and dismantled it brick by brick, damn her.

Unfortunately, he also knew there was nothing he could say or do to make her take her wall down. Just as Katri had begged him to bulldoze his, to support each other in their grief over Lena, yet he'd stubbornly refused. He hadn't been ready then, just as Anna wasn't ready now. She might never be.

And to prove her point, Anna said the words he'd never thought he'd hear her say to him.

"Goodbye, Brody."

Chapter Fifty-Six

Anna lay on her back, the covers pulled up over her head. She stared at the underside of her duvet. It was Sunday morning, and she'd got up three hours ago, but now she was back in here, at a loss for anything else to do. Would someone please tell her how to make it stop hurting, how to get that nice, calm, white bubble thing going again? That would be really helpful, thank you.

Oh, God, she was such a coward.

Especially after everything he'd told her.

He'd been wrong about her. Spencer had been wrong about her. She wasn't strong. She was pitiful. She was a jellyfish.

And whoever had said "knowledge is power" was also wrong. This knowledge of how she felt about Brody didn't make her any stronger. It didn't *change* anything. Because what she had told Brody was true. She didn't have it in her to love that way again. Not because she didn't want to but because she just . . . couldn't. It would break her. Weren't people always saying prevention was better than cure? This was the perfect example.

And here she was, *thinking* again, when she'd deliberately been trying to do anything but.

Anna sighed and felt her warm breath reflected back to her by the duvet cover. She lay there for ten more minutes before she flipped it back and stared at the ceiling. The second day of January was as gray and heavy as she felt, and she could just about make out the reflected shape of her sash windows on the painted plaster above her head.

Out of the corner of her eye, she could see her phone lying on the bedside table. She itched to reach out and pick it up, to dial the one source of comfort she'd found when things were dark and bleak, but that was impossible now, wasn't it? Pain and comfort had been rolled into one convenient package.

It seemed like a lifetime since she'd last talked to him. Not fourteen hours and twenty-five minutes . . . *No!*

Not those numbers. Those were the *wrong* numbers.

Anna threw the duvet off and got out of bed, something driving her. She found herself in front of Spencer's wardrobe and opened the doors, but there was no row of soothing shirts inside, only a higgledy-piggledy pile of ugly black sacks.

She pulled out the top one and rested it on the bed, then she plunged her fingernail into the stretchy black plastic, tearing the hole she'd made in the early hours of New Year's Day wider. It was very satisfying. She hooked both hands on either side of the rip and pulled outward. Spencer's shirts, which had been neatly folded and stacked, spilled onto the floor.

One at a time, she picked them up and returned them to their hangers, smoothing out the creases on the shoulders as she went. And then she disemboweled bag after bag, returning their innards to their proper places, until everything was right and neat and exactly the way it had been before—three years, nine months and ten days ago.

BRODY'S PHONE LAY in its new home on the kitchen counter. He glanced at it as he walked past. The screen was black and empty. When he'd got it, he'd thought of it as being a piece of equipment that would allow him to contact the outside world. It hadn't occurred to him—or mattered—if any communication could come back the other way. Now it was all he could think about.

In the past week, he'd called her a handful of times, not wanting to be too pushy. She hadn't replied. He'd described Anna as brave, amazing, kind . . . But now he knew he could add "stubborn" to that list. If he hadn't been feeling so dull and empty inside, he might have laughed about that. This level of pigheadedness made them the perfect match. But he wasn't finding it very funny at the moment. Not at all.

Brody thought for a moment then turned and headed for his study. He hadn't been in this room much this past week. Every time he sat in that old armchair it only made it seem all the more glaring that his phone remained silent, so he'd just stopped sitting there. He didn't want to be *that* guy. Watching, waiting. Pining.

In fact . . .

Brody stared at his armchair. If possible, it looked shabbier than it had done before. He stared for a few seconds more then walked over, picked it up by the arms and wrestled it out through his cottage and into the yard, where he dragged it into a secluded corner round the back of one of the outbuildings.

Once he got it in exactly the right spot, he marched into the workshop, picked a plastic container of fluid off the shelf and returned outside. He unscrewed the lid, poured the barbecue lighter all over the upholstery and arms—silently thanking the gods that the chair's age meant it was constructed of wood and metal and horsehair rather than toxic foam—and then he lit a match and tossed it onto the seat. The flames caught even before the match landed. He stood there, watching it burn, and a slow smile formed.

He felt the warmth of the flames on his face and chest and he thought about Anna. He'd hoped that they could go forward together, but no matter what she chose, he needed to be able to do it on his own.

The armchair crackled as the flames began to eat through the upholstery and into the padding underneath. Brody turned and walked back across the yard toward his house.

Moving forward.

That meant he had a few phone calls to make.

Chapter Fifty-Seven

The next day, Anna arrived far too early at Tullet's Garden Centre, having encountered a bewildering lack of traffic even for a Sunday afternoon in early January. She made her way to the café, opened a reading app on her phone and settled down to wait. She'd managed three chapters of her novel by the time her phone pinged to life—a text from Teresa: *ETA five minutes.*

Anna carried on reading, every now and then glancing up to the end of the café that merged into the sales floor, and after a few minutes she spotted Teresa navigating her bulky stroller through the display stands full of Wellington boots and gardening gloves. Anna stood up and was about to wave when she saw another figure alongside Teresa.

Gayle.

Their mother-in-law strolled behind Teresa, hair set, posture perfect. Gayle spotted Anna when they were about twenty feet from each other. She stopped briefly, her jaw tightening, then began walking again. It seemed that neither of them had been expecting an extra guest.

Anna turned to Teresa as she parked the stroller beside the table. She was looking nervous but resolute. She gave Anna a hug, while Gayle stood stiffly by, then Teresa pulled out a chair and sat down. Anna looked across at Gayle, and Gayle looked back at her, and in the absence of any other ideas, they both sat down too.

"Sorry for the subterfuge," Teresa began, but then corrected herself. "Well, maybe I'm not *very* sorry." She looked between Anna and Gayle, her eyes asking for understanding. "Something had to be done. We're family . . . And family gets through things. Family doesn't let stuff fester—at least they shouldn't."

Teresa was right, of course, but Anna wasn't sure this was going to do any good. Gayle hated her. She glanced across at her mother-in-law, who looked as if she'd just sucked a lemon. If she'd needed any confirmation, there it was.

"Right, I'm going to go and get us all some coffees. Cappuccinos?" Teresa took in both Gayle's and Anna's nods and added, "I'm going to leave this little man here rather than try and deal with a stroller and a tray, and while you're minding him, you two can talk. Okay?"

Anna looked nervously across the table at Gayle. Although this had to be the most uncomfortable coffee date ever, she knew Teresa was just trying to help, and she loved her for that. However, she didn't want Teresa to endanger her own relationship with Gayle and Richard.

But when Gayle turned to smile at her grandson as Teresa walked away, Anna realized she needn't worry. The balance of power had shifted in that relationship, thank goodness. From the warm look in Gayle's eyes as she gazed at Little Spencer, she wasn't about to do anything to jeopardize being able to spend as much time with him as Teresa would let her.

Anna breathed out, knowing that made what she was about

to say easier. Even though she hadn't come here prepared, it was suddenly clear to her what she needed to do. She couldn't control what her mother-in-law did, whether she chose to hold on to this grudge or not, but she could stop being a coward and take responsibility for her own part.

After a couple of moments of staring at the acrylic tabletop, she took a deep breath and said, "I would like to apologize, Gayle. For what I said to you on Spencer's birthday. I shouldn't have said those things, and I'm sorry that I shouted at you in front of the rest of the family. It was wrong of me to do that."

Gayle turned away from her grandson, looking slightly taken aback. "Th-thank you."

"And I want you to know that I didn't bring Jeremy"— Gayle's eyes narrowed at the mention of his name—"To the party to upset you or cause problems. I had intended on bringing Gabi, but plans changed at the last minute and Jeremy stepped in. I . . . I know him from my salsa class."

Gayle was watching her carefully. "But he's more than that, this man. He's not just a salsa partner?"

To deny this completely wouldn't have been honest. "He was. We went out to dinner a few times," she said calmly. "But there's nothing wrong with that, and at the party we didn't *do* anything. We didn't even touch each other. I wanted to be sensitive . . ."

Gayle huffed slightly. Her expression told Anna exactly what she thought about that. It was tempting to do what she always did—what *everyone* did—and go along with Gayle for a quiet life, but she knew she needed to draw a line in the sand now, or nothing would ever change. "I might not want to be on my own for the rest of my life, Gayle. Surely you can understand that?"

Gayle looked away. She did understand, Anna guessed. She just didn't want to.

Gayle spent a long time staring at her grandson, holding his hand and playing with his chubby fingers as he beamed back at her, and then, without looking around, she said, "I saw you with him, and I . . . I . . ." She turned and her voice dropped to a whisper. "I thought it was *him* at first, you see. Just for a split second. The same sort of height, the same color hair . . ."

"Oh . . ." Anna replied, her voice trailing away as she realized she didn't know how to respond to that. Did Jeremy look a little like Spencer from the back? She hadn't thought so, but maybe he did. "That must have been . . . hard."

Gayle's mouth wobbled slightly. "And then when I realized it wasn't him, that you'd chosen someone who looked so much like him, as if you'd just . . . replaced him . . ." She shook her head disbelievingly "I saw red." She took a moment to compose herself. "I am very sorry, Anna, for what I said to you that night. It was wrong, and I didn't mean it. I've wanted to tell you that for months now, but every time I thought about calling you or dropping round I . . . couldn't." Her gaze dropped to the tabletop. "I was just so ashamed of myself."

"I appreciate that, Gayle. Thank you. But it wasn't just the party, was it? Even before that I could sense that you were freezing me out. Why?"

"Because it didn't seem fair," Gayle muttered, eyes still downcast. "You could marry again, find someone new to love . . . But I'll never be able to replace my son." She looked up at Anna.

"And I could sense it coming," she said, looking both fearful and distraught. "I could tell you were getting ready to do that, and I suppose I was jealous that you could find someone to fill that hole in your life when I would never be able to. The easiest thing was to push you away, so I didn't have to deal with it."

Anna swallowed. This was something she definitely couldn't judge her mother-in-law for, especially as it was a Herculean effort to hold everything she'd been feeling since New Year's Eve at bay. "I understand that."

"I don't hate you, Anna, honestly I don't. In fact, if I didn't care, I wouldn't have been bothered about any of this, but I just got so wrapped up in how I was feeling that I didn't stop to . . ." She looked at Anna pleadingly. "I'm so sorry. Will you forgive me?"

As Anna regarded Gayle, she discovered she could. She nodded, but before they ended this discussion, she realized there was something else she needed to clear up, otherwise it was just going to rear its ugly head again in the future. "I'm not seeing Jeremy anymore," she said, and saw Gayle's expression brighten. "But I might find someone someday. If it *had* been me who had died instead of Spencer, if he was sitting with you here today, wouldn't you want him to be happy?"

Gayle initially stiffened at the reminder of what she'd said at the party to Anna, but as she thought of her son, her eyes misted. "Of course."

"Then why is it so wrong for me to want the same—whatever shape that happiness comes in, whether it's a man, or a new family, or something else?"

"I suppose that's reasonable, but . . ."

"But?" Anna prompted, not allowing her surprise at Gayle's agreement to show.

Gayle looked her straight in the eye. "I suppose I don't want you to replace him. I don't want you to forget him."

Anna leaned forward, tears suddenly hot behind her eyeballs. She wanted to reach for Gayle's hand but wasn't sure it would be welcome. "I will *never* forget Spencer," she said, then had to pause for a moment until she was able to speak again. "Could you?"

"No!"

"Then why do you assume *I* will?"

Gayle flashed that fierce but brittle look that Anna was starting to recognize. "But it *will* be like replacing him if you do find someone new, won't it? There will be another man beside you at family functions, another man sleeping on his side of the bed."

"You have a new baby to fuss over and love, to take a gazillion snaps of to fill new photo albums. Does that mean you'll love the son you lost less?" Gayle pressed her lips together and shook her head. Anna handed her a napkin from the holder on the edge of the table. "And neither will I," she said, then reached for a napkin herself and blew her nose. "I will always love Spencer. Always!"

Gayle dabbed under her eyes with a corner of the rough tissue. "He'll always be your first love," she said nodding, not really asking a question but stating a fact. "And you'll never love anyone the way you loved him." She looked at Anna with a mixture of hope and desperation in her eyes. "Because they won't be Spencer. They won't be *him*."

"No," Anna said, acknowledging the truth that no one ever

would quite be like Spencer, while at the same time her last conversation with Brody came back to haunt her.

I can't feel about you the way you want me to . . . Because you're not Spencer . . .

Was that what she really wanted? Always to know the best was behind her? She brushed the thought away and turned back to her mother-in-law.

"If we can, I'd like to put this behind us. And I'd like to remain part of your family because . . ." She breathed in, staving off the tears. ". . . because I love you all, and I know that's what Spencer would have wanted. But we've got to start cutting each other some slack, Gayle. Are you willing to do that, no matter what we've said and done in the past? Can we try and start again, let our love for him keep us together instead of pushing us apart?"

At that moment Teresa arrived with a tray of cappuccinos, muttering something about incompetent staff and temperamental coffee machines. She put the tray on the table, sat down and looked first at Anna then at Gayle. "Well?"

Anna looked at her mother-in-law too, aware Gayle had yet to answer her question.

"Yes," Gayle said. "I can do that. I'd *like* to do that . . ."

Anna rose and gave her mother-in-law a hug. Gayle, rather than being stiff and cold, softened a little and patted her, just once, on the back. Anna smiled as she pulled away and gave Teresa a sneaky wink. Oh, she had no doubt it wouldn't be smooth sailing with Gayle here on in, but she'd staked out her boundaries, quite effectively, she thought, and she was pleased about that.

Little Spencer gurgled at that moment, and instead of sitting down again, Anna went to crouch by the side of his stroller. "Hello there, young man," she said, grabbing his foot lightly and giving it a little wiggle. The baby turned his head and gave her a beaming smile.

For a moment, Anna couldn't do anything but stare at him. There was a cheekiness in his expression, a twinkle in his eye, that was so familiar. "Oh, my goodness!" she said, turning to Teresa and Gayle. "He really *does* look like Spencer!"

Chapter Fifty-Eight

She was already waiting for him in the coffee shop when he got there. Brody walked over to her table. She looked up as he drew close. "Hello," she said.

"Hi."

"Long time no see."

He nodded.

"What has it been? Five years?"

"Six, I think."

Katri motioned for him to sit opposite her. Her blond hair was loose around her shoulders, shorter than he remembered it, but her blue eyes were as sharp and observant as they'd ever been. "You look well," she said, with her customary forthrightness.

"Thank you."

"You weren't in a very good place last time we met."

"No," he replied. "I wasn't. And it only got worse . . ." He went on to tell her his story: the cottage, the isolation, everything.

She let him talk, and when he'd finished, she reached out and touched his arm. "Oh, Brody." That's what he'd loved about her once, that alongside the no-nonsense approach to life, she was warm and compassionate.

"But I'm here," he said, gesturing to the café, which sat on the edge of Richmond Park, and despite the damp Wednesday morning, was half-full. "I've been seeing someone—a professional. I realized I needed to let someone help me, that maybe there were some things I could do with talking about."

Katri put her coffee cup down and gave him a *Well, yeah!* kind of look. He couldn't help laughing softly. It was good to remember that it could be this way between them. The last couple of years of their marriage had been filled with tears and arguments, angry silences.

"I'm glad you got in touch," she said. "Especially about today."

He nodded. "I wanted to be here. I've missed too many years."

"Yes. I was cross with you about that, but now I'm starting to understand." She paused for a moment and Brody saw the tiny wobble at the corner of her lips, the slight sheen in her eyes, as she said, "She would have been twelve today. That hardly seems possible, does it?"

He shook his head, unable to answer.

"She would have been all grown-up and at middle school," Katri continued, smiling, even though a single tear was now running down her cheek. "Taking the bus on her own. Giving us attitude—because I am *sure* there would have been a whole lot of attitude . . ." She trailed off and swallowed.

"I have no doubt," Brody said.

Katri nodded, then straightened herself. "Peter is coming with me to the cemetery. I hope you don't mind."

"No. He should be there with you." Katri's new husband had seen her through the last few anniversaries of Lena's death, through the birthday visits to the grave every January twelfth that Brody had missed, and Brody was grateful to him for that. There was no reason why he shouldn't be part of this one. "But I

think I might wait until you've finished before I go to the grave.
I need to go alone."

She nodded. "Maybe next year."

"Yes, maybe."

She shifted in her chair, preparing to stand up, and Brody
cleared his throat. "I wanted to say . . ."

She stopped moving, looked at him. He held her gaze.

"I wanted to say that I'm sorry. Sorry that I pushed you away.
Sorry that I wasn't there for you when you needed me."

Katri was not the sentimental sort, but her eyes filled. "Thank
you," she said. "I think I needed to hear that. But it's okay, really.
I know you tried."

"Did I?"

"Yes. Once or twice." She sighed. "But it was so horribly
painful to even go there—for both of us. Eventually, you just
couldn't face it anymore."

Brody frowned. "I don't remember that. I just remember
being very, very angry."

Katri laughed gently. "Oh, yes. You were definitely angry."

"When I think back to that time, all I can picture is being
stuck behind this huge invisible wall, me on one side, everyone
else on the other."

She nodded. "But it's down now?"

He shrugged one shoulder. "In the process."

"I'm glad."

Something behind him caught her eye and she turned to see a
man standing outside the coffee shop, looking in their direction.
That must be Peter. "You're happy?" he asked.

Katri smiled and nodded. "I am."

"Good."

She stood and grabbed her handbag but paused to put an arm around him and kissed him softly on the cheek before she left. "I'll text you when we leave."

He nodded, and when the door had closed behind her, he went to order a coffee and sat back down. He had a bag with him, and he placed it on the table. Inside was a small wooden box. He lifted it out and removed a delicately carved figure from the packing material inside.

He'd wanted to make one of Lena, how he remembered her, with her bright smile and her inquisitive blue eyes, just like her mother's, but he hadn't been able to. Maybe one day, but not yet. So he'd made Pip instead. She stared up at him from the tabletop, sword in hand, feet planted wide. She looked ready for anything.

He'd almost finished his coffee when his phone beeped, signaling the arrival of the text message he'd been waiting for from Katri. He slugged back the dregs, put Pip back in her box and left the coffee shop, walking the short distance to the cemetery on the edge of the park.

It was picturesque, as cemeteries go, full of old gnarled trees and lichen-covered headstones. He followed the path round to a particularly pretty part of the gardens, where the graves were smaller, where there were more flowers and photographs and teddy bears. Brody lifted a bunch of yellow and white daisies from his bag and placed them at the foot of a small white marble headstone.

Sorry it's been a while, girl. Sorry, I haven't been to see you. I did my best, but it wasn't enough, I know that. All I can say is that I'm here now.

He stood there, saying nothing, doing nothing, as the rain

began to fall harder. He listened to the drops hit the leaves above his head, drowned out occasionally by the pitiful barking of a dog somewhere in the distance. When he was ready, he got the figure of Pip out of the box and laid it down beside the flowers. She would have a friend here now. Someone to keep her company.

Brody stood again. There was no happiness here, no joy to be found. He doubted he'd ever feel complete peace about what happened, but something was shifting, releasing. In that imaginary place he'd avoided for so long—his woodland glade with the pond—a tiny single shoot began to poke through the scorched earth. He took one last look at the words on the headstone, heaved a sigh and walked away. He had one more appointment in London before he headed home, something he knew he needed to do, but really wasn't looking forward to.

Chapter Fifty-Nine

Anna finished the vegetable chili she'd made for herself, setting her bowl down on the coffee table in front of her. It hadn't tasted as good as she'd wanted it to. But that had been the theme of the day, she supposed. She'd also had a big meeting at Block-Time, something she'd been looking forward to all throughout Christmas. It was really going to happen. She'd given her notice at Sundridge Plumbing and Heating to go to work for them, to oversee both the office and the development of her app. And for almost double her current salary. It was all a bit mind-boggling.

Even though Anna knew this was really huge, that this was a massive step forward, she couldn't quite seem to get excited about it the way she wanted to. For the last two weeks, ever since New Year's Eve, it had felt as if something was dragging her down, making her heavy and listless.

She had just got up to go and deliver her plate to the dishwasher when her phone rang. It was Gabi. "You must promise not to judge me . . ." she began.

Anna closed her eyes. "Oh, Gabs . . . What have you done now?"

"I . . . um . . . I phoned Lee's number a few nights ago."

Anna's eyelids snapped open. "Oh, Gabi! You didn't! That is a really, really bad—"

"No, Anna. Wait! I didn't call Lee—I called his *number.* It was late at night and I felt lonely and so I . . . I did what you did."

"You did what *I* did?"

"Yes. I called the number, even though I guessed it might have been given to someone new. I thought about what you did and thought that maybe . . . somehow . . . the magic would work for me too. So I waited until midnight and I dialed."

Until *midnight?* Anna slapped her palm to her forehead. Oh, dear. Gabi really had got sucked in by this idea, hadn't she? "And . . . ? What happened?"

Gabi exhaled. "Someone answered."

"They did?"

"Yes. And we talked. He gets insomnia too. Like me, he's lonely . . . His wife died. And can you believe he lives in Sevenoaks? That's only ten miles away!"

This *is why she needed to start work at BlockTime as soon as possible and develop that app,* Anna thought, *to find a safe way for people to meet.* Suddenly, she saw very clearly why Gabi had been so wary of Brody in the beginning. "Are you going to keep talking to him?"

"Um . . . I already did . . ." Anna could imagine Gabi wincing as she told her this. "He's calling this evening because I promised to do some shopping for him."

"Oh, Gabs . . . Don't spend any money on this guy! You hardly know him."

Instead of being affronted, Gabi started to laugh.

"What's funny?" Anna asked, not sure if she was irritated or confused or a little bit of both.

"He's not going to scam me!" Gabi replied. "I'm sending him a book of crossword puzzles. He had a hip operation and needs something to do."

A likely story, Anna thought.

Gabi giggled again. "He's eighty-three, Anna . . . and very sweet."

"Eighty-three," Anna echoed, and then she began to laugh too. Well, there wasn't much else she could do, could she? She was definitely in no place to judge.

"We're helping each other," Gabi added. "Even if he's not what I expected."

"That's wonderful," Anna said, and the more she thought about it, the more she realized how true that was. Gabi was living proof her app idea could work, even if Gabi had gone about it in her own unique way.

"Also," Gabi added more seriously, "he keeps talking about his 'rather nice' grandson, and I—"

Suddenly, everything went quiet. "Gabi? Gabs?" Anna said, her volume rising. "What's going on?"

"Turn the TV on! Turn it on right now! BBC One."

"But . . . What's this got to do with—"

"Just do it, Anna!"

Anna picked up the remote and jabbed a button to turn it on to the right channel. All she saw were the regular presenters of one of those early evening entertainment shows with features and news snippets, guests and occasionally a live band. A reporter was doing one of those interviews when an actor or singer had something to promote, the kind filmed not in the studio but in a stylish yet anonymous hotel room.

"Why have you told me to—?" Anna began to say to Gabi and then fell silent as the screen switched to a shot of the interviewee and she saw exactly why Gabi had . . .

It was Brody.

Brody was being interviewed in the stylish yet anonymous hotel room.

Anna sat back down on the sofa with a thump. It was similar to that immediate reaction she'd had seeing him at the top of the Shard, only this time it was more like falling, as if the floor had disappeared and the air beneath her was just about to let go and allow her to plummet downward. It was the strangest sensation.

Anna blinked, unable to tear her eyes away from the screen. The reporter had been doing some preamble, saying something about the well-known children's author revealing the reasons behind his disappearance from public life.

"So, you're back," the reporter said. "And so is Pip! I hear you're working on the final installment of the series and there are murmurings the book will be available to buy next year."

"Yes, as long as people are still interested in reading it," he said, and he didn't actually smile, but something in his eyes made it seem as if he had. Anna practically stopped breathing.

"I'm sure they are," the interviewer said.

Anna had always liked the woman before but now she wasn't so sure. She wasn't just interviewing Brody, she was fawning all over him! Look at her, flipping her hair . . .

"What's taken you so long to get around to writing the final installment in the series?"

"Almost a decade of writers' block will do it," he replied.

The shot cut to the reporter, looking thoughtful. "And what brought an end to that?"

"I met someone," Brody replied, then paused. Anna's heart began to hammer painfully. "Someone who reminded me how brave and resilient and adaptable human beings can be, how just when we think our story is over, there might still be an unexpected twist, giving us a different ending."

The reporter liked this. "A *happy* ending?" she asked, leaning in.

Brody shook his head, in the manner of someone refusing to be drawn. "And that's what Pip needed too . . . A different ending. I'd written myself into a corner, leaving her stuck in a dark and lonely place, but it suddenly became clear what the solution was—she needed someone else to help her climb out of it. I think we could all do with a little help like that from time to time."

He and the interviewer began to discuss the reasons he'd stopped writing—the accident and the disintegration of his marriage. Anna stared in fascination. It was so strange to hear that voice and at the same time to see him moving, his expression changing. It made everything seem vaguely unreal. The topic then moved on to the panic and agoraphobia that had marred his life. Anna felt so selfish for having missed it. She'd known there was something wrong . . .

"That's why I wanted to come forward after keeping silent for so long," he said. "So many people suffer with anxiety and panic in secret. I was too ashamed of what was happening to me to tell anyone, so I struggled alone, and things just got worse and worse. It's important to talk about mental health issues, so that people can understand that they're not alone, that they're not irrevocably broken. That there is hope. But like Pip, I couldn't do it on my own. I needed a helping hand."

"Are you currently receiving treatment for your anxiety?"

Brody nodded. "For more than six months now."

"And have you conquered it?"

"Getting there," Brody replied, a smile lifting his features.

Anna gripped onto the arm of the sofa for support. She'd never seen him smile before. It was so . . . so . . .

And then he was gone. The reporter was wrapping up and there were shots of the pair of presenters back in the studio. Anna stood up and moved toward the television, although she wasn't quite sure why.

"Anna?"

Anna almost jumped out of her skin at the muffled voice that seemed to be coming from somewhere near her midriff. She looked down and saw she was clutching her phone. Oh, yes. Gabi.

"Are you there?" Gabi asked, sounding shrill. "Did you see?"

"Yes." She felt like she was in a trance.

"He was talking about you, Anna."

Anna nodded dumbly. "I know."

"So . . ." Gabi took a breath, then carried on, sounding hesitant. "The big question is—are you going to call him?"

Chapter Sixty

It was close to eight a.m. when Anna turned into a narrow lane that climbed steeply out of the valley up a wild and windswept hill. She'd driven through the night and dawn was just about to break. Thank goodness for all the Google mapping she'd done after she'd found out who Brody really was. She was pretty sure she was in the right spot. She'd driven through Hexworthy and had just passed the little stone bridge that she *thought* was the one Brody described taking Lewis over most days.

Halfway up the winding hilly lane, she spotted a cottage and her pulse began to hammer as she slowed down and pulled her car into a large, cobbled yard. When she turned off the engine, the silence of the countryside around her was thick and complete.

Anna got out of the car and walked up to the cottage. She was so nervous she thought she might faint. It was an inconvenient time of day to be knocking on somebody's door, she knew, but she hadn't been able to make herself go to bed and wait until the morning before she'd set off.

She used the large brass knocker on the door to rap a few times and waited, but there was no dull thud of feet on stairs inside, no muffled rustling as someone made their way to the door. She looked up. One of the bedroom windows was open. He might be in. He could have seen her through the window, and maybe he just didn't want to answer.

What should she do now? Anna didn't know. But she did know that she wasn't ready to turn tail and flee again. She walked back out into the center of the yard and looked around. There were a few outbuildings and a wide path that led round the side of the house toward a small porch. Beyond that was a terrace with an old wrought-iron table and chairs. She sat down on one, facing the brightening sky down the valley, and waited.

BRODY STRODE DOWN the hill with Lewis in his wake. He'd woken up sometime around three and hadn't been able to get back to sleep again. An idea had been hovering around in his brain, yet it had refused to come into focus, even when he'd properly woken up. He'd finished writing the last volume of Pip's adventures yesterday, yet he had the feeling that something was missing: a character, a person.

He'd been too groggy for a run that early in the day, but a long walk had fit the bill. He'd been up to the top of the hill over the valley and, sitting on a small rocky outcrop, he'd watched the sunrise. Now he was definitely ready for some breakfast.

When he turned into the yard, he stopped. There was a strange car sitting there, a little silver hatchback, and from the creaks and groans of the metal, he guessed the engine had not long been turned off. He looked around but couldn't see the driver. He hadn't been expecting any deliveries today.

Lewis barked and ran off down the side of the house. Brody followed him. When he turned the corner onto the terrace, he saw a woman sitting at the wrought-iron table. She was wearing a coat, a gray scarf and a knitted purple beanie with a flower on the side.

"Anna?"

She looked up at him. Those eyes, that expression. Just like the picture on his phone. Brody started to wonder if he had actually got up and gone for a walk that morning. Maybe he'd dozed off again. Maybe he was dreaming.

"Are you real?" he asked as he walked toward her. A hint of a smile lit up her eyes and he realized he'd said that out loud. That was the problem with living on your own in the middle of nowhere. You forgot to filter stuff, said any old thing that came into your head.

"As real as you are," she replied, standing up.

Lewis was at her feet, looking up at her, and she bent down to make a fuss of him. He then flopped down contentedly at her feet and rested his chin on his paws.

What? How . . . ?

"I know what you're thinking," she said. "What am I doing here?"

She moved toward him and Brody began to feel light-headed.

Anna stopped when she was a few feet away and glanced down at the flagstones. "I lied to you," she said when she looked back up at him.

"It's okay," he said, realizing that it really was. "I lied to you too. Mostly by omission, but that didn't make it any more honest."

She pressed her lips together briefly. "I wish you'd told me about all your struggles. It wouldn't have changed anything, you know, about our relationship. I saw . . . that interview you did. You said you were doing better."

"A lot." He tried to smile. "There's a stranger in my yard and I'm not freaking out, so I'd say that's progress."

"A stranger . . ." Anna looked away, nodding gently. "I

suppose I deserve that. Especially after all you went through just to see me on New Year's Eve, and I just . . ." She trailed off, looking unbearably sad.

"You were scared," he said, but it was a fact, not a judgment.

"I was terrified. Of you, of everything I felt."

"Yes," he said. "Are you still?"

Anna nodded, but she stepped nearer. She looked up at him, right into his eyes. "Definitely. But I am certain of one thing . . . I don't want to say goodbye to you, Brody. I don't want to say it to you ever again." Tears filled her eyes, making her lashes dark and spiky. "Do you remember the first thing I ever said to you?"

"You said, 'I love you.'" He looked down at the ground momentarily. "But you weren't saying it to me. You were saying it to Spencer."

"But now I am saying it to you. Only, I didn't want to say it down a phone line. I wanted to say it like this." She stepped even closer, so they were almost touching. He could see the hesitation in her eyes, the fear. "I love you, Brody. I was just too scared to let myself see it, and then when I did . . ."

He nodded. He understood the weird things fear could make a person do. "It doesn't matter."

He reached out, his fingers hovering near her face, aware he was about to touch her for the very first time. Slowly, he brushed her jaw, her cheek, felt the softness as she looked into his eyes and blinked away her tears. She brought her hand up and covered his, held it. She was smiling now.

He kissed her tears away and when that was done, he kissed her properly. It had been so long since he'd made contact with another human being that the sensations were magnified. This didn't just feel like his first kiss with Anna; it felt like his first kiss ever.

But then she smiled at him, and it was a memory direct from his dream all those months ago. The smile said, *I know you. I am with you and for you. Always.* Warmth flooded through him. This was definitely not a stranger.

"Hello," she whispered through fresh tears, and her smile grew wider.

Brody smiled back. "Hello."

Acknowledgments

First thanks have to go to my lovely editor Emily Kitchin, who believed in me enough to want to publish this book after a few false starts—on my part, not hers—and has been unwavering in her enthusiasm for *The Last Goodbye* throughout the process, from first idea to final manuscript. Dude, we finally got this one in the bag! Many thanks too, to my US editor, Liz Stein, and to Molly Gendell. I so appreciate your wisdom and insight. Between the four of us, we really have polished this story to a shine!

I am also in awe of the wonderful, dynamic, energetic team at HQ, who are going from strength to strength, and I am really excited to be one of your authors. Thank you so much for believing in *The Last Goodbye* from the get-go—your enthusiasm blew me away. It really is an author's dream come true to have so many people so invested in a project, and I want to thank everyone who has worked on, or will work on, this book, even in the smallest way. Special thanks have to go to everyone in the PR and marketing teams, especially Jo Rose, Joe Thomas and Katrina Smedley, and most of all to the ever-innovative captain of our ship, Lisa Milton.

Massive, massive thanks to my wonderful agent, Amanda Preston, to whom this book is dedicated. It took a year and five started manuscripts for us to come up with the right story idea, but you cheered me on and kept me buoyant throughout. And not only did you know straightaway which of my final round of possible book ideas had legs, but you also came up with the last puzzle piece to the story cencept that truly unlocked its potential. This book would not even have existed if you hadn't said, "but what if it isn't him . . . ?" I can never thank you enough for all your hard work and support over the last few years (although I may attempt to repay you in chocolate and/or desserts, if that's okay?).

Also, huge thanks to my lovely friend Rachael Carter for talking to me about her family and Brazilian culture and customs. You are such a joy to know, and I'm so thankful for your generosity.

As always, I have to thank my family for all their love and support. Andy, Rose and Sian—you know you are my favorite people in the world, and I love you all to bits. Thanks to my sister, Kirsteen, for her unfailing support and understanding the woes and triumphs of being a writer.

And, as any writer knows, there is *family* family, and then there is *writing* family. I couldn't do this job without you all. Thank you for the laughs, the commiserations, the ranting on my behalf and the wine (because there always seems to be wine . . .). Big love especially to Susan Wilson, Heidi Rice, Daisy Cummins, Iona Grey, Donna Alward and Sheila Crichton, and to the wonderful members of the RNA—too many to name, but what a wonderful community to belong to!

And a few random last-minute mentions: to the staff of my local Caffè Nero, who have no idea that that table just inside the door is my unofficial office, and to my newfound family of nerdy, authentic, talented and outrageously funny writers and readers on #Booktok. I finally find my online tribe!

I know it's not always very fashionable to believe in God anymore, but I do, and I cannot begin to quantify the impact this has had on my life, my career and my creativity. Thank you to the One who gives me strength, love and inspiration.

About the author

About the book

Insights,
Interviews
& More . . .

Meet Fiona Lucas

About the author

Rose Loakes

FIONA LUCAS is an award-winning author of contemporary women's fiction. She has written heartwarming love stories and feel-good women's fiction as Fiona Harper for more than a decade. During her career, she's won numerous awards, including a Romantic Novel Award in 2018, and chalked up a No. 1 Kindle bestseller. Fiona lives in London with her husband and two daughters.

A Conversation with the Author

Where did the idea for The Last Goodbye *come from?*

It was a scene from the hit drama *The Good Wife* that got me thinking how strong the urge to have one last conversation with someone you've lost can be, especially when they're taken suddenly and unexpectedly. It made me think of how my mother-in-law kept my father-in-law's voice on her answering machine for years after he died. The idea of a widow phoning her dead husband's number just to hear his voicemail message grabbed me—but what if something impossible happened? There should be silence on the other end of the line, but what if someone answered?

What is your writing routine like? Tell us about your process.

I'm definitely a planner, but what I need to know most before I start writing is the emotional journeys that my characters are going to go on, because that is what shapes the plot for me. I dig deep into the characters and get to know them really well before ▶

3

A Conversation with the Author *(continued)*

I start writing, but then, as I go along, I have to work out what plot events will push them to grow and change— and sometimes pinning down what they're going to do and say on the page to make that journey is the hardest bit to work out!

You've been writing fiction for over a decade. How has your writing changed book by book?

I think the basic flavor of my writing hasn't changed much—I still write heartwarming, emotional books with a touch of humor. While I've written quite a few rom-coms in the past, and still love the flirtiness and freshness of those stories, more recently I've been drawn to writing books with darker and more emotionally complex storylines.

What was it like writing about Brody's career as a novelist, a world you know well? Is his writing process similar to yours in any ways?

I think Brody had a much more serious case of writer's block than I've ever had (thank goodness), but maybe that's my fears coming out on the page? He also writes a lot faster than

I do when inspiration strikes, so maybe there was a bit of wishful thinking going on there too!

What is the main thing you hope readers take away from The Last Goodbye?

That as human beings we have a tricky relationship with the past—it can be the source of our dearest memories but also our deepest pain. Whether we like it or not, the river of time keeps moving us forward, and to pretend it doesn't only bring us further misery. Somehow, we have to learn how to honor the past while still navigating our present and steering towards our futures—but it can be a rocky journey and take bravery and courage to do that. ⁓

Reading Group Guide

1. Is there anyone you've lost or are no longer in contact with that you would like to have one last conversation with? What would you like to ask them? What would you want them to know?

2. How are Anna's and Brody's emotional conditions at the start of the book similar? How are they different?

3. Gabi tells Anna she's like a zombie—is this true? How do you see this in her behavior?

4. Why do you think the tragedy in Brody's life led to his agoraphobia?

5. Gayle isn't always a likable character. Did you ever sympathize with her?

6. Why do you think Anna's first instinct was to run when she saw Brody at the top of the Shard?

7. While the book dealt with some difficult issues to do with grief and mental health, did you find the ending optimistic or uplifting?

What do you feel the message of the book was?

8. Anna complains that Gayle is stuck in the past, but can you move on after loss? How do you find the balance between holding dear memories close and living the best life you can in the present?

9. Why is Anna able to open up to Brody in a way she isn't able to speak to the others in her life, even those close to her or those who have also lost Spencer? What does their relationship, and Anna's inspiration for the app, say about the importance of human connection? ∽